A GYPSY'S POWER

"What is your name, milady?" Dante asked.

That was something Esme would not part with. "My name is none of your concern."

"I usually like to know the name of the ladies I kiss, but with you I'll make an exception."

"Why are you doing this?" she whispered.

She could barely think, let alone speak. His scent, his low sensual voice, his dark brooding eyes; the lethal combination turned her knees to jelly. How could this gypsy affect her in ways no other man had?

The gypsy lowered his head. "I'm going to kiss you because I want to. Have you never had an urge to do something you shouldn't?"

Her tongue darted out to lick her lips. She thought she heard him groan but chose to ignore it. "No, never."

The heat of his big body nearly overwhelmed her. She didn't like the feeling. Then the ability to think fled as the gypsy's mouth claimed hers.

Gypsy Lover

CONNIE MASON

LEISURE BOOKS NEW YORK CITY

A LEISURE BOOK®

May 2005

Published by

Dorchester Publishing Co., Inc.
200 Madison Avenue
New York, NY 10016

ISBN 0-8439-5462-0

Visit us on the web at www.dorchesterpub.com.

Prologue

Bedfordshire, England, 1785

An icy wind rustled through the trees, wailing like a banshee singing a sad song. A man and a woman, their heads bent against the wintry blast, trudged determinedly toward the lights spilling from the windows of a towering stone mansion. The large number of carriages parked in the courtyard and circular driveway of the ancestral home of the Marquis of Alston momentarily gave them pause.

They halted, looked at each other and then at the mansion, and with mute agreement continued forward. The woman pulled her cloak tighter around her, cradling the precious bundle she held close to her body.

The couple reached the gate. It was open and they walked through, wending their way around the parked carriages to the front door. Without hesitation, the man grasped the impressive brass door knocker and rapped sharply. The door opened; a liv-

1

eried footman stared down his nose at the couple.

"The servant entrance is in the rear," he said as he tried to close the door in their faces.

The man held it open with pure determination and the strength of his muscular arm. "We're here to see Viscount Knowles."

"His Lordship has already left on his honeymoon. We don't expect him to return for a full year."

The woman let out a startled cry. "He is wed?"

The footman tried to close the door again but the man pushed past him. "Then we will speak to his father. Tell Lord Alston that Sandor and Carlotta request an audience."

The footman eyed the couple with distaste. He could tell by their gaudy clothing that they were gypsies, and could think of no possible reason the marquis would want to speak to them. Still, the couple refused to leave, giving him no choice but to oblige them. If His Lordship wanted the couple tossed out on their ears, he would see to it himself. Besides, the gypsies appeared ready to create a disturbance, and the footman knew the marquis wouldn't want his guests disturbed on this happy occasion.

"Follow me," the footman said, leading them to a small anteroom near the front entry. "Wait here and warm yourselves by the fire while I advise the marquis of your presence."

The woman walked directly to the hearth while the man pulled up two chairs for them to sit on.

"Rest, Carlotta," Sandor said. "It's a long trek back to the caravan."

Carlotta opened her cloak and gently rocked the bundle in her arms. "Poor little lad. The viscount has a wife now, one who will give him legitimate heirs."

"The child will not suffer," Sandor vowed. He thumped his chest. "I, Sandor, will be his father."

"The marquis's hospitality is sadly lacking," Carlotta observed. "We were offered no refreshments while his guests gorge themselves on rich food and drink."

Sandor snorted. "Did you expect anything different? We are lucky to be out of the cold. I wouldn't have brought you here at all if you hadn't insisted."

Sandor lapsed into a moody silence while Carlotta crooned softly to the babe.

The door opened and a distinguished gentleman in his middle years stepped inside. "What are you doing here?" he demanded curtly.

Sandor stood, his gaze unwavering before the handsome nobleman. Despite the silver strands prominent in his thick black hair, the marquis appeared in vigorous health.

Sandor took the child from Carlotta's arms and held it out to the marquis. "Bid welcome to your grandson, my lord."

The marquis looked dispassionately upon the swaddled babe. A flicker of emotion barely registered before it was gone. "Why have you brought the boy here?"

Carlotta took the babe from Sandor's arms when it became apparent the marquis had no intention of taking the child. She held him against her ample breasts, her expression fiercely protective.

"My daughter died giving birth. 'Tis your son's right to see his child," Sandor said.

The marquis looked away. "My son had no idea he was to become a father. He wed the woman I had betrothed him to and left hours ago on an extended

3

wedding trip. If I have my way, Alexander will never know."

Aghast, Sandor asked, "You didn't tell him?"

"I thought it best to keep the knowledge from him. After you informed me your daughter was expecting my son's bastard, I threatened to disown him if he continued to see her, but I did not tell him about the child."

"I wondered why he never returned to our camp," Sandor mused.

"I sent him away to make sure he would never know about the child he sired. I know how gypsies are with children," Alston said. "You would never part with the boy, even if my son had wanted him." Something flashed in the marquis's eyes, an emotion not easily interpreted. "You *will* take good care of him, won't you?"

"We will give him the love you and your son deny him," Carlotta promised fiercely. She started toward the door. "Come, Sandor, let us leave the *gadje* to their party."

"Wait!" the marquis said. "I am not as heartless as you think. I wish to provide for the boy's education."

"Carlotta and I will provide Dante with everything he needs."

"You've named him Dante?"

"My daughter named her son Dante with her dying breath."

The marquis nodded. "It's a good name, a strong name. But I insist on paying for his education. It's the least I can do." He opened the door. "Wait here for me; I won't be long."

"We don't need His Lordship's money," Sandor sneered once they were alone. "Come, Carlotta, we must leave before he returns."

Carlotta hung back. She gazed deep into the flames dancing in the grate, her eyes seeing beyond the fire to something no one else could fathom. "Dante is meant for greatness," she intoned. "His fate has already been foretold. I have seen it in the stars and read it in his tiny palm. Dante must be prepared to meet the future. We can teach our grandson about life, but formal schooling will give him knowledge that we cannot."

"What foolishness, Carlotta. We can teach Dante everything he needs to know to survive. Dante is a Rom; that is his future."

"Do you doubt my ability to read the future, Sandor? I have not been wrong yet. Mark my words, Dante will rise above his humble beginning."

Sandor subsided. "Forgive me, Carlotta. If you say Dante is meant for greatness, I believe you. We will take the *gadjo's* money and give Dante the education he needs to achieve the prominence of which you speak."

The marquis returned. "Take this," he said, thrusting a weighty leather sack into Sandor's hands.

Sandor opened the sack and peered inside. "This is gold," he said, and quickly closed and tied the neck of the sack.

"For Dante," Alston said. "Spend it wisely. I will arrange for his entrance into Cambridge. Bring him to the school when he reaches the age of sixteen. He is to remain at Cambridge until he reaches his majority of twenty-one; then he may return to you."

Sandor opened his mouth to protest but closed it abruptly when Carlotta poked him in the ribs. "We will not disappoint you, my lord," she said, "nor will our grandson. Dante will lack for nothing."

The marquis's keen blue eyes probed Sandor. "I trust you to do well by Dante. You could run off with the gold and forget about sending him to school, but I would advise you against it. If I learn Dante is not at Cambridge when he reaches the required age, I have the means to track you down."

Sandor's eyes narrowed. "Why do you care? It's unlikely that you and your son will ever see Dante again."

"True, but Dante has my blood running through his veins and I want him educated. Do I make myself clear?"

"Very clear, my lord."

Dante let out a mewling sound and squirmed in Carlotta's arms.

"Is the boy sickly?" the marquis asked anxiously.

Carlotta smiled tenderly at the infant. "No, my lord, Dante is hale and hearty . . . and hungry. A woman in our caravan recently gave birth and has enough milk to feed both her daughter and Dante."

Sandor pushed Carlotta toward the door. "We must go, Carlotta. The hour grows late."

"Where do you go from here?" the marquis asked.

"We are Rom, my lord. We go where the wind takes us. We plan to remain in the meadow beyond Alston Park until spring and then head north for the summer."

Lord Alston moved toward the gypsy couple. "Bring Dante closer to the hearth. I should like to look at him before you leave."

Carlotta wanted to refuse but reluctantly sidled closer to the hearth. She held out Dante for His Lordship's inspection. Alston stared at the infant for several minutes, as if memorizing his features, and then he stepped aside to allow Sandor and Carlotta access to the door.

The couple left the room without a backward glance. The footman promptly opened the door and ushered them outside, into a blustery blast of icy air. Had either Sandor or Carlotta looked back, they would have seen the marquis outlined in the light spilling from the open door, watching them walk out of his life with his newborn grandson.

Chapter One

Dante prowled the grounds of Hawthorne Manor as the gypsy musicians and dancers performed for the *gadje* attending the party honoring Lord Hawthorne's birthday. Dante felt nothing but disgust for the men salivating over the Rom women as they spun and dipped, their colorful bell-trimmed skirts twirling high to expose their bare thighs.

Dante's elderly grandparents, Sandor and Carlotta, had set up a fortune-telling tent on the grounds at the behest of the earl. But Dante knew from experience that gypsies were held in low regard, and he stood guard nearby should they need his assistance. Dante loved his grandparents too dearly to let anything happen to them because of the unpredictability of *gadje* who did not understand their culture.

Leaning against a tree, Dante let his gaze roam over the earl's highborn guests. The crowd was composed mostly of London dandies and highborn women, who were dressed to the nines in fancy gowns that bared most of their breasts. His gaze singled out and lingered on a woman with rust-colored hair piled atop her head in a becoming style that emphasized her gleaming white shoulders and long, graceful neck. Her stylish gown of deep blue displayed her figure to perfection, and Dante spent a few lustful minutes wondering what she would look like unclothed.

As if aware of his silent perusal, the young woman turned her head in his direction. Their eyes met for one stunning moment before she turned away, releasing Dante from her spellbinding gaze. Reluctantly, Dante returned his attention to the dancers, particularly to Loretta, a buxom gypsy well known to him. A murmur went through the crowd as Loretta's skirts spun about her slender waist, baring her long, shapely legs.

Dante smiled; he knew the pleasure to be had between Loretta's golden thighs, for he had experienced her sweet passion many times since finishing his schooling at Cambridge. Dante frowned. Just thinking about those wasted years at university turned his mood sour. He would never understand why he had been forced to leave his loved ones and live among people who detested him for his golden skin and popularity with the ladies.

Those years away from his family had been the worst of his life, and all because of a promise Sandor and Carlotta had made to his noble grandfather. Oh, yes, he knew that his father and grandfather had abandoned him, but it mattered not. Sandor and Carlotta had given him all the love he needed. He hated the *gadjo* blood that flowed through his veins and tried not to dwell on that foreign part of him.

From the corner of his eye, Dante saw a flash of blue disappear down a path that wound around to a gazebo some distance from where the guests were gathered to watch the entertainment. Was the woman meeting a lover? Dante wondered. As if drawn by an invisible cord, he glanced one last time at Loretta's golden thighs before slipping off down the path after the woman in blue.

Dante trailed a safe distance behind her, then darted behind a tree when the woman entered the gazebo. He remained hidden for a long time, waiting for the woman's lover to appear, but no one came down the path to join her. Drawn by something he couldn't explain and plagued by curiosity, Dante stepped out from behind the tree and entered the gazebo.

He found the woman sitting on a cushioned bench, staring down at her hands. Dante cleared his throat. She looked up, saw Dante and gave a small cry of dismay. Jumping to her feet, she slowly backed away from him.

"Who are you? Why did you follow me here? Don't come any closer or I'll scream."

Dante's gaze roamed freely over her lush body. She was an incomparable beauty, her body lush and ripe, neither too tall nor too short. Dante imagined long, slim legs beneath her skirts. He looked into her eyes and realized they were an intense shade of violet; he had never seen eyes that color before.

"Is your lover late, milady?" he asked smoothly.

Lady Esme Harcourt stared at the gypsy with barely concealed contempt. She had heard enough stories about gypsies to know that this one was up to no good. Though he might be the most handsome man she'd ever seen, he was still a gypsy. Esme couldn't forget what had happened at a country fair when she was a child and a gypsy man had tried to separate her from her maid when her back was turned. She had run away screaming. Afterward, she'd been told that the gypsy wanted to steal her away. She had feared gypsies ever since, hated them even.

Esme studied this one in detail while his own avid gaze traveled the length of her body. Dressed simply in well-worn dark trousers, an open-neck white shirt and a gaudy crimson jacket, he could never have passed as one of the dandies at Lord Hawthorne's party. The red scarf tied jauntily around his neck drew her gaze to his face. He was handsome in a rugged sense, if one admired golden-skinned men with curly black hair, dark eyes and slashing eyebrows. Esme had to clench her fists to keep from sweeping an unruly curl away from his forehead.

She sensed something dark and brooding in him ready to burst to the surface, an unplumbed depth, a quality that most women would find attractive. Their eyes met; his were dark with promise and wicked with intent. She backed away from him as far as she could go until her back met the gazebo wall.

He prowled toward her and stopped, legs splayed, the picture of pure animal aggression, insolent and unleashed. Did the gypsy intend to attack her?

"What do you want?" she asked on a rising note of panic.

"I'm not sure." He glanced behind him. "Are you expecting someone?"

"Certainly not you," Esme returned. "I but wanted a few moments of privacy. Is that so difficult to understand? Kindly leave."

"Why should a beauty like you seek privacy? Like all noble-born *gadje*, you have everything handed to you on a silver platter."

Esme's eyes glared defiance. "And like all gypsies, you steal what you want." She squared her shoulders. "Are you going to hurt me?"

She saw the surprise in his eyes and knew immediately she had nothing to fear from him . . . physically. But he was still a gypsy, and everyone knew they couldn't be trusted.

"Why did you follow me?"

Dante shrugged. "Curiosity, I suppose. I saw you slip away and wondered about the type of lover you would take."

"Not that it is any of your business, but I have no lover. As I said, I simply wanted to be alone. And since the men were all drooling over that brazen dancer, I thought no one would notice if I wandered off."

"Is *your* man drooling over Loretta?"

Esme shrugged. She didn't care one way or the other what Calvin was doing. She wasn't all that fond of her intended. Her future husband had been chosen for her. Her deceased father and the Marquis of Alston had arranged long ago for her to wed the man who would inherit the marquisate. And Viscount Calvin Lonsdale was Lord Alston's heir. Fortunately, her uncle and guardian, Lord Parkton, did not seem to be pushing the match between her and Calvin.

"I take your silence as a yes," Dante said.

"You may take my silence as a sign that I wish to be alone."

Dante advanced a step. Reaching out, he ran the back of his finger down the smooth satin of her cheek. She inhaled sharply.

"Don't touch me."

"Are you frightened of me?"

"Shouldn't I be? You're a . . ." Her lips clamped together, fearing that her insult would anger him.

His full lips narrowed into a grim line. A rapid pulse beat against one cheek. "I believe you were about to call me a filthy gypsy."

"You said it, not I."

"Don't you think I can sense your contempt for me and my kind? Yet your men seem to enjoy our women," he sneered, thinking about his own father, who had impregnated his mother and denied the child of that union.

"I know nothing about your kind," Esme shot back. *Why wouldn't he leave?*

"Have you ever been kissed by a gypsy?" Dante had no idea why he was goading her except that her lips begged for kissing.

"You wouldn't dare!" Esme cried, apparently appalled by the idea of being kissed by a gypsy.

That was the wrong thing to say to Dante. "Wouldn't I? You're in for a treat, milady."

Esme tried to edge around him, visually measuring the distance between the gypsy and the entry. The gypsy was no small man. She'd been under the impression that gypsies were short and slender, but this man was tall; his broad shoulders and muscular body seemed to dominate the gazebo. A single glance told her that he was strong enough to do whatever he pleased to her.

She was nearly past him when he snagged her around the waist and drew her against him. "Not so fast, milady."

"I told you not to touch me."

She glanced hopefully over his shoulder, looking for help, but the path was deserted. They were truly alone. Strains of music wafted to her through the air, and she realized the gypsy dancers still held their audience in thrall. Was the gypsy the only one who had seen her slip away?

His lips were so close she felt his breath brush her cheek. His scent was not what she expected. Instead of garlic and unwashed flesh, he smelled of soap, mint and pine. And though his clothing was somewhat unorthodox, it was clean.

"What is your name, milady?" Dante asked.

That was something Esme would not part with. "My name is none of your concern."

"I usually like to know the name of the ladies I kiss, but with you I'll make an exception."

"Why are you doing this?" she whispered.

She could barely think, let alone speak. His scent, his low, sensual voice, his dark, brooding eyes—the lethal combination turned her knees to jelly. How could this gypsy affect her in ways no other man had? She couldn't bear to have Calvin touch her, nor any other man of her acquaintance.

The gypsy lowered his head. "I'm going to kiss you because I want to. Have you never had an urge to do something you shouldn't?"

Her tongue darted out to lick her lips. She thought she heard him groan but chose to ignore it. "No, never."

The heat of his big body nearly overwhelmed her. She didn't like the feeling. Then the ability to think fled as the gypsy's mouth claimed hers. Not just claimed but devoured. Never had Esme been kissed so thoroughly. Never had she felt so helpless, so over-whelmed . . . so aroused.

His tongue prodded her closed lips. She resisted, but only for a moment. Without conscious thought, her mouth opened to his probing tongue. She wanted to feel disgust, but instead her reaction was nothing but surprised pleasure. Kissing the gypsy was not what she expected. She was no expert, but she knew instinctively that the gypsy was a man of vast experience. A man who'd enjoyed many lovers. That thought jolted Esme back to reality. If anyone saw her kissing a gypsy, society would give her the cut direct.

An angry flush bloomed on her cheeks. How dare he treat her like a lightskirt? She was a lady, the daughter of an earl. She deserved respect, even from a gypsy . . . particularly from a gypsy. She shoved him away and twisted out of his embrace. Rage emanated from her in torrid waves.

Excitement raced through Dante, resulting in instant arousal. Any woman in the throes of anger stirred him, but this woman was magnificent in her rage. Her violet eyes literally smoked with contempt, angry color tinted her alabaster skin, and her small, pointed chin had risen defiantly. Though Dante had had many lovers, both gypsy and *gadjo*, he knew immediately that he wanted this mystery woman in his bed. Unfortunately, the contempt he read in her expression shriveled his arousal. He stepped away from her. He had never forced a woman in his life; they came to his bed willingly and always eager.

"I may have earned your anger, milady, but I do not deserve your contempt. I will bother you no longer."

Executing a mocking bow, he turned and strode

away. Her fingers splayed over her lips, Esme watched him leave. No man had ever treated her with such disrespect. She should tell Lord Hawthorne and let him deal with the gypsy. But what could His Lordship do? Gypsies lived by their own rules. She'd always been told they were thieves and pickpockets; their women lacked morals and modesty. Her gaze followed Dante's departing back. And at least one of their men was a womanizer.

Esme decided it was time to leave. Her exit, however, was blocked by the very man she had hoped to avoid.

"So this is where you disappeared to."

Esme swallowed a groan. Calvin Lonsdale was the last person she wanted to see. "I merely sought a few minutes of privacy."

"Your uncle sent me to find you."

"I was just about to return to the party. Have the gypsies left yet?"

"They're packing up now. Everyone is moving inside for the dancing. The first dance is mine."

"I really don't feel like dancing."

Calvin's thin lips turned down, changing his somewhat pleasant features into a mask of disapproval. "Your uncle will be annoyed with you if you don't dance with me. I am, after all, your betrothed."

"Not yet, Calvin, and maybe never. My uncle hasn't pressed for a betrothal in a long time."

"Your uncle wants to see you married well. I will become Marquis of Alston upon my uncle's death. Our marriage is what my uncle and your father wanted."

"You're not Lord Alston yet. Your uncle is in excellent health."

"He is old," Calvin reminded her.

He grasped her elbow and urged her down the path. Her intended was not a tall man; Esme and Calvin were nearly of the same height. Nor was he muscular. Esme suspected he padded his shoulders and other parts of his anatomy to make him appear more masculine than he was. Compared to the gypsy, Calvin was an insignificant male of meager proportions.

Esme didn't want him. If she couldn't marry for love, she wouldn't marry at all. Once she turned twenty-five, she could claim her inheritance and take charge of her own life. Esme believed love existed, for she had seen it in her parents. Unfortunately, their lives had been cut short and her aunt and uncle had become her guardians.

After her aunt's death, Uncle Daniel became her sole guardian. Esme knew her uncle loved her, but she wished he was not so determined to see her make a brilliant marriage.

Esme's silence must have sparked Calvin's temper. "Esme, what is it about me that you don't like?"

Esme stopped abruptly, forcing Calvin to halt beside her. "Do you love me, Calvin?"

"Love? Where did that come from? We are equals in rank and should rub along nicely together."

Esme continued walking. She wanted to do more than rub along with her husband. She wanted to love him. She could never love Calvin. They weren't compatible. They had nothing in common. Aside from being weak, he gambled and spent money he didn't have. Those were traits she couldn't admire. She'd heard he was so deep in debt it would take half his uncle's fortune to keep him out of debtor's prison. He spent money on the premise that he would inherit the marquisate despite the fact that the marquis was healthy and in no danger of dying any time soon.

Esme was strangely disappointed when they arrived at the house and found the gypsies gone and everyone assembled inside for the dancing. It was just as well, she thought. She didn't need to see the gypsy to remember how obnoxious and arrogant he was. If she never saw him again, it would be too soon.

Dante returned to the caravan with the entertainers and his grandparents. The small group made a merry and boisterous procession. There would be a celebration tonight with song and drink and dancing, and afterward, the men would pair off with the women and find a different kind of pleasure.

When they reached the campsite, Dante led his mount to the makeshift corral where he kept the horses he raised and sold at country fairs. It was an occupation he thoroughly enjoyed. The money from the sale of his horses would support his grandparents through the winter till the next spring fair.

Sandor joined Dante at the corral. "Where did you disappear to this afternoon?" Sandor asked. "Loretta said she saw you walk off during the dancing."

Dante shrugged, recalling with relish the kiss he had stolen from the English milady. He would have kissed her again but for her blatant disdain for him. No man or woman who held him in contempt was worth his time. But, sweet Lord, she was delicious. Delicious and forbidden.

"I needed exercise and decided to do a little exploring," Dante explained.

"You did seem restless. Even Carlotta noted your

restiveness. Are you all right? Perhaps it's time for you to wed and settle down. You seem to favor Loretta. Perhaps you should wed her."

Dante gave a snort of laughter. "Loretta favors many men. I am but one. Fear not, Grandfather; when I find a woman who pleases me, I will wed."

Sandor grinned, the loose skin around his eyes crinkling. "That's what I told Carlotta. But she wants to hold your babe in her arms before she dies."

"You and Grandmother have many years left, Grandfather. After I sell my horses at the Bedford Fair, I intend to buy a small cottage where you can settle down. Traveling is for young people."

"I cannot live like a *gadjo*. You know better than to suggest such a thing, Dante. I am Rom, and proud of it. I will die as I have lived, in my wagon. Will you take supper with us tonight?"

"Don't I always? I enjoy Carlotta's cooking too much to fix my own meals."

Sandor nodded and then said, "I am glad Loretta isn't the woman you wish to spend your life with. That one would lead you a merry chase."

Dante laughed, and for a brief moment the brooding darkness in his eyes cleared. "Loretta is too fond of men to remain faithful to one, Grandfather. I don't want a woman like that. When I place a babe in Carlotta's arms, I want to be sure it is mine."

Sandor walked away laughing. Dante turned his attention to his horses. They were his pride and joy; he pampered them excessively and never tired of grooming them. Three of his mares had foaled this year, and their offspring promised to be as handsome as their sire.

Connie Mason

"Your horses are more important to you than I am."

Dante glanced over his shoulder at Loretta and smiled. "Not necessarily," he teased.

Pursing her pouting red lips, Loretta stamped her foot. "You're impossible, Dante. You care nothing for me, and after all I have given you. You know I prefer you to my other lovers. Shall I come to your wagon tonight?"

"Not tonight, Loretta. I have other plans."

Loretta's eyes blazed with fury. "You are going to see one of *them*. How can you make love to those pale *gadjo* women?"

"Did I say I was going to visit a woman?"

"You don't have to. I am not deaf. I hear them brag to their friends about their handsome gypsy lover when I perform at their parties. I know you are the gypsy lover of whom they speak."

"I admit yours aren't the only favors I enjoy, and I also know you don't confine yourself to me. Leave it at that, Loretta. Now if you'll excuse me, Carlotta will be angry if I am late for supper."

Loretta stomped off, deliberately stopping to flirt with Rollo, one of Dante's friends. Dante could summon no jealousy as the couple disappeared inside Rollo's wagon.

Dante checked on his colts one last time before joining Sandor and Carlotta. He sat down on a stump and accepted a bowl of stew that had been simmering over the fire most of the afternoon. He ate with gusto, savoring Carlotta's cooking. All his appetites were robust. He had just swallowed the last bite of bread and gravy when a man rode into camp.

Dante immediately assumed a protective stance as he

rose to greet the stranger. The man dismounted. When Dante saw that he carried no weapon, he relaxed.

"Are you lost?" Sandor asked. "How can we help you?"

"My name is Trevor Dunst. I'm looking for Sandor and his wife Carlotta."

Dante stiffened. "What do you want with them? They have done nothing wrong."

"I mean them no harm," Dunst said. "I merely wish to question them about their grandson Dante."

Sandor pushed Dante aside. "What has Dante done?"

"Nothing that I am aware of. I was paid by his benefactor to find him."

Dante stepped forward. "Look no further. I am Dante. Who are you working for, and what does he want with me?"

"I am employed by your grandfather, the Marquis of Alston. He wants to see you."

Dante's lips curled in derision. "I have no desire to see that man."

"Perhaps you should reconsider, Dante," Carlotta put in.

"Why should I? He was ashamed of me. You and Sandor are the only relatives I wish to acknowledge."

"Is that what you want me to tell the marquis?" Dunst asked. "He is eager to see and speak to you."

"I don't want—"

"Perhaps you should go, Dante," Sandor advised. "It can't hurt to hear him out. He did pay for your education."

"An education I neither wanted nor needed," Dante scoffed. "I was an outsider at school, ridiculed by the sons of rich noblemen because of my gypsy heritage. They hated me as much as I despised them."

"But you did learn," Carlotta ventured.

"Yes, I learned, even how to be a gentleman, for all the good it will do me. I am Rom and will always be Rom."

Sandor and Carlotta exchanged meaningful glances. "We both feel you should find out what the marquis wants," Sandor advised. "He must have a reason for seeking you out."

Dante's stubborn nature reasserted itself. "I want nothing to do with the man."

"We are not far from Alston Park; what could it hurt?" Carlotta prodded. "The caravan will travel with you and camp in the meadow near His Lordship's holdings."

Dante could tell that his grandparents wanted him to answer the marquis's call, but it wouldn't be easy to face the man who had denied his existence. He held his noble father and grandfather in contempt. His father cared nothing for him. In all his twenty-eight years, Dante had neither seen nor heard from him. In Dante's mind the man didn't exist. Sandor and Carlotta were the only family he needed.

"I think you should call on the marquis," Sandor said. "I have a feeling it could be important."

"That man is nothing to me," Dante growled. "But for your sake, I will see him. If for no other reason than to tell him what I think of him."

Chapter Two

Dante could see the roof of Lord Alston's manor house from the meadow where they had camped after the summons. Dante had helped his grandparents set up their camp, killing as much time as he could before his visit to Alston Park. Thinking about his noble grandparent brought a sneer to Dante's lips. He was proud to be Rom and independent of the marquis's money. Dante treasured his independence, thoroughly enjoying a way of life unfettered by society's rules. He had the freedom to go where he pleased and do what he wanted.

Though Dante had agreed to see the marquis, he intended the visit to be a short one.

"It's time you left, Dante," Sandor said when his grandson appeared reluctant to leave. "His Lordship will be expecting you. I'm sure Mr. Dunst informed him of your imminent arrival."

"Very well, Grandfather, but I can assure you the visit will be of short duration. I'm not interested in anything the marquis has to say."

"Perhaps your father wishes to see you. He never has, you know."

A muscle ticked in Dante's jaw. "I am well aware of that. 'Tis one of the reasons I have no desire to see either my noble sire or grandfather."

Carlotta clucked her tongue. "Treat the marquis with respect, Dante, just as you treat us."

"I will try to remember that, Grandmother."

Dante selected a handsome bay named Condor from among his horses to carry him to Alston Manor. During the short ride, he wondered why a man who in the past had shown little desire to make his acquaintance had summoned him now.

Shrugging off the strange feeling of foreboding clenching his gut, Dante rode Condor down the long, tree-lined drive to the imposing front entrance of Alston Manor. Dimly he wondered if he would be directed to the servants' entrance and decided he would leave if that happened.

Dante dismounted. Immediately a young boy ran up to take the reins. "I won't be staying long," Dante said when the lad started to lead Condor off to the stables.

Confident of his ability to hold his own in any situation, Dante strode up the stairs and rapped sharply on the door. His knock was answered by an elderly man austerely dressed in black livery. He stood so straight Dante feared he would topple over backwards. The butler's keen blue eyes traveled over Dante's gypsy garb and then settled on his face. He smiled but said nothing as he opened the door wide enough for Dante to enter.

"I am here to see my . . . the marquis," Dante said.

"Wait here, milord. I will tell him you have arrived."

Taken aback, Dante stared at the butler. Why had the man given him a title? While he pondered that strange occurrence, he took in his surroundings. The foyer was immense; his entire wagon, horses included, would fit inside the elegant entranceway. Dante had been inside *gadjo* homes before, but the marquis's mansion was beyond magnificent.

Marble columns, graceful statuary, an impressive chandelier and white tile floors spoke volumes about the vastness of the marquis's wealth.

"His Lordship will see you now. Follow me, milord."

"The title you give me is misplaced," Dante corrected.

"As you say, milord," the butler replied.

Dante shrugged and followed the man down a short hallway. The butler stopped at an open door and stepped aside for Dante to enter.

"Come in, Dante," a voice from inside invited.

Dante made a quick survey of the room—a study, he decided, and a comfortable one—and then his gaze settled on the man seated behind a desk. The marquis rose; Dante was impressed by his height and noble bearing, but not enough to forgive the man for ignoring him these past twenty-eight years.

Dante approached the desk. Without preamble he said, "What do you want of me?"

The marquis seemed undaunted by Dante's abrupt manner. "You look just as I pictured you." His voice held a hint of sadness. "I recognize your father in you."

Dante gave a derisive laugh. "The man who gave me life is nothing to me. I am Rom."

"Sit down," Alston directed. "You and I have a great deal to talk about."

Dante glared at him. "I cannot imagine what we have to discuss. I am twenty-eight years old. Had you wanted to find me, you could have done so before now. Obviously, my father had no desire to locate the son he sired with a gypsy woman. To my knowledge, he never inquired about my mother after my birth. I never asked to be acknowledged, far from it, but he could have found me had he wanted to."

Alston returned his glare. "Your father never knew about you. I never told him."

Dante's disbelief was palpable. "How could he not know that his gypsy lover had conceived his child? My mother died giving birth to me—did you know that?"

"I knew, but Alexander did not. Had he known about you, he would not have wed the woman I chose for him. He truly cared for your mother. When your grandparents informed me that their daughter was carrying Alexander's child, I made a decision I have since lived to regret. I didn't tell Alex about you. What I did tell him was that I would disown him if he saw your mother again. He agreed, but he was not happy with my ultimatum. The marriage I arranged for him was not a good one. He and his wife lived separate lives."

"Where *is* my father? Does he still not know about my existence?"

"Alex died without issue ten years ago; his heart failed. You were in school at the time. After you left school, I lost track of you, but I was quite proud of your academic achievements."

"Did you not hear that I was reviled and snubbed by nearly all my classmates? I was a gypsy, you see, unworthy of their respect."

Alston nodded. "I heard, but you also made a friend or two, and graduated with honors."

That was true. Viscount Jason Brookworth and the young Earl of Carstairs had befriended him. "I did, and since I was mostly left to myself, I had a lot of time to study."

"I also heard you were popular with the ladies."

Another bone of contention with his classmates. "What is this about? I am no longer a schoolboy."

Alston sat back and folded his hands. "When Alex died without issue, my nephew, Viscount Lonsdale, became next in line to inherit."

Dante had no idea what Alston was getting at. "He's a lucky man, I wish him well."

"If you knew him, you would not say that. Calvin gambles to excess; he isn't worthy of my trust or the marquisate. When he visits, I get the impression that he cannot wait until I'm in my grave. Sometimes I think he'd like to hurry me along."

Dante said nothing, waiting for his grandfather to get to the point.

Alston stared into Dante's eyes, his own eyes keen and unwavering. "You are an honest man, Dante."

Startled, Dante asked, "How do you know that?"

"I have ways of finding out things. With money anything is possible. I had your family thoroughly investigated before Dunst found you."

Anger shot from Dante's black eyes. He started to rise. Alston waved him back into his seat.

"Sit down, Dante. I mean no harm to Sandor and Carlotta. They did a fine job raising you and honored my wishes to send you to university."

Dante resumed his seat. "Perhaps you should tell me what you want with me."

Alston sighed, drew a deep breath and said, "I have acknowledged you as my grandson, and the courts have approved. All the papers are in order. You are now my legal heir."

Dante leaped to his feet. "What! Why would you do such a thing?"

"Because I am convinced you would make a better marquis than my nephew."

"I am Rom. I want nothing to do with you and your kind."

"You are as prejudiced against my kind as your classmates were against you. Rom or not, you are my heir."

"What does your nephew think about that? I suspect he isn't happy with your decision. No happier than I am right now."

"I haven't told him yet. He thinks he is my only heir."

Great peals of laughter rolled through Dante. Though his mind was reeling, he couldn't help laughing at the absurd notion of becoming a marquis after Alston's death.

"Forgive me, my lord, but I find your jest amusing."

"This is no jest, Dante. 'Tis already done. You are now Viscount Dante Knowles. The title was your father's. On the occasion of my death, you will become Marquis of Alston. The courts have approved my petition, and I have the papers confirming your new station in life. You also have an estate of your own and wealth that has been accumulating in your name."

"I don't want any of it."

"Whether you accept or not is your decision. The money remains yours to claim."

Alston removed two documents from his desk drawer, each bearing an impressive seal. He handed one to Dante. "This document recognizes you as my grandson and acknowledges your claim to my title, estate and wealth. And this," he continued, giving him a second document, "is a copy of my will. If you read it you will find that you're my legitimate heir. Keep these documents with you, for the only other copy is with my solicitor."

Dante looked at the documents in his hands with loathing. "Why are you giving these to me?"

"Because they are yours. Keep them safe, Dante. Someday you may need them." He chuckled. "Perhaps I'll let Calvin wait to find out he's not my heir until my will is read after my death. Too bad I won't be around to see his reaction."

Dante tossed the documents on the desk. "I refuse the honor, milord. Let your nephew inherit. Once, you rejected me; now I am disavowing you."

Alston stood and stepped out from behind the desk. For the first time, Dante realized how frail the old man was despite his appearance of robust health. The marquis had to be in his seventies. Disappointment made the old man's face sag, and Dante almost felt sorry for him. Almost.

"I've regretted my past actions many times over," Alston said. "But I knew you would be better off with Sandor and Carlotta. My son was embarking on a marriage that I hoped would produce legitimate offspring; I knew his wife would never accept you in her home. Clair brought great wealth to the family; I did what I thought was right.

"When Alex died, all my hopes for heirs died with him. You are my only hope for the future. You carry my blood in your veins."

"I'm sorry," Dante said, backing away. "I cannot accept your generosity. Good-bye, milord."

Alston seemed to diminish before Dante's eyes. "You don't have to decide now, Dante. I don't intend to cock up my toes any time soon." He picked up the documents and extended them to Dante. "Take these with you. Discuss them with Sandor and Carlotta. They are practical people; let them guide you. No matter where you are or what you do, you now bear the title of viscount. Will you visit me again after you've had time to think about our conversation? I know this has come as a shock to you, but I pray you will find it in your heart to forgive an old man for his sins."

Shock scarcely described what Dante felt. He didn't want to be a viscount. And he didn't want to like his grandfather, but he couldn't deny the Alston blood flowing through his veins. As for forgiveness, that might be a long time coming. He accepted the documents and tucked them in his belt.

"I will consider everything you have said and done concerning my future, but it will make little difference. You ignored my existence for years. I have no wish to accept anything from you now."

"It matters not; you *are* a viscount," Alston said simply. "Acceptance isn't necessary."

It was difficult for Dante to summon enthusiasm. The marquis could give him the world, but it wouldn't make up for his neglect over the years.

"Will you come back, Dante? I . . . I would like to see you again. I would like you to move into Alston Manor and learn more about my interests and investments. I'm placing a great responsibility upon your shoulders by naming you my heir."

Dante refused to commit himself one way or another. "Good-bye, milord."

"Won't you call me grandfather? Hearing it just once would warm this old heart."

Dante paused at the door. What would it hurt to call the old man grandfather? "Good-bye, Grandfather."

Alston's answering smile was genuine. "Grayson will show you out."

Immediately the door opened. "This way, milord," Grayson said.

The stable lad was waiting at the front door with Dante's horse. Dante mounted quickly and rode away from Alston Manor. He had but to glance over his shoulder at the magnificent house and all it stood for to know that he wanted no part of it. He had no desire for the kind of life associated with a title and wealth.

Sandor and Carlotta were waiting for him when he returned to camp. The question in their eyes demanded an explanation, and though Dante didn't feel like talking about his visit with Lord Alston, his grandparents deserved to know what had occurred.

Dante unsaddled Condor and turned him into the corral before joining the only two people in the world he truly cared about. It was dinnertime; Sandor had snared two rabbits, spitted them, and was cooking them over the fire while Carlotta turned potatoes over in the coals. Both looked expectantly at Dante.

Dante dropped down on a bench, uncertain how to begin. What would his grandparents think of Lord Alston's generosity? Would they consider it a burden as he did or a blessing?

Sandor looked up from the spitted rabbits. "How did the visit go?"

"Not at all as I expected."

Carlotta sent Dante a sharp look. "Was the marquis not happy to see you?"

"He seemed genuinely glad to see me," Dante admitted. He removed the documents from his belt and spread them out on his knees. Aware that his grandparents couldn't read, Dante said, "Perhaps the visit would be better explained if I read these documents to you."

Sandor and Carlotta gave Dante their undivided attention. When Dante finished reading both documents, their expressions gave mute testimony to their shock.

"I have no intention of accepting," Dante said. "I owe the marquis nothing. His title and wealth can go to the devil, for all I care."

The silence was stunning. "Well, aren't you going to say anything?" Dante asked.

Sandor cleared his throat. "You are making a huge mistake, Grandson. You are dearer to me than my own life, and I would never tell you to do anything that goes against your beliefs, but you were meant for this honor. Why do you think His Lordship looked after your education?"

"I have read your palm, looked into the crystal ball and examined the stars," Carlotta intoned. "They all foretold a future far more exalted than what can be found in our humble caravan. I didn't understand what the signs meant at the time, but now I do."

"You actually want me to be happy about this? The man denied my existence, Grandmother."

"No, Dante, he did not. He gave you to us to raise. Have we been bad parents to you? Have you regretted His Lordship's decision to let us raise you?"

"No, never!"

"Then perhaps everything worked out for the

best," Carlotta continued. "You are the most fortunate of men."

"What did you tell the marquis?" Sandor asked.

"I told him I didn't want a title."

"What was his reply?"

Dante shrugged. "He said it was mine whether I accepted it or not."

"You didn't mention your father," Carlotta said. "Why aren't he and his children the marquis's heirs?"

"My father died without issue ten years ago."

"Ah, that explains a great deal."

"Lord Alston said he followed my progress until I left university and then he lost track of me. It wasn't until he learned his nephew was untrustworthy that he decided to make me his heir instead of Lord Lonsdale." The last words were uttered with a sneer.

"These documents look authentic," Sandor said, holding them up to examine the seals more closely.

"They are. No matter how I feel about it, I am now Viscount Knowles, heir to one of the most respected titles in the realm." He laughed. "Can you see now why I cannot claim such an honor? I will be vilified and picked to pieces by the *ton*. I am Rom, the lowest of the low."

"Are you afraid?" Sandor asked.

"Afraid? You know me better than that. I fear no one."

"You are ashamed of your heritage," Carlotta accused. "Have we not taught you to take pride in what you are?"

"You did indeed, Grandmother. I am proud of who I am, and prouder still of you and Grandfather. That's why I don't want to leave you and accept the burden Lord Alston offered me. You need me more than he does. Besides, Alston is years away from his final reward. I will make my decision when that day arrives and not before. As for my exalted title, no one knows of it but us. I intend to keep it that way."

Sandor patted his shoulder. "That is true, Dante. When the time comes, I know you will make the right decision."

"Your grandfather has learned there is a fair on Bedford Commons tomorrow. Everyone in the caravan wants to go. They don't want to pass up the opportunity to earn extra money before the winter. I will tell fortunes, and you can sell your horses."

"You don't have to go if you don't want to," Dante said. "I have enough cash set aside to see us through the winter and beyond."

"I know, Dante, but I want to go, and you need something to take your mind off everything that's happened."

"Very well, Grandmother, we will all attend the fair tomorrow."

The following morning Dante arose after a night in which he'd found little rest. The responsibility Lord Alston had placed upon him weighed heavily. Not even the money associated with his new title tempted him. He had everything he needed, things money couldn't buy.

The weather promised to be sunny and clear when Dante left his wagon shortly after dawn. He ate breakfast with Sandor and Carlotta, then helped them break camp.

"I'll help you hitch the horses to the wagons," Sandor said. "Rollo and Peter are preparing the mares and colts to take to Bedford. They are a handsome lot, Dante, and should attract a good deal of attention."

Once the horses were hitched to both his wagon and the brightly painted one belonging to his grand-parents, Dante saw to his own horses. Peter and Rollo, his two best friends, had them well in hand. Dante had sold off most of his horses this summer, leaving just five mares, a stallion he intended to keep along with two mares, and three young colts. The stallion gave him the most trouble, but he was a good breeder and Dante hated to part with him.

One by one the wagons left the campsite; Dante brought up the rear with his horses. It wasn't far to Bedford Commons, and the wagons reached their destination just as vendors were setting up their booths. They weren't happy to see the gypsy caravan descend on them, but there was little they could do about it. Besides, as one vendor remarked, the color-ful gypsies brought in more customers.

Dante found a place a short distance away from the booths to display his horses. Carlotta located a suit-able site nearby to tell fortunes.

Eager to sample everything the fair had to offer, Esme all but dragged her maid toward the fair-grounds. She hadn't been to a fair since last summer, and she loved the hustle and bustle of people and the excitement. She hoped there was a dancing bear like the one she'd seen at a fair near London last year.

"Hurry, Jane, the fair will be over before we get there."

Esme's maid gazed up at the sky, a hint of misgiving in her blue eyes. "Look up at the sky, milady. A moment ago it was blue, but now clouds are gathering overhead."

"You worry too much, Jane. Hurry, I don't want to miss a thing."

"I'm going as fast as I can without running, milady," Jane panted. "Ladies don't run, they float."

Esme nearly laughed out loud at Jane's rebuke. Jane had been both maid and companion to her for as long as she could remember and had taught her a great deal about etiquette and decorum, but at times like this her advice went unheeded.

Esme knew that if her uncle were home he would insist that a footman accompany them, but he had gone up to London for a few days, leaving her on her own.

Esme could have gone to London with her uncle, but she preferred country life to the big city. She knew that once she went to London for the Season, she would be caught up in round after round of balls, routs and musicales. Not exactly her cup of tea, but she tolerated them for her uncle's sake.

Esme heard music and hastened her steps. Excitement raced through her. The sights, the sounds, the mouthwatering smells of meat pies and other tempting food made her clap her hands in pure joy. She didn't know where to go or look first.

"Oh, look, milady, there's the dancing bear!" Jane cried.

They made their way through the crowd to where the bear was performing. They watched for a time and then wandered past stalls offering a variety of wares. Esme stopped to buy two violet ribbons for herself and a yellow one for Jane.

"It's going to rain," Jane pointed out. "Perhaps we

should head home. 'Tis a long walk back to your uncle's manor house."

Esme was having far too much fun to leave now. She glanced up at the sky and dismissed the dark clouds gathering overhead. "The rain is hours away, Jane. Oh, look, a fortune-teller! Would you like to have your fortune told?"

"Oh, no, I dare not."

"Come, don't be silly," Esme said, pulling Jane toward a gaily decorated wagon. An elderly woman with sparkling black eyes, gray hair and folds of wrinkled skin the color of old gold sat on the steps. A wizened old man stood nearby, hawking the woman's talents.

Esme recognized the gypsy couple from Lord Hawthorne's party and immediately conjured up the image of the bold gypsy who had dared to kiss her in the gazebo. She touched her lips, recalling the way his kiss had made her feel. A shudder of guilty pleasure slid down her spine as she cast a surreptitious glance around. Was the man she only dared dream about here? She hoped not.

Esme knew she couldn't face him again, not after the way she had responded to his kiss. A dreamy expression turned her eyes a deep violet. No man had ever made her feel the way the gypsy did, and she blamed herself for falling prey to his rough charm and handsome face. Her friends would be horrified if they found out she had been kissed by a gypsy.

Despite her prejudice against gypsies, Esme saw no harm in having her fortune told. Dismissing her foolish thoughts about the handsome gypsy, she grasped Jane's hand and boldly approached the gypsy wagon.

"We'd like our fortunes told," Esme said.

Carlotta stood. "Come inside, pretty lady, and I will tell your future."

"You go first, Jane," Esme said, producing a coin for her maid. "I'll wait here for you."

"Oh, no, milady, I couldn't."

"Go on, I don't mind waiting."

Carlotta led Jane up the steps and into the wagon. Esme waved her off and wandered over to inspect the wares at a nearby booth while she waited. She was so engrossed in the trinkets that she failed to notice the thinning crowds and darkening sky.

She started violently when a bolt of lightning lit the heavens, followed by a boom of thunder. Then the skies opened up. Wind-driven rain lashed through the trees, drenching the fairgrounds and everyone unfortunate enough not to have left before the storm arrived. People scattered like sheep, running every which way to escape the downpour.

Esme didn't know where to go, which way to turn. Buffeted by gusts of wind and rain and jostled by people anxious to reach the safety of their homes, she looked for the nearest shelter.

Dante was sprinting toward his wagon when he saw her. He recognized her immediately by the wisps of rust-colored hair escaping from her bonnet, which had been all but ruined by the wind and rain. She was soaked to the skin and appeared lost in the crowd of people rushing past her for cover. A man nearly knocked her over in his haste and she lost her footing, tottering back on her heels.

Dante immediately changed course, pushing through people exiting the fairgrounds to reach her.

Without missing a step, he scooped her into his arms and ran through the downpour to his wagon.

More startled than frightened, Esme groaned in dismay. "What are you doing?"

"Rescuing a damsel who lacks the wits to get out of the rain."

"I was waiting for my maid."

Dante sprinted up the steps, flung open the door to his wagon and carried her inside. "Where is your maid?"

"Having her fortune told."

He lowered her to her feet. "She's safe with Carlotta and Sandor." He closed the door, shutting them off from the tempest outside.

"I can't stay in here with you," Esme declared. "My reputation will be ruined if we are seen together."

Dante glanced out the window at the nearly deserted fairgrounds. "Who will see us? All your fancy friends left when the rain clouds began to gather. You should have followed them."

Esme shrugged off his rebuke and opened the door. The wind caught it and flung it out of her hand. Dante pushed past her and pulled it shut. "It looks like you're stuck here for a while."

Esme shivered, hugging herself with her arms.

"You're cold. I'll light the brazier." He knelt, fed coals into the stove and soon had a fire going.

Esme studied her surroundings while the gypsy was busy with the fire. Though the space was limited, every bit of it was utilized. She glanced at the bed and quickly looked away. Just thinking about the bed and the gypsy at the same time conjured all kinds of sinful thoughts. Thoughts she'd never had before she'd met the gypsy.

Dante backed away from the brazier and urged milady forward to soak up the heat. The moment he looked at her, he regretted it. Her thin summer dress was soaked through; it clung to the lush curves of her hips and thighs and breasts in a most disconcerting manner. This pale *gadjo* was doing to him what Loretta and her overt sensuality failed to do.

He wanted her.

Wanted her desperately.

Chapter Three

Dante's lust raged out of control. If he didn't turn his mind in another direction, he knew he would act rashly. He had never forced his attentions on a woman and he didn't intend to start now. But nothing in his code of ethics said he couldn't kiss a woman, or seduce her into his bed.

Grabbing a blanket from the bed, Dante placed it around milady's shoulders. Out of sight, out of mind, seemed a good adage to follow, at least until his lust subsided.

"That should warm you up," Dante said. "Sit down; we'll wait out the storm together."

Esme sat gingerly on the edge of the bed.

"I'm sorry, I didn't catch your name," Dante said.

"I didn't give it."

The rain pounding on the roof and the occasional bark of thunder were the only sounds in the wagon for several tense minutes.

"Would you like a cup of tea?" Dante offered as the

silence between them stretched. "It won't be any trouble."

Esme sent him an uncertain look. "I'd love a cup of tea."

Dante moved a kettle over the brazier, then rattled about in a cupboard until he found a teapot and two cups. He measured tea leaves into the pot and placed the cups on a small table. When the water began to bubble, he poured it in the pot and waited for the tea to steep.

"Do you live nearby?" Dante asked, hoping to learn more about the elusive milady.

"I live not far from here with my uncle," Esme replied.

"Do you ever go to London?"

Esme wrinkled her nose. "Only when I have to. My uncle and I usually go up to London for the Season."

"Are you married?"

Esme shook her head. "No, but I'm . . . almost betrothed."

Dante's dark brows arched upward. "Almost?" He poured the tea and handed her a cup. "Do you plan to wed your almost fiancé?"

Caught off guard by the personal nature of the gypsy's questions, Esme said, "Not if I can help it."

Before saying more than she intended, Esme clamped her lips together. She didn't want the gypsy to know anything about her. If their names were mentioned in the same breath, she would die of embarrassment. And Calvin would be livid. Esme stifled a grin. Seeing the look on Calvin's face would be almost worth the unsavory gossip that would follow. But no, she couldn't allow her name to be linked to that of a gypsy.

Dante observed the play of emotions on milady's expressive features and wondered what was going through her mind. "You sound as if you're not overly enthusiastic about your almost fiancé."

"I never said that," Esme replied defensively. "What woman wouldn't want to marry the heir to a marquisate?"

"I couldn't answer that," Dante replied. "You must be of noble birth to reach so high."

Esme drained her cup and set it down on the table. She had already told the gypsy more than she intended. She rose and moved to the window. "I should leave."

When no answer was forthcoming, she turned to see what the gypsy was doing and found him standing behind her, so close she could feel the heat radiating from his body to hers.

"You're crowding me," she said, struggling to keep the panic from her voice. The intimacy of the situation made her uncomfortable. Though she wasn't frightened of the gypsy, she most definitely didn't trust him. His kind weren't trustworthy.

"You don't like me, do you?" Dante asked in a low voice that made the fine hairs on the back of her neck stand up. "Is it just me you don't like or all Rom?"

"Since I've had no dealings with gypsies I cannot say."

"Liar," Dante said softly. "Do you remember our kiss?"

How could I forget? "No, I barely recall meeting you."

"It hasn't been all that long. Have you forgotten the gazebo where we shared that kiss?"

Vivid color flooded her face. Why was he being so irritating? "You are only saying these things to annoy me. I prefer to forget the gazebo and what happened there."

"Shall I remind you?"

Grasping her face between his hands, he tilted her head to one side. Lowering his lips to hers, he whispered, "Perhaps you will remember *this* kiss."

His breath heated her lips, and then he covered them with his, coaxing them apart with his tongue. It wasn't fair that something as warm and soft as the gypsy's lips should belong to a man forbidden to her, Esme thought.

Dante pulled her closer to him, melding their bodies together. From chest to thigh, his body molded the soft curves of hers. He was hard everywhere, and growing even harder in a private place she dared not think about.

His tongue swept across hers. Thrusting, retreating and then returning for more. Esme attempted to withhold any kind of physical reaction, but it was difficult. She could slow her racing pulse, her erratically pounding heart would eventually settle into a normal rhythm, but how could she stop the throbbing low in her belly or cool the fire in her blood?

Tossing caution to the wind, Esme leaned into him. Despite the wrongness of it, she wanted the gypsy's kiss. After today she would never see him again, and her life would go on as it had before she encountered him. Gypsies were wanderers. What were the chances of meeting him again?

Dante pulled away, holding her at arm's length. A frown creased his forehead, and she knew she'd crossed the line of decency.

"Milady, please tell me your name."

"Why? So you can find me again? I think not." She

pushed him away. "This is impossible! I don't know what got into me."

His smile chased the brooding darkness from his eyes. "I would love to get into you if you'd let me."

Esme stared at him a long time before she realized what he meant. Though she wasn't accustomed to words with sexual undertones, she wasn't completely innocent about such matters. She had made good use of her uncle's extensive library.

"How dare you!" Before he had time to react, she drew her arm back and dealt him a stinging blow across the face. "You disgust me." Without a by your leave, she tossed aside the blanket and swept past him. He grasped her arm before she reached the door. Tension charged the air. His voice stabbed at her, and the darkness returned to his eyes.

"Don't ever do that again."

"Release me. I want to leave."

His breath came unevenly. A violent tug-of-war was being waged in his chest. This woman aroused his lust and refused to assuage it. Finally sanity returned and he released her arm. She made a break for the door.

"What about your maid?" he called after her.

"She can find her own way home. It's but a short walk."

Dante stood in the doorway until he could no longer see her. He thought about following, but decided he would be wasting his time. It would be best if he never saw milady again. She had made damn certain he knew that she considered him, and all Rom, a bug beneath her dainty foot.

Within a half hour the summer storm passed and the sun came out. Except for the very muddy ground, the storm had done scant damage. Most of the stalls reopened and people began drifting back. Dante stepped outside and walked to his grandparents' wagon. He had one foot on the first step when the door opened and an attractive woman in her early thirties rushed past him. Milady's maid, Dante thought as he continued up the stairs and entered the wagon.

"Your clothing is wet," Carlotta said. "Come sit by the fire."

Kissing milady had created so much heat within him that Dante had failed to feel the dampness. He sat down on a bench, staring at his hands until he could put words to his thoughts.

"I think we should leave," he announced.

"Perhaps you're right. The storm has ruined the fair. We can return tomorrow," Carlotta said.

"No, I mean leave the area. Let's go to Scotland for the rest of the summer."

Carlotta and Sandor exchanged startled looks. "Has something besides your concern about your new title upset you?"

Carlotta read him so well. He looked away, then asked nonchalantly, "The woman who just left—did she say anything about herself?"

"Not much, other than that she was worried about her mistress. She ran out of here the moment the rain stopped."

"Did you read her fortune?"

"Of course, 'tis what I was paid to do." She shrugged her narrow shoulders. "The woman's palm held little of interest. She has been in service her entire life. She loves her mistress well and would do anything for her. All I could tell her was that one day she would find true love."

"Did she mention her mistress's name?"

"Why does the maid interest you, Dante? Do you know her mistress?"

Dante's silence provoked Carlotta's curiosity. "You *do* know the maid's mistress. Is she important to you?"

"Enough, Grandmother. I don't even know the lady's name."

"Too bad she didn't return to have her fortune read."

"Don't make something out of nothing," Dante growled.

"Give me your palm, Dante."

"You've read my palm countless times."

"But not recently."

"I know all I need to know."

"Very well, I will consult my crystal ball."

Dante rose. "I have to see to my horses."

"Sit down, Dante," Sandor ordered. "I'm beginning to think you have something to hide."

Dutifully Dante resumed his seat while Carlotta placed her crystal ball on the table between them. Dante saw nothing in the ball but mist. Carlotta, however, appeared puzzled by what she divined. As she peered closely into the ball, Carlotta's expression went from joy, to concern, to fear.

"What do you see?" Sandor asked.

"Many things," Carlotta whispered in a singsong voice unlike her own. She seemed completely immersed in the visions within the ball. "Dante will become Marquis of Alston sooner than he thinks. He will face grave danger and gain a wife." She gazed up at Dante, her eyes fixed on something beyond him. "You will find great joy with this woman once you convince her to wed you, Dante, but beware, beware. Evil lurks where you least expect it."

Dante shot to his feet. "Beware of what? What kind of evil? Really, Grandmother, this is preposterous. I will never become Marquis of Alston and have no intention of getting married. If I choose a wife, and that's a big if, she will not need convincing."

Carlotta blinked; her expression went blank, as if she were trying to regain her bearings. "That's all I can tell you."

"If Carlotta spoke of danger, you must take precautions to protect yourself and your wife," Sandor advised.

"I have no enemies," Dante maintained. He strode out the door. "I'm going to fetch the horses and hitch them to the wagon. I have a longing to travel. If you don't want to go to Scotland, we can head south to our winter campground."

"What do you think, Carlotta?" Sandor asked after Dante left.

"Dante is running from his future," Carlotta observed.

"How can we help him?"

"The decision lies with Dante. We must convince him to speak to the marquis again. His ascension to the marquisate is inevitable. The crystal ball never lies."

"What about the woman? Was her identity revealed to you?"

"No. I saw a beautiful woman with hair more rust than red. From the brief image granted me, I saw her contempt for all things Rom."

"That doesn't sound good. You spoke of danger. Who threatens our grandson?"

"I do not know. Go find our grandson, Sandor. It is too late in the year to travel north. Tell him we will travel south together after the fair if he will visit the marquis before we leave. I sense an unnamed evil surrounding the marquis."

Sandor moved to the door. "Very well, I will talk to our grandson."

Sandor found Dante with his horses. Dante nodded a greeting but offered nothing else.

"Your grandmother and I will take the caravan south if you agree to remain here until the fair ends. It's too late in the summer to travel north; the winters are too harsh."

Some of Dante's moodiness dropped away as he considered Sandor's request. "Very well, another two days at the Bedford Fair it is, but I will listen to no more of Grandmother's predictions."

Sandor cleared his throat. "There is one more thing."

Dante rolled his eyes. "Of course there is."

"Carlotta is still uneasy about what she saw in the crystal ball. She would like you to visit Lord Alston before we leave. The distance to Alston Manor is not so great that it will make a difference in our travel plans."

"Grandfather, I told you—"

"Dante, indulge your grandmother. When she feels something this strongly, it is wise to heed her. Life will be much easier for both of us if you do this for her. She asks so little of you."

Dante sighed. He couldn't deny his grandparents anything. In truth, they did ask little of him. "Very well, Grandfather. The fair runs two more days. After we leave here, the caravan can camp a night in the meadow near Alston Park while I visit His Lordship."

Sandor's lined face lifted in a smile. "Thank you, Dante. You have never disappointed us."

By the time the fair ended two days later, Dante had sold all his horses except one colt, two mares and his stallion. All things considered, it had been a good fair.

After a brief visit with Lord Alston to please his grandparents, Dante and the caravan would travel south, where they wintered every year near the small village of Heath.

Lord Alston stood before the open window in his study, gazing at the night sky as he wondered if he would ever see Dante again. There were many things he regretted in his life, but the one thing he regretted most was waiting all these years to meet his grandson. The boy had met all his expectations and more. But Dante was no longer a boy. He was a man with a strong will and superior intelligence.

Alston's gut feeling was that when the time came, Dante would refuse neither the marquisate nor the responsibility attached to the title. He must trust Dante to wield his power prudently, for he knew his nephew Lonsdale would not do the title justice. Dante was a far better choice. Alston was glad he'd had the foresight to change his will in Dante's favor, even though he only knew his grandson from reports he had received regularly from the university.

Alston moved to the sideboard, poured a measure of brandy into a snifter and sat down at his desk. His back to the window, he closed his eyes and relived his first meeting with his grandson. Dante had been resentful and angry and determined not to like him, but who could blame him? Dante had a great deal to digest right now and needed time to think things through.

A noise behind Alston broke through his reverie. He whirled in his chair and found himself facing a pistol-wielding intruder who had entered through the open window behind him.

"You!"

"Open the safe," the intruder hissed.

"Tell me what you want."

"The safe—open it."

Alston moved to the safe, twisted the dial several times and pulled open the heavy door.

"Move aside."

Alston stepped away. "I expected you to show up, but not like this?"

The intruder rummaged through the contents of the safe, cursing when he failed to find what he was looking for. "Where is it?"

"I have no idea what you're talking about."

The intruder prodded Alston backward with his pistol. "Empty your desk drawers."

Alston obeyed. "Why didn't you come in the front door instead of breaking in like a thief in the night?"

The man glared at Alston but said nothing. He searched through the contents of the drawers, cursing violently when he failed to find what he was looking for. "Where is it?"

"Where is what?"

"You're not a stupid man." He waved the pistol in Alston's face.

Alston said nothing.

The intruder shoved everything into the drawers and slammed them shut. Then he moved to close the safe.

The moment the man turned away from him, Alston lunged for his pistol. The intruder easily overpowered him. He pushed Alston down into his chair. "When did you begin to suspect me?"

"Just recently. I didn't want to believe it of you."

"Your copy of the will—where is it?"

The marquis smiled. "You're too late. I gave it to Dante."

"Bastard! You have to die."

In the last moments before the intruder placed the pistol against Alston's right temple and pulled the trigger, the marquis regretted his past and wished he had had more time with his grandson. His last wish was for Dante's happiness.

The pistol shot reverberated through the mansion. Before he escaped through the window, the intruder placed the pistol in Alston's right hand and his finger on the trigger.

The gypsies remained until the end of the fair and then traveled to the meadow beyond Alston Park, where they set up camp. Dante moved from wagon to wagon, helping where he could. Then he ate supper with his grandparents and sought his bed. He was surprised to find Loretta waiting for him, her naked body attractively arrayed atop the sheets.

"There's too much on my mind tonight for this, Loretta."

"You've been neglecting me, Dante," Loretta said, pouting. "You appeared troubled at the fair—let me help you relax." She held out her arms.

His gaze followed the ripe curves of her body, finally settling on her dusky nipples. Loretta was right. A woman might be just what he needed to take his mind off the woman who still haunted his dreams. He undressed quickly and climbed into bed. But the moment he took Loretta into his arms, he knew he had made a mistake. He didn't want Loretta. Convincing her to leave, however, was easier said than done.

Loretta slid on top of him, suggestively rubbing her lush body against his. Being a virile male with a powerful sexual drive, Dante responded to the stimulating sex play naturally and without volition.

"I'm tired, Loretta," Dante complained. "It's been a long day and I've got a lot on my mind. Another time, perhaps."

Loretta scooted down his body and curled her fingers around his sex. The musky scent of her arousal wafted up to taunt him. "You don't *feel* tired," she purred. "You feel ready for me."

Dante didn't stand a chance. Loretta straddled him, fitted his sex against her core and sat down hard. He went in easily, sliding deep on the moist cushion of her desire. From there it was all instinct. But his heart wasn't in it. Loretta's hair was dark, not rusty red, her body was golden, not a creamy porcelain, and she wasn't a virgin, which he strongly suspected milady was. Loretta had lost her innocence a long time ago, and he hadn't been the man who had taken it.

Thoughtful lover that he was, Dante saw to Loretta's pleasure before his own. However, tonight wasn't one of his better performances. Something was missing, and he knew exactly what it was. Loretta wasn't milady.

* * *

The following morning dawned as dark and dreary as Dante felt. After Loretta had crept back to her wagon, Dante tossed restlessly, unable to sleep. He feared he would never see milady again, and that put him in a foul mood. Even though she despised him for being Rom, he had felt her response to his kisses and knew she wasn't indifferent. Unfortunately, he would never get the chance to prove he was as good as her noble almost fiancé. Dante wondered what milady would say if she knew he had refused a title—an impressive one, at that.

"Come have breakfast with us," Carlotta called when Dante stepped from his wagon into the cool, misty morning.

Dante accepted a bowl of oatmeal from his grandmother and ate in silence.

"Will you visit the marquis this morning?" Sandor asked when Dante set his empty bowl aside.

"Yes. I want to get this over with. The sooner we leave this place, the better."

"You cannot escape your fate, Dante," Carlotta said.

Her gaze pierced him. A shiver raced along Dante's spine. "What do you see when you look at me, Grandmother?"

"Death," Carlotta whispered. Then she slumped against her husband. Sandor helped her into the wagon and lowered her onto the bed.

Dante rushed to his grandmother and knelt beside her. "Is she all right, Grandfather?"

"She's been having dreams about you and the marquis. She sees darkness and death in her dreams. She fears the death might be yours."

"Please do not fear for me, Grandmother," Dante pleaded. "If consulting the crystal ball upsets you, you must stop."

Carlotta touched his face. Her callused hands were dearer to him than his own life. He grasped one and held it against his lips. "I don't like to see you like this, Grandmother."

"Don't worry about me, Dante. I will be fine. You must go to the marquis. Do not put it off any longer. I will not rest easy until you return."

"I don't have to go to him," Dante ventured. "We can break camp and leave now."

Carlotta rose up on her elbows, her voice barely above a whisper. "No, you must go now. Please, Dante, listen to me. Dark forces are at work against the marquis."

"You had best go, boy," Sandor urged. "Do not upset your grandmother any more than she already is."

"Very well, but take good care of her while I'm gone. I shan't be long."

Dante's mind whirled with speculation as he mounted Condor and rode the short distance to Alston Manor. Something having to do with the marquis had upset his frail grandmother, and he wondered what he would find at the manor house.

Dante dismounted at the front entrance. No one came to take Condor's reins, so he tied them to a hitching post and climbed the steps to the door. He grasped the knocker and rapped sharply, but unlike the first time he came calling, no one answered. He rapped again, harder and louder. Dante was tempted to return to the campsite when Grayson answered the summons. The butler's face lit up when he saw Dante.

"Thank God you've come, milord!" Grasping

Dante's sleeve, he pulled him inside. "It's so sad, so terribly sad. The staff is devastated."

Dante felt the change the moment he entered the house. The spirit, the very soul had left. The house was an empty shell. Dante wished he had paid more attention to Carlotta's warning.

"What happened?"

"Two nights ago His Lordship put a bullet through his right temple. It was ghastly."

Dante felt the color drain from his face. His full lips narrowed into a thin line. A rapid pulse beat against his cheek. "It cannot be! Though I hardly knew the marquis, he didn't strike me as a man who would take his own life when he had so much to live for."

Grayson's upper lip trembled. "Exactly what I told the magistrate, milord. But since he found the pistol in the marquis's hand, he could draw no other conclusion. You've arrived just in time. The will is to be read this afternoon."

"Where was the body found?" Dante asked, unable to come to grips with Alston's suicide.

"His Lordship was in his study when I heard the shot. I was the first to arrive."

"What did you see? I want to know every detail."

"I found His Lordship's body slumped over his desk. A pistol was clutched in his right hand. It was such a shock."

"Think, Grayson, think hard. What else did you see?"

"Nothing. When I returned to the scene after the magistrate left, the room appeared in perfect order."

"Was the window open or shut?"

"Why, open, of course. The marquis enjoyed fresh air."

Dante thought a moment, then asked, "Did His Lordship favor his right hand or his left?"

"His left, milord." Grayson frowned; then his face lit up as comprehension dawned. "He wouldn't have shot himself in his right temple if he was left-handed!"

"Precisely. Let's keep this to ourselves for the time being. It's unlikely the magistrate will find the killer, since there are no clues. But I promise you this, Grayson. I *will* find the man who murdered my grandfather."

Grayson drew himself erect. "His Lordship trusted me, and so can you. This"—he gestured—"is all yours now, and everyone will know it as soon as the will is read."

"I assume my grandfather has already been interred."

"Yesterday morning; he was laid to rest in the family vault. We thought it best not to wait." Grayson looked pained. "The heat, you know."

"I must tell Sandor and Carlotta what has happened, but I will return. Instruct the solicitor to wait to read the will until I arrive. Who else will be here for the reading?"

"Viscount Lonsdale is already in residence, acting as though he owns the place. He attended the burial service. He still believes he's the marquis's heir."

Dante knew what he would do—what he had to do. He didn't know what Sandor and Carlotta would think of his plans, but he hoped they would approve. The marquis's murder had changed everything. He couldn't let the foul deed go unpunished.

Dante rode into camp. Everything looked just as

he had left it despite the fact that nothing would ever be the same for him. And Carlotta had known it. He dismounted and went directly to his grandparents' wagon. His gaze sought Carlotta, and what he saw in her face startled him.

"You know, don't you?"

Carlotta nodded slowly. "The marquis is dead."

Dante squared his shoulders, already feeling the weight of his responsibilities. "The magistrate pronounced Lord Alston's death a suicide, but I know different. I am the new Marquis of Alston, and I swear upon my grandfather's grave that I will find the killer and avenge his death."

Chapter Four

Dressed in his finest gypsy garb, Dante returned to Alston Park. He was admitted immediately by Grayson, who had stationed himself at the door.

"The solicitor and Viscount Lonsdale await you in the study, milord," Grayson said. "The viscount is in a foul mood. He cannot understand the delay."

Dante learned firsthand the degree of Lonsdale's rage when he heard shouting coming from the study. "I am the heir—I order you to begin now!" The words reverberated with the speaker's irritation and outrage.

Dante decided that the restrained voice that followed the outburst must belong to the solicitor. "Announce me and summon the staff. I'm sure His Lordship made provisions for each of them." He paused. "Don't reveal my name or title yet. Let Lonsdale wonder about me."

Dante accompanied Grayson to the study; the door was open. Grayson cleared his throat. "The guest we were expecting has arrived, Mr. Bartholomew."

The solicitor stood. Lonsdale whirled, his mouth dropping open when he saw Dante. "What is that gypsy doing here? What on earth could he have to do with Uncle Alston's will?"

"Please sit down, milord," Bartholomew said. "All will become clear after your uncle's will is read."

One by one the staff crowded into the study. Grayson maintained his stance at the door.

"Really, Bartholomew, this is above too much," Lonsdale chided. "Never say all these people are included in my uncle's will."

"Indeed they are," Bartholomew replied. "Shall we get on with it?"

"I suppose we may as well get this over with," Lonsdale said testily, "as soon as the gypsy is shown the door. He has no business here."

Bartholomew peered over the top of his spectacles at Lonsdale. "I beg to differ with you, milord." He glanced at Dante. "Do I have your permission to begin, milord?"

Dante acknowledged him with a wave of his hand. The solicitor cleared his throat and began reading. When he came to the part where Lord Alston acknowledged Dante as his grandson and legal heir, Lonsdale leaped to his feet. "What! Impossible! The old man wasn't in his right mind. Why would he legitimize a gypsy bastard and make him his heir when he had me?"

"Perhaps you should ask yourself that question, my lord," Dante replied.

Lonsdale looked down his long nose at Dante as if he were lower than dirt beneath his feet. "You are nothing but a thieving gypsy."

"A thieving gypsy *marquis*," Dante reminded him. "Please continue, Mr. Bartholomew."

"Yes, ahem. To each of his servants the marquis leaves the sum of five hundred pounds, and he requests that the new marquis keep the staff intact."

"What about me?" Lonsdale asked petulantly.

"The marquis leaves the sum of one thousand pounds a year to you, doled out at the discretion of his heir."

"What? Is that all? This is a travesty, an appalling travesty."

"Please let me continue," Bartholomew said. "The marquis knew you would be angry, but I wrote his wishes exactly as they were dictated to me."

"When did the old fool have time to change his will? It's been a year since he last saw you."

Dante sucked in a startled breath. Lonsdale couldn't have known that unless he had been keeping tabs on the marquis.

"His Lordship changed his will on his last visit to London," Bartholomew explained. "You see, milord, he kept track of his grandson over the years, had him educated and considered him capable of inheriting. If it makes you feel better, you're next in line to inherit if the new Lord Alston refuses the marquisate."

"I've heard enough!" Lonsdale spat, rising. "I fully intend to contest the will."

"You may try," Bartholomew said, shrugging, "but it will do you no good. All the documents are in order and have been approved by the king and the highest courts of the land. Lord Alston was quite thorough. He knew you would try to contest the will and took precautions to prevent it."

Bartholomew turned to Dante. "Apparently, you and I have the only copies of the documents recognizing you as Alston's grandson and heir, milord. Can you produce them?"

Dante removed the documents from his belt and placed them on the desk. "His Lordship gave these to me when I visited him several days ago. He told me I might need them to prove my identity."

Lonsdale grabbed the documents and quickly scanned them. Cursing, he tossed them back on the desk. "The only way the gypsy could have these documents in his possession is if he killed my uncle and stole them."

Bartholomew stared at Lonsdale through narrowed lids. "Your uncle's death was a suicide."

"So it was," Lonsdale muttered. "Forgive my lapse."

Dante's wits sharpened. Lonsdale's careless words marked him as a prime suspect in the murder. "If you have evidence suggesting that my grandfather was murdered, please share it with us, Lonsdale."

"No! No! I know nothing of the sort. I spoke out of anger. Can you blame me? I have just lost everything I considered mine. I was to be Alston's heir. What will I do now? How can I face society?"

"One thousand pounds a year isn't an insignificant legacy," Dante pointed out.

"It is when you consider the vastness of Uncle Alston's wealth. It's all yours now, gypsy. I hope you live to enjoy it, and that you produce an heir to leave it to. If not, it will become mine."

"I intend to take very good care of myself," Dante responded, rising to his feet. He stood a whole head taller than Lonsdale and twice as broad. Flinching,

Lonsdale edged toward the door. Grayson held it open and slammed it the moment he exited.

"He can find his own way out," Grayson sniffed.

Dante turned to address the staff. "I know five hundred pounds is a great deal of money, and that some of you may choose to leave, but I will be grateful if you remain. I know little about being a marquis and will need your help to make the adjustment. I don't even know the extent of the late Lord Alston's estate. Tell Grayson your wishes, and I will see that the provisions of the will are met."

One by one the servants filed out, talking among themselves about their sudden windfall and what they intended to do with it. Grayson was the last to leave.

"I will not desert you, milord," he said before slipping out the door and closing it behind him.

Dante sighed. "I must be mad to accept this kind of responsibility." He subsided into a chair opposite Bartholomew's. "The only time I stayed in one place for more than a few days were the years I spent at school, and I hated every minute of it. This will take some getting used to. I hope you can remain a few weeks to acquaint me with my grandfather's estate and financial investments, Mr. Bartholomew."

"Perhaps it would be best if I return to London and get all the estate papers in order for your perusal. By the way, Lord Alston had a reliable secretary. Mr. Champion has been away visiting his sick mother but should return soon. His Lordship's death will come as a shock to him, but he is loyal and will remain with you if you want him."

He cleared his throat. "There is, however, a codicil to the will I purposely did not mention earlier. I thought it best to wait for Lonsdale to leave before enlightening you, although he knows about it."

Dante frowned. What now? "That doesn't sound promising. What is it?"

"Alston had a very good friend, an earl who died several years ago. The earl had a daughter who now lives with her uncle. The two friends decided shortly after Alston's son Alexander died without issue, that Alston's heir, whoever that might be, should wed the earl's daughter. Since no other heir was available, the assumption was that Lord Lonsdale, as Alston's heir, would wed the current Lord Parkton's niece."

Dante went still. "Are you saying I am expected to wed a woman I do not know if I wish to inherit? A woman who was intended for Lonsdale?"

"The will states the girl is to wed Alston's heir. And that, milord, is you. Once Lord Parkton learns you are the new marquis, he will expect you to honor Lord Alston's wishes and wed his niece. It was your grandfather's fondest wish that you wed Lady Esme Harcourt after he made you his heir.

"If you prefer to ignore his wishes, the title and estate will revert to Lord Lonsdale," Bartholomew continued. "You will still inherit a substantial amount of money. In light of this new development, you may prefer to forgo the title, take the inheritance and leave. Personally, I think the marquisate may be nothing but a burden to you. Perhaps you should refuse it and let Lonsdale inherit."

"I was prepared to accept the title and the responsibility accompanying it, but taking a wife is more than I bargained for. What if the lady refuses to marry me?"

"Lord Alston's will clearly states that you must wed Lady Esme to inherit."

"I don't like it."

"I suspected as much. The title is yours to accept or reject. I'm sure Lonsdale will happily accept both the lady and the title if you aren't up to the challenge."

Dante bristled. He wasn't about to commit himself until he spoke with his grandparents. "I must speak with Carlotta and Sandor before I give you my answer. Grayson will see to your comfort while I'm gone. We will talk further at dinner tonight."

Carlotta and Sandor were waiting for him when he returned to the campsite. "Has the will been read?" Sandor asked.

Dante nodded. "Aside from the usual bequeathals, I am the sole heir to Lord Alston's estate. Alston's nephew showed up for the funeral and stayed for the reading. As you might expect, Lonsdale's reaction to Lord Alston's will was explosive."

"Come inside and tell us everything," Carlotta said.

Dante related every detail of the reading and what occurred afterward. When he finished, Sandor appeared shocked. "It doesn't seem right that Lord Alston should withhold the title if you refuse to wed his friend's daughter."

Sandor looked to his wife for an explanation. "I do not understand. Carlotta, can you tell us why the marquis would demand such a thing of Dante? Our grandson should be allowed to marry whom he wishes."

"Your brief meeting with your grandfather must have convinced him that you were worthy of the title, and that you would also suit the lady," Carlotta mused.

"Have you made a decision?" Sandor asked. "If it's money you want, this is your chance to claim your portion and walk away from the marquisate."

"I cannot do that, Grandfather. After meeting Lord Lonsdale, I'm convinced he had something to do with Grandfather Alston's death. He expected to inherit, and appeared shocked when he learned Lord Alston had another heir. I'm convinced Grandfather Alston's death was no suicide. If I took the money and left the title to Lonsdale, I could never live with myself. The power associated with my new title will help me find and bring Lord Alston's killer to justice.

"If I hadn't met the marquis, I might not have cared. But I no longer hate him as I once did. And Lord Alston certainly did not deserve to die as he did. I refuse to walk away from Alston Manor and let the murderer go free."

"What about the woman?" Sandor asked. "Are you willing to marry her?"

"Do I have a choice? Once I tell Mr. Bartholomew that I accept the title, I must honor Grandfather Alston's wishes. You taught me well, Grandfather. I suddenly find I am a man of honor."

Carlotta smiled. "You are but fulfilling your destiny."

"Let's talk about more practical things," Dante said. "Like where you are going to live. I want you both to move to Alston Park. Eventually I must go up to London. I know you don't like the city, but you should be reasonably happy in a grand manor."

Sandor held up his hand. "Say no more, son. Carlotta and I are not ready yet to sit back and toast our toes before a fire. We are wanderers, and so we shall remain."

"Grandfather, please reconsider. I will not always be near to take care of you and Grandmother."

"Do not worry about us, Dante," Carlotta said. "We are not doddering yet. Perhaps we will consider your offer at some point in the future. Meanwhile, you have a wife to court."

Dante snorted. "I don't even know what the woman looks like."

"Trust me, all will be well. But do not take my earlier warning lightly," Carlotta cautioned. "There is still an evil entity out there. Someone murdered Lord Alston, and he is likely to make you his next target. Be careful, Grandson."

"I take nothing you say lightly, Grandmother. I must go now, but I will return before you take the caravan south. I intend to see that you have enough money to keep you in comfort no matter where you go."

"How long will you remain at Alston Park?"

"Long enough to learn everything I need to know about the workings of society. Grandfather Alston's secretary and butler will coach me. I do not intend to face the *ton* or the woman Lord Alston wants me to wed before I am every bit as formidable as my grandfather, and have the information I need to take my place in the House of Lords."

"A wise move," Carlotta agreed.

"There is much to be done before I launch myself into society, such as acquiring the proper clothing," Dante continued. "Although I am proud of my heritage, I cannot appear as I am dressed today." His chin firmed, his voice hardened. "I intend to make my own way in society. Despite my responsibilities as marquis, I will remain my own man and follow my own dictates."

"Spoken like a true Rom," Sandor applauded. "You will do fine, Grandson. Your grandmother and I have never been prouder of you."

"How long do you intend to camp in the meadow?" Dante asked.

Carlotta squinted at the sky and sniffed the air. "Signs point to an early winter, which means the caravan should begin the journey south within a fortnight."

Dante's expression softened. "I shall miss you."

"And we you. Go now and fulfill your destiny. Become the marquis Lord Alston knew you would be. Show the *gadje* what a Rom is capable of. When we return in the spring, you can introduce us to your wife."

Wife. The thought of marrying a woman he did not know appalled Dante, but perhaps the two of them could find common ground in order to fulfill the late marquis's wishes.

Dante hugged his grandparents and bade them good-bye, then spoke to the friends he had grown up with. Everyone in the caravan knew he was leaving and why. Though most expressed pleasure at his good fortune, a few called him traitor for becoming a *gadjo*. With his fate all but decided for him, Dante returned to Alston Park.

Dante spent a month and more learning about his vast empire from his solicitor, including his estates, business dealings and income. In time he would demand a full financial accounting from Bartholomew and told the solicitor as much before he returned to London.

A tailor was summoned from London and returned to his business with orders for a wardrobe befitting Dante's new station in life. Luther Champion, the former Lord Alston's secretary, proved to be a fountain of information on the *ton*. Between visits to Sandor and Carlotta, Dante rode his Bedford estate, met his tenants and learned that his grandfather had been well liked and respected. No one could understand why a man in Alston's position would take his own life when he had everything to live for.

Their high opinion of the marquis made Dante more determined than ever to find his grandfather's killer.

The only thing that concerned him even remotely was courting the woman who would become his wife.

Was she beautiful? Ugly? High-strung? Haughty? Would she scorn him?

Would she consider him an unworthy Rom wearing the trappings of a marquis?

Finally Dante was ready to face society. Rigged out in style, he left for London with an entourage that included Grayson and Champion. Their destination was the Alston mansion he now owned in ultrafashionable Mayfair.

Chapter Five

Her arm gently resting on her uncle's sleeve, Esme waited patiently to be announced at the Harris' ball. She'd only been in Town a week and already invitations had begun arriving. Although the Season hadn't officially started, a large number of families were in Town for various reasons.

The Harris' ball was intended as a preseason event that would set the mood for festivities yet to come. Esme knew she would be exhausted before she could return to the country at the end of the Season.

"Lord Alston's new heir is supposed to be here tonight," Lord Parkton said. "He sent a note around asking to meet you."

Esme gave a huff of indignation. "Surely you don't expect me to wed a man I do not know."

"You've always known you were promised to Lord Alston's heir."

"I assumed that was Calvin."

70

"I thought you were unhappy with Lonsdale, my dear."

"I was, and well you know it, but we know nothing about the new marquis. Do you truly believe Alston committed suicide? I met him on several occasions, and he didn't appear to be a man bent on killing himself."

Parkton shrugged. "Alston was a private person. Who knew what he was thinking? Lonsdale was as surprised as everyone by the suicide. The viscount has kept to himself since the reading of the will. Can't blame him; discovering there is a new heir for the Alston title must have came as an unwelcome surprise. I suspected something had changed when I last spoke to Alston. He told me not to push for a marriage between you and Lonsdale."

"Does anyone know the new marquis? Has anyone seen him? Where did he come from all of a sudden? Why didn't Calvin know about him?"

Parkton sighed. "I wish I had answers to your questions, Esme. From what I've heard, Alston's heir is his bastard grandson. Alston acknowledged him in the courts, so now everything is legal. I'm as anxious to see the man as you are. He must be a good man, considering all the trouble Alston went to to recognize his grandson and make him his heir."

"I still don't like it," Esme whispered as a footman announced them. "I don't care what my father and the old marquis wanted, I won't marry a man I know nothing about, no matter how worthy the marquis considered him."

"You're not getting any younger, my dear. You have to settle on a husband soon. I was willing to wait until

Alston's heir inherited; now that day is at hand and your time has run out."

Esme's chin rose defiantly. *Not if I have anything to say about it.*

"Do not reject the man out of hand, Esme," Parkton continued. "Give him a chance to court you, to get to know you. You might find him to your liking."

Disgruntled at the hand fate had dealt her, Esme was barely civil to the gentlemen who came up to sign her dance card. As soon as the card was full, Lord Parkton said, "There's your friend Louise. I will leave you to chat with her while I greet some of my cronies."

Esme greeted Louise effusively. They had been friends ever since childhood. Louise was engaged to the Earl of Carstairs and was planning a lavish wedding in the spring.

"How are plans for your wedding progressing?" Esme asked. "And where is that handsome fiancé of yours?"

"Travis is still in the country." Louise pouted. "Family business, but he should be here for the Dunsworth musicale next week." She glanced behind Esme. "Where is Lord Lonsdale?"

"He's not here. No one has seen him since Lord Alston died and left his title and estate to an unknown grandson. He's probably off somewhere licking his wounded pride."

"Oh, I've heard all about it," Louise gushed. "Have you met the new marquis?"

"No. Do you know anyone who has?"

Louise shook her head, and then confided in a hushed voice, "Rumor has it the new heir is a bastard."

"I already know that much."

"But do you know his mother was a gypsy? The gossips are having a field day with it."

Esme blanched. "Uncle Daniel and I haven't been in Town long enough to hear rumors. Surely they cannot be true. I knew Lord Alston; he was proper to a fault. He would never let a gypsy inherit his estate. Even Calvin, with all his faults, would be a better choice."

"I wonder what Lonsdale thinks about being disinherited?" Louise said.

"The title meant a great deal to him."

"Perhaps losing you upset him more than losing the title," Louise suggested.

Esme could not stop the smile that came unbidden to her lips. "I sincerely doubt that."

"Your dowry is quite generous; he might need it now that he can no longer count on the Alston fortune."

"I don't want a man who wants me for my money," Esme replied. "It would be different if Calvin loved me and I loved him, but all I feel is relief. I never wanted to wed him."

"But everyone knows you are to wed the Alston heir. As things stand now, you'll be expected to marry the gypsy."

"In the first place," Esme huffed, "we don't know the new marquis is a gypsy. And in the second place, I don't have to marry anyone I don't want to."

"I wouldn't be too sure about that," Parkton said, joining them in time to hear Esme's remark. "I intend to see you wed according to your father's and Alston's wishes. I'm not an ogre, Esme. I just want to see you settled and happy."

"With a gypsy?" Esme returned.

"Whatever he is, I'm sure he's honorable and worthy of the title. Excuse me, ladies, I think I'll join the men in the card room."

Esme felt a sick headache coming on. Just thinking about having to wed a gypsy made her ill. She already knew one gypsy, and that was one too many. That despicable man had somehow gotten into her head and refused to leave. On those nights when sleep eluded her, she recalled the gypsy's handsome face and relived his kisses, much to her dismay. She also remembered his arrogance, his conceit. The impossible man thought he was God's gift to women, and expected them to fall into his arms.

Esme's thoughts were interrupted when young Lord Batterly claimed her for his dance and they joined the next reel. Though Esme enjoyed dancing, after four dances her head was pounding worse than before. When her current partner returned her to the sidelines, she sought out Louise and asked her to tell her uncle that she had a headache and was taking the carriage home, and she would send the carriage back for his use.

Esme was wending her way toward the door when an unaccountable stillness settled over the crowded ballroom. Glancing around, she noticed that everyone's attention was riveted on the entrance. She couldn't see over the heads of those in front of her, so she had no idea who or what had caused such a reaction.

Then she heard the footman announce a late guest.

"Lord Dante Knowles, the Marquis of Alston!"

Abruptly the crowd parted and Esme saw him. He

had his back to her, greeting the host and hostess. He was dressed in unrelieved black but for white linen spilling from his throat and wrists. A raven among a roomful of brightly dressed popinjays, Esme thought. He was tall, his shoulders broad; he possessed the physique of a man who needed no padding beneath his clothing to accentuate his masculinity.

Something about him seemed familiar, but she couldn't quite decide what. Perhaps it was the intense, brooding energy emanating from him, or maybe . . . He turned around; Esme gasped and nearly fainted.

The gypsy! *Her* gypsy. *He* was the new Marquis of Alston? Esme wanted to disappear into the woodwork. There was no possibility of marriage between them, for she would never wed a man whose ego was exceeded only by his arrogance. A bastard *and* a gypsy. What had the old marquis been thinking?

Esme tried to slink away where she could watch the *ton's* reaction to the gypsy. A woman standing next to her began fanning herself. Her female companion whispered loudly enough for Esme to hear, "I always thought there was something special about Dante. He's the most marvelous lover. A marquis . . . well, well, who would have thought?"

Esme edged closer, trying not to look as if she was eavesdropping.

"Have you really had him in your bed, Margaret?"

"I have indeed, Penny, more than once. Homer left me behind to languish in the country last spring while he went off to Town. I met Dante at a country fair. After meeting him, I didn't mind Homer's leaving me behind."

"Can you introduce me?" Penny asked. "My husband doesn't intend to come up to London until Parliament opens."

"Of course. I imagine Dante will appreciate all the friends he can get. He won't have an easy time finding friends among the *ton*—male friends, that is. Women will flock to him in droves. Just look at him; he's gorgeous." Margaret gave a delicate shiver. "And sooo talented in bed."

The two women strolled off, leaving Esme utterly confused. But as she watched the scene unfold, she realized that every woman, from the youngest debutante to the oldest matron, was clearly swooning over the gypsy. The men, however, appeared more cautious. But the gypsy's exalted title soon had the gentlemen eager to meet him as well.

Esme recognized the man who accompanied the gypsy. He was Viscount Brookworth, a man reputed to be a prolific womanizer. Esme supposed that men of the same ilk gravitated toward one another.

Then Uncle Daniel found her. "Lord Alston is here, my dear." He grasped her arm and gently steered her toward the gypsy. "I'm sure the marquis is eager to meet his future bride."

Esme dug in her heels. "Can't this wait for another time, Uncle? I really don't feel well."

"So your friend Louise informed me. I'm sure it's only nerves. After you meet the marquis, you may go home, if you still wish to leave."

"Please, Uncle, I—"

It was too late; the gypsy turned in her direction and looked directly at her. Their gazes locked and held. Esme was the first to look away.

* * *

Aside from being nervous, Dante didn't feel as out of place as he'd thought he would. All he had to do was remember he was a marquis and outranked nearly everyone here tonight. Besides, he had been coached and prepared for this night by Grayson and Luther Champion.

Dante had met few people during the week he had been in Town. It had been a lucky day, however, when he ran into Brookworth, his friend from university. While Brookworth had been shocked by Dante's new station in life, he appeared pleased with his friend's good fortune. He had taken Dante to the most popular gentlemen's clubs, showed him the ropes, so to speak, and introduced him to some influential people. Brookworth had told him not to worry about being accepted by the *ton*; his rank demanded respect. No one would dare give a marquis a cut direct.

Dante's attention sharpened as he recognized a few women he had known previously. They were ladies he had met at country fairs and later bedded. They hadn't cared that he was a gypsy. All they cared about was the hardness of his cock and how well he pleasured them. He wondered if Esme Harcourt would feel the same way. Or did she consider herself too high in the instep for a gypsy?

"You're not going to have any problems with the ladies." Brookworth grinned. "Look at them; they are all drooling over you. Too bad you're promised to the Harcourt chit."

"What do you know about Esme Harcourt?" Dante asked.

"Not much. She prefers the country and only

comes to Town occasionally. Her uncle, the Earl of Parkton, is her guardian. If I remember correctly, she's easy on the eyes, but it's been a long time since I've seen her."

Dante heaved a sigh as he searched the crowd. At first his gaze passed over her, and then it snapped back, as if an invisible force pulled his eyes in her direction. Their gazes met, locked; he felt the hairs on the back of his neck stand at attention. The blood ran hot through his veins and settled in his nether regions. She was the first to look away.

"It's milady." He spoke aloud though he hadn't meant to.

"Who? Do you see someone you know?" Brookworth asked.

Dante was about to point milady out to his friend, but realized it was too late. She and the older man with her were nearly upon them.

"Lord Alston, allow me to introduce myself. I am Daniel Harcourt, the Earl of Parkton, and this is my niece, Lady Esme Harcourt."

Dante lost the ability to speak. *His* milady was the woman he was supposed to marry? Impossible! The woman hated him. She held him in the utmost contempt. He wondered if he should pretend not to know her or admit to having met her before.

Brookworth jumped in to fill the silence. "Lady Harcourt, how nice to see you again." He poked Dante in the ribs.

Dante remembered his manners in time to shake the earl's hand and acknowledge milady. He looked into her eyes, saw her dismay and decided to deny having met her. When she offered her hand, he took it in his and barely touched his lips to her fingers.

She jerked her hand away so fast he found himself kissing air.

"Lady Esme, my pleasure," Dante said smoothly.

Her violet eyes were vibrant against her porcelain skin and rusty red hair. Dressed in a shimmering silver ball gown, her hair held in place by a glittering tiara, she looked like a princess.

A very angry and somewhat confused princess.

"My lord," Parkton went on. "You are aware, of course, of your grandfather's wishes concerning my niece, and I suspect you would like to become better acquainted with her."

"I would indeed," Dante allowed, assuming his most cultured voice.

"Then you have my permission to take Esme for a stroll in the garden, as long as you do not wander too far from the house. Even though you and Esme will wed one day, her reputation must be protected."

"Uncle," Esme began, "my head is splitting. I want to go home."

"Perhaps a breath of fresh air is just what you need," Dante said. "It's quite pleasant out tonight." He cupped Esme's elbow. "With your permission, my lord, I would very much like to take Lady Esme outside for a breath of air. It's stifling in here."

"Off you go then," Parkton said. "Don't mind Esme—she's a little shy."

"This way, milady," Dante said, guiding her toward the open French doors. As they sailed out the doors, Dante leaned over and whispered in her ear, "Shy? Your uncle doesn't know you if he thinks you are shy."

"How did this happen?" Esme hissed. "How did you become Lord Alston's heir? Calvin must be furious; I haven't seen him since the will was read."

"Are you referring to your almost betrothed?"

He guided her down the stairs to the extensive garden, where hundreds of glowing lanterns lent a magical quality to the night. Several couples were strolling along the main path. Too many people for a private conversation, Dante thought as he swerved off onto a narrow, less traveled path, taking Esme with him. Then he pulled her behind a hedge.

"Uncle Daniel said we should remain within sight of the house," Esme hissed. "He believes we are strangers."

Dante's lips curved upward. His grin was too wicked for Esme's peace of mind. "But we aren't strangers, are we, milady? I have held you in my arms, kissed you, tasted your passion."

Highly affronted, Esme retreated, until the hedge pressed against her backside. "No one knows that but you and I, and I prefer to keep it that way." She glared at him. "Why didn't you tell me you were Alston's heir? Why did Lord Alston let Calvin think he was going to inherit?"

"I met my grandfather for the first time at the end of the Bedford Fair. Until that time I had no idea he had made me his heir. I've always known I was Alston's bastard grandson, but up to that point, we had never met."

"What kind of pressure did you put on Lord Alston to make him disown Calvin?"

"You do know how to hurt a man," Dante mocked. "I used no pressure. I knew nothing about the will until a few days before Alston's death. He sent a Runner to find me. I was told my grandfather wished to see me. That's when I learned he had made me his heir. He told me he didn't trust Lonsdale to do justice to the title. I always wondered why the marquis paid to send me to university, and now I know." He laughed. "He called me a man of honor."

Esme shook her head. "I understand none of this."

"Neither do I."

"You're a gypsy. How could Lord Alston think you trustworthy? Calvin may have his faults, but I've never known him to steal for a living."

"He may have done worse," Dante muttered.

"What did you say?"

"Nothing, but let's get one thing clear. I bred and sold horses to support myself and my grandparents. While not all Rom are honest, I've done nothing to be ashamed of."

Esme thought otherwise. "How can you say you are no thief when you stole a kiss from me the first time we met?"

"You gave it willingly."

"I did no such thing! How dare you think I would allow a gypsy to kiss me when Calvin has never—"

"Calvin is a fool," Dante charged. "You are no longer his almost betrothed. I am the Marquis of Alston, the man you will wed."

Esme was happy she was no longer expected to marry Calvin, but she wasn't about to let the gypsy know that. "You're mad if you think I'm going to marry you. Just the thought makes me ill."

Dante's eyes narrowed. The play of shadows and moonlight on the dark planes of his face made Esme catch her breath. No wonder women fell over themselves for his attention. He was too handsome, a demon in the guise of virile masculinity. Dark, mysterious, sensually intriguing.

"What you mean is that marrying a *Rom* sickens

you. Admit it, you consider me dirt beneath your dainty slipper."

Esme flushed. She wouldn't exactly put it that way, but he had come close to the truth. She wouldn't marry him, no matter what her uncle said. She would become the laughingstock of the *ton*. The man had been born far beneath her, and no title could change that.

Dante recognized contempt when he saw it. Esme despised his Rom heritage even though her body responded to his. Marrying her would make his life a living hell. She would find a *gadjo* lover before the ink was dry on their marriage papers. Would Mr. Bartholomew consider the terms of his grandfather's will met if Dante offered for the lady and was refused?

Dante knew that pursuing a woman who held him in contempt was an exercise in futility. However, he remembered Carlotta telling him that fools walked in where angels feared to tread, and Dante was no angel. A slow smile stretched his lips. If he seduced Esme to his bed, she would have to wed him.

Did he want her enough to seduce her?

His cock stirred relentlessly, providing him with the answer.

Dante reached for her. The hedge prevented her from retreating, and he easily swept her into his arms. "We're a perfect fit," he whispered into her ear. "And you smell good, too. Everything about you arouses me."

"Any woman would arouse you," she shot back. "You're a womanizer. I have ears, and your reputation preceded you."

Dante ran the back of his finger down the silken

surface of her cheek. Moving closer, he whispered against her lips, "I'm a lover, not a womanizer."

Esme shrugged. "Womanizer, lover—I see no difference."

"A womanizer beds women for his own personal satisfaction, while a lover gives as well as receives pleasure. A lover never leaves a woman wanting."

"Harumph!" Esme snorted. "You give yourself too much credit. I've never heard a more arrogant statement." She pushed against his chest. "If I don't return to the house soon, Uncle Daniel will come looking for me."

"We'll return in a moment. I *do* intend to court you, you know. Our marriage was destined long before we met."

Esme shook her head. "I refuse to be seen with you."

Anger stiffened Dante's spine. Esme Harcourt had a lesson to learn, and he was just the man to teach it. No matter how she felt about him, he wasn't going to release her until he was good and ready. She felt too good in his arms, and he desperately wanted to kiss those lush, pouting lips.

"I'm going to kiss you, milady."

"You don't have my permission, milord."

"I don't need permission. You are my betrothed."

"Not yet and maybe never."

"My kiss or the betrothal?"

"Both."

Esme's gaze was drawn to his eyes. Moonlight turned them into pools of black velvet, so intense she couldn't look away, could scarcely breathe or think. Her gaze slid down to his lips. They were full, moist and slightly tilted. She watched in dismay as his mouth descended on hers, covered it, molding, coaxing, pulling a response from her despite her reluctance.

She parted her lips on a gasp of pleasure. The tip of his tongue stroked the edge of her teeth, ventured further, brushed the inside of her cheek in a burning, mind-stealing exploration. The kiss stole her will, made her light-headed, and she clung to him in a desperate bid for balance. She felt something hard probing against her . . . and gasped.

Dante pressed the rigid length of his sex against her softness, rotating his hips as his mouth possessed hers with wicked skill. Esme moaned into his mouth. This couldn't go on. She didn't want to become another of the gypsy's conquests. She wanted nothing to do with him. When his hands found her aching breasts, cupped them, gently squeezed her nipples, Esme feared she was in deep trouble. *She liked it too much.*

How could a thieving gypsy's kisses arouse her? She had kissed a few men, but their kisses had left her cold. The gypsy's kisses left her deliciously breathless and tingling in forbidden places. To her utter mortification, she wound her arms around his neck and kissed him back. When his tongue stroked in and out of her mouth in blatant imitation of the sex act, she wanted to melt into him, absorb him into her pores. In a moment of madness, she wanted to feel his naked skin against hers.

That forbidden thought returned her to sanity and renewed her resolve to resist the gypsy's seduction. Summoning her willpower, she gave him a mighty shove. Either she was stronger than she thought or he let her go, for his hands slid away from her breasts.

"Did I frighten you?" Dante asked.

She shook her head, looked into his dark, fathomless eyes and said, "No . . . I've frightened myself. I cannot think when you kiss me."

Her answer renewed Dante's faith in his seductive charms. At least she felt something for him besides contempt. Why it mattered, Dante had no idea. The violet-eyed beauty had intrigued him from the beginning. He had wanted her well before he knew who she was, and he still wanted her.

"At least we are a match in one way," Dante said. "Beneath your disdain lies a spark of passion. I can feel it when I touch you, taste it in your kiss. I vow that one day you will want me as much as I want you. Most married couples don't even have that much."

"You assume too much," Esme charged, edging away from him. "I will never marry you."

"Is it Lonsdale? Do you love that . . ." he was going to say killer but changed it to "popinjay?"

"No . . . no . . . no! I don't love Calvin. I'm glad I'm no longer expected to marry him."

For some reason, her admission made Dante smile. His fingers curled around her arm. "I'll return you to the ball. You are right—if we don't return soon, your uncle will think I've compromised your virtue." His tone mocked her. "I *am* a gypsy, after all."

"Yes, you are," Esme returned on a huff of indignation.

The path was narrow. Their bodies touched as he escorted her to the main path and back to the ballroom. She tried to edge away but there was no room. She felt the heat of him through her clothes and his. Everything about him exuded power and arrogance. Apparently, he was a man who always got his way. He wanted her sexually and expected her to fall into his arms.

Even she had to admit the gypsy was exciting. He had but to touch her to send fire pulsing through her veins.

They reached the house and climbed the stairs to the veranda. To Esme's dismay, everyone turned to look at them when they entered the ballroom. Instead of taking Esme to her uncle, Dante immediately swept her into a waltz that had just begun.

"I didn't know gypsies waltzed," Esme said insultingly.

"Gypsies might not waltz, but marquises do," Dante replied.

Esme had nothing to say to that. When the dance ended, Dante guided her to where Parkton stood at the edge of the dance floor.

"If you hadn't returned when you did, I would have come looking for you," Parkton said with a hint of censure. "May I remind you, Alston, that you and my niece are not yet formally engaged? Proper decorum must be observed until then. I know you had a somewhat . . . unorthodox upbringing, but I'm sure you have been apprised of the workings of society."

"Indeed, my lord. Please forgive my breach of etiquette. I hadn't meant to keep Lady Esme out that long, but it seemed we had a great deal to talk about."

Parkton nodded, apparently mollified. "I'm glad you two found common ground. I intend to do all I can to promote the match between you."

"Uncle Daniel, must we discuss this now?" Esme asked.

"Of course not, my dear. We can discuss it another time, if you wish. Although the sudden change of heirs has left me rather confused, Alston, I want to see my niece settled in a good marriage."

"Uncle!"

Parkton brushed her admonition aside. "Esme can do no better than a marquis, but I want to make sure she will fare well with you on a personal basis. I'm sure you understand, my lord. Ordinarily I wouldn't approve of a gyp . . . ahem, a man I know little about, but your grandfather trusted you enough to make you his heir, so I can do no less."

"You may say gypsy if you wish, my lord," Dante said, pinning him with the intensity of his dark gaze. "I cannot hide who I am. Gypsy or no, I still have Grandfather Alston's blood flowing through my veins."

"Indeed," Parkton blustered. "And you outrank an earl. Why don't you meet me at White's tomorrow? Say around four? We'll find a private corner and discuss"—his gaze slid to Esme—"the betrothal."

"I shall be delighted," Dante said.

"I want to go home," Esme cut in. "My headache has intensified. Good night, gyp . . . Lord Alston."

"Good night, milady," Dante replied, bowing deeply. "Perhaps you will do me the honor of riding with me in my carriage tomorrow morning. You could show me the sights."

"I'm sorry, I don't—"

"Esme would be delighted," Parkton interrupted. "You may pick her up at ten."

Whipping around, Esme gave Dante her back as she marched away. Parkton followed in her wake.

"What did you say to make the lady angry?" Brookworth asked, sidling up to Dante.

"It's not what I said," Dante replied. "It's what I am."

Chapter Six

Dante was in a cheerful mood the following morning as he drove his carriage around to the Parkton townhouse. Though not as large as the Alston mansion, the Parkton residence was elegant nonetheless. Dante was too new to his title not to be impressed by London's upper crust and its extravagances. Many times in the past weeks he had wished himself back in his cramped wagon, which held everything he needed in the world. He would be there now, enjoying the simple life, if not for his grandfather's murder.

Dante drove the carriage up to the curb and set the brake. Though he missed his nomadic life, there were advantages to being wealthy and titled that he *did* enjoy. Like this elegant carriage, for instance, and the other equipage he had inherited.

At precisely ten o'clock, Dante grasped the brass knocker and rapped on the door. A young footman answered his summons.

"Would you please inform Lady Esme that Lord Alston is here?" Dante said, handing the man his hat and cane—unnecessary items he had little use for, but Grayson had insisted upon both.

The footman returned Dante's hat and cane. "Milady isn't in to anyone this morning."

Dante frowned. What kind of game was Esme playing now?

"Alston, I'm afraid my niece is ill."

Dante gazed past the footman to Parkton, who stood poised at the foot the staircase. With a nod, the earl dismissed the footman.

"Is Lady Esme truly ill, or is she ashamed to be seen with me?" Dante asked. He knew her better than her uncle.

"No, no, you misjudge my niece," Parkton denied. "If you recall, Esme wasn't feeling well when we left the ball last night." He shrugged. "Women and their ailments defy my understanding."

Women like milady were a puzzle to Dante as well.

"I'll have a talk with Esme before our appointment at White's at four. Don't be late; we have a great deal to discuss."

"I'll be there," Dante said. He glanced one last time at the staircase to make sure Esme hadn't changed her mind, then turned and stormed off.

The snub stung. Dante knew precisely why she had declined his company this morning. She was embarrassed to be seen with a gypsy. Dante was acquainted with ladies of the *ton* who would happily welcome him to their beds. When Dante reached the curb, he turned and looked back toward the house. From the corner of his eye he saw a curtain flutter at a second-floor window, and then a face appeared in the opening. Milady's face. He bowed and tipped his hat.

The face disappeared and the curtain fluttered

back into place. Dante smiled to himself as he sprang lightly into his carriage and drove off. But instead of returning home, he decided to enjoy a drive through Hyde Park. He hadn't been there yet, and from what he'd heard, it was *the* place to be seen.

"He's gone," Esme said with a sigh of relief.

"Your uncle is not going to be pleased with your behavior," Jane predicted. "One does not snub a marquis. And His Lordship is almost your fiancé."

"I am not going to marry a gypsy," Esme protested.

Jane sighed. "Gypsy or nay, you have to admit the man is devilishly handsome."

"He's a devil, all right," Esme muttered. "Find me something to wear, Jane. It's a fine day for a stroll in the park."

A knock sounded on the door. "Esme, may I come in? I promise I won't overtax you."

"Uncle Daniel," Esme hissed as she dove into bed and pulled the covers up to her chin. "Come in, Uncle."

Parkton strode into the room. "How are you feeling?"

"My head still hurts. Cook gave me a powder for the pain, but it hasn't helped. I think I'll rest in bed today."

"I hope your illness isn't due to your reluctance to accompany Alston this morning. Truthfully, the man has impressed me on many levels. I should know more about him after our meeting at White's later today. I will see you at dinner. I hope you'll feel well enough to join me."

Esme gave him a wan smile. "What are you about today, Uncle?"

"I have a busy day. As soon as Parliament opens, I'll

be drumming up support for a bill I hope to get passed."

"Then I shall see you tonight."

Parkton hesitated. "After my meeting with the marquis today, I hope to announce your betrothal and set a wedding date."

"How do you know the gypsy is an honorable man, Uncle? You can't betroth me to a man we know nothing about. We need time to learn whether Alston can live up to his grandfather's expectations."

"I have heard nothing detrimental about him, but you're right. Our conversation today should tell me a lot about his character. Well, I'm off now. Have a care for your health, my dear. We don't want Alston thinking you're sickly, do we?"

Personally, Esme didn't care. The moment her uncle left the house, she jumped out of bed, fuming over the plight of women as Jane dressed her. An hour later, properly dressed and wearing a fetching bonnet, Esme set out for Hyde Park with Jane in tow. The hour was still too early to be fashionable, but Esme didn't care. She preferred the park when it was less crowded.

"Did you bring the bread to feed the ducks?" Esme asked. Feeding the ducks was one of her favorite things to do in the park, except for riding.

Esme had nearly reached the pond when she heard someone hail her. Turning, she saw Viscount Lonsdale hurrying to catch up with her.

"I hoped I'd see you here today," Lonsdale said when he finally reached her.

"Good morning, my lord," Esme said coolly. "You've certainly made yourself scarce since your uncle's death. Wherever have you been?"

"I avoided society after the reading of the will. I needed to pull myself together. The shock my uncle dealt me nearly destroyed me. I hadn't a clue about the gypsy until the will was read. I cannot imagine why Uncle Alston bypassed me in favor of a gypsy bastard. It's unthinkable! I have never been more humiliated in my life."

"Don't you have any idea why Lord Alston favored his illegitimate grandson over you?"

Lonsdale shook his head. "As I said before, I had always assumed I was Uncle Alton's sole heir, and he never said anything to refute my assumption. Upon occasion he lectured me about my debts, and even hinted that he was going to change his will, but I thought it was his way of warning me about my excesses. I knew nothing about the gypsy, or that Uncle Alston even had an illegitimate grandson."

"I understand Lord Alston had the gypsy educated," Esme ventured.

"So I've heard. Brookworth has already spread the word. It seems the gypsy found a friendly face or two in Town. His reputation with women has preceded him. It disgusts me to think that highborn women would cavort with a gypsy.

"I intend to speak to your uncle today about announcing our engagement. I cannot believe Parkton would let you wed a man carrying gypsy blood in his veins. I still want you, Esme. Ours would be a marriage between equals. My bloodlines are impeccable. My mother, remember, was Uncle Alston's sister."

Esme lowered her gaze to where Lonsdale gripped her arm. "Release me, Calvin, you're hurting me."

"Not until you promise to marry me. I may not be the Marquis of Alston, but at least I am no gypsy." He tugged her arm. "Come away with me to Gretna Green. We'll be married before your uncle can interfere."

Esme heard the crunch of wheels and tried to pull away so they wouldn't be run down by the conveyance approaching from behind them. Apparently, Lonsdale was so intent upon persuading her to elope that he did not hear the sound.

"Calvin, a carriage—"

"All the arrangements are made," Calvin said. "I've hired a comfortable coach to carry us to Scotland. You can even take your maid along if you'd feel more comfortable."

The carriage rolled to a stop. Behind her, Esme heard Jane gasp, but she was too involved in escaping Calvin to wonder at the cause of Jane's distress.

"Remove your hands from milady," a cool voice demanded.

Esme's head whipped around. The gypsy! A groan of dismay gurgled from her throat as he leaped to the ground. What was he doing here? Despite her surprise, Esme realize she was glad to see the gypsy at this particular moment. Calvin seemed determined to haul her off to Scotland with or without her consent.

Lonsdale sneered at Dante. "Go away. You took everything else that was mine, but you can't have Esme."

Esme finally managed to jerk free of his grip. "Don't be ridiculous, Calvin. I told you countless times that I had no intention of marrying you, but you refused to listen."

Lonsdale sent Esme a disgusted look. "Never say you want a man with questionable bloodlines. If you wed a gypsy, you will be given the cut direct."

Esme sighed. "I am marrying no one. Please leave, Calvin."

Dante's hands curled into fists. "I suggest you do as the lady says before I show you just how uncivilized this gypsy can be."

"You don't frighten me, Alston," Lonsdale snarled.

Nevertheless, he backed away, step by cautious step, as Dante advanced toward him. Then, like the coward he was, he turned and fled. "You win this time, but you haven't heard the last from me," he called over his shoulder.

Esme rubbed her arms. "Are you all right?" Dante asked. "Shall I go after him and teach him a lesson he won't soon forget?"

"I'm fine."

"What did he want?"

"He wanted me to elope with him to Gretna Green."

Dante's brows shot upward. "And you, of course, preferred me as your groom."

"I want neither of you."

He guided her toward his carriage. "You look shaken. I'll take you home."

"I'm perfectly capable of finding my own way home."

Dante swept her into his arms and placed her in his carriage. Then he gave Jane an apologetic smile. "There is only room for two; Lady Esme will meet you at home."

"But—" Jane protested. The rest of her sentence was lost as Dante climbed onto the driver's bench and the carriage rattled off.

Instead of leaving the park, Dante headed toward Rotten Row.

"I thought you were taking me home."

"I am . . . but we should talk first."

"About what?"

"Lying, for one thing. You said you were ill this morning."

Her chin tilted upward. "I was. I felt better after you left and thought some fresh air would help clear my head."

"I don't believe you, but I'll let it pass for now." His expression turned grim. "Tell me what you were doing with Lonsdale. Did you arrange to meet him in the park today?"

"Absolutely not! It was a chance meeting."

"Stay away from him. You don't know what he's like."

Esme's eyes widened. "Whatever are you talking about? I've known Calvin for years. I'm sure Uncle Daniel considers him trustworthy."

"He may trust Lonsdale, but I don't. I'm *ordering* you to stay away from him."

"You're *ordering* me? My lord gypsy, no one orders me about. If I want to see Calvin, I shall." She had no intention of seeing Calvin again, but the arrogant gypsy didn't have to know that.

"The man is a . . ." No, he couldn't accuse Lonsdale yet, not until he had proof.

"A what? Do you know something I don't about Calvin?"

"Perhaps," he hedged. "Nevertheless, you will obey me. Now you may tell me why you are making such a fuss about being courted by me. Are you in love with another man?"

"What if I am?" Esme challenged.

They were alone, too late for early riders and too

early for the fashionable crowd. Dante pulled the carriage to the side of the road and grasped her shoulders. "If there *is* another man, I intend to banish him from your mind."

"Arrogant gypsy," Esme muttered.

"Do you know Lady Dimwiddy?"

"Vaguely."

"After you left the ball, she invited me to share her bed. And she wasn't the only one who sought my attention. *They* seem to like me—why can't you?"

Esme worried her bottom lip as she pondered her answer. "You are too bold, too sure of yourself. I don't want to be added to your long list of lovers." She glared at him. "Which lady did you honor with your exalted presence?"

Dante chuckled. "None of them." He shrugged expansively. "Or perhaps all of them. Apparently, it makes no difference to you." He looked into her vibrant violet eyes and was immediately drawn into them. The woman was too dangerous to be roaming the streets, where unsuspecting men could fall victim to her charms.

Before Esme could protest, he pulled off her bonnet and ran his fingers through her hair, spreading the vivid strands over her shoulders.

"What are you doing?" Esme gasped, diving for her bonnet, which had fallen to the floor of the carriage.

"I've wanted to do this since the day I met you. Your hair is glorious. Not red, not rust, but somewhere in between." He buried his nose in it. "It smells delicious."

Esme's breath caught. If any other man touched her like this, he would feel the sharp edge of her temper. What made the gypsy different from the others?

Calvin was handsome—not as handsome as the gypsy, of course—but she had never wanted to be touched by him or to touch him.

Dante's hands cupped her face. She stared into his eyes, so dark, so intense, so utterly captivating that she couldn't look away. She saw his head lower toward hers, watched his lips descend. His scent was fresh and clean; she remembered it from the last time he had kissed her. Her thoughts scattered as his lips claimed hers and his arms drew her close.

She spread her hands against his chest, intending to push him away, but when she felt his heart beating against her palm and the heat emanating from his body through the layers of his clothing, the will to resist dissolved.

This was wrong. But how could something that felt so right be wrong? The sense of floating, of her heart not beating while she knew it was pounding, were strange manifestations of an emotion completely foreign to her.

At first the kiss was gentle as Dante brushed his lips against hers, once, twice. Then he claimed them with a fierceness that stirred her more than his gentleness. When his tongue searched for hers and found it, she reacted strongly to the scent and taste of him, to the melding of their breath. Not even when she remembered that the man kissing her was a gypsy did she stop him by word or deed. Curling her hands against his chest, she gave in to the wicked desire plaguing her, surrendering fully to his passion. She'd deal with her traitorous body later.

At last he drew back; she took a shaky breath. Her hand flew to her mouth, and she stared at him while he watched her with those mysterious dark eyes.

"That wasn't so bad, was it, milady?"

"I didn't like it." Her lie fell easily from her lips.

Dante laughed. "A man of my experience knows when a woman enjoys a kiss, and you, milady, thoroughly enjoyed being kissed. Once we are wed, I will kiss you whenever you wish." He leered at her. "And do a lot of other things you will enjoy, too."

"I would enjoy nothing with you," Esme retorted.

"I know when a woman is ripe for bedding." His fingers curled around her breast. She nearly jumped out of her skin.

She slapped his hand away. "Don't do that! Take me home. Uncle Daniel is going to hear about your attack upon my virtue."

"We shall wed soon; get used to the idea," Dante replied.

"You're mad!" Esme charged. "Will you take me home or must I walk?"

Dante sighed. This was going to be harder than he'd thought. What truly surprised him was the fact that he wanted to marry Esme. He wouldn't need other women in his life with Esme as his marchioness. The challenge energized him, gave him the will to continue the farce of being a marquis when at heart he was a free soul who hated living in a mansion with servants in his way every time he turned around.

Dante took up the reins just as another carriage drew abreast of them and stopped. A lady leaned over the side of the open carriage and waved.

"Lord Alston, Lady Esme, how fortunate to meet you here."

"Lady Harrison," Dante greeted.

"I'm having a week-long house party at my country estate the first week in September. There will be hunting and gaming for the gentlemen and games and outings for the ladies. And a grand ball to culminate the event. The invitations went out before you inherited the marquisate, Lord Alston. If you are free, please join us. And you too, Lady Esme," she added as an afterthought. "You know where I live, my lord," she said coyly.

"I will check with my secretary to see if I am free, my lady," Dante hedged.

"I am otherwise engaged," Esme said, "but thank you for the invitation."

Lady Harrison gave Dante a dazzling smile and motioned her driver to continue. Dante ignored Esme's pointed look as he flicked his whip lightly against the horse's rump. The animal set off at a leisurely pace.

"Is Lady Harrison one of your lovers?" Esme asked.

Dante refused to be goaded. "I met the lady at a fair."

"She hinted that you are or had been intimate."

A smile stretched Dante's sensual lips. "Are you jealous, milady?"

"Of you? Hardly. I don't care how many lovers you take as long as you don't add me to your list."

"I have every intention of adding you. Yours will be the last name on the list. After we wed, there will be no other women."

Esme had nothing to say to that. What could one say to a man who had just promised to be faithful to his marriage vows?

The ride to the Parkton townhouse was both short and silent. Dante pulled up to the curb and leaped lightly to the ground. Grasping Esme's tiny waist, he swung her to the sidewalk. They strolled to the gate together. Dante opened the gate and Esme slipped through.

"Do you enjoy riding, milady?" Dante asked as they approached the door. "I enjoy early-morning rides myself. Would you care to join me tomorrow, weather permitting?"

"I love to ride," Esme admitted, "but tomorrow isn't a good time for me."

Amusement colored his words. "Will any day be a good time? No, don't answer that, I already know the answer. I shall call on you tomorrow afternoon. Good day, milady."

Esme didn't go inside immediately. She turned and watched the gypsy stride away. She was confused by the emotional turmoil she felt when she was with him. She didn't even like the gypsy. He had stolen Calvin's inheritance, and that wasn't right. Not that she was overly fond of Calvin, but she knew the difference between right and wrong. But something besides Calvin's lost title was bothering her. The gypsy sparked sensations she had never felt before, and that frightened her.

Esme watched Dante climb into the carriage and take up the reins. She started to turn away when the thunder of horses' hooves caught her attention. Then she saw it. A large black coach rumbled down the street at an accelerated speed, aiming directly for Dante's lighter carriage.

Esme screamed a warning, but it was too late. The cumbersome coach sideswiped Dante's carriage, sending it crashing onto its side. Esme's heart plummeted when she saw Dante fly into the air and hit the street with a sickening thud. He lay there without moving.

Esme's scream brought a bevy of servants streaming out the door. "Lord Alston has been injured," she cried, trying to make herself heard over the screeching horse still attached to the carriage. She took off at a run, followed by two footmen and the butler.

Dante knew he had been injured when the sudden explosion of pain took his breath away. His head hurt like the very devil, but the most severe pain radiated from his right shoulder. It was either broken or dislocated. He hoped it was the latter. He tried to move and nearly blacked out from the pain, barely aware of Esme kneeling beside him, her face a mask of concern.

"Send someone for the physician," Esme ordered crisply. "We need to get His Lordship into the house. And see to the horse. The poor animal could be hurt."

Dante had enough presence of mind to say, "Be careful—my shoulder may be broken."

"There could be other broken bones besides your shoulder," Esme replied. "Fetch a blanket, Jamison; we'll use it to carry His Lordship into the house."

The footman hurried off, returning a few minutes later with a sturdy woolen blanket. Dante stifled a groan as he was eased onto the blanket, lifted and carried into the house and up the stairs to a guest bedroom. The whole process was painful, and by the time Dante had been placed on the bed, he was barely conscious.

Dante had no idea how long he had drifted in and out of consciousness, but every time he awakened, he knew that Esme hovered over him, placing cold cloths on a bump of mammoth proportions rising on his forehead. His first true awareness was when the physician entered the room, introduced himself as Dr. Adams and ordered everyone out.

"Well, my lord, let's see what injuries you have sustained besides a lump on your head. I was told you were in a carriage accident."

"I don't recall exactly what happened," Dante muttered.

"Hmmm, that's a pretty nasty bump. Do you remember your name?"

"Of course, I'm Dante Knowles, the Marquis of Alston."

"Very good. Where do you hurt besides your head?"

"Right shoulder," Dante grunted. "It's either broken or dislocated."

Dr. Adams probed gently. Dante gritted his teeth, then let out a yelp when Adams tried to move his right arm.

"Dislocated," Adams murmured. "I'm going to need help snapping it back into place." He left the bedchamber and returned with the same two footmen who had carried Dante upstairs.

"Be careful removing his shirt," Adams advised. "He'll need a nightshirt after I'm finished."

Dante felt helpless and hated it. If Carlotta were here, she would have fixed him up without all this fuss.

One of the footmen left to fetch a nightshirt while the other removed Dante's shirt. Then he helped the doctor ease Dante out of bed and onto a stool. Adams took a stance behind Dante and ordered the footman to hold Dante's left shoulder steady. Dante braced himself as Adams placed his knee in the middle of his back, grabbed his right shoulder and pulled it into place. The loud snap that followed made the footman wince and turn pale.

"Done," Adams said. He fashioned a sling to hold Dante's arm in place and fastened it behind his neck. "The shoulder will be good as new in a fortnight."

Sweating profusely, Dante rose and wobbled over to the bed. Now that his shoulder was where it belonged, he could concentrate on his splitting headache.

"I'll leave a powder for your headache," Adams said, as if reading Dante's mind. The footman handed Adams a nightshirt. "Once we get you into this contraption, I will examine you for bruises."

"I'll survive the bruises, Dr. Adams," Dante said. "As for the nightshirt, I won't need it, for I intend to return home immediately. My secretary will see that you are paid for your services."

"You should remain in bed for a day or two," Adams insisted. "You could have a concussion. I'm sure Lord Parkton will extend his hospitality to you."

"Unacceptable."

"I really must insist that you remain in bed at least twenty-four hours," Adams pressed.

"I don't think—"

Dante's words were cut off by Parkton, who had just entered the bedchamber. "I just learned about your accident, Alston. I've already dispatched people to find the careless driver who struck your carriage, and I've sent a note around to your residence."

"Lord Alston has sustained multiple injuries, including a possible concussion and a dislocated right shoulder," Adams said. "He is a stubborn man. He insists upon leaving against my express wishes that he remain in bed."

"I won't hear of your leaving, Alston," Parkton said. "You must follow the physician's orders. We still haven't had our talk. If you feel well enough, we can converse later today without your having to leave the bed."

Dante knew when he had been defeated. He supposed he could remain in bed a day if it would help his splitting head and heal his arm faster.

"Very well, but one day in bed is all I can tolerate. I intend to investigate the accident and find the responsible party."

Assured of his patient's cooperation, Adams packed up to leave. "Send for me if you need me. Good day, Lord Parkton, Lord Alston."

"You need help getting into that nightshirt," Parkton said, nodding to the footmen, who stood waiting for instructions.

Cursing his inability to help himself, Dante soon found himself divested of his clothing and dressed in a nightshirt, a garment he never wore, then tucked into bed.

Parkton dismissed the servants and pulled a chair up to the bed. "What can you tell me about the accident, Alston?"

"Not much. All I recall is climbing into my carriage and then flying through the air."

"I know exactly how it happened." Esme stood in the doorway. "Dr. Adams said it was all right to come in."

"You saw the accident?" Dante asked, trying to sit up. Parkton helped him into a sitting position and motioned Esme forward. She walked to the bed, her concerned gaze skimming over Dante. "Are you all right?"

"I'm fine. My shoulder wasn't broken, just dislocated. Once my head stops pounding, I shall be as good as new. Tell me what you saw."

"For some reason, I turned around before I entered the house and watched you climb into your carriage. I saw a black coach with its shades pulled down bearing down on you. It could have passed you easily, there was enough room, but the driver deliberately veered into your carriage."

"Was there a marking on the coach?" Dante asked.

"No, it was plain black."

"Did you see the driver?" Parkton asked.

"He wore a muffler and knit cap pulled low over his forehead. I wouldn't be able to identify him if I saw him walking on the street. It was no accident. Someone made a deliberate attempt upon Lord Alston's life."

"Do you have enemies, Alston?" Parkton asked.

Dante said nothing. To his knowledge, he had but one enemy.

The man who'd killed his grandfather.

Chapter Seven

Dante was sleeping so soundly when Parkton looked in on him later that afternoon that the earl decided their conversation could wait. Dante slept on, not awakening until he heard the hall clock strike midnight. He couldn't believe he had slept so soundly, but the rest had done him good. The pain in his head had dulled to a low ache, and his shoulder didn't throb nearly as much as it had.

The fire in the hearth provided enough light for Dante to see a napkin-covered tray sitting on a nearby table. He suddenly realized he was hungry. He sat on the edge of the bed a few moments before attempting to stand. He rose, wobbled a bit, but soon found his balance. A tempting array of cold meats, cheese and bread met his gaze when he removed the napkin.

Dante pulled up a chair and began eating with his left hand. Cursing his clumsiness, he eased his right arm out of the sling, discovered he could use it without causing excessive pain and polished off the entire tray of food, washing it down with the wine that had also been provided.

Once his stomach was full, Dante felt his strength returning and began stomping around the bedroom to work the stiffness from his legs. Despite the doctor's orders, he felt that remaining in bed an entire day was a waste of time. He was never ill, suffered only insignificant injuries during his reckless youth.

Dante felt silly in the nightshirt. If he intended to return to bed, he didn't need excessive material impeding his movements. He lifted the nightshirt over his left arm and head, then eased it over his right arm and tossed it aside.

The door opened. Esme stepped inside. "Are you all right? I heard you stomping around in here and . . ." She gasped. "My word, you're naked!"

As dearly as Esme wanted to leave, she could not make her legs move or force her eyes to look elsewhere. The gypsy's swarthy body was magnificently fashioned, perfectly proportioned; she didn't know where to look first.

His arms were roped with muscle. His chest was broad, his hips narrow, and his legs were long and sturdy. The very essence of the man made her feel giddy. The way he moved, his every gesture exuded sensuality. He was a sexual animal that made her think of sinful things. Things she knew little about.

Though he must have known she was staring at him, he didn't move; he merely smiled at her. His mouth was well shaped, deceptively tender. His hair and slanted brows were as black as a raven's wing. Even 'as she fought the wicked urge to stare at him, her gaze drifted downward to his . . . Oh, my! She'd seen male appendages in books and on statues, but the huge member jutting forth from a nest of black hair was beyond anything she could have imagined.

She swallowed the lump in her throat as she attempted to leave. Unfortunately, her feet refused to move. "Forgive me . . . I didn't mean . . ."

With great effort, she managed to look away, though it was a struggle to keep her gaze from returning to the extraordinary display of lust-inspiring male strength. Were all men so extravagantly endowed? Somehow she doubted it. She took a small step backward.

Dante knew he should have dived into the bed when Esme appeared, but he had been as startled as she. And afterward, the way her eyes devoured him had kept him rooted in place. He glanced down at his cock, smiling wryly when he saw it had risen admirably to the occasion. Only when he saw Esme back toward the door did he react. Three long strides took him to her side. He shut the door and turned her away from it. Then he stared at her with the same intensity with which she had looked at him.

She was dressed in something long and white that floated about her slim legs and clung to her unfettered breasts. The material was so fine he could see the proud thrust of her ruby nipples through it. His gaze shifted downward, to the rust-colored triangle between her thighs.

Esme blinked. "Why did you shut the door?"

"Did you like what you saw, love?" he drawled. "I very much like what I see."

"I . . . I . . . should leave. I only meant to look in on you to make sure you were all right."

"Esme, sweet Esme, deny it all you want, but you

are ready for love, and I can't think of a better time or place." He took her hand and led her to the bed.

Esme pushed against his chest. Caught off guard, Dante fell onto the bed, pulling Esme with him. She fell on top of him. A jolt of pain slashed through his injured shoulder, but it was quickly forgotten as her soft breasts flattened against his chest.

"Stop, gypsy! You'll hurt yourself."

"My name is Dante. Say it? Why must you think of me as a gypsy instead of a man worthy of your attention?"

"Because a gypsy is what you are," she argued. "I don't want to hurt you, gypsy, but I will if you don't unhand me."

Dante's lips flattened. "My name is Dante. Say it."

Silence.

"If you don't say my name, I will strip you naked and kiss you all over, until you want me as badly as I want you."

Apparently, Esme realized he wasn't jesting. "Dante. There, I said it. Now what are you going to do?"

Dante grinned. "Strip you naked and kiss you all over."

"You lied!"

"So I did. Are you going to scream? If we are found together, there will be an immediate wedding whether you want one or not."

"You are a—"

"I am, aren't I? But I promise not to do anything you don't want me to do. You can tell me to stop at any time and I will."

She sent him a skeptical look. "I don't believe you."

"Try me. Let me kiss you. If you don't enjoy it, just tell me and I'll release you."

He flipped her over in one graceful motion, bringing her beneath him. Then he pushed her hair aside and lowered his lips to her exposed throat, stroking his tongue across her flesh. He felt her gasp and smiled. This was the woman he was going to marry; he could see no reason to wait for their wedding night. But he would keep his word even if it killed him. The first time she said stop, he would. He prayed that she would not.

Dante nipped the lobe of her ear as he reached down between their bodies, his agile fingers raising her nightgown inch by slow inch. His mouth slanted over hers, tasting, seeking, finding her tongue with his. She tasted so sweet, so innocent, he could scarcely control his randy cock.

His hand stroked downward over the quivering flesh of her bare stomach, coming to rest on the nest of curls between her legs. His fingers came away damp. Reaching further, he traced the damp folds of her sex with a talented fingertip. She stiffened but didn't utter the word that would stop him. He had promised to cease if she asked, but thus far the word hadn't crossed her lips.

His kisses continued hot and demanding as he accustomed her to a lover's touch. His tongue probed her mouth evocatively as he boldly opened her tender petals and slid one finger slowly, steadily into her tight sheath. Her body arched provocatively under his. He rose up on his left elbow and gazed into her eyes, his brows raised. When she said nothing, he took her mouth again as his finger pressed and withdrew inside her, once, twice . . . again.

He stroked again, then opened her wider and pressed another finger beside the first. Her hips tilted, lifted into his touch. He smiled inwardly. He still hadn't heard the word that would end this blissful interlude.

Overwhelmed by his kisses, her senses fractured by a multitude of sensations, Esme responded instinctively to Dante's intimate caresses, opening to the penetration of his fingers.

"Relax," Dante whispered against her lips. "You taste so sweet and feel like heaven. Let's get this nightgown off of you. I want to taste your breasts."

Esme opened her mouth to protest but groaned instead. To her disgust, she even helped him remove her nightgown. If she was going to stop him, it was now or never. Then his mouth found her breasts and coherent thought fled. He licked the firm mounds and suckled her nipples until they tautened into aching nubs.

The feeling was so intense, she couldn't begin to describe it. His fingers played between her legs. Her hips rose, shifted as his fingers moved in and out, stroking, withdrawing, plunging deep again. She responded instinctively to the intimate caresses, thighs easing, relaxing.

He lifted his body over hers, spreading her thighs with his knees. Easing his fingers from her, he guided the throbbing head of his erection into her soft, melting core. He pressed in; she gasped. He paused, resting just inside her body, lavishing kisses upon her lush mouth, engaging her senses, demanding all her attention.

He looked down into her eyes, saw her confusion and suffered a moment of guilt for instigating this seduction, but he quickly banished it from his mind. He had given Esme every opportunity to stop him, but she'd said nothing to make him think she didn't want this.

She was breathing heavily, her eyes glazed with passion. Nothing in her expression suggested she wasn't enjoying what he was doing to her. "Brace yourself, love. I am going to take you to paradise."

"You'll hurt yourself," Esme said breathlessly. "Your headache, your shoulder—"

"Let me worry about that. Do you want me to stop?" Though it would cost him dearly, he would end this if she asked it of him.

Her hips moved fractionally, as if trying to pull him deeper inside. "Sto . . . Oh, God, I must be as mad as you are. I cannot say the word."

"Thank God. This may hurt a bit, but I'll try to be gentle."

His gaze never leaving hers, he eased back slightly, flexed his hips sharply and drove deep into her body with one powerful thrust. He felt the resistance of her maidenhead give way, felt her hot slickness surround him, felt her clamp tight about his throbbing sex. At last he knew the true meaning of heaven.

He caught Esme's cry in his mouth, felt her stiffen beneath him. Laboring for breath, his body in agony, Dante forced himself to remain still, restraining the need to thrust home, to plunder her sweet warmth, to conquer and claim her and make her his. Reluctantly he released her mouth, lifted his head and gazed down at her.

She drew in a huge, shuddering breath; her breasts pressed against his chest, increasing his torture. His aching cock jerked inside her. Her eyes lifted to his, so deep a violet they were almost black. She blinked, blinked again and tried to shift away. "That hurt."

He was in agony. "No, don't move. Just . . . wait a moment until I gain control of myself."

She let out another shuddering sigh. He touched her lips with his, brushing soft kisses across her mouth . . . felt her resistance fall away, felt her body soften beneath him.

Felt her surrender, tasted her need.

The sweetness of the moment nearly unmanned Dante. He was filled with a heady sense of rightness, of belonging. He kissed her deeply and began to thrust. His hunger for her was so intense, so primitive, that it robbed him of thought, of speech. Her rhythm adjusted to his, mirroring his movement. Soon their bodies were so attuned, he didn't know where his left off and hers began. They were one.

His blood thundered and his body cried for release as he plunged ever faster, the heat of their bodies fusing them together.

"Oh, my," Esme gasped. "What's happening? I feel . . . I need . . . I can't explain it."

Dante chuckled briefly, harshly, against her ear. "I know what you need, love." He increased the tempo of his thrusts. He was so close to climax, he feared he would leave her behind, and that wasn't acceptable to the infamous gypsy lover. Working his hand between their bodies, he found the center of her tension and rubbed the swollen nub until shudders wracked her.

Esme felt as if Dante had delved deeply into a secret part of her, a part she hadn't known existed. Her heart pounded as she answered the tempo of his thrusts with increasing vigor. With each surge, he touched something deeper, richer, and her control came close to splintering. She moaned over and over, beyond caring about anything except attaining a goal she desired above all else.

Intense, pounding fever gripped her senses, held them captive. For one glorious moment, she felt as if the man making love to her truly cared for her. Then her thoughts scattered. She became a willing captive to pleasure, spasming in glorious climax.

When she subsided, Dante was still moving on her, his dark eyes observing her with fierce male triumph. Then he threw his head back, the muscles in his neck cording, his hips pounding her into the mattress as he found his own pleasure.

His frenzy dragged her deeper into ecstasy. She writhed, sobbed, clung to his shoulders as his hot seed bathed her. She heard his muffled shout, felt him relax against her and then lie still. When he raised his head and stared into her eyes, they were glazed with spent passion.

Esme glanced away. She couldn't bear the look of conquest shining from his eyes. Anger welled, burst. She had been seduced by a gypsy who had lived up to his reputation this night.

She lurched up from the bed. "Damn you! I didn't want that."

"I didn't hear you say stop."

"Would you have?"

"Though it might have killed me, I would have stopped at any point if you had asked."

She reached for her nightgown. "You are too experienced for me and you knew it. I didn't have a chance against you."

Dante said quietly, "I gave you every opportunity to stop me, my love."

Esme bristled. "Don't call me your love. I don't even like you."

She pulled on her nightgown and tossed him his nightshirt. Dante let it lie where it landed. "I don't sleep in clothing."

Dante leaned up on his right arm, muttered a curse and fell back on the bed.

Esme heard him curse and looked back. He was holding his arm, a pained expression on his face.

"Foolish man," she clucked. "I warned you. You hurt yourself, didn't you? Where's your sling?"

Dante shrugged. Esme found it lying on the floor next to the bed and flung it at him. "Put this on."

"Why? I thought you didn't care about me."

"I don't, but I would help an animal if it was suffering." She placed the sling around his neck and shoved his arm into it.

"Ouch! You deliberately hurt me."

"Be quiet. Do you want my uncle bursting in here?"

"It doesn't matter. We're to be married."

"I haven't agreed to marry you yet."

"You don't have a choice. I've ruined you, and your uncle will demand that I do the right thing."

"Arrogant gypsy," Esme huffed. "I don't wish to marry you. Neither you nor Uncle Daniel can force me to the altar."

Dante's mouth turned up into a grim smile. "You think not?" He sent her a piercing look. "As I pointed out, I've already ruined you."

She froze him with a look so cold he shivered. "Who's going to tell him?"

Dante knew he would never say anything to Parkton about tonight. It wasn't in his nature to spread tales about his lovers. He would never shame Esme in such a manner.

"Don't worry, I won't tell your uncle that we are lovers."

"We are *not* lovers! One time does not constitute an affair." She glared at him. "Perhaps I *should* have married Calvin. *He* never tried to seduce me."

Dante chuckled. "I didn't just try, I succeeded."

Refusing to be goaded, Esme opened the door, peeked into the hallway, saw that no one was about and flounced off.

Dante sprawled on the bed wide awake, wondering how things had gone wrong so quickly. He didn't regret seducing Esme; it would have happened sooner or later. Her passion had stunned him, and he was still reeling over that revelation. He smiled. Who would have thought an innocent virgin could be so responsive? He had expected Esme to be untouched, and was grateful his expectations had been met. But he was incredulous that she would refuse his proposal after letting him love her.

He had seduced her, for God's sake! No woman in her right mind would refuse to wed her seducer if he offered for her hand. If she had no intention of marrying him, why hadn't she stopped him?

Abruptly Dante's mind turned to his recent close call with death. What if Esme had been in the carriage when the accident happened? With that frightening thought preying on his mind, Dante drifted off to sleep.

Dante managed to dress himself the next morning despite his aching shoulder. His head still hurt, but he decided he could live with the temporary pain. Why hadn't he noticed it when he was making love to Esme?

A footman he recalled from the day before showed him to the breakfast room. The sunny chamber was empty but for servants setting breakfast out on the sideboard. "Is Lady Esme still abed?" he asked the footman.

"Aye, milord. Lord Parkton should be down shortly. Do you prefer coffee or tea?"

"Coffee, please, Jamison. It is Jamison, isn't it?"

Jamison beamed. "It is indeed, milord." He poured coffee into Dante's cup.

Dante waved away the cream pitcher Jamison offered. He liked his coffee black and strong. He was holding the cup in his left hand and sipping awkwardly when Parkton strolled into the dining room.

"What are you doing out of bed, Alston?"

"Eating breakfast. I feel well enough today to return home. Not that I don't appreciate your hospitality."

"You know what's best, I suppose. This will give us time to have that talk we missed. You were sleeping so soundly yesterday, I didn't want to wake you."

The men helped themselves from the sideboard and began eating. When they finished, Parkton sat back and studied Dante through narrowed lids. "Shall we discuss the attempt upon your life? Apparently, someone wants you out of the way. Do you know who?"

Dante hesitated. "No. I have no enemies. Until I inherited the title, I didn't stay in one place long enough to collect enemies."

"I see. Do you still intend to marry Esme?"

"She doesn't want a gypsy. She considers me unworthy of her."

"Esme will come around. Shall I order her to marry you?"

"I don't want her that way. Besides," Dante mused, "if my life is in danger, this wouldn't be a good time to take a wife. It would distress me no end to see her hurt on my account."

"You could be right. Before we continue talking, please answer my question. Do you still intend to marry Esme?"

"Of course. Initially I was upset that Grandfather had picked out a bride for me, but after I met Esme, I knew he was right. She is the perfect wife for me . . . if she can get over her prejudice. But I'm not going to demand that we wed until I'm certain no harm will come to her because of me."

"You are a wise man, Alston, and a thoughtful one," Parkton said. He rose. "If you need help, please don't hesitate to contact me. I will do all I can to aid your courtship of Esme."

"Thank you, but I want a willing wife, not one forced to the altar."

"Esme was promised to Alston's heir after your father died without issue. I intend to carry through with her father's wishes. If you'll excuse me, I have an appointment I cannot be late for. I'll instruct my coachman to take you home when you are ready to leave."

Dante sipped his coffee, recalling his seduction of Esme. After last night, he knew there was something special between them; he just had to convince milady. Dante couldn't help smiling. He couldn't recall when a woman had pleased him so much, despite the twinge of guilt he harbored for seducing her. However, the knowledge that she had not tried to stop him alleviated his guilt somewhat.

"What are you doing out of bed?" Esme asked from the doorway. Dante noted immediately that her cheeks were reddened, and that her eyes did not quite meet his. Was she ashamed of what they had done last night?

"I don't want to overstay my welcome. Besides, I need to find out who tried to kill me."

"Perhaps your accident really was an accident," Esme mused as she moved to the sideboard to fill her plate. Jamison rushed to fill her cup with steaming tea.

"Is that what you think?"

Esme shrugged. "Perhaps."

Dante rose. "It doesn't make sense." He dismissed Jamison with a look, then moved to stand beside Esme. "About last night . . ."

Esme glared up at him. "I do not wish to talk about it. Even though you had your way with me, I have no intention of marrying you, nor do I wish to see you again."

Perhaps it would be best, Dante thought, to give Esme time to come to grips with their mutual attraction. "If you have no desire to see me again, I shall comply with your wishes."

Esme's head snapped up. "You will?"

"Milady's wish is my command."

"But . . ."

He took her hand, turned it palm up and raised it to his lips. "You will miss me," he said, sending her a warm smile, "as I will miss you."

"I won't miss you at all. Your arrogance is insufferable. I suspect you'll find another woman to warm your bed before the day is out."

"Do you really think so?"

His teasing voice set her teeth on edge. Had last

night meant nothing to him? It angered her to think he had used her and she had let him. She certainly hadn't expected him to agree so readily to her request that he not see her again. Last night he had been eager to wed her; had he given up already?

"I expected no less from a gypsy," she huffed. "Good day, my lord."

Dante's hasty exit left Esme stunned. How could he treat her this way when she had given him her innocence?

Lacking an explanation, Esme stared at the door Dante had vanished behind. He was gone, and she didn't expect him to return. Last night he'd said they would wed. What had changed his mind? The answer came to her in a rush of shame. Her inexperience had made him lose interest. Food turned to straw in her mouth.

Esme told herself she should have welcomed Dante's rejection. It was what she wanted, wasn't it? Why should she seek the gypsy's admiration when she didn't even like him?

But the question that bothered her most remained unanswered. Why hadn't she stopped Dante last night? She refused to admit she had wanted the gypsy to make love to her, that she had enjoyed every moment in his arms.

The only explanation she would accept was that the man had seduced her and taken advantage of her innocence. That explanation was the only way to salvage her pride. If she never saw the man again, it would be too soon.

Dante encountered Jamison outside the breakfast room and asked him about his horse and carriage.

He had heard the animal's terrible cries and feared the worst. Jamison directed him to the stables behind the townhouse, where he found Condor munching contentedly on hay, but his carriage was nowhere to be found.

"His Lordship sent yer carriage to the blacksmith for repair, milord," the stableman replied to Dante's inquiry. "But yer horse is right as rain."

Dante scowled at his injured right arm and squelched his request for a saddle so he could ride home.

"Lord Parkton instructed that ye were to be taken home in his carriage," the stableman said. "I'll fetch John Coachman."

Dante examined his horse more closely during the stableman's short absence. Condor did indeed seem in fine fettle. Then the coachman arrived, and Dante settled into Lord Parkton's carriage. Though the ride was a short one, his mind returned to the events of the previous night.

Esme had been everything he had imagined . . . and more. He had seduced her, knowing she was an innocent, and the only thing he regretted about it was that she still considered him beneath her.

His title meant nothing to her; she looked at him and saw only a gypsy. Nevertheless, they *would* marry.

Grayson was overjoyed to see Dante when he walked into the house. "We feared the worst when we received word of your accident, milord." His gaze went to the purpling bruise on Dante's forehead.

"It's nothing, Grayson, hardly bothers me at all. And the arm will be as good as new in a few days."

"That's good to hear, milord. Is there anything I can do for you?"

"Yes, in fact, there is. Fetch Luther Champion. I'll wait for him in my study."

Grayson left immediately to fetch Dante's secretary. When Champion arrived from the cubbyhole that served as his office, Dante dictated two notes and arranged to have them delivered.

Dante was still in his study an hour later when visitors were announced. Dante rose to greet Lords Brookworth and Carstairs. "That was fast."

"Your note said you were injured in a freak accident and needed our help," Brookworth replied, "so we came straightaway."

"I'm fine but for a few scrapes and bruises."

"It's good to see you again," Carstairs greeted. "It's been a long time. Brookworth told me about your new title. Welcome to society."

"Thank you, Carstairs. It's good to know you remembered our friendship from Cambridge," Dante replied. "But for you and Brookworth, I wouldn't have had any friends at university."

"How did you happen to fall into the title?" Carstairs asked. "You were never forthcoming about your people, as I recall."

"I didn't try to hide my gypsy heritage," Dante reminded them. "I've always known my grandfather was the Marquis of Alston, and that he abandoned me when I was born. It was something I preferred not to mention."

"Apparently, the marquis hadn't forgotten you, after all. I heard his only son died without issue," Brookworth noted. "We all assumed Viscount Lonsdale was Alston's heir." He grinned. "I'll bet Lonsdale was shocked when he learned he wasn't Alston's heir." He gave a bark of laughter. "That means Lonsdale lost Lady Esme to you, as well. He must have been livid."

"Beyond livid. I need help, and you two are the only ones I can count on."

"Ask away," Brookworth said.

"What happened to me yesterday was no accident. A deliberate attempt was made on my life. I need your eyes and ears to help me find the culprit. I want to be certain no harm will come to Lady Esme because of me."

"Are you really going to marry Lady Esme? You aren't betrothed yet, so you could always cry off," Brookworth ventured. "Perhaps you'll find someone more to your liking."

Dante grinned. "I'm going to confide in you because I know what I say will go no farther. Grandfather Alston left a codicil to his will. If I don't marry Lady Esme, Lonsdale stands to inherit. Giving up the title is out of the question. You see," he said, lowering his voice, "I suspect Lonsdale helped my grandfather to his final reward. And," he added, "Lonsdale is the only person who stands to gain from my death. If I die, or if Lady Esme refuses to wed me, Lonsdale will inherit. I cannot let him have the title, no matter how much I might prefer my former life."

"You are a marquis, old man," Brookworth drawled. "So get used to it. As for Lonsdale, we'll keep an eye on the bloke for you. Never did like the man. He scatters his vowels around like seeds in the wind."

"I thought your grandfather's death was a suicide," Carstairs ventured.

"I have good reason to believe Grandfather was murdered," Dante explained.

Silence filled the room. Finally, Brookworth said, "I'm sure I speak for Carstairs when I say we will help in any way we can."

"Here, here," Carstairs rejoined. "Now tell us about your life since we left our school days behind."

The next hour or so was spent catching up. When the men departed, Dante no longer felt alone in a world totally foreign to him. He had rediscovered two friends he could trust.

Chapter Eight

Esme could not banish the feeling that Dante had abandoned her. She tried not to let it bother her, but as the day progressed, her displeasure with the gypsy increased. A slow drizzle that had begun in mid-morning prevented her from going out, which disgruntled her even more. With nothing to occupy her mind but Dante and what had taken place last night in his bed, Esme decided she needed something to distract her and went in search of a book.

Her uncle's library was extensive; it didn't take long to find a book of poems and settle down before the fire to read. Since Esme wasn't expecting callers on such a raw day, she was surprised when Jamison informed her that Lord Lonsdale had arrived.

"Show him into the library, Jamison, and ask Jane to attend me."

"I'm already here," Lonsdale said. "I didn't think you'd send me away, so I followed Jamison. Forgive my boldness."

"What are you doing abroad on such a dismal day?" Esme asked.

Lonsdale took a seat very close to Esme. "I had to see you. There is something about Alston you should know."

Esme's attention sharpened. "Actually, I know very little about him."

"That makes my information even more important," Lonsdale said. He moistened his lips and glanced furtively toward the open door. "I don't want your maid to hear this. You know how servants talk."

"Really, Calvin, what is this all about?"

"I know of no way to break it gently, so I'll just tell you straight out. I believe the gypsy killed his grandfather for his title and wealth."

"What! Why would you say such a thing? Lord Alston committed suicide."

"That's what the authorities think, but I'm not so certain. Uncle Alston had no reason to kill himself. He was in good health and had everything to live for. He wasn't in debt and had no enemies, nor was he melancholy. Suicide just doesn't make sense."

Esme had to agreed. She couldn't picture Dante as a killer, but now that the notion had been planted in her head, she could not let it drop.

"Tell me what you know."

Calvin shifted nervously. "I don't actually *know* anything, except that the gypsy called on my uncle one evening shortly before his death. I also learned from Uncle Alston's solicitor that he changed his will in the gypsy's favor about a year ago. I believe"—Lonsdale leaned closer—"that Uncle Alston regretted his decision and told the gypsy he was going to change the will back again. I further believe the gypsy came through an open window a few nights later and killed my uncle, making it look like suicide."

Stunned speechless, Esme could do little more than stare at Calvin. He made it all sound so plausible.

"Did you tell anyone about your theory? Uncle Daniel should know."

"I've told no one but you. I cannot accuse a man without proof. But when I find it, I'll use it to drive Alston from England." He paused for effect. "You cannot marry the gypsy, Esme. He might be a murderer."

Esme recoiled, unwilling to believe that Dante could be a cold-blooded killer. But what if he were? What if Calvin found the proof he sought?

"I don't intend to marry Dante, and I've told him as much."

Calvin looked skeptical. "What did he say to that?"

Esme's cheeks flamed when she recalled how callously Dante had abandoned her. "It didn't seem to disturb him overmuch."

Calvin snorted. "That's hard to believe."

Now that Esme thought about it, Dante's easy acquiescence seemed out of character, especially after . . . after . . . Her cheeks flaming, she looked away.

"Your uncle will insist that you wed the gypsy no matter how you feel about it. That's why Alston gave in so easily."

Jane chose that moment to enter the library, panting for lack of breath. "I'm sorry, milady, I was sorting through your laundry and Jamison couldn't find me."

"Sit down and catch your breath, Jane," Esme invited.

Jane chose a chair in a far corner and focused her gaze out the window.

"You haven't heard everything yet," Calvin hissed to Esme. "There's so much more I need to tell you."

"You may speak freely in front of Jane."

"Please, Esme, this is important. Your life could depend upon it. Send your maid away."

Indecision weighed heavily on Esme. Finally, she said, "Jane, would you please fetch my shawl? It's a bit chilly in here. And take your time."

Jane sent Esme a measuring look but did as she was told.

"Now then," Esme said briskly. "What can't you say in front of Jane?"

He leaned closer. "Elope with me. I cannot bear to see you in danger. Once we are wed, there is nothing your uncle or anyone else can do about it. I'm a titled gentleman, not a gypsy interloper. We will manage very nicely together."

Esme didn't want the sort of convenient arrangement Calvin suggested. She wanted more. She wanted . . . what Dante had given her last night. She shook her head to clear it of such treacherous thoughts.

"You know I can't. Uncle Daniel would be livid."

"How would he feel if you were dead?"

Esme would agree to nothing without confronting Dante first. He deserved the benefit of the doubt. She didn't want to believe that the first lover she'd ever had was a murderer. But if she was wrong about him, she needed to be wary. Either way, eloping with Calvin would solve nothing.

"We were meant to be together," Calvin argued. "We've known for many years that we were betrothed. Doesn't it stand to reason that Uncle Alston would have told me if he meant to disinherit me in favor of a baseborn gypsy? Perhaps he changed his will for some perceived slight I dealt him, but then decided to reinstate me when he got over his pique. The gypsy killed him before he could accomplish the change. It's all so simple, I'm surprised I didn't think of it sooner."

It did seem rather simple, Esme thought. And entirely plausible. "I can't elope with you, Calvin, but I'll ask Uncle Daniel to look into the matter."

Calvin stood, pulling Esme with him. Before she knew what he intended, he pulled her against him and kissed her. Though his kiss wasn't repulsive, it did nothing for her. But when his tongue thrust forcefully into her mouth, she nearly gagged. Why hadn't she felt the same revulsion when Dante kissed her? Esme vowed not to let her emotions blind her. She refused to be gulled by either Calvin or Dante.

Esme pressed her hands against Calvin's chest and pushed him away. "Stop it! Jane could return at any moment."

"Forgive me. My feelings for you are so strong, I couldn't help myself."

Jane entered the room just then and placed the shawl around Esme's shoulders. When Jane moved away, Calvin hissed into Esme's ear, "There's more, but it can wait for another day." Then he stepped back and bowed politely. "I'll be in touch, Esme. Good day."

"Good day, Calvin."

"The marquis isn't going to approve of the viscount sniffing around you," Jane warned. "I don't understand you, Lady Esme. You've never been fond of Lord Lonsdale, but now you are whispering together like conspirators."

Esme had always encouraged Jane to speak freely, since she was more companion than servant, but just this once she wished Jane had kept her opinion to herself.

"I am not betrothed to the marquis. In fact, he does not appear anxious to take a wife. As for Lord Lonsdale, we were not conspiring. You may go, Jane. I intend to sit here and read until teatime."

The book lay unopened in her lap long after Jane had left. How could she read with so much on her mind? She had to confront Dante with Calvin's accusations.

Dante had not seen Esme in several days, and during that time no more attempts had been made on his life. Neither he nor his friends Brookworth and Carstairs turned up anything of importance about his assailant or the reason behind the carriage collision.

Dante felt confident that society was beginning to accept him, thanks to his two friends. They had accompanied him to all the gentlemen's clubs worthy of his attention and introduced him around. In a few short days Dante had learned whose friendship to court and whose to avoid. He felt out of place with the young dandies who wasted their time gambling, wenching and carousing. More than a few had empty pockets, or so Brookworth had told him, and were looking for rich heiresses to marry.

Then Dante learned from Brookworth that Lonsdale had been seen at White's the same day as his accident. He had been heard to brag that he would soon have the blunt to pay off all his personal debts.

When Dante returned home that night after an evening at Brooks's, he found a note from Mr.

Bartholomew asking him to call on him at his convenience. It was too late to do so that night, but Dante started out for the solicitor's office after breakfast the following morning.

Bartholomew greeted him warmly. "Please sit down, Lord Alston. Can I get you anything?"

"No, thank you, Bartholomew. Is there a problem with my grandfather's will you wish to discuss?"

"Not exactly. Have you made Lady Esme's acquaintance yet?"

"I have indeed."

"Is she willing to marry you?"

"Lord Parkton assures me she will wed me, but I don't want to force her to the altar. I prefer a willing bride. Regrettably, she can't see past my gypsy heritage."

Bartholomew sighed. "I was afraid of that."

Dante's eyes narrowed. "Is there something you haven't told me?"

"I didn't mention it before because I believed you and Lord Parkton would arrange the marriage in a prompt manner. The codicil in your grandfather's will gave you six months from the date of his death to wed Lady Esme. If you haven't convinced her to marry you by then, you will lose the title to Lonsdale."

"Does he know that?"

"I'm afraid so. He came to my office a few days ago and asked to see the will. I had no reason to deny him. Forgive me for not telling you this at the reading of the will."

Dante felt anger rising inside him and ruthlessly tamped it down. Bartholomew's reasons for not mentioning this new development before now seemed puny at best. What was going on here?

"I fully expect to wed milady before the six months' deadline, but there has been a glitch in the courting. An attempt was made on my life."

Bartholomew half rose from his chair. "What happened? Are you all right?"

"I'm fine." Then Dante proceeded to tell Bartholomew what had happened and briefly mentioned the injuries he had received.

"Why would anyone wish to kill you?" the solicitor asked.

"I don't know. There are no leads. I suspect Lonsdale but have no solid proof."

"Lonsdale," Bartholomew repeated almost eagerly. "You could be right. He has the most to gain."

"Proving it is going to be difficult," Dante pointed out. "It's been over a week and no further attempts have been made. Perhaps the accident was just that."

"Do you intend to proceed with your courtship?"

"That is my intention. In the short time I've known Lady Esme, I've come to care for her a great deal." Dante rose. "I'll keep you informed of my progress. But rest assured there will be a wedding. Good day, Bartholomew."

They shook hands, and Dante left. A note from Esme was waiting for him when he returned home. She wanted him to call on her. Dante was surprised at her request, but unpredictability was one of her charms.

Dante presented himself at Lord Parkton's townhouse at two that afternoon. Jamison ushered him into the parlor. Dante found Esme standing before the window, her back ramrod straight. Fear surged through him. He knew immediately that something had upset her.

He reached her in three long strides. Grasping her

shoulders, he searched her face. She shied away from him as if in fear.

"What is it? What has happened?"

Esme slid a glance at Jane, who was trying her best not to be seen as eavesdropping. Dante sensed that Esme didn't want to talk in front of her maid. "It's a fine day. Shall we walk in the park?"

Esme's eyes lit up. "That's a wonderful idea. Would you please fetch our shawls, Jane?"

Jane left immediately. "Can't we leave her behind?" Dante asked.

"No, but she can sit on the bench while we stroll around the lake."

Jane arrived with their shawls and the small party walked the short distance to the park. Jane hung behind a short distance, giving Dante a chance for a private word with Esme.

"What is this all about? You're upset."

Esme remained silent. But when they approached an unoccupied bench, Esme waited for Jane to catch up and suggested that she rest on the bench while they strolled around the lake.

"Finally," Dante breathed. "What is it that can only be said in private?"

Dante wondered why she refused to meet his eyes. Her hands, he noticed, were clenched at her sides. "Did something happen to you? Tell me you're all right."

"I'm fine," Esme said with a coolness that confused him. After a long silence, she met his gaze. "I have to know. Did you kill your grandfather?"

Dante halted, his body tense with indignation. "Who suggested such a terrible thing? What possible reason would I have to kill my grandfather?"

"Perhaps he was going to change his will in Calvin's favor and you found out about it."

"Impossible! My grandfather was a stranger to me until the day he sent for me and told me he had recognized my birth in the courts and made me his heir."

Esme searched his face. "Maybe you wanted to push him along to his reward in order to gain his power and wealth."

"Who put that crazy idea in your head? Was it Lonsdale?" Esme didn't answer. He gave her arm a little shake. "You're to stay away from him, do you hear?"

Esme pulled her arm free. "You have no right to tell me what to do. You've all but ignored me since you . . . since we . . ."

". . . made love? There was a reason for that."

She turned away. "I don't want to hear it."

Grasping her shoulders, he spun her around to face him. "I haven't abandoned you, Esme. You're mine, and not just because your father and my grandfather willed it. I've been inside you. No other man can say that."

"How dare you!" She spun away and began walking back to Jane. He caught up with her. "Calvin wants me to marry him, and perhaps I shall," she taunted. It was a lie, but she was too angry to care.

Dante's temper flared. "What did you say?"

"I've known Calvin a long time, but you are a stranger *and* a gypsy."

"Do you actually think I killed my grandfather?"

She looked away. "I don't know you well enough to say."

Dante wanted to tell her whom he suspected of doing the deed but feared she would think he was merely being vindictive.

"I thought you didn't like Lonsdale."

"I . . . like him better than I like you, my lord gypsy."

Dante sighed. This conversation was getting him nowhere. Lonsdale was deliberately trying to transfer suspicion to him. If he didn't find something to connect the viscount to his grandfather's death, and Lonsdale kept spreading rumors, he would not only lose the respect of his peers but he would also lose Esme, and he couldn't let that happen. It was time to retreat and regroup.

"I'll see you home," Dante said curtly.

Esme knew she had angered Dante; but he had given her nothing to disprove Calvin's accusation. She wondered why Lord Alston's death wasn't being investigated if murder was suspected. She would ask her uncle about it straightaway.

Esme turned her face away. How could she have been so wrong about Dante? Making love with him had been the most perfect experience of her life. She had wanted him. But now she realized she knew nothing about him.

When they reached the Parkton townhouse, Dante took his leave of her and strode off. Esme watched him walk away, admiring the way his jacket clung to his muscled arms and broad back. His legs were long and muscular and well shaped, the epitome of masculinity. Turning away from the disturbing sight, Esme opened the front gate.

"Esme!"

Esme glanced over her shoulder, surprised to see

Calvin hurrying up the walk. "Go on inside, Jane, I'll speak to Calvin and join you in a moment," she said.

"I hoped I'd catch you alone," Calvin said when he reached her. "Thank you for dismissing Jane."

"What is it this time, Calvin?"

"You were walking in the park with the gypsy." His tone held a wealth of censure.

Had he been following me? "Do you have a problem with that?"

"Indeed I do. I think I'm being watched by those two friends of Alston's. Do you have any idea why?"

Esme was stunned, though she wouldn't put it past Dante to do such a thing. "You must be imagining things."

"Indeed not," Calvin huffed. "Brookworth and Carstairs seem to be everywhere I am. The gypsy is up to something, I know it!"

"We can't talk here," Esme warned. "The neighbors will gossip."

"Are you going to the Cowper ball tonight?"

"I believe Uncle Daniel received an invitation and intends for us to attend. Why?"

"I need to tell you what I recently learned about my uncle's will. Will you meet me in the Cowper garden tonight? You should be able to slip outside without any trouble."

Esme sighed. She and Calvin had known one another a very long time. If he had a legitimate complaint about Dante, she wanted to hear it.

Although Esme didn't want to think ill of Dante, she had to know more of Calvin's suspicions. She would be lying if she said she wasn't half in love with Dante. Still, it wasn't too late to cut all ties with him . . . if he really was a murderer.

"Very well, Calvin. I'll try to slip away, but what you have to say had better be important."

Calvin suppressed a smug smile. "Oh, it is, I assure you." He hurried off, looking too pleased with himself for Esme's peace of mind.

"Has my uncle returned home yet?" she asked Jamison as she handed him her bonnet and cloak.

"Indeed, milady. He's in the study."

"Thank you. I'll announce myself."

The study door was closed. She rapped once and opened the door. "Might I have a word with you, Uncle Daniel?"

Parkton raised his head and smiled at her. "Come in, my dear. I always have time for you. What can I do for you?"

"Have you heard any gossip concerning Lord Alston's death?"

"Oh, that. Nasty stuff, what? I've heard rumblings and promptly put them to rest. The marquis had no reason to kill his grandfather. Besides, the lad isn't capable of murder."

He sent her a sharp look. "Who repeated those lies to you?"

She ignored the question. "Perhaps you should investigate nonetheless. What if the rumors are true? You wouldn't want me to wed a murderer, would you?"

Parkton chuckled. "So that's what this is all about. You still want to cry off. Forget it, Esme. Lord Alston's faith in his grandson is good enough for me. I'm thinking of holding a ball to announce your betrothal as soon as Alston gives the go ahead."

Esme thought it best not to mention Calvin's name in connection to the rumors. Uncle Daniel might think they were the rumblings of a jealous man. That might indeed be true, but Esme owed it to herself to look into the matter and make up her own mind.

"I hope your trust isn't misplaced, Uncle."

"Yes, well, don't worry your little head about it. I have complete faith in Alston. I won't be here for tea, but I shall be waiting in the foyer at precisely nine o'clock tonight to take you to the Cowper ball. Don't keep me waiting."

"I never do," Esme said in parting.

Dante prepared for the Cowper ball with meticulous care. Simpson, his new valet, made sure he was appropriately decked out in evening dress. As the finishing touch, Simpson was forming the perfect knot in Dante's cravat.

Dante knew that Esme and her uncle would attend the ball, for Parkton had told him. Despite being angry with Esme, Dante wanted to make a good impression. He would have offered to pick up Esme and Parkton in his carriage if their parting earlier today had been less acrimonious. He knew he shouldn't have been so abrupt, but milady's suspicion had hurt him more than he cared to admit.

Tonight Dante planned to disabuse her of those perverse ideas that Lonsdale had planted in her mind.

"The cravat is perfect now, milord," Simpson said, stepping away. "I do think, however, that you could have chosen a color other than black tonight. You will look a crow among peacocks."

"Thank you for your opinion, Simpson," Dante said dryly. "There was a not too distant time when I dressed in every color of the rainbow. Since inheriting the title, I prefer not to imitate those strutting dandies who seek to draw attention to themselves." He headed out the door. "No need to wait up for me, Simpson. I can undress myself."

Dante strode from his chamber and down the stairs. Brookworth was standing in the foyer. "Have you been waiting long?" Dante asked.

"Just got here, old man. You look splendid. Simpson must be working out for you."

Grayson handed him his hat. "He is indeed. Thank you for recommending him."

"Shall we walk?" Brookworth suggested. "It's such a nice night, and the carriages will be backed up for blocks."

"A good idea. It will give us time to talk."

"What's on your mind?" Brookworth asked as they strolled down the street.

"Lonsdale, who else? The man is smarter than I gave him credit for. He suggested to Esme that I had murdered my grandfather."

Brookworth halted abruptly. "Good God! She didn't believe him, did she?"

"It put doubts in her mind. Have you learned anything to connect Lonsdale with my grandfather's death?"

"Not yet. I spoke with Carstairs today, and he hasn't learned anything, either. Lonsdale is clever, I'll give him that. If he's guilty, he's covered his tracks very well indeed."

"You cannot imagine how shocked I was when Esme accused me of murder."

"You really do care for her, don't you? You're not pursuing her just for the title or wealth, are you?"

Dante gave him a wry smile. "If I can't change her

prejudice against me, we have no future. And whether you believe it or not, I do want a future with Esme. So to answer your question, yes, I care for her. Unfortunately, she doesn't share my feelings. She never will, with Lonsdale planting false rumors in her ear."

"Do you recall," Brookworth reminisced, "how the women flocked to you during our years at university? We all referred to you as the gypsy lover."

"My popularity with women gave my classmates one more reason to scorn me," Dante remembered.

"Long after our university days, I heard rumors about your continued success with women."

Dante chuckled. "I admit I have been invited into more bedrooms in the past seven or eight years than most men see in a lifetime."

"Lucky devil."

"There's the Cowper mansion," Dante said, eager to end talk of his personal life. "The line of carriages stretches for blocks."

"Look! Parkton and his niece are just now alighting from their carriage," Brookworth pointed out. "If you hurry you can catch up with them."

Hastening his steps, Dante was closing the distance when he saw Lonsdale sidle up beside Esme. Dante spit out a curse as Lonsdale leaned down and whispered something to Esme. Jealousy exploded in his head when she smiled at Lonsdale and nodded. Lengthening his steps, he caught up with them.

"Lady Esme, will you save the first waltz for me?"

"She's promised me the first waltz," Lonsdale snapped.

Dante sent Lonsdale a withering look. "Milady was mistaken. The first waltz belongs to me."

"A rousing gypsy dance would suit you better," Esme said.

Her guts churned. She had no reason to insult Dante and felt terrible about it. What was wrong with her? Dante seemed to rub her the wrong way. He stimulated her sexually and mentally and made her feel jittery and unsure of herself. Every time they were together, she wanted to insult him, while at the same time she ached to throw herself into his arms and kiss him. He stirred perplexing emotions within her.

I've been inside you.

His words played over and over in her mind, adding to her confusion.

Why had she let Dante make love to her?

"Milady," Dante murmured into her ear, "If you recall, I not only waltz but I do it very well. Among other things, which I'm sure you already know."

He extended his arm. "Shall we go in together? We are, after all, a couple."

Too stunned to protest, Esme rested her hand on his sleeve. They entered the house together.

"Esme, don't forget your promise!" Lonsdale called after her.

Chapter Nine

Dante's mouth flattened. "What precisely did you promise Lonsdale?"

"Nothing that concerns you."

Dante had no time for further words as a footman appeared to take their wraps. Dante's first glimpse of Esme's gown stole his breath. The elegant gold sheath, beaded with pearls at the low neckline, flowed enticingly over her stunning figure. Instead of an elaborate headdress that would have concealed her magnificent dark red hair, her mass of ringlets was held in place by a pearl-studded gold tiara.

"You look beautiful," he whispered. Then they were being announced and there was no more time for compliments, no matter how well deserved. They passed through the reception line and were welcomed by the Cowpers. When they advanced into the crush of people, Dante wanted to turn and flee.

He doubted he would ever feel comfortable at this sort of formal gathering. The appraising looks he received made it apparent that he was still being inspected and judged. Although many would never forgive him for being a gypsy, he really didn't care.

Immediately Brookworth and Carstairs came up to join him. Carstairs was accompanied by his fiancée, Esme's best friend, Lady Louise. Lord Parkton excused himself and headed for the game room. "Enjoy yourselves," he said in parting.

While Esme chatted with Lady Louise, Dante pulled Carstairs and Brookworth aside for a private word. A few minutes later, Brookworth drifted away, as did Louise and Carstairs. "Would you care for something to drink, milady?" Dante asked.

Esme shook her head. "Not now, thank you. You don't have to hover, my lord. I shall join a group of friends while you seek your own amusement."

Dante refused to leave Esme's side. He hoped his daunting presence would dissuade Lonsdale from approaching Esme. Though Dante had no idea what Esme had promised Lonsdale, he was determined to keep them apart. Meanwhile, he had to convince milady that he hadn't killed his grandfather.

Esme had just introduced Dante to a group of her friends when the music began. The first set was a waltz. "Milady, this is our dance, I believe."

Before Esme could protest, Dante swept her onto the dance floor. He had learned all the popular dances during his month-long stay at Alston Park before entering society. Grayson had hired a dance teacher to prepare him for his London debut.

"You're holding me too tight," Esme protested. "It isn't proper."

"It feels proper," Dante said, laughing at her with his eyes. "Smile," he said; "everyone is watching us. I think I'm being tested. The *ton* can't decide whether or not to accept me. But they have no choice, you see. I'm a marquis."

"You are a gypsy," Esme retorted, smiling through clenched teeth.

"So I am." He grinned. "A gypsy marquis. A rather remarkable combination, don't you agree?"

The waltz ended. They waited on the dance floor for the second dance of the set to begin. When it did, Dante swept Esme across the floor in graceful dips and turns.

"You waltz remarkably well for a gypsy," Esme said grudgingly.

"Gypsies learn to dance at an early age. I know you've seen Rom perform before audiences; music is a big part of our lives."

The conversation tapered off as the music ended and the last dance of the set began. Dante knew he was holding Esme closer than society allowed, but it had been so long since he'd held her in his arms, he couldn't resist. If everything worked as he planned tonight, he would do more than hold her.

As the last strains of music died, Dante maneuvered Esme to the edge of the dance floor and ducked with her into a hallway.

"What are you doing? I promised the next set to Lord Batterly."

Ignoring her protests, Dante swept Esme down the hallway and through a door that opened into a small, unoccupied chamber. Dante closed the door, turned the key in the lock and placed it in his vest pocket.

"We cannot be in here alone, Dante," Esme warned. "If you knew anything about society, you'd realize that I'll be ruined if we're found together."

Dante laughed. "What a short memory you have,

my love. I've already ruined you. I took your maidenhead. While you may have forgotten, I have not."

Esme groaned. Did the gypsy have no shame? Why did he keep throwing her indiscretion in her face? Folding her arms across her chest, she said, "How did you know this room would be unoccupied?"

"I asked Brookworth if he knew of a place where you and I might engage in a private conversation. He directed me here."

"Say what you have to say, then unlock the door. I wish to leave."

Dante stalked toward her until he stood so close she could feel the heat of his body, smell the masculine scent of him.

"What must I say to make you believe I had no part in my grandfather's death?"

Esme searched his face. "Do you believe your grandfather committed suicide?"

A distant look came into Dante's eyes. Silence throbbed between them. When he finally spoke, his voice was harsh with emotion. "No, I don't believe Grandfather Alston took his own life."

Esme felt her knees buckle but forced herself to go on. "Did you kill him?" she whispered.

"No!" His sharp denial exploded into the silence.

"If he was murdered, do you know who killed him?"

No answer was forthcoming. She sucked in a shocked breath as comprehension dawned. "You do know, don't you?"

"I know I didn't do it. Enough of this—I didn't bring you here to be interrogated."

"Why are we here?"

"For this."

Esme gasped as Dante pulled her against his chest and slid a hand up her neck. Threading his fingers in her hair, he all but ruined the complicated coiffure Jane had toiled over, and sent her tiara to the floor. With a firm tug, he tipped her head back and whispered against her lips, "I've missed you."

Before she could form a protest, he slanted his mouth over hers. Unwilling to fall victim to the gypsy's seduction, Esme pressed her lips together, denying him access.

He slid his tongue along the seam of her lips. When they didn't open to his insistent probing, he lifted his head and stared down at her. His eyes were laughing at her again. Her heart flew against her ribcage so hard she feared it would burst free.

"Part your lips, milady."

"No, I . . ."

Dante grinned. "You just did." And with those words he reclaimed her mouth, his tongue gliding inside with little resistance.

"I want you." His voice sounded husky, hinting of dark desires. "I want to hold you, possess you. I want to anoint every inch of your skin with my mouth, touch you all over, make your body sing, bury my tongue in your most secret places."

He kissed her even as he whispered words of passion and longing. Esme was utterly lost. His gravelly voice brought a rush of warmth in her belly, a tingling over her skin, a tremor in her legs. How could she hope to resist the infamous gypsy lover? She couldn't.

When he bore her down upon the soft carpet before the hearth, Esme could find neither the will nor the desire to call a halt. The warm glow of the fire was so intimate, the fragrance of burning pine wafting through the room so erotic that Esme could think of no better place for a seduction.

Seduction!

She sat up, attempting to push him away. "What do you think you're doing?"

"I *know* what I'm doing. I'm going to love you."

"I don't want—"

The sentence died before it was born as he stretched out beside her, drew her into his arms and pressed tiny, nipping kisses on her mouth. Whatever she was going to say was lost in a haze of passion so raw she began to tremble. He tugged down the low neckline of her gown, baring her breasts. She felt his fingers dance upon her nipples, felt them swell and throb. Then his mouth replaced his fingers. He suckled her; she cried out and arched against him. He showed her no mercy.

Closing her eyes, she clenched her hands into fists as passion pulled her into its relentless grip. Her pulse accelerated as he grasped the hem of her skirt and lifted it up, revealing white stocking-clad ankles.

"I wish I could strip you naked," he said wistfully. "The next time we make love, there will be no clothing between us."

With rough impatience, he nudged her skirt upward, seeking the center of her pleasure. Dante's first glimpse of the reddish curling hair at the juncture of her thighs made his stomach clench with desperate need.

He sent her an inscrutable look, shifted her skirt out of the way and with his palms lifted her buttocks at the same time as he lowered his head.

"What are you doing?" Her voice rose on a note of panic.

147

"Watch and see."

His head dipped. He kissed her stomach. She moaned softly. He straightened up, his eyes never leaving hers as he tore off his jacket and vest and unbuttoned his shirt. When he returned to her, he drew her legs up, bent his head and blew a warm breath against the heated flesh of her inner thighs. Then his tongue flicked out to lick along her moist crevice.

"Dante! You can't! Please . . ."

"I intend to please you, love, please you very well indeed. Relax, I want to taste your sweet nectar. I promise you'll like what I'm going to do."

She tried to shift away. He wouldn't let her move. Holding her still, he hooked his arms under her thighs and draped her legs over his shoulders. His tongue found her again, slipping between the folds of her sex, gently stroking. The pleasure almost shattered her. With a breathless moan, Esme put both hands in his hair, not to push him away as she ought but to hold his face between her burning thighs. He assuaged her need, sucking her feminine nub into his mouth, his onslaught slow and steady, unmindful of her bucking. She stifled a sob when, moments later, his tongue slid deep inside her, tasting, thrusting, giving her the most exquisite pleasure she had ever known.

Esme went wild, arching against his mouth, her hips moving in an elemental rhythm as old as time. The torture ended abruptly when she climaxed, soaring into throbbing, mindless release. She arched against his mouth, her frenzy ending in what felt like a shower of sparks.

Even as she spiraled downward, Dante released her legs and moved upward. Parting her knees, he fastened his mouth on hers and nudged her open with his aching erection. She clung to him, her breathing rapid and shallow, matching his. Beads of perspiration ran down his face as he thrust hard, delving deep. His blood thundered and his body cried for release as he plunged and withdrew, deeper, faster, feeling the heat igniting between them.

He heard her sob, realized she was going to climax again and rose up on his elbows so he could watch her face. He thrust again, once, twice; color flooded her face, her body convulsed and she cried out. Then he set them both free. With a final thrust, sensation exploded inside him, lights shattered behind his eyes, and his seed spilled.

He fell against her, dragging in shallow, shuddering breaths, his heart pounding so wildly he feared it would burst through his chest. Once they were wed, they could explore their passion every night; he sensed that sex with Esme would never grow stale. He rested his head against her forehead, willing her to feel the same emotions he was feeling, but she denied him that pleasure. Her eyes, when they opened, were blazing with fury.

"Damn you! You seduced me after I promised myself it wouldn't happen again." She pushed against him. "Get off me!"

With marked reluctance, Dante rolled away and gained his feet. When he offered Esme his hand, she ignored it and rose without his help. "My hair is a mess," she complained as she smoothed her skirts down and pushed her breasts back into her bodice. "I can't leave the room looking like this."

Unrepentant, Dante said, "I believe the ladies' withdrawing room is nearby."

Esme glared at him. "You planned all of this, didn't you?"

"I . . . needed you," Dante offered lamely.

"Why me, when you could have any woman here tonight?"

"I wanted you. You're my fiancée."

"You don't have a fiancée," Esme charged. "And you're not likely to have one."

"I'll speak with your uncle tonight and purchase a special license tomorrow," Dante said, pulling on his jacket and tying his hopelessly wrinkled neckcloth. "I'll let you know as soon as the arrangements are finalized."

"Don't bother, my lord. I cannot marry a man I do not trust. Too many questions have been raised about you, and you have given me no acceptable answers."

"Esme, this is ridiculous. You have to marry me. I've made love to you; there could be consequences."

"I won't be bullied into marriage," Esme retorted. She picked up her tiara and shoved past him. "After I repair my hair, I'm going to ask Uncle Daniel to take me home."

"I've never known a more stubborn woman in all my days." Disgust colored his words. "How many times must I tell you I had nothing to do with my grandfather's death?"

"Until I believe you," Esme shot back. She opened the door.

"Wait! Let me check the corridor first." He stuck his head out the door, saw no one and allowed her to brush past him.

Esme headed toward the withdrawing room, praying she would meet no one she knew. She didn't. In fact, the room was empty but for a maid stationed there to help ladies in need of attention.

"Would you be so kind as to help me with my hair?" Esme asked. "The dance was so strenuous, my coiffure is absolutely ruined."

The maid smiled, seated Esme at a dressing table and picked up a brush. When Esme left the withdrawing room, the talented maid had returned Esme's hair to its former glory.

Because Esme didn't want to cross the ballroom to reach her uncle in the card room, she edged along the perimeter, skillfully avoiding the crush gathered around the dance floor.

"Esme, there you are! I wondered where you had gotten off to."

Calvin. He came up beside her and wound her arm through his. "Where were you going in such a hurry?"

"To the card room to ask Uncle Daniel to take me home."

"But you just got here."

"I've suddenly developed a headache."

Leaning down, he whispered into her ear, "I need a private word with you. You promised, remember?"

"Can't it wait for another time? I've had my fill of private words."

Calvin sent her a puzzled glance. "This can't wait. Besides, I just came from the card room and Parkton was winning. He's not going to want to leave. Let me take you home. It will give us a chance to have our talk."

Esme wasn't convinced.

"A footman can carry a message to Parkton," Lonsdale urged. "I assure you he won't mind if I take you home."

Esme was on the verge of refusing when she spied

Dante heading toward the card room, probably to speak with Uncle Daniel. "Very well, I'll leave a message for my uncle on my way out. I can't stay here a moment longer."

What she didn't tell Calvin was that the gypsy and her uncle were probably setting a date for her marriage at this very minute. She allowed Calvin to escort her to the foyer to collect their wraps. Before they left, Esme asked a footman to deliver a verbal message to her uncle. Then Calvin swept her outside and into his closed carriage. He lingered a moment to give his coachman the direction, then joined her.

The carriage rattled off down the street. "This is as private as we're going to be, Calvin," Esme said. "What is it you wish to tell me?"

"It's about the gypsy."

Esme sighed. "Of course it is." Now her head was really beginning to hurt.

"I visited my uncle's solicitor and demanded to read the will in its entirety," Lonsdale confided. "I learned there was a codicil that wasn't revealed at the reading."

Esme pretended interest. What could the codicil possibly mean to her? "Why should that concern me?"

"Because it involves your future, Esme," Calvin said. "If Alston doesn't marry you within six months, the marquisate will revert to me."

Esme forced herself to breathe in and out, willing her heart to keep beating as she recalled everything that had happened between her and Dante. He didn't care one damn bit about her. Greed had dictated his actions since the moment they'd met. Well, maybe not the first time they met, for in the beginning he hadn't known who she was.

Or had he? Had his seduction been carefully planned and executed? A sob caught in her throat. How could he deceive her like that? Why hadn't he told her about the codicil instead of making her believe she meant something to him? A derisive snort exploded from her throat. The gypsy lover was simply living up to his reputation. Seducing women fed his ego. He was a sexual predator who thrived on amusing himself with women. How could she have been so stupid as to believe he truly wanted her?

"Esme, are you all right?" Lonsdale asked. "Did you hear what I said?"

"I heard," Esme whispered. "Dante will lose everything if I don't marry him within six months."

"Yes, well, not quite everything. He'll still inherit a handsome sum. He's using you, my dear. He's courting you to fulfill the terms of my uncle's will and for no other reason. You do believe me, don't you?"

Esme nodded. "It makes perfect sense."

Calvin leaned close. "There's a way to get even with him, to deny him what he has lied and perhaps killed for."

Esme looked at Calvin's familiar face and wondered what she had found objectionable about him. His features were pleasant, though he appeared dull and plain compared to Dante's handsome face, powerful form and vibrant spirit.

After Dante had made love to her tonight, Esme had realized that marrying the gypsy was the only way she would ever satisfy her craving for him. She had felt on insatiable desire for him, his touch, his kisses.

But his betrayal had gone too far. He could have told her at any point during their acquaintance that marrying her had not merely been the wish of her parents and his grandfather, but that his entire future as a marquis depended upon it. Until Calvin had told her the truth, she'd assumed Dante wanted her for herself. It hurt to know that it was the title he wanted, not her.

Even though Esme had disparaged Dante because of his gypsy blood, at some point she'd begun to realize that his ancestry made little difference in her feelings for him. In time she would have capitulated and married him, but not now. Under no circumstances would she marry Dante, knowing he had tricked her. He could lose everything and go back to living in a wagon, for all she cared.

Calvin was far more deserving of the title than the gypsy. Abruptly Esme realized what Calvin had said.

"What are you suggesting, Calvin?"

"There's only one way to foil Alston, my dear. You know your uncle will insist that you wed the scoundrel, so we have to act quickly."

"Yes, of course, but how—"

"I took the liberty of purchasing a special license."

Esme groaned. Did all men carry special licenses with them?

"We don't have to go to Scotland to be married," Calvin said. "We will leave immediately for my hunting lodge south of London, near the village of Heath. I'm sure the local vicar will be happy to marry us. Everyone will assume we eloped to Gretna Green, so we should be quite safe at Heath until we return to London and announce our marriage.

"I cannot wait to see the gypsy's face when he learns the title and power have been snatched from him." He puffed up his chest. "I have long anticipated the day I would inherit Uncle Alstons wealth."

Esme worried her bottom lip with her teeth. Eloping with Calvin seemed a bit drastic, but she could think of no other way to thwart Dante. Besides, if Dante had killed his grandfather as Calvin suspected, marrying him could place her own life in danger.

"Don't keep me in suspense, Esme. Say you'll marry me. We can leave tonight."

Esme stared at him, hesitating.

"Never say you care for the gypsy, that you prefer him over me." He grimaced, his distaste palpable. "He's a bloody gypsy—how could you bear for him to . . . to touch you?"

Letting Dante touch me is easier than you think. "I cannot leave tonight. I have no clothes, nothing to wear but my ball gown."

"We both know Alston will come after you," Calvin argued. "We cannot delay."

Esme was so angry with Dante that Calvin's logic began to make sense to her. She wanted to see Dante punished, and marrying Calvin would certainly do just that. She never stopped to think how marriage to Calvin would affect her own life, or that she would be tied forever to a man she was merely fond of. She could think no further than the fact that Dante had lied, perhaps committed murder, and seduced her for his own enjoyment and profit.

"Very well, but take me home first so I can change and pack a bag. Uncle Daniel won't be home for hours yet. No one will know I'm gone till morning."

"What about your maid?"

"We'll take Jane with us."

"That wouldn't be wise," Calvin advised. "Leave your maid behind; she can tell Parkton that we eloped to Gretna Green. That will throw Alston off our trail if he tries to follow."

Oh, he'll follow, all right. "Perhaps you're right," Esme agreed. She had the nagging feeling that there was something wrong with the whole plan, but she couldn't quite put her finger on it. Maybe it would come to her on their journey to Heath. Right now her emotions were too raw to think clearly.

The carriage pulled up before the Parkton townhouse. "Hurry," Calvin urged.

"I won't be long," Esme promised.

A sleepy footman opened the door and handed Esme a lamp to light her way up the stairs. Jane, who had been dozing in a chair, awakened immediately. "You're home early, milady." She peered closely at Esme. "Something is wrong. You look upset."

"Help me get out of my ball gown and into a traveling costume," Esme ordered. "Then pack a bag with a few changes of clothing and other essentials I might need for a short trip."

Jane's mouth gaped open. "What are you about, Lady Esme?"

Esme's chin tilted upward. "I'm eloping with Calvin."

"You're doing no such thing!"

"Yes, I am. You don't understand, Jane. Dante has used me. He's not what he seems. I will not marry him under any circumstances. You're to tell my uncle in the morning that Calvin and I eloped to Gretna Green."

The lie nearly choked her, but it had to be said in order to send Dante off in the wrong direction.

"You're not yourself, my lady. Don't do this while you're in an overwrought state. Wait until tomorrow, when you've had time to think this through. By then you'll remember that Lord Lonsdale isn't your favorite person."

Esme tossed off her gown, removed her tiara and strode to her wardrobe. If Jane wouldn't help her, she'd help herself. She chose a dark traveling dress and struggled into it. Jane sighed and lent a hand.

"If you're bent on committing this folly, I'll pack a bag for you and one for myself," Jane said.

"No, you're to stay behind and tell Uncle Daniel and the gypsy where I've gone, but not until tomorrow. Mind now—it's very important that you wait."

Jane folded her arms over her ample chest. "You're making a big mistake."

"Let me worry about that. Uncle Daniel expects me to wed Dante, and I cannot do it. He murdered his grandfather."

The color drained from Jane's face. "I don't believe it! Who told you such a thing?"

Esme found her bag in the back of her wardrobe and began throwing clothing into it. Jane pushed her aside and took over the task.

"If you insist on doing this, the least I can do is see to your packing. But don't think for a minute that Lord Alston won't come after you. He cares about you. I can see it in his eyes."

"Ha! What you see is greed . . . and lust. I don't have time for a lengthy discussion. I'll explain everything when I return as Calvin's wife."

"You're fooling yourself, milady, if you think you'll be happy with Lord Lonsdale. You care for the marquis, more than you want to admit."

"That's enough, Jane! My mind is made up. Just tell Dante and my uncle exactly what I told you. Gretna

Green, remember that. But you're to say nothing until tomorrow."

Jane nodded, sniffling into her handkerchief. Esme picked up her bag and cloak and left a sobbing Jane behind. The footman on duty dozed on a bench but awoke when Esme opened the door.

"Milady, where are you going?"

"To Gretna Green," Esme called gaily, "with Viscount Lonsdale."

The footman was so startled he merely stared at Esme as she sailed out the door.

Esme climbed into the waiting carriage, settled back against the squabs and wondered if she was making a grave mistake.

Jane waited until the carriage pulled away from the curb before rushing down the stairs and sending the footman to fetch Lord Parkton at the Cowper ball. There was no way she was going to wait until tomorrow to inform His Lordship of Lady Esme's rash decision to elope with Lord Lonsdale.

Dante's smile was jaunty as he stood at the edge of the card room. He had just made love to Esme and was eager to inform Lord Parkton that he was ready to set the date. As luck would have it, Parkton had been deeply engaged in his game and was only now able to extricate himself for a private word with Dante. They left the card room together and sought out a secluded alcove.

"Where is Esme?" Parkton asked. "She sent word that she was going home."

"That's impossible. I saw her go into the ladies' withdrawing room just a short while ago. I'll find her as soon as we set a date for the wedding. The sooner it can be arranged, the better. I'll purchase a special license tomorrow."

Parkton searched Dante's face until Dante began to fidget under his intense scrutiny. Finally he said, "So that's the way of things, is it?"

Dante had no intention of questioning Parkton's meaning.

"Very well, let's plan this wedding," Parkton said. "Does two weeks from Saturday next suit you?"

"That suits me just fine, if Esme is agreeable."

"Esme will agree," Parkton assured him. "Leave all the arrangements to me. The bishop himself will marry you in the cathedral before all the prominent members of the *ton*. Just show up on time with the special license."

Happiness burst through Dante. "Excuse me, my lord, I'm eager to find my betrothed and tell her the good news." They shook hands, but before Dante strode off to find Esme, a footman approached them.

"Lord Parkton, your footman is waiting in the foyer; he wishes to speak to you. He said it was urgent."

Dante and Parkton exchanged troubled glances before moving in unison to the foyer.

"Grimes, what is amiss?" Parkton asked anxiously.

Grimes looked so grim when he saw Parkton that Dante's heart began to pound. *What has Esme done now?*

"Milord, please forgive me for intruding, but Jane sent me straightaway to find you. She said it couldn't wait until morning."

"Spit it out, man!" Parkton all but shouted.

" 'Tis Lady Esme, milord. She eloped with Lord Lonsdale."

"What do you mean, she eloped with Lonsdale?" Dante demanded.

"Just that, milord. She returned home from the ball, had Jane pack a bag for her and left in Lord Lonsdale's carriage. Jane wasn't to tell you until tomorrow, but she sent me to inform you straightaway."

Dante spit out a curse and headed for the door.

"Alston, where are you going?" Parkton called after him.

"To fetch Esme. She's mine—Lonsdale can't have her."

"Good luck," Parkton called. "I fear you're going to need it."

Chapter Ten

Dante didn't leave London immediately. After he had spoken at length with Jane, he took advantage of Lord Parkton's connections and purchased a special license to marry from the bishop. Despite the delay, Dante felt confident that he would catch up with Esme, for Lonsdale wouldn't be able to travel over rough roads during the darkest part of night and would be forced to stop at an inn. Dante hoped to catch up with them before Lonsdale coaxed Esme into his bed. There was no horse faster than Condor.

The knowledge that Lonsdale and Esme would be alone at an inn goaded Dante into a fine anger. Would they anticipate their marriage and share a bed? Would Esme enjoy Lonsdale's kisses? He shook aside his dismal thoughts and urged Condor to a faster gallop.

Carlotta sat on a bench, staring into her crystal ball. The images she saw inside the misty sphere made her gasp and cry out. Sandor glanced at her from across the wagon, shivering when he saw the look of terror on Carlotta's pale face.

"What do you see, Carlotta?"

"Our grandson needs help," she whispered.

"Is Dante in danger?"

"He could be."

"What can we do?"

Carlotta closed her eyes, concentrating fiercely, trying to clarify her vision of Dante. Her eyes popped open, her hands shook. "Dante is riding north for a reason I do not understand."

"North? This late in the year?"

"He is making a grave mistake. Every fiber of my being tells me Dante should ride south, to us." She struggled to her feet. "If Dante continues on a northern course, he stands to lose everything, including his true love."

"Shall I ride after him?"

Carlotta shook her head. "I will try to reach him in another way. See that I am not disturbed."

Sandor retreated to a far corner of the wagon while Carlotta became so still she appeared to stop breathing. Then she turned her palms up, and her lips began to move in a silent chant.

As Dante headed north out of London, he felt strangely apprehensive. Even Condor appeared in some distress, for he frequently threw his head back and snorted, which wasn't at all like him.

Dante had scarcely left the environs of the city when he was plagued by a voice inside his head. The inner voice—his conscience?—urged him to travel south instead of north. Why should he ride south when he knew Esme and Lonsdale were on their way to Gretna Green?

Condor began acting up again. The usually obedient animal refused to take directions and kept pulling at the reins. That gave Dante his first inkling that he should rethink the situation. It was almost as if someone were trying to communicate with him. Having lived with Carlotta all his life, Dante had learned to heed his intuition.

Dante reined in and dismounted, allowing Condor to crop grass while he sat on a rock and let his mind wander back to the moment he had learned that Esme had run off with Lonsdale. Recalling his conversation with Jane, he remembered thinking it odd that Esme had openly revealed her destination to a maid *and* a footman. She'd been quite emphatic, Jane had said.

Why would Esme want him and Parkton to know where she and Lonsdale were going? The answer, when it came, was clear. Esme knew he would follow and had deliberately sent him racing off in the wrong direction.

The longer Dante thought about it, the more his gut told him he should be riding south instead of north. If he was wrong, he would lose Esme forever, but if he was right, he could stop a travesty from happening.

"Which shall it be, Condor? North or south?"

As if the horse understood, Condor whickered softly and rolled his head around to the south. It was more than enough to convince Dante to follow his gut. Thank God he had listened to his conscience before he left London behind.

* * *

"We're going to stop at an inn," Lonsdale told Esme. She was half asleep, her head lolling against the squabs. "The horses need a rest and so do you. Besides, we could both use something to eat."

"Let's keep going," Esme said, none too eager to be alone in an inn with Calvin.

"I'm so tired I can barely hold the reins in my hands," Lonsdale replied. "I know this road. There's a country inn not far ahead."

If Calvin thought to share a room with her, he was in for a shock, Esme thought, fully awake now. "I hope you don't expect to—"

"There it is!" Calvin interrupted, turning the horses in to the courtyard of the Hart and Horn.

Dawn was just breaking. A sleepy-eyed lad came out to greet them. "Ho there, lad, run in and rouse the innkeeper."

"Aye, sir," the lad answered, stumbling off.

Some minutes passed before the innkeeper appeared. "There you are, good sir," Calvin called. "We need a room and a meal."

"It's too early to open the kitchen; the cook hasn't even arrived yet," the innkeeper growled. "As to the room, you are welcome to it as long as you can pay."

Calvin produced a crown from his pocket and flipped it to the innkeeper. "Is it worth a crown to find us something to eat?"

The innkeeper caught it handily. "Aye, I suppose I can provide a cold collation. Come along, then."

Calvin helped Esme down, picked up her bag and escorted her into the inn. Only a few souls too drunk to take themselves home the night before remained in the common room, their heads resting on scarred tables.

"You want one room or two?" the innkeeper asked.

"Two."

"One."

Esme and Calvin spoke at the same time. "Which will it be? One or two?"

"Two," Esme replied, silencing Calvin with a look.

The innkeeper reached beneath a counter. "Here are the keys. The first two rooms on the right at the top of the stairs. Choose as you please."

"About the food," Calvin reminded him.

"Aye, sit yourselves down at a table, I'll bring it directly." He shuffled off, grumbling to himself about the early hour and inconsiderate guests.

"Why can't we share a room?" Calvin complained once they were seated. "I've waited a long time for this day."

"We'll have a lifetime together after we're married."

Truth to tell, Esme didn't want to think of being intimate with Calvin. That scenario was so unpalatable she nearly lost her appetite, and began to devise ways to keep him from her bed. When the innkeeper set a platter of cold meat, bread and mugs of ale in front of them, Esme was almost too tired to eat. Calvin ate ravenously while she picked at her food.

Esme yawned and pushed her plate away. "I'm exhausted, Calvin. Give me the key to my room; I'd like to retire."

Calvin rose, walked around the table and assisted Esme to her feet. "I'll see you to your room."

Calvin picked up Esme's bag and escorted her up the stairs. He stopped before the first door on the right and unlocked it. Esme stepped into a chamber devoid of light but for streaks of breaking dawn filtering through a window.

"I'll light the candle," Calvin said. He dropped her bag and fumbled for a sulfur match. Esme shivered and walked to the window, spreading the drapes wide to admit more light. She didn't hear the soft click of the key turning in the lock, for her mind was on Dante and the wild goose chase she had sent him on.

The candle flared, chasing away the darkness. Esme turned from the window, vaguely aware of a bed and various pieces of furniture. The room looked clean, if spartan, but she was too tired to care.

"Thank you," Esme said. "I'll be ready to leave after a few hours' sleep."

"There's no hurry. We can take supper together later, spend the night here and be on our way early tomorrow morning."

"Very well, I'll be ready when you are. Good night, Calvin."

Calvin stalked toward her. "I'm not leaving, Esme."

Esme blinked. "Wh . . . what? Surely you're jesting. We're not married."

Calvin laughed. "What difference will a few days make?"

"A great deal of difference. I'm not going to sleep with you until we're wed."

The corners of Calvin's lips turned down. "Don't be such a prude. I've wanted you for as long as I can remember. I had high hopes for us. With the Alston title and wealth, we would have been feted and fawned over by society. Then the gypsy had to ruin everything," he said fiercely. "Well, he can't have you, and I won't let your uncle try to annul our marriage. Besides, the gypsy won't want you after I've had you."

He advanced toward her. She scooted around him toward the door. He didn't try to follow, and she soon learned why. The door was locked and Calvin had the key.

"Open the door this very minute!" Esme demanded. "There's no way I'm going to sleep with you now."

And maybe never, Esme thought. She was beginning to regret her rash decision to elope. She should have confronted Dante about what she had learned instead of rushing off half-cocked, feeling hurt and betrayed. How did she even know Calvin wasn't lying?

Calvin grasped Esme's arm and pulled her away from the door. "I don't understand you, Esme. Why are you fighting this? Our marriage was meant to be. *We* were meant to be. I'm a good lover, you'll see."

"That's something I'll learn after we're married," Esme insisted. "Until then, we'll sleep apart."

He yanked her roughly against him. "Enough of this foolishness. I'm making you mine right now."

His lips claimed hers with ruthless determination. His tongue plundered her mouth; she gagged at the unpleasant taste and clamped down hard on it. Calvin yelped and thrust her away.

"Why did you do that? If you want to play rough, I shall be happy to oblige." He reached for her. Esme whirled away, grabbed a poker from the hearth and wielded it like a weapon.

"I don't want to hurt you, but I will," she warned. "What's wrong with you, Calvin? You've never been a violent man. Why can't you accept my refusal with good humor? I'm exhausted . . . we both are. Neither of us will be able to enjoy our first time together. We'll be wed soon, and then I'll have no reason to avoid your bed. Wouldn't you rather have a willing wife than one you had to force?"

Calvin seemed to mull over her words. "What if we can be wed this very day?"

Esme's eyes widened. "What are you saying?"

"It's simple, really. I'll find a country vicar to marry us. You'll be mine before nightfall." He leered at her. "That's what you want, isn't it?"

"I thought we'd be wed when we reached your hunting lodge."

"I can't wait that long. We passed through a village during the night. There's no reason we can't be wed there later today and return here to consummate our wedding vows." The idea seemed to please Calvin, for his mood changed from surly to extremely pleased with himself in a matter of moments.

Agreeing with Calvin seemed to be the only way to get him out of her room. "Very well, but only if I can remain here and rest while you fetch the vicar. I'm too exhausted to travel further today."

Esme used the first excuse she could think of to delay what she had begun to think of as the worst mistake of her life. What would she do when Calvin returned with the vicar?

Calvin grinned. "Very well, I agree. I'll sleep a few hours and leave after lunch," he said as he unlocked the door. "I shan't be long. Enjoy your rest, for I intend to keep you very busy in my bed tonight."

Esme closed and locked the door. Trembling, she leaned against the panel and released a long sigh. What was she going to do? Marrying Calvin no longer seemed a good idea. Why should she marry anyone? She wanted neither Calvin nor Dante. Thinking about her options was giving her a headache. Deciding to solve her dilemma later, she undressed down to her shift and crawled into bed.

* * *

Hunger gnawed at Dante. Every instinct he possessed told him he was close to his prey. But he could go no further without stopping to rest his horse.

Dante had ridden all night and all morning; he was so weary he could scarcely keep his eyes open. Condor's strength was beginning to flag when Dante arrived at the Hart and Horn Inn. He rode into the courtyard, dismounted and gave instructions to the stable lad for the care and feeding of his horse.

Dante didn't intend to linger at the inn beyond a couple of hours for he didn't know Lonsdale's destination. His gut told him that of all the roads leading south out of London, he had followed the right one—the road leading to Heath, where the gypsy caravan wintered. He intended to ask the innkeeper if Lonsdale and Esme had stopped to change horses or buy a meal.

Dante entered the common room and sat down at a table near the fire. There was a definite chill in the air these days, and the warmth emanating from the hearth was welcome.

The innkeeper shuffled up to him. "Will you be wanting to eat, sir?"

"I do, good sir. I haven't eaten since yesterday and would like something substantial."

"The cook has prepared a tasty meat pie."

"That will do."

"Warm yourself by the fire while you wait. Would you like ale?"

"Aye."

Dante folded his arms on the table, lowered his head and closed his eyes. He must have fallen asleep, for he awakened to the sound of voices. Blinking sleep from his eyes, Dante lifted his head and glanced around, more than a little shocked to see Lonsdale and the innkeeper conversing near the front door. Dante immediately turned to face the hearth, scarcely daring to breathe as he eavesdropped on the conversation.

"I shall return as soon as I can with a clergyman," he heard Lonsdale say. "My fiancée and I intend to be married right here at the Hart and Horn. After the ceremony, we will spend our wedding night here. Perhaps your cook can prepare a celebratory supper."

"A wedding? Here?" the innkeeper gasped. "It would be an honor, milord, but why not take your lady to the village and be married in the chapel?"

"My lady is exhausted." He guffawed and poked the innkeeper in the ribs. "She wants to remain here to rest up for our wedding night."

The innkeeper nodded enthusiastically. "Right you are, milord."

If Lonsdale hadn't left immediately, Dante would have leaped off the bench and ripped out his throat. With concerted effort, he kept his wits about him and remained seated. Though he was weary, his mind was working perfectly. Lonsdale was gone and Esme was still here. A smile stretched his lips. Esme wouldn't be here long if he had his way, and he usually did.

The innkeeper arrived with Dante's food. It was a veritable feast and Dante dug in, eating everything placed before him. As he ate and drank, his exhaustion dropped away; he had been revived by the belief that Esme would soon be his again.

Dante paid the innkeeper and then asked a few

subtle questions. "While I was waiting for my food I dozed off, but I thought I heard someone arranging a wedding."

"Aye. Lord Lonsdale and his lady wish to be wed immediately. Do you know His Lordship?"

"I know him very well. I am the Marquis of Alston, the lady's brother. I'm supposed to be Lonsdale's best man. I was afraid I wouldn't arrive in time."

"You've plenty of time, milord. Lord Lonsdale went to the village to fetch the vicar. I know Reverend Dickens, and it will take a great deal of persuasion to get him to come out here to perform the ceremony."

"I would like to inform my sister that I have arrived," Dante said. "Could you direct me to her room?"

"That I could, milord. Lord Lonsdale ordered lunch for his lady before he left." He glanced toward the kitchen; a young serving girl carrying a tray had just exited. "I believe Tillie is carrying the tray up to milady now. You can follow her, if you wish."

Dante flipped the innkeeper a coin. "Thank you, my good man. I believe I'll do just that. My sister and I can have a nice chat while we wait for Lonsdale's return."

The innkeeper drifted into the yard as Dante mounted the stairs behind the maid. She stopped before the first door on the right and rapped lightly.

Dante moved behind the maid, startling her. "It's all right, miss," he said. "I'll take the tray in to my sister myself. She's expecting me." He offered the girl a coin. Without a second thought, she smiled and handed Dante the tray. Bobbing a curtsy, she took herself off.

Dante heard Esme moving around inside the room. As her steps neared the door, he braced himself to push his way into the room before she slammed the door in his face.

Esme had awoken slowly, feeling as if she had just gotten to sleep. Earlier Calvin had called to her through the door that he was leaving for the village. He had also mentioned that he would order lunch for her.

Now the maid had arrived with her food, and Esme hurriedly pulled on her robe before opening the door. "Please put the tray on the table," she directed, "and take my travel costume with you to be pressed. I'll need it . . . *You!*"

Dante slammed the door closed with his foot, then set the tray on the table and locked the door, pocketing the key. His features set in hard lines, he glowered at her. She clutched the edges of her robe together. She had never feared the gypsy before, but his fierce expression now was truly frightening. She backed away from him.

"How did you find me?"

"Truthfully, I don't know. Blind luck, I suppose."

"Did you speak with Jane? You should be on your way to Gretna Green."

He advanced toward her, the intensity of his dark gaze slamming into her. "Two and two didn't add up. Why did you run away?"

Pretending nonchalance, Esme edged around him to inspect her lunch tray. "Can't this wait? I'm hungry."

"By all means, eat." His voice rang harsh with censure.

Esme sat down and picked at her food, hoping to put off the confrontation with Dante. She needed to compose herself before she explained her reason for eloping with Calvin. Though she pretended to ignore Dante, her eyes followed him as he paced the small room, impatience rolling off him in angry waves.

The moment of confrontation arrived sooner than she would have liked. Dante spun around, his expression even fiercer than when he had first arrived. Maybe making him wait hadn't been such a good idea. She turned her face up to his.

"Very well, have your say."

"Why did you leave with Lonsdale? We had just made love. I went to speak to your uncle about setting a wedding date. What were you thinking?" he demanded.

Not given to meekness, Esme shot up from her chair and marched up to him, hands on hips, her expression mutinous. "Making love to me meant nothing to you! *I* mean nothing to you!"

"Where did you get that idea?" He scowled at her, his eyes blazing with fury. "What did Lonsdale tell you to make you run away?"

"The truth!" Esme lashed out. "If you don't marry me within six months of your grandfather's death, you will lose your title to Calvin. You don't care about me; you just want to be a marquis." Her next words challenged him. "Deny it if you can."

Dante's mouth flattened; his eyes were shuttered. "If you think I wanted you because of Grandfather Alston's will, you don't know a damn thing. Our attraction began long before I knew who you were. Have you forgotten the Bedford Fair?"

Esme's cheeks flamed. "You don't seriously believe I could have tender feelings for a gypsy, do you?"

A muscle ticked in Dante's cheek; a feral growl rumbled from his throat and escaped through his clenched teeth. He grasped her shoulders, his fingers biting into her flesh.

"You will never forgive or forget my gypsy blood, will you? My ancestry will always stand between us. It doesn't matter how attracted to me you are, or how much you enjoy making love with me, for you will always see me through the eyes of prejudice."

Esme didn't deny it, though his accusation was no longer true. Dante's gypsy heritage had begun to matter less and less to her, despite an upbringing that emphasized the importance of noble blood. She didn't care about his title or bloodlines; she had begun to think of him first as a man she cared about.

"I'm more interested in talking about your grandfather's will," Esme said in an effort to change the subject. "Did you court me because you were forced to, or because you truly wanted to marry me?"

Dante hesitated. Baring his heart to Esme could bring him a world of hurt. He wasn't ready to give her that power. Not when she'd shown him nothing but contempt.

"As I said before, I didn't accept the title willingly. I could relinquish it tomorrow and feel no regret."

"But you won't."

"No, I won't. But the reason has nothing to do with you." His arms left her shoulders, dropped to her waist and pulled her against him. "Never doubt, milady, that I want you. It doesn't matter to me that you've slept with Lonsdale, for I will still have you. You're mine. I made you mine first."

Esme tried to twist from his grasp, but Dante's strength defeated her. "You took what you wanted without my consent."

A chuckle rumbled from Dante's chest. "That's not how I remember it."

"Arrogant oaf."

Dante glanced at the rumpled bed, then back to her. "Did you sleep with Lonsdale to hurt me? Or did he force you?"

"I refused to sleep with him until we were wed," Esme muttered. "That's why he rushed off to find a clergyman. We're going to be wed today by special license."

His heart soared. She hadn't slept with Lonsdale! His arms tightened around her. "That marriage will never happen," he said fiercely. He was thrilled to hear she hadn't been seduced by Lonsdale and vowed she never would be. "We'll be gone long before Lonsdale returns. But first, I intend to show you how much I want you."

"Surely you're not going to—"

"Oh, yes, milady, that's precisely what I intend."

Grasping the belt of her robe, he pulled the knot free and peeled the garment over her shoulders and down her arms. She stood before him in her shift, which hid nothing from him. He looked his fill before reaching for the hem and slowly raising it upward.

She grasped his hands. "Don't do this, Dante."

He shoved her hands aside. "Tell me you don't want me."

She opened her mouth; he filled it with his tongue. He kissed her passionately, his lips demanding a response, his tongue delving, tasting, teasing, his hands sliding around to cup her breasts, playfully tweaking her nipples. He tore his mouth from hers when he heard her moan, then raised his head and gazed into her eyes.

"Tell me you don't want me," he repeated.

"Damn you, you're not playing fair!"

"I'm not playing, love. I mean business."

He slipped off his jacket and unbuttoned his shirt.

Esme stared at his magnificent chest, her gaze following the line of dark hair that marched down his torso to the top of his trousers. She tried to conceal her fascination, but it was difficult. Dante possessed a dynamic presence, an inherent virility that spoke to her on a sexual level. She recalled the first time she had seen him. Clad in gypsy garb, he'd been no less impressive than he was now, dressed like a gentleman, his dark features stark with desire.

He was too masculine to be considered classically handsome. His mixed heritage had come together to form strong, bold features, softened by mesmerizing dark eyes shadowed by thick black lashes. He exuded power. It was inherent in his movements, the innate authority of his stance, the arrogant tilt of his head. He cared not that he had the look of a gypsy about him, for he had never denied his heritage; in fact he was proud of it.

Esme looked away from that masculine splendor, her teeth catching at the plush curve of her bottom lip, thinking how easy it was for him to seduce her. The thought had no sooner formed than he grasped the hem of her shift and flipped it over her head and away.

"Now, sweet *gadjo*, I'm going to make love to you. You can deny it all you want, but the glazed look in your eyes tells me more than those lying lips of yours."

Esme's gaze roamed freely as he finished undressing. This was the first time she had seen him naked in daylight. Fully aroused, his thick sex jutted out from a forest of black hair at his groin. She swallowed hard and looked away.

She yelped as he scooped her into his arms and carried her to the rumpled bed. When he placed her on the edge, she tried to scoot away, but he caught her foot and dragged her beneath him.

"There's no escaping me, love. When we leave this room, you'll never again doubt to whom you belong."

Her mind drifted away as his maddening kisses and talented hands drove her to distraction.

Chapter Eleven

"Lonsdale can't have you," Dante whispered against the heat of her skin as he kissed a path from one hipbone to the other.

Her lancing ache of doubt over his involvement in his grandfather's death dissolved with Esme's growing desire. This man, this gypsy she barely knew, possessed the power to steal her will and scramble her brains.

He kissed his way to the tops of her thighs, and then stopped to press her legs wide with his palms. She shivered as his hot breath whispered over her intimate flesh. She feared not just the onslaught of his passion but the quickening of her own, and tried to push him away.

He raised his head and murmured huskily, "I intend to taste all of you, and I won't be stopped."

Esme lost the battle along with her will as his tongue slid over her plump nether lips and delved within. She arched and cried out. He anchored her hips in place, wreaking havoc on her senses with his mouth and talented tongue.

Pleasure. More pleasure than she could stand. Her shivers grew to tremors, then exploded in shudders of unspeakable ecstasy as his nimble tongue slid within, delved deep and around, flicking relentlessly at the core of her sex, driving her inexorably upward. Then she was flying, reaching for the diamond-studded stars.

Esme shattered, spiraling into a flowing sea of radiance that spread from her core to the tips of her toes and fingers.

Dante watched her ride the downward current to satiation, his tongue finally retreating with her last spasm.

"You're lying to yourself if you think Lonsdale will satisfy you," he said as he slowly moved up her body. "Do you love him?"

Esme said nothing.

His hand slid beneath the pale curve of her breast, caressing it with long fingers, gently pulling on the elongated nipple. "Tell me. You must feel something for him."

She blinked. A long pause ensued. "I can't think when you're touching me like that."

He bent over her breast, touched one satiny tip with his tongue, then stroked the sensitive bud. "You mean like this?"

"Oh, yes," she said on a gasp.

His mouth sealed over hers; his knees spread her thighs wide. Gently he adjusted her position, moving his hands down her stomach until his hand slid through the matted curls of her sex. He found the feminine bud of her desire and worked her gently, caressing, teasing the sensitive nub with his fingertips.

Esme felt renewed desire pound through her as Dante's fingers delved into the exposed cleft, then slipped lower to probe the slick entrance. She felt her body turning heavy; her senses were coming alive again, awareness centered on the delicate stroking of his fingers.

"Turn over," he rasped.

Esme's eyes flew open. "What?"

"Turn over. Don't worry, I won't hurt you."

Swallowing a frisson of fear, Esme flopped over on her stomach. Dante raised her hips and knelt behind her. She felt the heavy weight of his sex rising between her thighs, felt him open her swollen lips, felt his thick sex probe her entrance.

"You're ready for me again," Dante murmured against her nape.

The engorged tip of his shaft slid inside, paused, then continued the downward slide into her tight passage, inch by slow inch. She wanted to scream at him, to tell him to hurry. Her insides throbbed with wanting. Then his hands found her breasts, creating a new sensation.

"Dante . . ."

"I know. Hang on, love, I'm going to take you on the ride of your life."

He thrust hard. She caught on quickly, moving her hips to meet his downward strokes. He felt so large inside her, she feared she would burst, but she stretched and closed around him with little difficulty, the clenching walls of her sex creating a delightful friction.

"Heaven, pure heaven." Dante repeated the words over and over again, pounding harder, deeper, clasping her hips and pulling her into his hard thrusts.

She ached, she throbbed. Hot pulsing pleasure burst through her. Each thrust sent her into spasms, each withdrawal left her in agony. She cried out his name, asked for more, her mind going blank and primal. Pleasure lanced through her, increasing until there was no beginning or end. It mounted until she was clawing her way to the top again.

He gave her more. He took her higher than he ever had before, thrusting her to the pinnacle. Just when she wanted to relax into a puddle of molten liquid, he began to move again, increasing his speed, becoming less controlled, more intense.

"Come fly with me, love," he panted into her ear.

They flew . . . up, up and away.

Esme opened her eyes, aware that Dante was lying beside her, sound asleep. She rose up on her elbows and gazed down at him. Sunlight bronzed his strong cheekbones and jaw and shadowed the stark planes of his face. Stubble darkened his chin and the dent below his full bottom lip. Her fingers itched to touch that masculine roughness.

From the moment of their first meeting, Esme had sensed something dark and hurtful hovering over him. Occasionally she had glimpsed a wounded vulnerability in his intense black eyes, a brief flash that was quickly dispatched by the wicked grin always lurking on his face. She knew he'd been abandoned by his father and grandfather, and he'd admitted that he cared nothing about the Alston title and wealth. Yet he had accepted his inheritance. Why?

Would he kill for it?

A shudder wracked her body. She glanced at him again. Her gypsy lover looked so young and carefree in sleep that she couldn't help reaching out to smooth a lock of crisp black hair from his forehead. A shocked cry escaped her lips when he grasped her wrist.

"You're awake!"

"I have been for some time. Did you see anything you liked?"

Gnawing at her bottom lip, she shook her head.

"Liar." He sighed and climbed out of bed. "I feel as if I could sleep a week, but I don't have that luxury." Grasping her arms, he pulled her up. "Get up, love; we need to leave before Lonsdale returns."

"Where are you taking me?"

"You'll find out."

"I should return to London. I don't want Uncle Daniel to worry about me."

He gave a snort of derision. "You should have thought of that before you eloped with Lonsdale. Parkton knew I'd find you and entrusted me with your care."

"He doesn't know what I know," Esme retorted. "If he did, he'd never agree to our marriage."

"Get dressed," Dante barked. While he donned his clothes, Esme hesitated, as if uncertain what to do.

"Please leave. I want to wash your scent from my body."

Dante grinned. "I like the way you smell. It marks you as mine."

"Dante—"

"Very well, I'll wait below. My horse will have to carry both of us, but I'm sure he's up to it." He opened the door. "Don't be long. If Lonsdale returns and challenges me, you know who will win."

Esme picked up the candlestick and threw it. The door closed behind Dante just in time; the candlestick hit it with a resounding bang and crashed to the floor. She uttered an unladylike oath as she turned to the washstand for a hasty wash. She knew Calvin wouldn't stand a chance against Dante. The gypsy was not only a celebrated lover; his toned body proclaimed him capable of feats of great strength.

Where would he take her if not London?

Dante should have been exuberant, but his mood was less than merry. He could make love to Esme till doomsday, and even if she enjoyed every minute of it, she'd still consider him unworthy. He would never be anything more than her gypsy lover. He wouldn't force Esme to marry him, he decided. But before he returned her to London, he would show her something of how he'd lived before he'd inherited the title.

Dante entered the common room to await Esme. Although there were more customers now, Dante found an unoccupied table. The innkeeper approached him shortly.

"Did you enjoy your visit with your sister, milord?"

"Immensely," Dante replied.

"My cook is preparing the wedding feast as we speak."

Dante sighed. "My good sir, I fear the wedding is off. My sister changed her mind and will be leaving with me as soon as she is ready."

The innkeeper's mouth gaped open. "Are you sure, milord? Perhaps milady should wait for Lord Lonsdale's return and work out their differences."

"Alas, she is rather piqued and refuses to wait. Tell Lord Lonsdale we will discuss this further in London."

The innkeeper wandered off, shaking his head and muttering about the inconsistency of women, especially highborn women. Dante had to agree, for nothing in his past had prepared him for a woman like Esme.

The object of his thoughts appeared at the top of the stairs. Dante mounted the steps to meet her. "Good, you're ready," he said. He grasped her bag with one hand and her elbow with the other. "Shall we go?"

They descended the stairs together. The innkeeper met them at the door. "Are you sure you want to do this, milady? Lord Lonsdale is going to be disappointed after all the trouble he went to."

Esme cast a withering glance at Dante when he answered for her. "I'm afraid my sister's mind is made up."

"You'll need a carriage for the lady," the innkeeper advised. "The livery in the village rents both carriages and horses, should she prefer to ride. Perhaps you'll meet Lord Lonsdale on the road and offer your own explanation as to why the wedding was called off."

Not if I have anything to say about it. "Thank you, my good man," Dante replied as he pulled a coin from his pocket and flipped it to the innkeeper. "That's for your trouble."

"I'll see that your horse is brought around, milord," the innkeeper said as he pocketed the coin and went off whistling.

When the stable lad brought Condor around, Dante spoke a few words into the animal's ear as he attached Esme's bag to the saddle.

"Are you sure your horse can carry the additional weight?" Esme asked.

"We won't be traveling far."

Grasping her waist, he hoisted her onto Condor's back and mounted behind her. Condor took the extra weight without complaint as Dante reined him south along the road to Heath.

"This isn't the way to London," Esme said. "I have a right to know where you're taking me."

"You lost that right when you ran off with Lonsdale and sent me in the wrong direction. You think I'm too far beneath you to become your husband even though I'm a marquis, one of the highest ranks in the kingdom."

"And you forgot to tell me you were required to marry me in order to keep your inheritance. No one can force me to wed a gypsy."

Dante gritted his teeth. There it was again, Esme's prejudice against his heritage. "I didn't hear you complaining when I made love to you."

Esme wished she had a retort worthy of Dante's insult. Letting Dante make love to her had seemed inexplicably right at the time; his talented hands and mouth had driven every thought from her mind but the pleasure he gave her. She had been innocent the first time he had seduced her; now she couldn't resist him.

If Calvin hadn't revealed the terms of Lord Alston's will, Esme would have believed that Dante truly cared for her. What a dolt she had been. She'd always been told gypsies were liars and thieves, and it seemed Dante was no exception. He'd lied to her about his feelings for her, and snatched the title from Calvin, and then he'd stolen her heart.

* * *

It was late afternoon by the time Viscount Lonsdale returned to the Hart and Horn with Reverend Dickens in tow. Strutting into the inn, Lonsdale sought out the innkeeper.

"Where is my bride-to-be? Is she awaiting me in her chamber?"

"Er . . . not exactly, milord," the innkeeper replied, looking uncomfortable.

Calvin felt the first stirrings of alarm. "Where is she?"

"The lady left with her brother, milord."

"Brother? *Brother?* Esme has no brother. What nonsense is this?"

"Surely you're mistaken, milord. I heard the Marquis of Alston quite distinctly, and he said he was milady's brother. They spoke in private for some time before he emerged from milady's chamber. He informed me that she had changed her mind about the wedding and intended to return with him to London."

"Damn you!" Lonsdale screeched. "How could you have let her leave?"

"See here," Reverend Dickens interrupted. "You told me the lady was willing."

"She was! She is! That bastard Alston kidnapped her from under my nose."

"The lady went willingly enough," the innkeeper said defensively.

"You will return me to town immediately," the reverend insisted. "You no longer have need of my services. I knew I shouldn't have let you drag me out here." Turning on his heel, he returned to the carriage to await Lonsdale.

Rage simmered through Lonsdale. How had Alston found them? Instead of being halfway to Gretna Green, Alston had stolen Esme away from him.

Blast and damn! There was no way he was going to let Alston steal everything that belonged to him. He had fawned over his uncle to the point of nausea, kowtowed to his wishes and made himself available at a moment's notice. And his reward had been disinheritance. What was a measly thousand pounds a year when he could have had everything? The gypsy was going to pay for this travesty.

"Innkeeper, are you sure Lord Alston said he was taking Lady Esme to London?"

"Aye, milord, he did indeed." He scratched his furry chin. "Funny thing, though, the stable lad said His Lordship and the lady turned south, toward the coast."

Lonsdale's fists clenched. "Are you sure?"

"Oh, aye. Elmer's not the smartest lad, but he knows his directions." He glanced toward Lonsdale's carriage. "You'd best get the reverend back to town. He doesn't look too happy about this."

Lonsdale spit out a curse. *Damn the gypsy and damn my uncle for changing his will!* If Alston convinced Esme to marry him, all would be lost.

Dante and Esme reached Heath as dusk settled over the land. Esme's stomach growled, reminding her that she hadn't eaten since lunch. "Are we going to stop at an inn for the night?"

"No, we're too close to our destination to halt now."

"If memory serves, the only town between Heath and Brighton is Lewes."

Dante seemed unconcerned as they left the village of Heath behind. Esme was half asleep, lolling against Dante's broad chest when the mouthwatering aroma of food cooking over an open fire drifted to her on a frigid breeze. She perked up immediately and sniffed the air. Then she saw a thin line of smoke rising above the treetops. She turned to mention it to Dante, but was forestalled when he turned Condor down a narrow lane.

Alarm spread through Esme. "Where are we going?"

Dante merely smiled at her. She began to worry in earnest when the rutted road led them deep into the forest. She couldn't imagine what mischief he had in mind, didn't even want to think about it.

At length they emerged into a clearing dotted with campfires. Squinting through a haze of blue smoke, Esme spotted several wagons and people milling about them. The hodgepodge of men, women and children were dressed in colorful gypsy garb, some cooking over campfires while others talked and laughed together in groups. Barking dogs heralded their arrival.

"What are we doing here?" Esme asked.

Dante didn't answer; he was staring at a small, wizened woman stirring something in a kettle over a fire pit. She looked up, saw Dante and rushed toward him, his name on her lips. Dante dismounted, swept the woman up into his arm and hugged her fiercely.

Esme recognized the woman as the fortune-teller from the Bedford Fair, whom she knew to be Dante's grandmother. Dante's grandfather came up to join them. After engaging in a short conversation, Dante returned to his horse and lifted Esme down.

"Grandmother, Grandfather, give welcome to Lady Esme Harcourt. She is going to be our guest."

Esme sent Dante a startled look but managed a greeting and a smile for the elderly couple.

"I am Carlotta and this is Sandor," Carlotta said, introducing herself and her husband by name. "Welcome to our humble home. We hope you will enjoy your visit."

That's unlikely, Esme thought sourly. But since she didn't want to hurt Dante's grandparents feelings, she kept her thoughts to herself.

"Dante!" A woman's high-pitched squeal rent the air. Moments later, a young woman leaped into Dante's arms. He caught her and accepted the exuberant kiss she planted on his lips.

"You've come back! I knew you couldn't stay away."

Laughing, Dante set her away from him. "Behave, Loretta."

Esme watched the scene with ill humor. Apparently, Dante and Loretta had been lovers once. Did he intend to take up with her again? Esme told herself she didn't care. She had no intention of marrying the gypsy. Gypsies didn't belong in polite society. Dante should return to his people and marry Loretta. This was the kind of life he was accustomed to, the life he deserved. Calvin would make a much better marquis.

Dante turned to Esme. "Loretta, this is Lady Esme Harcourt."

"What is that *gadjo* doing here?" Loretta spat.

"I shall leave immediately," Esme replied huffily. "I don't belong here."

Dante grasped her arm when she turned to leave.

"You're not going anywhere." He faced Carlotta. "Grandmother, Lady Esme has been riding a long time; we are both tired and hungry. Show milady where she can wash while I greet my friends."

Carlotta wound Esme's arm in hers and led her off toward her brightly decorated wagon. "I'm so glad Dante found you, milady," she confided. "Thank God my message got through to him. Riding north would have been a grave mistake."

Esme sent Carlotta a puzzled look. "You sent Dante a message? How?"

"It was a mental message, milady."

Esme knew Carlotta was a fortune-teller and wondered if she had powers beyond chicanery. It had long been held that gypsy fortune-tellers employed trickery to persuade unsuspecting clients to part with their coin. The few times Esme had visited fortune-tellers had been strictly for fun. She had never believed a word they said.

"Sandor and I share this wagon," Carlotta said, urging Esme up the stairs. "You'll find water and clean towels on the washstand. No one will bother you. Come out when you're ready. The rabbit stew simmering over the fire will be ready directly."

Esme ducked into the wagon. A candle sitting on a small table chased away the dark shadows as dusk thickened into night. She looked around, noting that no space was wasted in the wagon. It was charming in a gaudy sort of way.

A knock sounded on the door. "It's Sandor, milady. I have your bag. May I come in?"

Esme opened the door to admit Dante's grandfather. Fine age lines crisscrossed his dark features, but his open smile made him appear ageless. "Thank you," she said as he placed her bag inside the door.

"I hope you enjoy your stay, milady," Sandor said. "Dante must have had a reason for bringing you here."

"I already know the reason. He wishes to marry me," Esme retorted. "Lord Alston's will demands that we wed. Should Dante fail to convince me, the title he inherited will be passed on to Lord Lonsdale."

Sandor's wounded expression made Esme regret her words. "Please forgive me," she murmured. "I'm hungry and tired and spoke rashly."

Sandor accepted her apology with a nod and backed out the door, closing it softly behind him. Esme sighed. She certainly wasn't endearing herself to Dante's family. Nothing she'd heard or knew about gypsies was flattering, but Sandor and Carlotta had been nothing but kind and welcoming to her.

Esme located the pitcher of fresh water and poured some into the bowl. Using soap and a washcloth she found nearby, she began to scrub the road dust from her skin. What she really wanted was a nice warm bath, but she supposed that would have to wait until she returned to London, which she hoped would be very soon.

Before Esme left the wagon, she brushed her hair and tied it back with a ribbon. When she rejoined Carlotta and Sandor, Dante was waiting for her.

"There you are," Dante said. "I hope you're as hungry as I am. Grandmother is an excellent cook."

A table had been placed near the banked fire, complete with eating utensils and flanked by a pair of benches. Dante escorted Esme to a bench and joined her. Carlotta dished up four bowls of stew and placed them on the table. Then she ducked into the wagon and returned with a loaf of bread.

The stew smelled so good, Esme wanted to dig in immediately, but she waited until Carlotta rejoined them. The first spoonful was pure heaven; she closed her eyes, savoring the taste. She was about to take another spoonful when Sandor passed the loaf of bread to her. When it became obvious she was unsure what to do with it, Dante took it from her, broke off a large chunk with his hands and handed it to her.

"We don't stand on ceremony here," he said as he broke off a hunk for himself.

When Dante dipped the bread in the stew to soak up the delicious broth, Esme did the same. She couldn't recall when anything had tasted as good as this simple rabbit stew. She even accepted a second helping before declaring herself full.

"I imagine you'd like to retire," Dante said, pushing away from the table. "I'll show you where you're to sleep."

"What I'd really like is a bath," Esme said wistfully.

"A hip bath is the best I can offer," Dante said. "I'll fetch water from the creek and heat it over the campfire. Come, I'll take you to your wagon."

The hip bath turned out to be a washtub Dante unfastened from the back of the wagon and brought inside. Before he left, he lit the brazier. Warmth spread through the wagon, chasing away the chill of the night.

After the water was heated, Dante filled the tub and fetched Esme's bag from Carlotta's wagon. When Dante seemed in no hurry to leave, Esme realized why.

"Whose wagon is this?"

"Mine. I gave the use of it to Rollo, but now it is mine again. Unless"—he grinned—"you'd prefer to share a wagon with Loretta?"

Esme sent him a withering look. "No, thank you. How long are we to remain here?"

Dante shrugged. "I'm not sure."

"Where will you sleep?"

Dante's dark brows shot upward. "Is that an invitation?"

"Indeed not. Nothing you do or say will convince me to marry you. Will you please leave now? My bathwater is growing cold."

"I can stay and wash your back."

"I can manage. Please go, Dante. I'm exhausted."

Dante departed reluctantly. He had no idea what had possessed him to bring Esme here instead of London. He knew she had no use for his people, but he had wanted her to meet Carlotta and Sandor. He wanted her to know that there were good people in every culture.

Dante was heading over to speak to his grandmother when Loretta planted herself in front of him.

"Are you mad, Dante? Why did you bring a *gadjo* into our midst? Is she your mistress?"

"What is to me is none of your business, Loretta. She has nothing to do with you."

Loretta sidled close to him, rubbing herself against his hard body. "I've missed you." She gestured toward Esme's wagon. "Are you going to share a bed with the *gadjo*?"

"Perhaps," he hedged.

Loretta wound her arms around his neck, pulling his head down for her kiss. "That pale Englishwoman cannot satisfy you as well as I can. If you are looking for a place to sleep, you may share my bed." Then she kissed him, her mouth lingering on his suggestively.

Dante tried to push Loretta away, but she clung to him with tenacious greed. Since he didn't want to use physical force, he simply refused to cooperate. Eventually, he thought, the kiss would come to a natural end.

Esme finished her bath and pulled on her nightgown and robe, feeling better than she had since she'd left London. The tub took up so much floor space, she barely had room to get into bed. She wondered if Dante was coming back to carry it away. She also wondered where the privy was, since she hadn't found a chamber pot in the wagon. Her need was urgent, so she decided to find Carlotta and ask her about it.

Esme hesitated at the open doorway, wondering if she should dress before leaving the wagon. Since no one seemed to be about, she threw her cloak over her nightclothes and descended the three steps to the ground. She took two steps toward Carlotta's wagon and stopped in her tracks when she saw Dante and Loretta locked in a passionate embrace, their mouths fused in a searing kiss.

Esme must have made a sound, for Dante abruptly thrust Loretta away from him. "Esme, do you need something?"

"I wanted you to remove the tub," Esme said coolly, "but I see you are busy."

"Carry it away yourself," Loretta spat. "There are no servants among us. The Rom do for themselves."

"That's enough, Loretta," Dante warned. "I'll take care of it, Esme."

Esme turned away, fuming over the way women seemed to flock to Dante. Esme nodded and continued on to Carlotta's wagon.

Esme found Carlotta sitting on the steps of her wagon with Sandor. Carlotta welcomed her with a warm smile. "May I have a private word with you?" Esme asked, sending Sandor an apologetic smile.

Sandor stood. "I will go to our grandson; he looks in need of rescuing."

Esme glanced at Dante, saw he was still conversing with his lover, and turned away. It seemed that the gypsy didn't have it in him to devote himself to one woman. Cursing her stupidity, Esme realized she should have known better than to think Dante cared for her. The only reason he had made love to her was because passion satisfied his lustful nature. She didn't want a man on those terms.

Esme settled beside Carlotta on the steps. The old woman patted her hand. "Does your wagon suit you, milady?"

"It's . . . comfortable," Esme admitted. She leaned closer, her cheeks coloring with embarrassment. "I came to ask about the . . . the privy. I couldn't find a chamber pot in the wagon."

"Ahhh," Carlotta said knowingly. "We Rom are not as refined in our habits as *gadje*." She gestured expansively toward the surrounding forest. "We live off the land and use it for many purposes.

"The men usually go off to the left of the encampment and the women to the right. We bathe in the creek until it gets too cold, then we forgo bathing until weather permits. Except Dante—he's always had a particular fondness for clean skin. I think he developed the habit of frequent bathing at university.

195

That's why he was able to produce a tub for you when you asked. He used it regularly during the winter months."

Esme glanced toward the forest, shocked by what Carlotta had revealed. She was learning more about gypsies than she cared to know. But the call of nature was too urgent for her to ignore.

She glanced at the dark forest and shivered. The long shadows looked like gargoyles reaching out to drag her into their clutches. Gulping back her fear, she thanked Carlotta and headed off toward those beckoning monsters. She hesitated when she reached the edge of the clearing, then plunged into the dark, groping shadows.

Later, her needs assuaged, Esme laughed at her fear and started back to camp. She had taken but two steps when a figure rose up before her. Esme shrieked and stepped back. Slowly the figure took on a feminine shape. The woman moved from the deep shadows into moonlight filtering through a break in the trees.

"Loretta! You frightened me," Esme said on a shaky breath. She attempted to edge around the gypsy woman.

Loretta grasped her arm, digging her fingers into Esme's flesh. "You don't belong here, *gadjo.* Return to your people; Dante is mine. He has always been mine."

Esme laughed. "Dante doesn't have it in him to be faithful to one woman. Surely you must know that by now."

Loretta tossed her long ebony hair. "Dante always returns to me. I want you to leave."

"I would love to. Dante brought me here against my will."

"Bah! Dante is obsessed with you. But I can fix that."

Suddenly she drew a wicked-looking dagger from beneath her clothing and rushed at Esme. The will to live fueled Esme's survival instincts. Catching Loretta's wrist, Esme tried to wrest the blade from her grasp. While the gypsy's strength was formidable, so was Esme's. Faced with her own mortality, she waged a fierce fight.

They struggled several minutes, until an unexpected surge of adrenaline kicked in, giving Esme a source of renewed strength. With a mighty shove, she pushed Loretta to the ground and ran, zigzagging around trees until she emerged into the clearing. She was shaking and out of breath when she reached her wagon. Rushing inside, she slammed the door and shot home the bolt.

Her sigh of relief died in her throat when she saw Dante stretched out on the bed, a dangerously wicked gleam in his eyes.

Chapter Twelve

"Your lover tried to kill me!" Esme shouted, still shaking from her close encounter with death.

Dante shot up from the bed. "What in blazes are you talking about?"

"Ask Loretta. She pulled a knife on me." Esme observed him through narrowed eyes. "What is it about you that makes women so desperate for your attention?"

His jaw set in grim lines, Dante lifted Esme away from the door, released the bolt and pulled it open.

She followed him outside. "What are you going to do?"

"Find Loretta and get to the bottom of this. How dare she threaten you!"

Esme grasped his arm. "Wait! I have a better solution. Return me to London. I'm not wanted here."

"I wanted you to get to know Carlotta and Sandor. They're my family; I wanted you to know them as I do. I hoped that knowing them might change your rigid ideas about gypsies."

"I have no doubt you love your grandparents, and they seem to be good people, but I don't belong here. After Loretta's attempt on my life, I'm afraid to go into the woods alone to . . . to tend to personal needs."

"You won't have to go anywhere alone," Dante proposed, "for I will accompany you."

Esme gave an exasperated sigh. "Be realistic, Dante. You cannot be with me every minute of every day."

His expression hardened. "Perhaps not, but I can warn Loretta that such behavior will not be tolerated by me. Spend a few more days with my grandparents—that's all I ask. I promised your uncle I would return you safely to London, and so I shall."

"It's late. You can speak with Loretta tomorrow."

"This can't wait. I won't be long."

Dante strode off, anger radiating from him with every step. Light streaming through Loretta's window told him that she hadn't retired. He climbed the steps and rapped sharply on the door.

"Who is it?"

"Dante."

Loretta flung open the door, a welcoming smile on her face. Grasping Dante's arm, she drew him inside and closed the door.

"I knew you would come."

"I'm here, but not for the reason you think. What in blazes were you thinking? Did you believe attacking Esme would endear you to me?"

"She told you," Loretta spat.

"Did you believe she wouldn't?"

"The lady doesn't want you, Dante. Are you so blind that you cannot see it? She cringes whenever

199

one of our people approaches her. It was never my intention to hurt her. I simply wanted to scare her into leaving."

Dante searched the fiery beauty's face for a hint of the truth. He knew Loretta to be fiercely jealous, but would she kill?

"What you and I had together was nothing but sex," Dante told her softly. "You knew I bedded other women, and I knew you bedded other men, so what is it about Esme that arouses your jealousy?"

Loretta's exotic beauty took on an expression of dark vengeance as she glowered at Dante. "I never worried about the other women; they meant nothing to you. But this one is different. She alone of all the women in your past has touched your heart.

"Listen to me, Dante, for I speak the truth. Your tender feelings for the *gadjo* are misplaced. Her eyes betray her. They show naught but contempt for you and our people. Ask Carlotta if you do not believe me."

Dante feared Loretta's words were true but preferred not to dwell on them. He still held high hopes of changing Esme's mind about his people. No, that wasn't true; he held diminishing hopes and little else.

"What did you expect to gain by attacking Esme? Even if she goes back to London, it will change nothing between you and me."

"You have to wed someone," Loretta returned. "You and I are compatible in all ways. A highborn lady will never wed a gypsy. No matter what, you will always be a gypsy, Dante. Milady will not have you, and you'll come crawling back to me."

Dante's temper flared. "Nonetheless, that does not give you license to kill Esme, or even threaten her.

GET UP TO 5 FREE BOOKS!

Sign up for one of our book clubs today, and we'll send you
FREE* BOOKS
just for trying it out...**with no obligation to buy, ever!**

HISTORICAL ROMANCE BOOK CLUB

Travel from the Scottish Highlands to the American West, the decadent ballrooms of Regency England to Viking ships. Your shipments will include authors such as CONNIE MASON, CASSIE EDWARDS, LYNSAY SANDS, LEIGH GREENWOOD, and many, many more.

LOVE SPELL BOOK CLUB

Bring a little magic into your life with the romances of Love Spell—fun contemporaries, paranormals, time-travels, futuristics, and more. Your shipments will include authors such as KATIE MACALISTER, SUSAN GRANT, NINA BANGS, SANDRA HILL, and more.

As a book club member you also receive the following **special benefits:**

- **30% OFF all orders through our website & telecenter!**
  (Plus, you still get 1 book FREE for every 5 books you buy!)
- **Exclusive access to** special discounts!
- **Convenient** home delivery **and 10 days to return any books you don't want to keep.**

There is **no minimum number of books to buy**, and you may cancel membership at any time. See back to sign up!

*Please include $2.00 for shipping and handling.

YES! ☐

Sign me up for the **Historical Romance Book Club** and send my THREE FREE BOOKS! If I choose to stay in the club, I will pay only $13.50* each month, a savings of $6.47!

YES! ☐

Sign me up for the **Love Spell Book Club** and send my TWO FREE BOOKS! If I choose to stay in the club, I will pay only $8.50* each month, a savings of $5.48!

NAME: _____

ADDRESS: _____

_____

TELEPHONE: _____

E-MAIL: _____

☐ **I WANT TO PAY BY CREDIT CARD.**

☐ VISA   ☐ MasterCard   ☐ DISCOVER

ACCOUNT #: _____

EXPIRATION DATE: _____

SIGNATURE: _____

Send this card along with $2.00 shipping & handling for each club you wish to join, to:

**Romance Book Clubs
20 Academy Street
Norwalk, CT 06850-4032**

Or fax (must include credit card information!) to: 610.995.9274. You can also sign up online at www.dorchesterpub.com.

*Plus $2.00 for shipping. Offer open to residents of the U.S. and Canada only. Canadian residents please call 1.800.481.9191 for pricing information.

If under 18, a parent or guardian must sign. Terms, prices and conditions subject to change. Subscription subject to acceptance. Dorchester Publishing reserves the right to reject any order or cancel any subscription.

JOIN NOW!

Make another attempt on her life and you'll be very sorry. Is that clear?"

Loretta tossed her head, sending her mane of coal-black hair cascading over her shoulders. Hands on hips, she sidled up to Dante. The scent of female arousal made him take a step backwards. At one time, that would have been all the invitation he needed to toss Loretta on the bed and take what she so generously offered. But things had changed since those carefree days. Esme had come into his life.

"Those enticements might have worked in the past, but I have changed," Dante declared.

"Bah! You're a man, aren't you? Even marquises have their needs." Her arms snaked around his waist. "Let me satisfy them. We've always been good together."

He pushed her away. "I'm not here for sex, Loretta. I suggest that you set your sights on Rollo. He will have you despite your faults. All I want from you is your promise to keep away from Esme while she is here with us. Try to hurt her again and I'll have you banished from the caravan. Sandor will agree with me, for he does not condone violence."

Pouting, Loretta whirled away. "Very well, I promise."

Dante didn't believe her. Until he returned Esme to London, he vowed to be extra vigilant of her. Leaving Loretta to her brooding, Dante returned to his wagon and Esme. He was exhausted. He hadn't slept since he'd left London. The door wasn't latched. Dante opened it and stepped inside. Esme rose when he entered.

"Did you see Loretta? What did she say?"

"She said she didn't intend to hurt you."

"And you believed her?"

"No. That's why I issued her a stern warning. I don't think she will try to hurt you again."

Esme searched his face. "You don't sound convinced."

Dante shrugged. "Nothing is ever certain with Loretta. Rest assured that I will be watching her closely. Let's go to bed—I'm exhausted."

"You're sleeping here?"

Dante stripped off his coat and shirt. "I just want to sleep; I'm too tired to do either of us any good."

He sat on the edge of the bed and removed his shoes and stockings. Esme watched him warily. He did appear weary. Perhaps he really did intend to sleep. She didn't want him touching her again, for she knew what would follow.

Dante didn't bother pulling off his trousers. He merely eased back on the bed, rolled over, groaned and fell asleep. Esme couldn't decide whether she was relieved or disappointed. Keeping a wary eye on him, she removed her robe and climbed into bed, too. A few minutes later she was sleeping as soundly as Dante.

Dante was gone when Esme awakened the following morning. She had actually slept well, comforted by the warmth of Dante's large body beside her. Delicious cooking smells drifting through the open window convinced her to dress and find her breakfast.

Esme's meager wardrobe was beginning to look the worse for wear, but she managed to find a skirt and blouse in her bag that were only slightly wrinkled and pulled them on after performing her morning ablutions. She brushed her hair out and let it hang loose, since there was no one to help her dress it in a more elaborate style. When she finished, she stepped down from the wagon and glanced around her.

The campsite was a beehive of activity. Barking dogs chased children; men were doing chores while women bent over cook fires. Esme skirted around a group of men and headed off to the woods, embarrassment coloring her cheeks. It was upsetting to know that everyone realize where she was going and for what purpose. Privacy seemed nonexistent in a gypsy community.

Nothing untoward happened in the woods. Esme finished her business and found Dante waiting for her at the edge of the clearing. "What are you doing here? This side is for women."

"I said I would protect you while you're here and I meant it. Carlotta has prepared breakfast; let's not keep her waiting."

"I'll join you as soon as I wash my hands in the creek," Esme replied.

Dante walked her to the creek, waited while she washed her hands, then escorted her to Carlotta's wagon. The cool, unpolluted air had given Esme a ravenous appetite. She ate heartily of eggs, bangers, cooked oats and bread. When she had eaten her fill, she thanked Carlotta and headed back to her wagon.

Dante caught up with her. "I'd like to introduce you to some of my friends." He grasped her hand and pulled her off toward a group of women seated around a table.

Though everyone greeted her politely, there appeared to be considerable speculation about her place in Dante's life and in their community. Nevertheless, the women tried to interest her in their activities, making trinkets and stringing glass beads to sell at fairs.

Apprehensive at first, Esme joined in and discovered she liked the women, whose chatter and dreams differed little from those of women in her own culture.

"Watch out for Loretta," a woman named Serena whispered. "She is jealous of Dante's attention to you. She considers him her property."

"I already learned that the hard way," Esme confided without further elaboration.

To Esme's surprise, the day passed pleasantly. True to his word, Dante hovered nearby during most of the day, refusing to let her out of his sight. But there had been no need, for Loretta kept her distance, jabbing Esme with nothing more than the dark threat in her eyes.

After supper that night, several men built a fire in the center of the campsite while others gathered around with an assortment of musical instruments.

"You're in for a treat," Dante said.

"What's happening?" Esme wondered as men, women and children began gathering around the central campfire.

"Watch and see."

The first haunting strains of a violin drew Esme closer. The music, softly melodic at first, soon became more spirited, enticing eager dancers into the area around the campfire. Loretta was one of them. The tempo increased; the dancers created a mad swirl of colorful skirts and flashing legs. Women whirled, baring ankles, thighs, a gleaming hint of a bare buttock, while men leaped high. The dance was a tempting display of brazen sexuality. Esme could not look away.

Suddenly Loretta appeared before Dante, swaying like a reed before the wind, inviting him to join her with a beckoning finger and a seductive roll of her hips. Laughing, Dante leaped into the rousing dance. Esme couldn't help admiring the fluent moves of the dancers, the near frenzy of their enthusiasm. She began to clap her hands and stomp her feet in time to the music.

Suddenly Dante stood before her, offering his hand. Taunted by the glint of challenge in his eyes, she placed her hand in his and let him pull her into the dance.

Then, realizing what was expected of her, she whispered, "Dante, I can't. I don't know what to do."

"Follow my lead," Dante replied, twirling her about until her skirts billowed out around her knees.

The magic of the music, the madness of the moment, seized Esme, imbuing her spirit with a wildness she hadn't known she possessed. Her feet seemed to fly over the ground as she followed Dante's expert lead. How she wished she had tinkling bells on her skirts like the other women, so she could dance to her own tempo. The music reached a wild crescendo, and with it the dancers. Dante grasped Esme's waist, lifted her high and whirled her about in time to the crashing finale.

They were both panting heavily as the dancers began to disperse, their eyes locked in sensual combat, bodies tense with unspoken need. Instead of releasing her, Dante swept her into his arms and carried her away from the campfire. Knowing laughter followed in their wake, but neither was aware of it.

Dante's body burned; his skin was on fire. He was so aroused he could scarcely walk. His wagon was so far away he feared he wouldn't make it. The moment darkness swallowed them, he wanted to bear her to the ground, throw up her skirts and thrust his randy cock inside her. Fortunately, a small portion of his good sense remained intact as he strode purposefully toward the privacy of their wagon.

While most of the Rom were amused by Dante's impatient need, Loretta was not. Rage darkened her lovely features into an ugly grimace; a low growl issued from her throat. Infuriated by Dante's attention to another woman, she headed off into the forest to rant at the trees. She was well into her tirade when a strange man materialized before her. Startled, she tried to run, but he caught her arm.

When she opened her mouth to scream, he covered it and whispered into her ear, "I'm not going to hurt you. Did you mean what you said? Do you really want to be rid of Lady Esme?"

Loretta went still.

"I'll remove my hand if you promise not to scream."

Loretta nodded vigorously. The man removed his hand.

Loretta drew in a shaky breath. "Who are you? You're not one of us."

"I will explain later. I surmised from your cursing that you want to be rid of the lady who has captured your man's attention. I want to help you."

"Why? Do you intend to kill milady?"

"Indeed not. Like you, I don't want her gypsy lover to have her. If Alston weds her, he will never return to you or his family. But if he loses her, he will lose his title and return to your loving arms. You'd like that, wouldn't you?"

"I want Dante," Loretta said fiercely. "Tell me how that may be."

The *gadjo* drew her deeper into the forest. "Here's what you must do . . ."

Dante carried Esme into the wagon, slammed the door with his foot and let her slide down his body. She began unbuttoning his shirt before her feet touched the floor.

Mad for each other, they tore at their clothing with deft haste, hands manipulating buttons and ties with one purpose in mind: to strip one another naked in the shortest amount of time.

"I cannot believe how desperately I want you," Dante rasped. "I wanted to throw you to the ground and ravish you long before we reached our wagon."

The beauty of his finely honed body made Esme's throat go dry. Her stomach clenched painfully. "I would have let you," she panted. She pulled him toward the bed. "Hurry. You've ignited a fever inside me; I can't wait."

They tumbled to the bed in a tangle of arms and legs, their mouths fused together in mutual need. His tongue played with hers, touching the tip, sucking it into his mouth, stroking the underside.

After he had sated his hunger with her taste, he bent to kiss her breasts, moving his lips up the cleft between to the rapidly beating pulse in her throat, savoring the salty sweetness of her skin. His mouth returned to the lush roundness of her breasts, lashing the erect rosy nipples with the rough surface of his tongue.

They didn't talk. Each knew what the other wanted and strove toward that end. A rush of heat swept over Esme; she felt as if her skin was too tight for her flesh.

She hadn't realized how desperate she was for this, for Dante, until the sexual heat of the dance created a burning hunger inside her.

Esme's hands were shaking as she reached up to touch his chest. His skin felt hot and smooth; his muscles rippled beneath her fingertips. When she felt his straining arousal rising against her feminine warmth, she was desperate to have him inside her.

Esme flicked the tip of her tongue across the velvety lobe of his ear, chuckling in satisfaction as his hips jerked against her. He raised his head, a wicked grin teasing the corners of his mouth.

"You're going to pay for that," he said.

When he slid his weight between her thighs, her knees eased open to receive him. "Now," she gasped. "Please, Dante."

With one finger he traced a path down her stomach, searching through the russet curls to the aching crest between her thighs. He massaged it gently, around and around, until she wanted to scream with frustration. His finger slid lower, parting the moist petals of her sex, delving inside.

Esme gasped, clutching his shoulders, desperate to feel him fill and stretch her. Then his mouth found her and her mind shut down. She became a shivering mass of raw sensation as Dante plied his mouth and tongue to the most sensitive part of her. She writhed, she whimpered, she held his head in place, afraid she would die if he stopped now.

He didn't.

His tongue played a sexual melody at the portals of her sex, then delved deep inside to taste and tease. He was relentlessly thorough, holding her hips in place to keep her from squirming out of his reach.

Esme felt the tremors begin and braced herself for the inevitable rush of ecstasy, so eager for it she could scarcely breathe.

Her hips hiked suddenly and a roaring began in her ears. She heard the breath leave her lungs, and a sob reverberated like thunder in her ears. Her gut clenched and she climaxed, soaring to the heavens and beyond. Dante held her as she slowly floated back to earth.

When he rose up to push his erection into her body, Esme suddenly realized she wanted to be more than a recipient of Dante's passion. She wanted to give him the same kind of pleasure he had given her. Taking him by surprise, she flipped him on his back and straddled him. "It's your turn," she murmured.

Dante grinned. "I have no objection to being ridden."

She stared into his eyes, her face flushed with power as she scooted down his body, allowing his sex to spring free. She lowered her head.

Dante grasped her shoulders. "Esme . . . You don't have to do that."

"I want to." She was too far gone in passion to want anything else. She might be embarrassed tomorrow for becoming someone she didn't recognize, but she'd worry about that later. What she wanted, what she needed, was to taste Dante, to savor his skin, to drive him mad with desire. Tomorrow, yes, tomorrow she would find a way to break the gypsy's spell and become herself again.

Grasping his staff in both hands, Esme covered the tip with her mouth, gently moving up and down on him. She heard him groan, felt his body tense as she ran her tongue along the seam at the tip and then down one side and up the other.

A low growl gurgled in his throat as his hands clamped her shoulders to pull her body up over his. Lifting her slightly, he flexed his hips and lowered her onto his rampant shaft. She took all of him, stretching to fit around him. When he started to move, she moved with him, arching and straining to meet the violence of his passion.

Dante lost himself inside her; nothing existed but the grinding of their bodies, the thrusting of his cock inside her as they reached for completion. Esme writhed, cried out and went still. He heard the breath go out of her lungs, then a sob catch in her throat. As she drifted downward, he felt her damp body trembling in his arms. Only then did he feel free to unleash the tempest building inside him.

Tension held his body taut, every muscle within him constricted. Grasping her bottom in his hands, he moved her against him, with him, thrusting hard and deep. Thunder pounded in his head, his groin and every limb, until the storm broke and his climax ripped through him like gale-driven wind.

His heart was still thumping in his chest when she eased off him and curled away from him, giving him her back. When he tried to turn her to face him, she resisted.

"Esme, what is it?"

Silence.

"Did I hurt you?"

"You made me forget who I am and why I cannot marry you."

Bitterness colored his words. "No, milady, I made you forget who *I* am. For a suspended moment in time, you forgot I am Rom."

Hiding his hurt behind a cold smile, Dante left the

bed and began pulling on his clothes in angry jerks. He had been insulted for the last time by this proud beauty who was so unwilling to accept him for who he was. He was through with her, finished. From this day forward, Esme could do what she pleased, even wed Lonsdale. He didn't care. He should have known that the grandfather who had abandoned him would set him an impossible task. Though he had expected resistance, he hadn't counted on being accepted as a lover but rejected as a husband.

"I'll return you to London as soon as I end my visit with my grandparents," Dante said in a voice devoid of emotion. "Meanwhile, I'll not trouble you with my unwelcome presence. I trust you can persevere a few more days with people you despise."

"I don't despise your people," Esme protested. "I'm confused. I want to believe you didn't kill Lord Alston, but nothing you've said so far has convinced me of your innocence. I don't think Calvin would lie about your involvement unless he had good reason. And I don't believe you want to marry me for the right reasons."

Dante shrugged. "Believe what you want."

"It's not that simple."

"I'll tell you how simple it is. Would you marry me if Lonsdale hadn't filled your head with his accusations?"

Silence.

Dante snorted. "I thought not. You can't get past the fact that I have gypsy blood. Very well, I accept that." He opened the door. "Sleep well, milady. One word of warning before I leave: Don't be in a hurry to marry Lonsdale. I intend to prove that he was the one who killed my grandfather."

* * *

Sleep proved impossible. Dante's parting words had left Esme more confused than ever. Could Calvin be the guilty party? He had always wanted the marquisate. Would he have killed for it?

Dante made her feel the kind of pleasure she had never felt before. He made her heart beat faster and her blood flow hot and thick through her veins. She suspected that no man would ever make love to her like Dante. But admitting that did little to reassure Esme. Knowing Dante, he probably made love to every woman the same way he made love to her. It was what he did best. On that depressing note, Esme drifted off to sleep.

Dante was nowhere in sight when Esme left the wagon the following morning. When she asked about him, Carlotta informed her that Dante, Rollo and Peter had gone to check on the horses.

Esme accepted a plate of food from Carlotta and took it to her wagon. The atmosphere was not conducive to friendly conversation this morning. What had Dante told his grandparents about their less than amicable parting last night? She wished Calvin had never voiced his suspicions to her. Her heart told her Dante wasn't capable of murder, while at the same time her mind considered the possibility that he was. Had Calvin told her the truth? Or had he lied because he coveted Dante's inheritance?

Despite her confusion, Esme feared she had lost someone important to her. Her distrust and prejudice, aided and abetted by Calvin, had caused her to lose someone she had begun to really care for.

Was it too late for her and Dante? Had she ruined a relationship that could have made her happy? She was having more than second thoughts. She was beginning to regret her foolish prejudices and rash actions. Could she and Dante recapture what she had so carelessly discarded?

A knock on the door sent Esme's hopes soaring. Had Dante returned to give her a second chance? She rushed to the door, and was disappointed to find Loretta standing on the steps.

"What do you want?"

"I met a man in the forest. He's a friend of yours. I'll take you to him if you wish."

"Does this man have a name?"

"He said to tell you Calvin wishes to speak with you."

"Calvin! Here? How did he find me?"

"I wouldn't know."

Esme ran the gamut of emotions. Should she speak to Calvin and tell him she intended to reconcile with Dante? Or should she ignore him and hope he'd go away? In the end, she decided on the former. Calvin should know that Dante was the man she wanted.

Esme stepped out the door. "Very well, I'll speak with Calvin. Just point me in the right direction. I'll find him."

Loretta accompanied Esme to the edge of the clearing. "I left him near the berry patch. Just follow the path."

Esme found the path and entered the cool dimness of the forest. But when she reached the berry patch, Calvin was nowhere in sight. Puzzled and a little put out, she turned to walk back to camp. A hand closed around her upper arm.

"Esme, don't go."

"Calvin. Why were you hiding?"

"I've come to rescue you."

"I don't need rescuing."

"Never say you're happy living with gypsies." He shuddered. "Come along, my dear. I still have the special license. Let's finish what we started."

"I've changed my mind. I no longer wish to marry you."

"Don't tell me you intend to wed the gypsy," Calvin spat indignantly.

"I'm not telling you anything," Esme retorted. "I'll be returning to London with Dante soon."

"No, you won't. You're coming with me."

Esme would have issued a scathing reply if Calvin hadn't covered her mouth with his hand. "Don't fight me. I'm doing this for your own good."

Though Esme struggled, Calvin found a reserve of strength inside himself as he dragged her through the forest to his carriage and tumbled her inside.

Chapter Thirteen

Dante decided to return to the caravan, leaving Peter and Rollo behind to make minor repairs to the corral. He intended to escort Esme to London within the next day or two and wanted to spend as much time as possible with his grandparents before he left. As for Esme, he had meant what he'd said the night before. He was through with her. He hadn't wanted Lord Alston's title or money in the first place and wouldn't miss them if Lonsdale inherited.

If only he could prove that Lonsdale had killed his grandfather, the man would hang instead of marrying Esme. Immersed in his thoughts, Dante had no idea he was the target of a gunman until it was too late. By the time he recognized the metallic click of a pistol being cocked, the shot had already been fired. The force of the bullet sent him reeling backward. Clinging tenaciously to his horse with his powerful thighs, Dante retained his seat through pure determination.

Glancing down, he saw blood blooming on his upper right chest. Then he felt a burning pain so sharp he nearly lost consciousness.

"Take me home, Condor," he gasped, leaning over his mount's withers as darkness blurred his vision and then totally consumed him.

Condor carried Dante directly to Carlotta and Sandor's wagon. He stopped, pawing the ground and snorting. Sandor came out of the wagon to investigate as Dante began a slow slide to the ground. Sandor stopped his fall and called for help. Several men came running to help Sandor ease Dante from the saddle.

Carlotta arrived on Sandor's heels, saw blood smearing Dante's shirt and took charge. "Be careful—he's hurt. Carry him inside his wagon."

"What happened?" Loretta asked when she saw Dante being carried into his wagon.

"Looks like a bullet wound," Sandor replied.

Loretta's hand flew to her mouth. "Someone shot Dante? Who would do such a thing?"

"We don't know. Move aside, Dante needs me," Carlotta said, pushing past Loretta.

"Let me help," Loretta offered.

"There is nothing you can do right now except find Lady Esme and tell her what happened."

A flash of triumph darkened Loretta's eyes. "Milady is gone."

Carlotta sent Loretta a distracted look. "I do not have time for this now. We will speak later."

Sandor removed Dante's shirt; Carlotta used it to stanch the flow of blood.

"The bullet needs to come out," she said, her eyes meeting Sandor's in unspoken concern.

"How bad is it?"

Carlotta lifted the pad she had fashioned to press against the wound and carefully probed it with a blunt fingertip. "The bleeding has slowed; it's safe to assume the bullet missed a major bleeder. Fetch my medical supplies, whiskey, a kettle of boiling water and clean cloths."

Sandor moved quickly for a man of his advanced age as he returned to his wagon to collect the items Carlotta had requested.

"I'll put the kettle on to boil and bring it as soon as it's ready," Loretta offered. She and most of the Rom had gathered in knots outside the wagon to await word of Dante.

Sandor grunted approval and hastened back to Carlotta.

Loretta appeared with the kettle of boiling water in time to see Carlotta pour whiskey over a long, slender blade. Then she carefully washed the wound and dried it, unaware that Loretta had remained.

"Hold him still, Sandor," Carlotta said. "If the bullet hasn't shattered, and I can rid the wound of foreign material, there's a good chance it won't fester."

Sandor gripped Dante's shoulders, preventing him from thrashing about in his unconscious state as Carlotta probed for the bullet. Dante moaned and fought the pain. "It went in deep," Carlotta muttered.

She let out a sigh when she found the bullet and lifted it out. Then she returned to look for foreign material that could cause infection. When she was finished, she poured whiskey into the open wound. Dante stiffened and cried out, still unconscious. Her hands were sure and steady as she stitched the

217

wound, smeared it with a salve made of dried herbs and applied a bandage.

"Will he be all right?" Loretta asked, wringing her hands. "Who could have done such a thing?"

Carlotta spared Loretta an impatient glance. "Dante is a strong man—he will recover. As for who hurt him"—she shrugged—"perhaps my crystal ball will give me the answer."

"It could have been an accident," Sandor suggested. "A hunter's bullet gone astray or—"

Carlotta gave her head a vigorous shake. " 'Twas no accident. Someone wants our grandson dead. He's been in danger ever since he inherited the marquisate, but he wouldn't listen to me."

Loretta's cry resounded loudly in the cramped wagon. Carlotta speared her with a probing look. "What are you hiding from us? Do you know who shot Dante?"

"No, how could I know?" She drew a shuddering breath. "I wanted to tell you before, but you wouldn't listen. A man came for Lady Esme; she returned to London with him. I'm not sure if that has anything to do with the shooting, but I thought you should know."

"I saw no stranger in camp," Sandor said. "When did this happen?"

Loretta lowered her gaze, the lies falling easily from her lips. "Milady met a man in the forest today. I saw her and followed because I was curious and did not trust her. She met him near the berry patch and accompanied him to a carriage parked on the main road. Then they drove off together."

Carlotta rounded on her. "Why did you wait to tell us this?"

"There was no time. Dante had been injured and needed your full attention. Besides, who cares if the *gadjo* left? Not I. She doesn't want Dante, and he's better off without her."

"Time will tell," Carlotta said cryptically.

"Grandmother?"

Carlotta knelt beside the bed, feeling Dante's forehead for fever. "Don't try to talk."

Dante licked his parched lips. "Water."

Loretta poured water into a cup and held it to Dante's lips.

"What happened?" he asked once his thirst had been quenched.

"What do you remember?" Sandor asked.

Dante's brow furrowed. "I was returning to camp and . . . Damn and blast! I was shot!" He tried to sit up, groaned and fell back. "How serious is it?"

"You were lucky. The bullet missed major bleeders and lodged against a bone. I removed it and all the foreign material I could find. Barring any setbacks, you should be up and around in a few days."

"Thank you, Grandmother. I'm sure my survival is due to your excellent doctoring skills."

"I will take care of Dante," Loretta said, stepping forward.

Dante glanced past Loretta. "Where is Esme?"

Carlotta and Sandor exchanged meaningful glances.

"What is it? Has something happened to Esme? Does the attempt on my life have anything to do with her?"

"Probably," Loretta spat. "The fancy *gadjo* slut left our encampment with a man."

Dante stared at her. Intense pain must be playing

219

havoc with his hearing, he thought. "What did you say?"

Loretta happily repeated her statement, adding, "I saw her meet a man in the forest earlier today. They left together in a carriage. When I returned to camp, I learned you had been shot."

Dante closed his eyes, trying to think past the pain. He didn't have to be told whom Esme had left with. How had Lonsdale found them?

Dante had thought he wouldn't care if Esme left him. Hadn't he told her he was through with her, that she was free to do as she pleased? At the time, he had meant it. But now that she was gone . . .

"Dante needs rest," Carlotta said, shooing everyone out of the wagon.

Once they were alone, Carlotta poured a measure of laudanum into a glass and held it to Dante's lips. "Drink it all; healing sleep is what you need right now."

Dante wrinkled his nose. "Laudanum. I don't—"

Carlotta took advantage of Dante's open mouth to pour the potion down his throat. He swallowed, gagged, but managed to keep it down.

"That's not fair, Grandmother."

Carlotta patted his cheek. "I know you are upset about milady leaving, but there is nothing you can do about it now. Get well first and then decide."

"There is nothing to decide, Grandmother. Esme won't have me under any circumstances, and I've washed my hands of her. I would have preferred that she had told me she was leaving, but she was free to do as she pleased."

"We will speak of this later."

Dante's eyelids were growing so heavy he couldn't

find the energy to reply. Closing his eyes, he surrendered to a drug-induced sleep.

Carlotta watched over him as he slept, a diminutive protector of her grandson's heart. Though she had no way of knowing what was in Esme's heart, she knew what was in her grandson's. He had been hurt by more than the bullet.

Dreams plagued Dante. Dreams of Esme. He saw her with Lonsdale, beside him as he aimed a pistol at Dante and pulled the trigger. He cried out in his sleep. Carlotta placed a cool hand on his forehead and murmured soothingly into his ear. He immediately calmed, his sleep becoming more peaceful.

Rage simmered through Esme. Calvin had forced her inside his carriage, then locked the doors and disappeared for some time. When he'd returned, he'd refused to listen to reason. They were now hurtling down the road at breakneck speed.

"I'll never forgive you for this, Calvin."

"You should thank me for saving you from your own folly. I had to get you away from that abominable place. The gypsies were holding you prisoner."

"That's not true!"

Sadness seared through Esme when she recalled her last words to Dante. After they had made love, she had insulted him, accused him of terrible things. She knew she had hurt him by the look on his face. She'd cringed inwardly when he told her he was through with her, and that she could do as she wished, even marry Calvin. Her heart had gone with him when he walked away.

How could she have been so stupid? It hadn't

taken Esme long to realize she had made a terrible mistake: It was Dante she wanted, not Calvin, never Calvin. She had been anxious for Dante to return to camp so she could apologize and tell him she was ready to marry him. The only reason she had met with Calvin was to tell him she loved Dante and to send her erstwhile suitor on his way.

The pain of loss brought a groan to her lips. Was it too late for her and Dante? Had she killed whatever feeling he had for her?"

"Now, now, Esme, don't upset yourself. You didn't want to stay there anyway."

"How do you know what I wanted? Stop the carriage!"

"I will, at the next village we come to with a church."

"I'm not going to marry you, Calvin. I didn't come with you of my own accord—you forced me. I'll never consent to become your wife, and no clergyman will conduct a ceremony without the consent of both parties."

"Think carefully before you refuse, Esme. If you don't return to London a married woman, the scandal will ruin you."

"I don't give a fig about society. I've always preferred country living anyway. Listen carefully, Calvin, for I'm not going to say this again. I . . . will . . . not . . . marry . . . you."

"You have no choice."

"I have several choices, and none of them involve you."

Esme seriously doubted that Dante would follow her after their volatile parting. She had said and done so many foolish things, and one of them was disparaging Dante and his people. Another was letting Calvin convince her that Dante was responsible for his grandfather's death. How could she have been so gullible?

Calvin clasped his hands over his stomach and smiled—a supremely satisfied grin that set Esme's teeth on edge. "Loretta heard you and the gypsy arguing this morning. He left you rather abruptly, I understand, so I doubt he will follow us. He cares nothing for you."

"Loretta! I should have known. Did she conspire with you to lure me away?"

"What does it matter? You're lucky to be rid of him. He'll never keep the title; he doesn't deserve it."

"You already have a title. Why do you need another?" Esme demanded.

Calvin's glittering gaze sent a shiver down her spine. His voice held a sharp edge as his eyes narrowed on her. "I need the money more than the title. I'm deep in dun territory and can't find my way out. I could end up in debtor's prison if I can't get my hands on Uncle Alston's blunt. You wouldn't want that to happen, would you?"

"Would you kill for your uncle's money?" Esme whispered.

Startled, Calvin jerked upright, his fierce scowl a chilling warning that she had gone too far. "I'm going to pretend you didn't say that, Esme. You've known me long enough to know I'm not a killer."

"What makes you think your uncle was murdered, and why do you suspect Dante?" Esme said in a rush.

"The gypsy had just cause. He knew Uncle Alston had changed his will in his favor, and he was too greedy to wait for my uncle to die of natural causes."

"That doesn't make sense," Esme argued. "Dante knew nothing about the will; he told me he hadn't known his grandfather prior to the changes Lord Alston made in the will."

"He's lying."

"I believe him. Can you prove otherwise?"

"If I could, I'd set the law on him," Calvin muttered. "Why do you believe him and not me? All gypsies are liars." A look of utter distaste crossed his features. "Don't tell me you are lovers. Did he force you?"

"No!" Esme flushed and looked away. "What we did or didn't do is none of your concern."

"I can't believe it of you," Calvin spat.

"It doesn't matter what you think. Once I wed Dante, the marquisate will be beyond your reach."

A smirk stretched Calvin's thin lips. "I'm next in line to inherit after your lover, should something unforeseen happen to him before he produces an heir."

Esme sat up a little straighter. "What mischief are you planning?"

"Me? Why, nothing. When I carried you off, I thought I was saving you from making a grave mistake. I wanted us to marry and spend our lives together. Until Uncle Alston changed his will, we knew we would wed one day."

"Not true, Calvin. I never intended to marry you." Her chin rose slightly. "Even Uncle Daniel began to realize that we would not suit, for he stopped pressing me to set a date."

"Why did you elope with me if that's how you felt?"

Esme wondered that herself. "I suppose I was angry with Dante and wanted to hurt him. And . . ." She paused, realizing she was about to speak those hurtful words that still haunted her. "I despised Dante's gypsy blood."

Calvin snorted. "Obviously, you've worked through your prejudice if you let him bed you."

"I don't wish to speak of it, Calvin. Dante is a better man than you'll ever be."

"I'm glad I learned, before I married you that you and the gypsy have been lovers."

Esme subsided against the squabs, refusing to be goaded by Calvin. The moment Dante returned to London, she intended to do everything within her power to convince him that she loved him, and that his gypsy blood enriched who he was. She never would have let him make love to her if she didn't have strong feelings for him. She should have realized that from the beginning.

The following morning found Esme squirming in a chair, hands folded in her lap as Uncle Daniel paced before her, lecturing her on her lack of good sense, her reckless nature and her stubbornness. When she and Calvin had returned to London the night before, he had unceremoniously dumped her on her doorstep. A footman had opened the door to her knock and informed her that her uncle was out. Grateful for the reprieve, she had climbed the stairs to her chamber.

The reprieve was short-lived, however, for Jane burst into her room moments later. "We were worried sick about you, milady," Jane scolded.

Esme hadn't been ready then to discuss her misadventures, so she'd cut Jane short by saying she was exhausted and they would talk tomorrow. After a restless night, Jane had wakened her the following morning with a summons from her uncle. When Esme had arrived in Lord Parkton's study, she'd known she was in for a tedious lecture, but a well-deserved one.

Parkton stopped pacing and planted himself in front of her. "It was irresponsible of you to elope with Lonsdale. What in God's name were you thinking?"

Esme shrugged. "I suppose I wasn't thinking. But if you recall, you were the one who wanted me to marry Calvin."

"And if *you* recall, I stopped pressing you some time ago. I spoke with Lord Alston a few weeks before his death. He advised me to delay your engagement to Lonsdale. He didn't have time to elaborate due to a previous appointment, but we agreed to meet at a later date. Unfortunately, he killed himself before our meeting took place.

"After the reading of the will, I understood why he advised against rushing you to the altar. For reasons unknown to anyone, Alston changed his will in favor of his illegitimate grandson."

Esme's head shot up. "Why did you say nothing to me about this?"

"I saw no need after Alston's death. If you had been enamored of Lonsdale, I would have spoken sooner, but if you told me once, you told me a dozen times that you had no intention of wedding Lonsdale."

He cleared his throat. "I'm still waiting to hear why you ran off with a man you barely tolerated."

"I had a . . . falling out with Lord Alston. Angry words were exchanged."

"Angry words? Explain yourself."

"Dante doesn't want me for myself. He has to marry

me to keep the Alston title and fortune. His grandfather placed a provision to that effect in his will."

"So you thought to thwart Alston by marrying Lonsdale. Thank God he found you before you reached Gretna Green."

Esme swallowed past the lump in her throat. She owed her uncle the truth. "Calvin believes Dante had a hand in Lord Alston's death. When I question Dante about it, he denied it, but did not vindicate himself. I didn't know what to think. Suddenly, marrying Calvin seemed like the lesser of two evils."

Parkton whipped his head around to stare at Esme. "Never say you wed Lonsdale! Please tell me Alston found you in time."

"Calvin and I . . . we didn't go to Gretna Green. We wanted everyone to think that, but we went south instead. Calvin keeps a hunting lodge near Heath. We planned to be married there by a local vicar."

Parkton staggered to the nearest chair. "I had no idea you could be so devious. Poor Alston—you deliberately sent him to Gretna Green. Am I to congratulate you on your marriage to Lonsdale?"

"No. Dante found us in time. By that time I had already decided I didn't want to marry Calvin. Dante found me at an inn near Heath and forced me to leave with him."

Parkton looked completely befuddled. "How did Alston know to ride south?"

Esme shrugged, as puzzled about that as her uncle. "I don't know. It's all rather strange."

"Am I to assume that you and Alston are now man and wife? For your sake, I hope he's done the right thing. The gossip about your absence could be brutal. It's best if we keep Lonsdale completely out of this. No one has to know you left town with him."

Taking a deep breath, Esme said, "I'm not married, Uncle. Dante took me to meet his grandparents. While we were there, Dante tried to convince me to marry him. I refused."

Parkton rose abruptly. "You what? I thought you had more sense than that, Esme."

Esme launched into an explanation. "I *did* change my mind, Uncle, but I never got the chance to tell Dante before—"

"What are you trying to say, Esme? Where is Alston now?"

"I don't know."

"If Alston didn't bring you, how did you get here?"

Esme had a hard time finding an explanation that wouldn't result in a duel between her uncle and Calvin. How could she tell Uncle Daniel that Calvin had dragged her away from the caravan against her will?

"Calvin showed up at the gypsy camp. I asked him to take me back to London."

"Why? Surely Alston did not approve of that arrangement. I understand none of this."

Neither do I. "Dante didn't know I'd left; I didn't tell him. We'd argued and I thought it best to leave, but during the return trip to London, I began to have doubts. I realize now that I made a grave error. I'm ready to marry Dante now if he'll have me."

"I'm happy you've come to your senses. Lord Alston's choice of heir was good enough for me. I like the current Lord Alston better than I do Lonsdale. He comes from good English stock regardless of his gypsy blood."

"If he'll still have me," Esme reminded him. "I . . . was rather nasty to him. I don't understand what happens to me when I'm with Dante. I can't seem to control my tongue."

Or any other part of me.

"We must find out his intentions regarding your betrothal as soon as possible. I'll send a note off to Alston and ask him to call on me." His expression turned grave. "Leaving the gypsy camp without Alston's knowledge—and with another man, no less—may prove difficult to explain. Let's hope Alston doesn't cry off."

"Crying off could lose him everything. Did you know Calvin will inherit if Dante fails to gain my hand in marriage? I'm sure that's why Calvin was so eager to elope with me."

"I believe I did know that, but I foresaw no difficulty. If you weren't so stubborn, you would already be the Marchioness of Alston."

He paused, sending her an assessing look. "We've always had an exceptionally close relationship, my dear, so I hope you will feel free to confide in me. How do you really feel about Alston? Is marrying him abhorrent to you?"

"I . . ." She looked up at him through a fringe of feathery lashes. "I don't hate him. I . . . care for him. But I fear my careless words have convinced Dante that I believe him unworthy because of his gypsy blood. I need to speak to him as soon as he returns to London to convince him otherwise."

"Very well. I'll dash a note off immediately and ask him to call upon us."

Esme reached up and kissed his cheek. "Thank you, Uncle Daniel. I'm lucky to have you."

Esme moved restlessly from room to room after Parkton left, wondering what Dante had made of her disappearance. The need to see him became so compelling that she fetched her reticule and pelisse and ran from the house without telling anyone where she was going. By the time she reached the Alston mansion, she was panting so hard she had to stop and catch her breath before reaching for the brass knocker.

A footman answered the summons, apparently startled to see an unaccompanied female standing on the doorstep.

"How may I help you, miss?"

"Would you please inform Lord Alston that Lady Esme would like to speak with him? It's rather urgent."

"I'm sorry, milady, Lord Alston isn't in."

Esme stepped past the footman. "I'll wait."

"Well, I . . . uh . . . that is . . . I'll fetch Grayson."

Esme was left standing in the impressive foyer as the footman hurried off. A few minutes later an elderly man impeccably dressed in Alston livery appeared. She recognized Grayson from past visits with her uncle to the Alston country estate. He seemed surprised to see her.

"Lady Esme, Grimes informed me you wished to speak to Lord Alston. Please forgive my boldness, but I thought you and His Lordship were together." He cleared his throat. "I haven't heard from him since he left London. Didn't he catch up with you and Lord Lonsdale in time to prevent . . ." His sentence trailed off.

"Oh, he found me, Grayson, but . . . we became separated. Hasn't he returned yet?" Esme asked, thinking it strange that Grayson knew so much about his employer's business.

Grayson's gray brows drew together. "His Lordship hasn't returned to London. I find this all very unsettling, if you'll pardon my saying so. I was under the impression . . . I expected . . ." He shrugged. "I'll inform His Lordship that you called the moment he arrives."

A frisson of apprehension slid down Esme's spine. Dante should have returned by now. He couldn't have been very far behind her . . . unless he had been glad to be rid of her and had not followed. A sob caught in her throat.

What if Dante never returned to London?

Dante's recovery had been delayed by an energy-sapping fever despite Carlotta's careful handling of his wound. Though the fever wasn't life-threatening, it was debilitating. During the endless days spent sweating out his fever, Dante's anger grew and expanded, until he had convinced himself that he never wanted to see Esme again. They had been in lust with each other. While she loved his cock and how he made her feel, she had never considered him good enough to marry.

Since learning that Esme had left with Lonsdale, Dante had come to a painful conclusion: Lonsdale had shot him and Esme had conspired with him. But they had made a serious mistake in trying to kill him. Dante was very much alive, and soon he would be ready to find and destroy his enemies.

"I've brought your lunch, Dante."

Dante struggled into a sitting position as Loretta set his tray down. This was his first day without fever, and despite a lingering weakness, he was eager to be up and about.

"What pap did you bring me today?" he complained.

"Chicken broth, but Carlotta added bread to your menu," Loretta said. "Shall I feed you?"

Dante waved her aside. "You've been very attentive during my illness, Loretta, and I appreciate it, but I am capable of feeding myself now. Will you ask Carlotta if I might have some meat? My stomach is touching my backbone. I intend to return to London soon and need something more substantial than broth if I'm to build up my strength."

"Bah! Why would you return to London? Not to see that bitch who betrayed you, I hope. I'm not the only one who believes the *gadjo* was responsible for the attempt upon your life. She and that Lonsdale bastard probably planned your death so he could inherit. He *is* next in line to inherit, isn't he?"

As much as Dante wanted to deny it, he couldn't. All the pieces of the puzzle fit—the attempts upon his life and Esme's refusal to marry him despite their intimacy. Esme had probably been waiting for Lonsdale to do him in, and once he did, she and Lonsdale intended to enjoy the fruits of their evil scheme.

The knowledge of her conniving hurt more than his wound. What a fool he'd been to lose his heart to a *gadjo*. How could he have thought that Esme would overlook his gypsy blood and treat him as an equal?

"Don't rub it in," Dante growled. "Give me that damn broth."

Dante drank the broth and ate the bread with ill humor. When he finished, he thrust the bowl at Loretta. "Tell Carlotta I need solid food. No more flavored water."

Loretta gave him a wounded look. Immediately Dante regretted his gruffness. Loretta had scarcely left his bedside since he'd been wounded.

"Forgive me, Loretta. As you can tell, I'm in a foul mood. If I don't leave this bed soon, I'll go mad. Go now and bring me something to fill the empty place in my stomach."

After Loretta left, Dante swung his legs out of bed and sat on the edge. Though his wound hadn't fully healed, his head didn't swim when he tried to sit up. That was progress. Taking a deep breath, he attempted to stand, finding it easier than he expected. Though still weak, he was far from helpless. Tomorrow he would venture outside and begin his slow trek back to health so he could wreak vengeance on his enemies.

Disregarding Carlotta's objection, Dante left his wagon the following morning. He asked for a hearty breakfast and ate every morsel. From that moment on, his recovery was fairly straightforward. He didn't even wait for Carlotta to remove the stitches from his wound before climbing on Condor's back and riding around the campsite. Other than an unaccustomed stiffness from lying in bed so long, Dante felt no discomfort and considered himself healed enough to return to London.

Two days later, Dante informed his grandparents that he intended to leave the following day.

"You won't do anything foolish, will you?" Carlotta asked.

"That depends on what you consider foolish," Dante replied, summoning a cocky grin for his devoted grandmother.

"You know what I'm talking about," Carlotta admonished. "You don't know for certain that Lady Esme conspired with Lord Lonsdale."

Dante's words crackled with emnity. "I know

enough. Don't worry, I won't hurt her physically. That's not my way. She *will* feel my wrath, however. As for Lonsdale, spare him no pity, for I won't."

"I consulted my crystal ball," Carlotta revealed, "but alas, no clear picture formed."

"Forget the crystal ball, Grandmother. I don't need a seer to tell me who wants me dead. When I return to London, I intend to make two people very, very sorry they misjudged my will to survive."

"Take me with you!" Loretta cried, clinging to his arm. "I won't get in your way, I promise. I've never been to London and would love to see the sights."

"Loretta, I don't think—"

"Please, Dante, don't say no. All I'm asking is that you let me stay in your home while you conclude your business in London. Then we can return to the caravan together."

Dante shrugged. "Why not, as long as you remember that all you're getting is a place to sleep and regular meals. What I do and where I go is none of your concern. In return, I'll not interfere with your comings and goings."

"Is that wise, Dante?" Carlotta asked once Loretta left to pack her meager belongings. "Loretta is trouble. She's very possessive of you. She'll want to skewer the first lady who flirts with you."

Dante laughed. "London is a big city, large enough to keep Loretta occupied while I tend to business. I'll even spend some of my grandfather's money on new clothing for her. That should keep her out of my hair for a while. Besides, she might prove amusing."

Sandor shook his head. "You always did like to live dangerously. Be careful, my son. Once your enemy learns you're alive, he might be tempted to make another attempt on your life."

Dante's dark eyes burned with an inner fire that did not bode well for Calvin Lonsdale. "I hope he does."

Chapter Fourteen

Ten days after Esme's return to London, Uncle Daniel came home with the news that Lord Alston had returned to London that very day. Esme's first inclination was to go to him and unburden her heart, but Uncle Daniel forbade it. Instead, he sent a note around telling Dante that they were to attend the Hogarths ball tonight and expected to see him there.

Esme was nervous about their meeting. How would he react when she told him she was willing to marry him? More importantly, what had kept him away from London so long?

That night Esme took particular care dressing, selecting a leaf-green, shoulder-baring confection cut low over her breasts and cinched at her narrow waist with a dark green sash. Jane had arranged her russet locks in a becoming upswept style that emphasized her slender neck.

Dante hadn't arrived yet when they entered the Hogarths' crowded ballroom. Parkton left to check the card room while Esme headed for a group of friends. Lonsdale intercepted her before she reached them.

"If you're looking for Alston, forget it," he said. "I doubt he will show up."

Esme glared at him. "Why do you say that?"

"He has no reason to return. You told him you wouldn't marry him, so he has nothing to gain by coming to London."

"I've already told you that I've changed my mind. Tonight I intend to tell Dante I'm willing to marry him."

Calvin smirked. "Perhaps he won't have you."

A commotion near the door brought the conversation to a halt. Then the footman announced the Marquis of Alston. Esme gave Calvin an "I told you so" look and set off on a path to intercept Dante.

He looked thinner, Esme thought, and paler than she recalled. She didn't have time to ponder the change in his appearance as she stepped into his path and smiled up at him.

"Where have you been?" she asked. "I've been waiting for you."

Dante affected a formal bow, his expression one of bored politeness. "Lady Esme." Esme had expected a cool reception, but this was icy. "Please excuse me."

He stepped around Esme and headed directly toward a knot of women, including Lady Harrison and Lady Wilton. His public rebuff was painfully embarrassing. Esme heard a buzzing in her ears and realized it came from people who had heard Dante's chilly greeting. They were staring at her, some with pity and others with glee, as if they couldn't wait to spread gossip about her awkward encounter with the Marquis of Alston.

Esme wanted to slink away, to disappear into the woodwork, but her pride wouldn't let her. Angling her chin upward, she looked for a friend, spotted Lady Louise and headed in her direction. From the corner of her eye, Esme saw Dante lead Lady Harrison onto the dance floor. Apparently, he wanted to prove to the *ton* that he and Esme were no longer an item.

Before Esme could reach Louise, Lord Carstairs led the lady onto the dance floor. Swerving, Esme made for the refreshment table.

Calvin stepped into her path, grasped her arm and hissed, "I need to talk to you. It's important."

"I've nothing to say to you, Calvin."

His hand tightened on her arm, a spark of triumph in his eyes. "Alston no longer seems interested."

Esme pulled free. "All will be well again once I explain."

"You can't marry him," Calvin insisted. He looked almost desperate. "I need the Alston blunt more than he does. What does he know about being a titled gentleman?"

"Release me, Calvin. You're beginning to annoy me. People are staring at us."

He released her arm.

Esme spun on her heel and returned to the ballroom, waiting for a chance to have a private word with Dante. She danced when asked, smiled without heart and made polite conversation, all the while trying to keep track of Dante. He appeared to be having a good time, which was more than she could say for herself.

When she saw Dante step out onto the balcony alone, she seized the opportunity. Excusing herself from a group she had been chatting with, she hurried after him.

The balcony was deserted; Dante was nowhere in sight. Shivering in the cool air, she was about to give up and return inside when she spied him standing in the garden in a patch of moonlight. She found the steps and descended quickly, before anyone saw her.

"Dante."

Dante heard but didn't acknowledge her. Esme was the last person he wanted to talk to. He'd gone to great lengths tonight to show her he didn't need her, and felt that he had succeeded. Margaret Harrison had invited him to her home for an assignation, and he was seriously thinking of accepting. Then he recognized Esme's familiar scent and knew she was standing behind him.

"Dante, didn't you hear me?"

He turned to face her, his expression devoid of emotion. "My hearing is exceptional, thank you. What do you want? But before you answer, know that we have nothing to discuss. You made your contempt for me very clear back in Heath."

"I wanted to ask your forgiveness for treating you like . . . like . . ."

". . . a gypsy?" he supplied. "Like a man unworthy of your hand? I know that's how you regard me, but I never suspected you hated me enough to plan my death."

"What? Are you mad?"

"Not at all. We have nothing to discuss, milady."

"Yes, we do. After our argument, I realized how foolish I had been. I really do care for you, Dante."

Dante laughed in her face. "Do you? Then why did you leave with Lonsdale?"

"I didn't leave with him."

Dante's brows arched upward. "Didn't you? That's not what I heard."

"I did leave, but . . ."

"But what?"

"Calvin forced me."

Dante threw his head back and laughed. "Of course he did. Congratulations. Am I to assume you are now Lonsdale's wife?"

"You may assume no such thing! I didn't marry Calvin. I don't even like him."

"Tell that to someone who will believe you. You and Lonsdale planned to wed and share my grandfather's wealth. You never wanted to marry me. I'm a gypsy, remember? And to make sure I wouldn't interfere with your plans, you and Lonsdale conspired to get me out of the way."

Esme backed away from him. "What are you accusing me of? I was waiting for you to return to camp after our argument to tell you I was willing to set a date for our wedding." She reached out to him, her hand curling into a fist. She dropped it when he stepped beyond her reach. "I want to marry you, Dante. I wouldn't have made love with you if I didn't lo . . . care for you. Why won't you believe me?"

"You're too late, milady. I don't want you. You've insulted me one too many times. I was a fool to think you could care for me. You only wanted me for a lover; the world is full of women like you.

"I've asked my solicitor to look for ways to circumvent the marriage clause in Grandfather's will. Perhaps I won't need to marry you to keep my inheritance." His face as cold as a winter wind, he added, "I don't need you. I've lived twenty-eight years without a title, and I can do so again if Bartholomew fails to find a loophole. You were wrong to listen to Lonsdale. I wanted you for yourself, not because of the inheritance. But now I don't want you at all."

Dante hardened his heart against Esme's strangled sob. "Why can't we forget what went before and start over?"

"It's too late, milady. In case you're wondering why I'm still walking among the living, it's due to my grandmother's healing skills."

Esme's brow furrowed. "What are you talking about?"

"Shall I show you the bullet wound? It's not pretty."

"You were wounded?"

"That innocent act will get you nowhere, milady. One day I shall prove that you and Lonsdale planned my death."

Esme's throat worked soundlessly. Several minutes passed before she could speak. "You were shot? When? How? What makes you think I had anything to do with it?"

"I can put two and two together, milady," Dante sneered. "I happen to have had a very good education. I was shot shortly after you and Lonsdale were seen together in the forest. Need I say more?"

Someone had shot Dante! Nearly incoherent with rage, Esme began tearing at his evening clothes. "Where were you wounded? Are you all right?"

He grasped her wrists. "Leave off, milady. One might think you cared."

"I do care, Dante. I swear I had nothing to do with your shooting."

Dante's lips twisted into a mocking grin. "I expected you to deny it, and you haven't disappointed me."

"Don't do this to us, Dante."

"There is no us. You've destroyed everything we might have had together. Yes, I did need to marry you to fulfill the conditions of my grandfather's will, but a title is something I can live without. I truly wanted you, milady, but no longer. And now I wish you good night."

Esme watched Dante leave, her head bowed beneath the weight of her despair. She had destroyed a relationship that could have developed into something beautiful. Dashing away her tears, Esme squared her shoulders and made a solemn vow to herself. Somehow, some way, she would make Dante love her. Though her prospects of success were slim, she refused to give up. If Dante had cared deeply for her once, he could do so again.

It had taken Esme a long time to realize that her feelings for Dante were genuine, and that she loved him despite her initial misgivings. She wanted him to love her in return.

Esme made her way back to the ball deep in thought. Had Calvin shot Dante? She had to consider the possibility, for Calvin had the most to gain from Dante's death. He might have had time to do it while she was locked up in the coach, she supposed.

Esme returned to the ballroom in time to see Dante leave with Lady Harrison clinging to his arm. The thought of Dante holding, kissing, loving another woman nearly broke her heart. A few minutes later she sought out her uncle and asked to be taken home. The evening had been an unqualified disaster.

When Dante left the ball, he had every intention of accompanying Margaret to her townhouse and making love to her until Esme became but a distant memory. Margaret's husband was in the country, and she was as eager for an illicit liaison as Dante was.

But something strange happened when he stepped into the cold night air. He realized he didn't want Margaret. In fact, he didn't want a romantic liaison of any kind right now. He had too many things to accomplish before he lost the title to Lonsdale—unless, of course, Bartholomew could find a legal way to circumvent the marriage clause in his grandfather's will. Dante was determined to find evidence to prove that Lonsdale had murdered Lord Alston and had planned Dante's own death as well.

When Lady Margaret's carriage was brought around, Dante assisted her inside but didn't enter himself.

"Get in, my lord." Margaret licked her lips with the tip of her tongue in such a lascivious manner, it could be mistaken for nothing but sexual innuendo. "I can't wait to taste you." She rolled her eyes. "There is a great deal we can do in a carriage." She sent him a beckoning look. "What a delicious thought."

Dante closed the door and stepped back from the curb. "I just recalled an appointment. Perhaps another time, my lady."

"What?" Margaret screeched. "You're leaving me?"

"Forgive me, but my appointment cannot wait."

"At this time of night? Gypsy lover, bah! I expected you to live up to your name, my lord. Has inheriting a title tamed you?"

Disdaining an answer, Dante nodded to the coachman. The carriage pulled away from the curb and into the roadway. Margaret leaned out the window, her display of fury stunning. "Bastard," she hissed.

Dante didn't blame Margaret for being angry. He had agreed to the assignation because he believed that bed games would improve his disposition. But his confrontation with Esme in the garden had unsettled him too much to enjoy bed sport with anyone except Esme.

Betrayal was an ugly word. Dante hadn't wanted to believe that Esme had helped Calvin plan his death, but everything he'd seen, heard and surmised had led to that conclusion. He wanted nothing more to do with the lying witch.

Since Dante's mansion was but two blocks away from the Hogarths' he had walked to the ball. He was glad for the walk home now, for the cold night air helped clear the cobwebs from his head.

Esme had truly seemed shocked when he told her he'd been shot. He had almost believed her innocent, but he had experienced milady's acting skills before. All those times they had made love, she had pretended to enjoy it.

Dante reached his mansion. Grayson opened the door to him. "Where is Loretta?" he asked the butler.

Grayson rolled his eyes. "In her room, milord."

"Good. Good night, Grayson. I won't need you any more tonight."

Dante accepted the candlestick Grayson offered and climbed the stairs to his chamber. He must have been mad to bring Loretta to London. True to his word, he had outfitted her befitting a lady and turned her as loose on London. He didn't intend to delve too deeply into her activities; he really didn't care what she did, as long as she didn't interfere in his life.

Dante entered his room, closed the door and placed the candlestick on the bureau. Dante blessed

Grayson for building the fire up in the hearth as he undressed and climbed into bed. Even the bed felt toasty. When a warm, naked body nestled into the curve of his body, Dante realized why the sheets were not cold. He wasn't the only one occupying his bed.

Dante reared out of bed and reached for the candlestick, bringing it close to the bed.

"Blast and damn! What are you doing here, Loretta? If I wanted company in bed, I would have asked for it. Get out."

"Don't make me leave, Dante," Loretta purred. "You look like you need me tonight."

"You're wrong. I don't need a woman . . . any woman," he added for emphasis.

"You saw *her* tonight, didn't you? I hope you punished her for what she did to you. You almost died, Dante. She helped plan your death."

"Whatever happens between milady and me is none of your concern. Don't make me sorry I brought you to London."

"You really are besotted, aren't you, Dante?"

"You're wrong, Loretta. I cannot stand the sight of Lady Esme Harcourt."

"Ha!" Loretta laughed, rolling out of bed. "Tell that to someone who will believe you. It's time you learned you mean nothing to the lady. You're dirt beneath her dainty feet."

She flounced off, parading her nakedness before Dante as she stormed from the room.

Dante wanted to laugh. Besotted? He certainly was *not* besotted. He was still too raw inside to feel anything but . . . but what?

Damn Esme! Damn her to everlasting hell for chewing him up and spitting him out.

Chapter Fifteen

Two days after the Hogarth ball, Lord Parkton walked into the back parlor where Esme was staring listlessly out the window. "I'm sorry, Esme, I tried, but Alston refuses to see me," he said.

"I didn't expect he would, Uncle. He's very angry with me."

Parkton cleared his throat. "I didn't want to tell you this, but I fear I must. Lonsdale is telling everyone that you ran off with him to get married but changed your mind at the last minute. He's saying that you and he stayed at an inn without benefit of a chaperon."

"What does Calvin hope to gain by spreading malicious gossip?"

"I'm not sure. Apparently, the talk I had with him did little good. Lonsdale is a bitter man. It appears he'll go to any length to seize the Alston title and wealth for himself. You are the key to everything he wants, my dear."

"I told Calvin that I intended to marry Dante. He's angry. I think he's spreading gossip to ruin me."

"We'll see about that," Parkton muttered beneath his breath.

"What did you say, Uncle?"

"I don't want you to fret, Esme," he hedged. "I refuse to stand by and see your reputation ruined. I'll make this come out right, you'll see."

Esme sent her uncle a fond smile, though she seriously doubted he could do anything to help. Dante didn't want her, and she didn't blame him. And she wasn't about to marry Calvin.

If only she could make Dante believe in her innocence.

Her face set in determined lines, Esme marched up to the Alston mansion later that day with one purpose in mind. She was going to speak with Dante even if she had to wait all day. She grasped the brass door knocker and rapped sharply.

Grimes answered the door. "Lady Esme, how may I help you?"

"Please inform Lord Alston that I wish to speak with him."

Grimes asked her to wait, then disappeared down a long hallway.

A shuffle of feet and whisper of skirts drew Esme's attention toward the staircase. What she saw left her virtually speechless. Loretta, decked out like a lady, tripped gaily down the stairs. She paused when she saw Esme and then continued to the bottom landing.

"What are you doing here?" Loretta demanded.

"I might ask you the same," Esme shot back.

"Unlike you, I don't consider myself too good for Dante. He brought me to London so that I might give him the comfort you denied him."

Esme flinched. Loretta's words stung.

"Is Dante in? I need to speak with him."

"He doesn't want to see you."

"I prefer to hear that from him."

"Loretta speaks the truth," Dante said from behind her.

Esme whirled, drinking in the sight of him. Her heart was pounding so hard, she feared that Dante could hear it. His face, hawkish with high, well-defined cheekbones, sturdy jaw and full lips, had settled into a frown. Not even his dark, mysterious eyes, so heavily lashed and set beneath gently curved brows, could soften the harsh lines of his disapproving expression.

"You have nothing to say that I wish to hear," Dante continued. "You said it all before you left me wounded and near death."

"I didn't know," Esme asserted once again.

"Did you not?" Dante mocked.

Loretta joined Dante, pressing her lush curves against his side. "If not for me, Dante would be dead. I nursed him back to health."

Dante sent Loretta an amused smile but did not contradict her, even though it was Carlotta's skill that had saved his life. To prove his disregard for Esme, he placed an arm around Loretta's shoulders. He saw Esme wince, and almost lost the façade he had adopted to prove he no longer cared for her.

Dante knew why Esme was here. He had heard the gossip Lonsdale was circulating about her, and knew it was damaging her reputation. She had Lonsdale to thank for involving her in a scandal, for Dante would never have muddied her name. But since Dante was reconciled to losing his title, he saw no reason to stop Esme from marrying his rival.

"May we speak in private?" Esme asked, sliding a glance at Loretta.

"I see no need," Dante bit out.

Unfortunately, his heart didn't agree. He still wanted Esme. Oh, yes, very much, but pride held him stiff and unyielding. He tightened his arm around Loretta in an effort to prevent himself from reaching for Esme and kissing her senseless. He knew that would only lead to more heartache. He had bared his heart to her, and she had rejected him. Now she came begging when her reputation was being shredded by gossip.

If he thought Esme truly cared for him, he would relent without protest and marry her immediately. But even then, there would always be a doubt in her mind about his grandfather's death.

Dante hardened his heart as he recalled exploring every inch of her lush body, heard in his mind her blissful cries as she shattered in his arms. If he allowed himself to dwell on their lovemaking, he knew he would lose the battle to protect his heart.

If Esme wanted a marquis for a husband, she had but to wait for Lonsdale to propose after the title went to him. The thought of Esme intimately entwined on a bed with Lonsdale made him wince inwardly, and he thrust the image away. Soon he would be simply Dante the gypsy once again, unless Bartholomew could find a way around the terms of his grandfather's will.

"All I ask is a few minutes of your time," Esme said.

"You could have had all of my time," he shot back. "It was your choice to leave me."

"No. I told you, Calvin took that choice from me."

Dante shrugged. "So you said. Excuse me, please; I'm late for an appointment with my solicitor."

A smug smile curving her lush lips, Loretta marched to the door and opened it, inviting Esme to leave. Her head held high, Esme left without a backward glance.

It took all of Dante's strength to keep from bolting after her. He wanted her, needed her, but couldn't bear the thought of a lifetime of being made to feel inferior.

"Good riddance," Loretta gloated after slamming the door on Esme. "You won't have to worry about *her* again."

Dante stared at Loretta, aware that bringing the gypsy woman to London had been a mistake, but he'd been hurt and confused and had let himself be persuaded. "You can't stay here, Loretta. Pack your things and be ready to leave tomorrow."

Loretta stamped her foot. "No! I want to stay with you."

"You'll be much happier with the caravan. People like us don't belong in London."

Loretta brightened immediately. "Will you be returning with me?"

"Not now."

"I'll wait."

"We'll discuss this later; I really do have an appointment."

So saying, he brushed past her, leaving her standing alone in the foyer.

* * *

A sly-eyed clerk ushered Dante into Bartholomew's office and left somewhat reluctantly.

"I hope you have good news for me," Dante began.

"Please be seated, my lord," Bartholomew invited.

"I think I'll stand for this," Dante said. He could tell by the look on the solicitor's face that the news wasn't good.

"Very well, if you insist. Rest assured that I have exhausted every resource at my disposal on your behalf. However . . ."

"Out with it, man."

Bartholomew cleared his throat. "Your grandfather's will is ironclad. There is no way to break it or circumvent the marriage codicil to the will. He must have been very sure that you and Lady Esme would suit, else he wouldn't have dictated those terms. I did question him about the codicil when he rewrote his will, but he was adamant. He wanted you to wed the woman of his choice."

"I see. Thank you for trying."

"Are you sure there is no possibility of a marriage between you and Lady Esme?"

"The lady is willing but I am not," Dante informed him.

For some reason, Dante's words seemed to please Bartholomew.

"May I ask why?"

"My reasons are my own. I'll be in touch."

Dante found Grayson waiting for him in the foyer when he returned home. "You have a visitor, milord. I tried to tell him you weren't home, but he insisted on waiting. I fear you'll have to see him."

"Who is it? I'm in no mood for idle chatter."

Connie Mason

Dante knew he was being abrupt, but after talking to Bartholomew, he wanted to be alone to think. He was no closer to linking Lonsdale to his grandfather's murder and the attacks upon his own life than he had been a few weeks ago.

"I'm sorry, milord. I know you told me you didn't wish to see Lord Parkton, but he wouldn't take no for an answer. I put him in the study."

Dante groaned. What next? First Esme, now Parkton. Add Loretta into the mix and he was in one devil of a situation. He opened the door to his study and stepped inside. Parkton rose when he entered out of respect for Dante's higher rank.

"Please be seated," Dante said. He went immediately to the sideboard, poured brandy in two snifters and handed one to Parkton. Perching on the edge of his desk, Dante swirled the amber liquid and took a deep swallow before speaking. "What can I do for you, Lord Parkton?"

"I think you know, Alston. Have you heard the gossip circulating about Esme?"

Dante tossed back the rest of his brandy. "I've heard."

"What are you going to do about it?"

Dante set his glass down. "I beg your pardon? Shouldn't you place the blame where it belongs? Esme made her wishes perfectly clear. She prefers Lonsdale."

"Esme doesn't want Lonsdale. She told me she was willing to marry you but you rejected her."

"Did Esme tell you the reason my return to London was delayed?"

Dante knew by Parkton's puzzled look that she had not told her uncle the complete truth. "I was shot by

252

an unknown assailant while visiting my grandparents. I have good reason to believe that Esme and Lonsdale conspired together to kill me."

"That's preposterous!" Parkton sputtered, shooting up from his chair. "What reason would Esme have to want you dead?"

"It's simple, really. Lonsdale will inherit if I am dead."

"You're mad! Esme isn't capable of that kind of treachery."

Dante gave a mirthless laugh. "Would Esme elope with a man she didn't like?"

"My niece can be stubborn and a bit reckless, but she would never deliberately hurt anyone. You do her a grave injustice." Parkton paused to catch his breath. "If you don't marry Esme, you will lose everything to Lonsdale. Are you prepared to return to your former life?"

"I can return to my former life with no regrets. As Dante the gypsy, I will be free from the strictures of society."

"You leave me but one alternative, Alston. Since you are so set against wedding Esme, I must seek a betrothal between Esme and Lonsdale. I hoped it wouldn't come to that, but I cannot allow Esme's reputation to be ruined. I didn't want her to marry Lonsdale, but it's essential that she marry someone,"

Unwelcome pictures began forming in Dante's mind, fueled by Parkton's words. Though he knew they deserved each other, he couldn't bear the thought of Esme lying in Lonsdale's arms, giving him her body and everything else Dante had lost because of his pride.

It suddenly occurred to Dante just how much he

was sacrificing and who would benefit if he gave up the marquisate. The last person in the world he wanted to gain from his loss was Viscount Lonsdale. But wasn't that exactly what would happen if he refused to wed Esme? He could well imagine Lonsdale's glee when Parkton offered Esme to him.

Damn and blast! Lonsdale must not have Esme. He wouldn't allow it. Throwing away everything his grandfather had left to him suddenly seemed like a stupid thing to do. There was a great deal he could accomplish with the Alston title and fortune. He could take his seat in Parliament and try to effect changes to help the downtrodden.

"Your silence speaks for itself," Parkton said. "Obviously, you never cared for my niece. Perhaps she would be better off with Lonsdale after all." He reached for the doorknob.

"Wait!" Dante couldn't let it end like this. His intuition told him Lonsdale had killed Lord Alston and was responsible for the attempts upon his own life. He couldn't let the man win. Giving up now, when marrying Esme would keep Lonsdale from seizing power, was an unwise decision.

Parkton turned, his expression hopeful. "Have you changed your mind?"

"Perhaps, but I must speak with Esme first. I want her to understand what I expect from the marriage."

"So be it," Parkton agreed. "We will expect you for tea. Don't be late."

"Grayson will see you to the door."

Dante stared at the closed door long after Parkton had departed. His body burned and his loins tightened at the thought of having Esme in his bed every night. She would be his forever, to make love to whenever he wanted her. Though he had no qualms about making love to Esme, he knew better than to trust her. He vowed to watch her every move. If she so much as looked sideways at Lonsdale, he would confine her to the house. He wouldn't give her the opportunity to conspire against him again.

What Esme needed was a child to keep her occupied. A smile stretched his lips. Getting Esme with child would be his pleasure.

Parkton returned home in time to join Esme for lunch. He kissed her forehead and waited to be served before dismissing Jamison so that he might speak freely.

"I saw Alston this morning," Parkton began.

Esme's fork stopped midway to her mouth. "I thought he refused to see you."

"Not this time."

Esme chewed thoughtfully. "I don't know why you bothered. His mistress is living with him."

That seemed to startle Parkton. "Are you sure? I saw nothing to prove your claim."

"I saw her with my own eyes."

"You visited Alston? That wasn't well done of you, Esme. I hoped you took your maid with you."

Silence.

Parkton sighed. "Your impulsiveness is the bane of my existence."

"Dante doesn't want me."

"He's changed his mind. He's coming for tea today. I expect him to offer for you, and I want you to accept. It's either him or Lonsdale."

Esme's mouth gaped open. "What did you say to change Dante's mind? He was adamantly opposed to our marriage when I spoke with him. It was obvious that he and Loretta were together."

"I know nothing about Loretta; I only know that he is willing to wed you."

A note of bitterness crept into her voice. "Dante must have decided he wants the title after all. He accused me of conspiring with Calvin to kill him."

"So he said. Did you?"

"No! How can you ask such a thing? I didn't even know Dante had been shot until he told me."

"Bloody hell! Do you think Lonsdale capable of murder?"

Esme hesitated. How well did she know Calvin? Was he capable of evil? "Honestly, Uncle, I don't think so. I know Calvin was counting on inheriting from his uncle, but I don't believe he's capable of murder."

"Dante's grandfather was free to leave his estate to whomever he chose; it was not entailed. Apparently, he'd been thinking about his grandson for some time and considered him better suited than Lonsdale. He knew more about these two men than we do. I believe we should accept the man he chose, but I don't like the idea that Alston believes you conspired with Lonsdale."

"I had no part in any conspiracy, Uncle Daniel."

"I believe you; now you'll have to convince Alston." He paused, his brow furrowing in thought. "Beginning a marriage with distrust of one's partner doesn't bode well for the future. I don't want to see you hurt, my dear. Perhaps I was wrong to approach Alston. You could always return to the country until the *ton* finds someone else to gossip about."

Esme seriously considered her options. She didn't mind the gossip, nor would she mind going back home; she'd always loved the country. What she did mind was leaving Dante. Despite his low opinion of her, she loved him too dearly to leave him to Loretta.

"I wouldn't mind returning to the country, Uncle, but if I did, it would look as if I had something to hide. Dante will believe the worst of me."

"But if you marry him, he could make your life miserable, my dear."

"Not if I convince him that I . . . I care for him."

Parkton's eyebrows arched upward. "*Do* you care for him? Somehow I find that hard to believe after learning that you left the caravan with Lonsdale."

Esme lowered her gaze to study her fingers. "I tried to convince myself that Dante's gypsy blood mattered. I wanted to believe he was too far beneath me to become a serious suitor."

She returned her gaze to her uncle. "When I finally realized my thinking was wrongheaded, it was too late. I regret leaving the gypsy camp with Calvin"— she still didn't want to tell her uncle she'd been forced—"and after that, Dante wouldn't have me."

Parkton shook his head. "I understand none of this, Esme. I know you were alone with both Alston and Lonsdale, and though I have no idea what took place while you were with either, I suspect it would be in your best interests to marry Alston. In his best interests too."

A tinge of red crept up Esme's neck. Uncle Daniel had good reason to insist upon a marriage between her and Dante, but she wasn't about to admit to the intimacies they had shared. Besides, she doubted that her uncle would want to hear about her indiscretions.

"I have no intention of turning down Dante's offer, Uncle. I have no illusions, however, about his reasons for proposing. Giving up everything he's inherited and resuming his former life would be difficult."

"It's settled, then?"

"Yes. I suppose I'll learn precisely what Dante expects from our marriage before he makes his offer," she mused.

Parkton's relief was palpable. "I'll take tea with you and then make myself scarce."

Esme stood and pecked his cheek. "Thank you, Uncle. I'll instruct cook to prepare something special for tea."

Parkton watched Esme leave, wondering why he still had reservations about the marriage. He wanted his niece to be happy, but that prospect looked doubtful as long as Alston believed Esme guilty of plotting his death.

Dante arrived at the appointed hour and was ushered into the drawing room. Parkton greeted him profusely, but it was to Esme that Dante directed his gaze. His heart lurched in his chest. He had always thought her an exceptional beauty, but today she seemed to glow. Her russet hair shone with a vibrancy that made her skin appear luminous.

She wore a pale blue velvet gown with a scoop neckline and long fitted sleeves that suited her perfectly. He had never wanted her more, or trusted her less. He marveled to think that anyone who looked like Esme could be capable of treachery. But despite his suspicions, he was committed to wed the bewitching beauty, but only under his own terms.

"Welcome, Lord Alston," Parkton greeted.

Reluctantly Dante took his gaze from Esme. "Good

day, my lord." He returned his attention to Esme, bowing slightly. "Milady."

"Just in time," Parkton said. "Tea will be served directly. Please be seated."

Dante selected a chair between Esme and her uncle, his expression showing nothing of his thoughts. He couldn't afford to give his emotions free rein. He wanted Esme and her uncle to believe he wasn't anxious for this marriage.

A servant arrived with the tea cart; Esme poured. "Milk or sugar or both?" she asked.

"Both," Dante replied.

Their eyes met and clung as she handed him his teacup. He felt a jolt of awareness and had to force himself to look away. In an effort to defuse the tension pulsing between them, he helped himself to a tiny sandwich, a slice of lemon cake and a biscuit.

Parkton attempted to make small talk. Dante had enough presence of mind to nod occasionally and murmur a reply. Esme was curiously quiet. After several tries at conversation, Parkton rose and excused himself.

"I have some paperwork awaiting me in my study," he said. "I'm sure you and Esme have a great deal to discuss."

Dante swallowed the last bite of sandwich and returned his cup and plate to the cart. He cleared his throat. "I'm sure you know why I'm here, milady."

"My uncle told me to expect an offer."

"Then I won't disappoint him. I've asked you this question before, milady, but you have always found a reason to refuse."

"I know," Esme replied. "Are you going to ask again?"

Dante was drawn so deeply into the violet fire of her eyes that for a brief moment he felt totally consumed by it. "Do you want me to?"

"I believe I do."

"Very well, but this time my proposal comes with terms."

He watched her face redden and wondered what she was thinking. He knew she was angry when her violet eyes turned dark purple.

She rose abruptly and stalked toward him, hands on hips. "Terms? You dare to dictate to me?"

He rose to meet her, looming several inches above her. "Either you agree or the marriage is off."

"I didn't hear you propose, my lord."

"Milady, will you do me the honor of becoming my wife?" His mocking tone raised her ire several degrees.

"Only if you accept my terms."

"*Your* terms? Now, that's an interesting concept."

"State your terms and then I'll present mine," Esme said.

"Very well. First, you are to have no contact with Lonsdale."

"Agreed. Any others?"

"Yes. Our marriage won't be in name only. I need an heir, more than one, to ensure that Lonsdale won't inherit if one of his attempts to murder me succeeds."

Dante imagined that he saw steam coming from the top of Esme's head.

"Let me get this straight," she said with a calm that belied her rising temper. "You're marrying me in order to secure your inheritance, and then you intend to turn me into a broodmare."

"You said it, not I."

She began to pace, then whirled around to confront him. "Anything else?"

"That about covers it." He thought a moment, then added, "Oh, I almost forgot. You will not betray our marriage vows, nor show disrespect for my grandparents."

"Such arrogance deserves a comeuppance. Now I'll tell you my terms," Esme shot back. "First, you are to send Loretta packing. I won't tolerate your mistress in my home. Second, you, too, will not betray your marriage vows or take a mistress."

His mouth twitched, but he managed to suppress his smile. The thought that he would want any woman but Esme was amusing. "Anything else?"

She tapped her chin. "You have to trust me."

Dante frowned. "You've set me a difficult task. In the past, you've given me too many reasons not to trust you. As for your other terms, I have no problem with them."

Esme gaped at him. "You'll send Loretta away?"

"I already have."

"And you'll remain faithful?"

"I said I would."

"But you don't trust me."

"No. What about *my* terms?"

"I agree to all of them."

"Even to having my children?"

She nodded slowly, almost shyly. "I doubt there is anything I can do to stop the course of nature. If you don't trust me, I'm surprised you want to . . . to . . ."

"Bed you?" He laughed. "I'm a man, Esme, and I just promised to remain faithful to our marriage vows."

"Then we're in agreement. I will marry you, Dante."

"I never doubted it for a moment," he said dryly.

His need for her blazed inside him like a roaring fire. He wanted to take her in his arms that instant, bear her to the floor and make love to her until they were both sated.

"Shall we seal our engagement with a kiss?"

"If you insist."

"Oh, yes, milady, I insist."

Esme stared into his glittering dark eyes, desire for him overflowing her heart. Trembling, she waited for his kiss, eager to taste him again. He didn't disappoint her. His kiss was beyond thrilling. It was everything, and more, that a woman could want.

Chapter Sixteen

Esme had but a week to prepare for her wedding. It was to be a late-afternoon affair with only close friends in attendance. Handwritten invitations had been delivered by messenger to a select list of people. Lady Louise had consented to act as maid of honor, and Dante had asked Lord Carstairs to be his best man. Uncle Daniel was to give her away, and Reverend Cooke, a family friend, had agreed to perform the marriage rites. After much discussion, everyone agreed to hold the wedding at the Parkton townhouse.

The announcement of her marriage to Dante was to appear in the *Times* the same day as the ceremony. The gypsy caravan had started south for the winter, so Dante's grandparents couldn't possibly reach London in time. He had asked that only three people be added to the guest list on his account: Lords Carstairs and Brookworth, and Mr. Bartholomew.

With but a week to select a pattern and have a wedding dress made, Esme decided instead to wear a gown from her own wardrobe. She had not yet worn it, and it seemed appropriate to the occasion.

Esme hadn't seen Dante since he'd proposed and sealed their bargain with a kiss that had left her eagerly awaiting her wedding night. She had wanted the kiss to go on forever, but of course it had to end.

When the day of her wedding arrived, Esme began having second thoughts. Would Dante ever look at her with love instead of lust? Loving a man who distrusted her could make her life a living hell.

A knock sounded on the door. Uncle Daniel asked permission to enter. Jane opened the portal.

Smiling fondly, Parkton entered the room. "You look magnificent, my dear. Alston is a lucky man. I hope he realizes it. Are you ready? The guests are here, Alston has arrived, and Reverend Cooke is waiting."

Esme dragged in a steadying breath. "As ready as I'll ever be, Uncle."

He offered his arm. She clutched it desperately, glad for the support. Of a sudden her knees wobbled like jelly. Once they spoke their vows, she and Dante would be forever bound together. Her steps faltered.

"You're not having second thoughts, are you?" Parkton asked. "We can always call this off."

Esme squared her shoulders. Marrying Dante had as many advantages as disadvantages. He had promised to remain faithful to his vows; she would be the only woman in his bed. The biggest disadvantage was his distrust of her, something she hoped to change. All in all, she had more to gain than lose by marrying him.

Dante fidgeted nervously as he waited for his bride to descend the stairs. This would be a happier occasion if he trusted Esme. He had to be mad to marry a woman he didn't trust. But when it came down to marrying Esme or letting Lonsdale inherit, the choice had been an easy one. He had thought he could walk away from the title and leave Esme to Lonsdale, but the reality was that he couldn't.

He wanted Esme more than he had ever wanted anyone or anything, including the title. He had promised to remain faithful, and he would, but he'd never let Esme know how deeply he cared for her. Admitting his feelings would give her the power to destroy him. Now, as he waited for her to appear at the head of the stairs, he vowed to guard his heart lest she break it.

The buzz of conversation stopped; Dante's gaze moved toward the staircase. Esme and her uncle stood at the top landing, ready to descend. Dante saw her anxious gaze pass over the guests until she found him. A tremulous smile curved her lips as she started down the stairs on her uncle's arm.

Dante's breath caught in his throat. It seemed as if Esme floated on air, as ethereal as an angel, as beautiful as a goddess. *A treacherous goddess,* he thought, and then quickly banished the thought.

Her gold brocade gown featured a fitted torso and long train. A pearl necklace rested against porcelain skin bared by a square neckline that exposed the enticing tops of her rounded breasts. The effect of her bright russet hair, partially covered by a veil of lace that trailed down her back and was held in place by a gold circlet, against the gold backdrop was stunningly beautiful. In her hand she carried a small bouquet of fall flowers tied with a large white ribbon.

Esme's smile seemed to waver when she reached

him. When Parkton placed her arm on his, Dante noted that she was trembling. Was she as uncertain about this marriage as he was? He gazed down at her, searching her face for answers.

Esme couldn't take her eyes off Dante. His dark, exotic features never failed to thrill her. From the moment of their first meeting, the attraction between them had been intense, even though she had tried to deny it. Dante's gypsy blood no longer was an issue between them. He was everything a woman could want in a man.

He was dressed formally today in black, with yards of pristine lace cascading from his shirtfront and sleeves. His head was bare, his black hair clubbed at his neck. But when she looked into those dark, unfathomable eyes, Esme felt a chill creep down her spine.

Dante's inscrutable eyes gave away nothing of his feelings. Esme's breath faltered. His expression served to reinforce her belief that he was marrying her for the wrong reasons. Dear God, what was she getting herself into?

Despite her reservations, Esme whispered her vows and listened intently as Dante spoke his loud and clear. Carstairs produced a ring and handed it to Dante. With a smile far too cool and controlled, Dante slid it on her finger. Moments later, they were pronounced husband and wife.

Esme stared at Dante, uncertain what to do next. The guests seemed to expect something, but what? Dante answered her unspoken question when he turned her toward him and brushed his mouth against hers in a teasing kiss. Then they were surrounded and separated by the crowd of well-wishers. As Esme smiled and nodded, her gaze kept straying to Dante, wishing she could read his mind.

Esme's life had changed forever today, but only time would tell if she had made the right choice. While her heart told her Dante was the only man who could make her happy, her mind advised against wearing her heart on her sleeve. If Dante knew how much she loved him, he could use that knowledge to hurt her. She had to remember that he hadn't married her for love.

Dinner was announced. The guests gravitated to the dining room. Dante joined her and offered his arm. "Milady."

"Milord," she answered, placing her hand on his arm. "The title is yours now; no one can take it from you."

"Does that make you happy, Esme? You are a marchioness now. The title sets you apart from most women."

"Marrying for love is more important that an exalted title."

He stopped, his dark eyes glowing as they gazed into hers. "Did *you* marry for love?"

"Did *you* marry for love?" Esme shot back.

His mouth smiled, but his eyes did not. "I believe we've reached an impasse. Shall we go in to supper?"

The mood throughout the wedding feast was subdued. Dante was an unknown entity. He hadn't yet proved himself to the *ton,* and some of the guests were still leery of his gypsy blood despite his title.

Esme ate sparingly, hardly tasting the food that cook and her helpers had spent all day preparing. All she remembered afterward was that the feast was sumptuous and the cake a masterpiece. Countless toasts were made, until Esme's head was spinning from too much wine and too little food. After what seemed like hours, Dante stood, thanked everyone and announced that it was time for them to leave.

In a daze, Esme followed Dante to the front door. When Jane started to follow, Dante told her she wasn't needed tonight, that she should wait until the morrow and accompany Esme's baggage to Dante's townhouse. Before Esme could protest, Dante wrapped her cloak about her shoulders, picked up the small bag Jane had prepared and hustled her out the door.

The cold air helped clear her head. Before Dante handed her into his carriage, she turned and waved to her uncle, who stood in the open door, concern etched upon his features. Dante climbed in beside her and the carriage eased forward, clattering down the street toward the Alston mansion.

"Are you all right?" Dante asked as he settled against the squabs.

"Of course; why wouldn't I be?"

"You were unusually quiet during supper. Do you regret marrying me?"

Esme gazed at him through shuttered eyes. "Should I?"

He shrugged. "You're a marchioness; what more could you want?"

Your love. "Your trust."

"Trust has to be earned. Can you honestly say that *you* trust *me*? You still believe I was responsible for my grandfather's death."

"And you believe I conspired with Calvin to kill you."

268

"So once again we come to an impasse."

"Not necessarily. I don't believe you killed your grandfather. You're not capable of murder."

Dante sent her a startled look. "What changed your mind? I thought Lonsdale had convinced you of my guilt."

"I neither trust nor believe Calvin."

Dante stiffened. "What did he do to you besides spread malicious gossip?"

"He's proved untrustworthy in many ways. Calvin isn't half the man you are."

Dante grinned. "Is that a compliment? Dare I believe you aren't too displeased with your choice of husband? You could have wed Lonsdale, you know."

"Whether you believe me or not, I wanted this marriage, Dante."

"Why?"

"Because . . ." She paused, choosing her words carefully. "Maybe because you please me in bed." Esme was determined to guard her heart until she knew where she stood in Dante's affections.

The light went out of Dante's eyes. What had he expected her to say? That she was passionately in love with him?

"If that's all you expect of me, then you won't be disappointed. My passion is yours to command."

But not your heart.

Esme was unprepared when he scooped her up and settled her onto his lap. She didn't resist. How could she, when she aching for his touch?

"That wasn't much of a kiss I gave you to seal our vows," Dante murmured. "I can do better."

His mouth claimed hers with a possessiveness that

startled her. His kiss was savage in its intensity, consuming, a fair warning of his intentions this night. His hands roamed over her body, beneath her cloak but over her gown, seeking the lush curves that would soon be his to lay bare. Esme's head was spinning when he abruptly removed her from his lap.

They had reached their destination, and Esme hadn't even been aware that the carriage had stopped. The coachman opened the door and put down the steps. Dante exited first and handed Esme down.

"Welcome to your new home, milady."

The front door opened before they reached it. Esme walked inside, then halted, surprised to see that the entire staff had turned out to greet her. Grayson, whom she already knew, introduced each servant in turn, beginning with Mrs. Winters, the housekeeper, and continuing on to the maids, footmen, cook and her helpers. After the introductions, Grayson dismissed the staff with a wave. Dante took Esme's hand and led her toward the stairs.

Grayson stopped Dante with look. "What is it, Grayson?"

"You have visitors. They are waiting for you in the study."

Grayson's expression convinced Dante that he should see the visitors immediately. "Very well. Show milady to the master suite and see that her bag is delivered to her chamber." He turned to Esme. "This shouldn't take long."

Dante watched Esme ascend the stairs before turning away. Whoever was waiting for him was going to get short shrift, for a man's wedding night was no time to be greeting visitors.

Dante walked into the study, his churlish mood lifting the moment he saw who awaited him. "Grandmother! Grandfather!"

Carlotta gathered Dante in her arms and held him tightly, while Sandor patted him on the back repeatedly, as if to assure himself that he was well and whole.

"I thought you were at your winter campground. Had I known you were coming, I would have delayed my wedding."

"I told you so," Carlotta said to Sandor. "My crystal ball never lies." She sent Dante a sheepish look. "We knew about your wedding but did not want to interfere where we were not wanted."

"Not wanted! I will always want you," Dante said fiercely. "You are the only parents I have ever known; no one will look down their nose at you as long as I am alive."

Sandor spread his hands. "We are gypsies. We have no illusions about our place in this world. We do not want to shame you before the *ton*."

"As if you could," Dante scoffed. "I doubt society will ever accept me despite my exalted rank." He shrugged. "It matters not. I will probably make my home at one of my country estates. I have more than one property, I'm told, and intend to visit London only when Parliament is in session."

"Has your wound healed properly? I worried that you left before you were well enough to ride."

"I'm fine, Grandmother. Where did you leave your wagon? I didn't see it when I arrived home."

"Grayson told us to take it around to the mews," Sandor said. He glanced at Carlotta. "We should go. This is Dante's wedding night."

271

Connie Mason

"Nonsense. This is your home as well as mine," Dante replied. "The house is large enough for you to have your own suite. I'd like to keep you with me always, but I know you are wanderers."

"It's our life," Sandor said simply. He looked at Carlotta. "What do you say, wife? Shall we stay with our grandson for a while, or return to our people now that we know Dante is well?"

Carlotta searched Dante's face. "I sense danger. We cannot leave yet."

Dante grinned. "I can take care of myself, Grandmother, but Esme and I welcome your company."

"I'm happy for you, Dante. My fondest wish for you was a love match."

Dante hated to disappoint Carlotta, but she had to know the truth. "Ours isn't a love match, Grandmother. We married because Grandfather Alston's will made my inheritance dependent upon it."

"Is that the only reason?"

"Lord Parkton was going to offer Esme to Lonsdale," Dante admitted. "There was no way in hell I would allow that to happen. You know I never wanted the title or fortune, but I was determined to keep it out of Lonsdale's hands. The only way to do that was to wed Esme."

"Why do you deny your love for milady?"

Dante looked away; Carlotta read him too easily. "There is no love involved. I don't trust Esme. She has said nothing to convince me she didn't conspire with Lonsdale to kill me."

"On the other hand, you have no evidence to connect her to the crime," Carlotta reminded him.

Dante sighed and glanced at the door.

Sandor took the hint. "Our grandson wishes to join his bride, Carlotta. We are interrupting his wedding night."

"We will speak further tomorrow," Dante said. "Grayson will show you to the east wing and see that you have everything you need."

He yanked on the bell pull. When Grayson appeared, Dante issued instructions, then bade his grandparents good night. Moments later, Dante took the stairs two at a time. This was his wedding night, and Esme awaited him.

Dante entered the bedchamber and closed the door firmly behind him. Esme arose from a chair beside the fire. The sight of her stole his breath away. He wanted to toss her on the bed, lift her skirts and thrust himself inside her. Inhaling deeply, he forced a calm he didn't feel.

"Who were your visitors?" Esme asked.

"My grandparents; they're going to stay with us awhile."

"What a shame they didn't arrive in time for the wedding."

"You don't mind them staying with us?"

Esme looked startled. "Of course not—why should I? I like your grandparents."

"They're gypsies," Dante reminded her.

"So are you, but I married you." She walked slowly toward him. He met her halfway.

"I'm glad you didn't undress," he whispered. "I wanted to do that for you."

Esme's violet eyes glittered. "I had no choice. You refused to allow Jane to accompany me, and I cannot reach the fastenings on my dress."

He held out his arms and brought her against him. He tasted her lips; his tongue explored her mouth, tentatively at first, then with growing urgency.

Abruptly he broke off the kiss and turned her around. "Let's get these clothes off you." He felt her tremble as he worked the buttons free at the back of her gown, his fingers lingering possessively on her skin. He wanted her naked in his arms, every lush inch of her bared to his hands and mouth. He disrobed her with swift urgency, his fingers uncharacteristically clumsy. It had been so long; he couldn't wait to be inside her. He was hard as stone and growing harder. But he could be patient; he wanted to give Esme as much pleasure as he intended to take.

To slow himself down, he took several deep breaths. Once he regained control, he began kissing her breasts. He felt her shudder, felt her nipples swell and harden. His lips moved toward the throbbing pulse in her throat and nuzzled it. She was sweet, so very sweet.

He pulled her toward the bed. She resisted. "Wait." Her hands went to the buttons of his coat, her eyes pleading.

He removed her hands and quickly stripped himself to the waist. Her gaze lingered on the bulge straining against his trousers.

"You want me," she whispered.

"I've never denied that."

"We can make this marriage work if you give it a chance."

He ripped open the buttons of his trousers and stepped out of them. "You talk too much." Reaching for her, he lifted her high and dropped her on the bed. The bed squeaked in protest as he stretched out beside her.

She touched his chest in a lingering caress. He shivered, trying to control the spasms her touch created. Her hand continued its downward exploration, along the skin stretched taut over the ridged muscles of his hard body, leaving fire in its wake.

He pulled her against him, melding their bodies, breast to breast, loins to loins, kindling a blaze he feared would take a lifetime to extinguish. Passion flared, spiraling out of control, so great it threatened to consume him. His mouth found hers, ravaged it, insatiable, wanting more. Nothing mattered but this moment as their bodies forged an unbreakable link.

His hand slid downward, his middle finger thrusting deep into her moist core. Her sensitive flesh enveloped his finger completely. She waited in impatient hunger while his circling thrusts built her passion to a crescendo of raging need.

She inhaled sharply; she felt her breasts swelling against his chest. She moved her hand to his turgid sex, closed around it. He was hot and smooth, silky velvet over a hard, thick shaft. "Dante, I want . . ."

Dante's body jerked, his sex pulsing against her palm. "If you're trying to kill me, you're succeeding."

"I don't want you dead, I want you inside me."

"Not yet."

He removed her hand and loomed over her, the hard glint in his eyes a blatant signal of his need. A dark and heated desire hung heavy in the air as he slid down her body. His mouth found her breasts, his tongue her nipples, suckling each in turn until Esme feared they would burst from the pleasure his mouth was creating.

She watched in breathless anticipation as his mouth left her breasts, breathing fire on her skin as he wandered downward, past her navel to the tuft of hair between her legs. His tongue slipped between the folds of her sex. Esme cried out, writhing, lifting her hips to meet his questing mouth. Dante caught her hips, held her still so that he could lave her at his leisure, tasting and nipping playfully. Esme feared she would die of pleasure, and then his lips closed around the throbbing bud of her desire.

He sucked it between his teeth, nibbling it; Esme couldn't muffle her scream as she exploded into tiny shards of fractured light. Driven nearly wild, she squirmed to escape the blinding pleasure; it was too much, too intense, too overwhelming. But there was no escape. Dante held her steady and continued to nip and suck that little bud until every last burst of carnal pleasure subsided.

Only then did he lift his head and come over her, kissing her roughly, passionately, leaving the taste of her own body on her lips as he parted her thighs with his knees. The kiss went on and on as he pressed the tip of his erection against her heated center.

"No matter how much you lie to me, I want you more than I've desired any other woman," he whispered against her lips.

"I've never lied to you, Dante, except when I told you I didn't want to marry you. It wasn't easy for me to admit the truth."

He thrust upward, the hardness of him filling her, his jaw clamped, his eyes watchful. "What *is* the truth?"

"I love you, Dante. I suppose . . . I always have."

"So you say," Dante answered in a strained voice.

Esme brought her legs around his hips and flung her arms around his neck; she felt his sweat-slick muscles flex as he thrust again. How could she have ever thought Dante wasn't good enough for her? If there were any way she could change the past, she would. Then he began to thrust and withdraw, destroying thought, making her writhe and cry out, her reawakened passion asserting itself in the most elemental way. Waves of intense heat started at the juncture of her thighs and shot up through her veins.

"You're mine," Dante growled. "No other man will ever know you this way."

He pumped faster, harder, plunging deep, his jaw clamped, his body straining. Esme tilted her hips, giving him unlimited access to the very core of her. Seconds before she found release again, she heard his shallow breathing, felt the shudder that wracked him, saw the grimace of pleasure that twisted his features as he buried himself deep with a single stroke and gave up his essence to her.

Dante moaned and collapsed. His body felt heavy, languid, spent. He withdrew, his sex glistening and wet, a once mighty sword now sated and limp. With a groan, he lifted himself off and away from her.

Dante had wanted to prolong the pleasure, to savor every nuance of their joining, but raw need had conquered him. A deep, burning hunger had built swiftly inside him, destroying his control. Now, as his body still shuddered with the aftermath of pleasure, one glaring fact remained.

He would kill any man who tried to take Esme from him.

He might not trust her, she might consider him inferior to her, but she was his.

Wrapped in each other's arms, they drifted off to sleep.

It was still night when Dante woke. The chamber was dark but for the glowing embers in the fireplace. He could feel the chill in the air and brought the covers up over Esme before he climbed out of bed and built up the fire. Then he walked to the washstand, poured water from a pitcher into a bowl and washed himself. By the time he rejoined Esme, he was thoroughly chilled and shivering.

"You're cold," Esme murmured. "Where did you go?"

"I thought you were sleeping. I left the bed to build up the fire. Go back to sleep."

She snuggled against him. "I can't."

A tortured groan rumbled from Dante's chest. "Neither can I with you plastered against me."

"Then neither of us are going to get any sleep tonight," Esme promised as she rolled on top of him.

He pulled her head down to his and kissed her, at the same time rolling her beneath him. Esme muttered a frustrated groan when he lifted himself off her and left the bed. "Where are you going now?"

He walked to the washstand, wet a cloth and returned to the bed. Then he pulled the cover down and carefully washed all traces of himself from between her legs. "I want to make you more comfortable before we begin again." When he finished, he tossed the cloth aside and took her into his arms. "Now where were we?"

Esme rolled on top of him again. "Right here." This time she initiated the kiss. Dante's arms went around her, but she squirmed out of his grasp and scooted down his body, her flesh scorching his as she kissed her way down his chest, past his navel to his . . .

Bloody hell! He nearly arched off the bed when she took the head of his erection in her mouth and ran her tongue around the rim and then down the distended length of his sex. Dante feared he would die on the spot when she sucked and then blew on the engorged tip.

"You're killing me, woman!"

She glanced at him through long, sooty lashes, her violet eyes seductively dark and provocative. "If I *did* want you dead, this would be a perfect time. You do like this, don't you?" Her mouth returned to him, sucking him deep into her throat.

Dante growled, pulled her up and rolled her atop him so that she straddled him. "You've had your way long enough, milady."

He opened her with his fingers, flexed his hips and thrust deep; the throbbing depths of her body welcomed him. With each stroke, Esme pressed downward, drawing him into her deepest core. Head thrown back, she rode him ruthlessly, desperately seeking that place of final fulfillment. His fingers slipped between their bodies, finding the source of her need, stroking it into a hard nub.

Esme was nearly insensate as tumultuous sensations built and multiplied, hastened by the delicious stroking of Dante's fingers, his hardness filling her, stretching her. Pleasure spiraled upward until she could bear it no longer. Arching her back, she convulsed uncontrollably, and then fell against him, muffling her cries in the curve of his neck.

Dante continued with a low growl, driving hard into her quivering center until a raw sound ripped from his throat and he pulsed violently inside her.

They remained locked together for a long, breathless moment, neither of them wanting to break the spell that joined them. Esme could have remained that way forever. Her eyes were closed, damp lashes clinging to her cheeks. When he lifted her away from him, she bit her lip to keep from moaning a protest.

Long after Dante had fallen asleep again, Esme lay awake, plagued by emotions plummeting out of control. Dante had bedded her like a man in love. Did the gypsy lover make love to all women with the same relentless ardor? How could she restore his trust in her?

The answer came quickly. To earn Dante's trust, she had to learn who had been behind the attempts on his life.

The task she set for herself wouldn't be an easy one, especially since Dante had forbidden her to see or speak to Calvin. Though Esme hated to go against Dante's wishes, it was necessary if their marriage was to survive.

With her plans more or less set, Esme curled herself around her husband's body and drifted off to sleep.

Chapter Seventeen

Dante was gone when Esme awoke the next morning. She stretched and smiled, warming from head to toe when she recalled her wedding night. Since Dante had married her for the wrong reasons, she hadn't known what to expect, but Dante's loving had exceeded her wildest dreams. Still smiling, she climbed out of bed and rang for Jane.

Jane opened the door and bustled inside. "His Lordship told me to let you sleep as long as you liked," she said, opening the blinds and gathering up discarded clothing. "Would you like a bath? There's water heating in the kitchen."

"I'd love a bath. When did you arrive?"

"Early this morning with the baggage." She probed Esme with a hard look. "Are you all right? You seemed a bit dazed when you left your uncle's townhouse after the wedding."

"I'm fine, Jane, truly. You thought Dante might hurt me, didn't you?"

"After everything that's happened, I wasn't sure.

But I can see you're satisfied with the match. I'm happy for you, milady."

Esme's smile faded. "There's a catch. My husband doesn't trust me. But I intend to change his opinion very soon."

Jane's attention sharpened. "What are you planning now? Nothing good, I suspect. Don't go looking for trouble."

"Trouble already exists, Jane. There is no way our marriage can thrive without trust, and I intend for this marriage to be a happy one. I'm going to fix it, Jane, just you wait and see."

Jane flung up her hands. "You worry me, milady."

"Dante is the one in danger, not I. Attempts have been made on his life, and I intend to find the culprit before the next attempt succeeds."

"Lord have mercy on us all," Jane muttered. "Let Lord Alston handle this. Think about that while I fetch your bathwater."

Esme's thoughts turned to Dante. Where was he now? If something happened to Dante before he produced an heir, Calvin would inherit. That was a frightening thought. She had to stop Calvin before he struck again, or else proved he was innocent of shooting Dante, which was looking more and more doubtful.

Servants arrived with the tub and hot water. Once all was in readiness, Esme climbed into her bath and let Jane minister to her.

"His Lordship's grandparents arrived last night," Jane said conversationally.

"I know. I'm looking forward to seeing them again."

"Have you had time to explore the mansion? It's

enormous. Lord Alston must be vastly wealthy. The housekeeper showed me around the kitchen and servants' quarters this morning. I can't wait to see the rest of the house."

Feeling clean and relaxed, Esme stepped out of the tub. Jane wrapped a towel around her and dried her hair.

"What will you wear today, milady? Most of your clothes are still packed, but I did manage to press the yellow morning dress and the blue day gown while you were sleeping."

"The blue, I think," Esme replied. "Hurry with my hair, I'm starving."

Jane smirked. "I wonder why."

Esme ignored her. "Don't do anything fancy with my hair. I'll wear it down, tied back with a ribbon."

"All done," Jane said a few minutes later, standing back to inspect Esme's appearance. "You'll do. I'll stay here and unpack your trunks while you're at breakfast. Will you be going out today?"

"I don't know. I need to speak to Dante before I make plans."

Esme found her way downstairs but had to be directed by a footman to the sun-drenched breakfast room at the back of the house. Apparently, everyone had eaten and left, for she was the only one dining this morning.

Grayson hovered at her elbow. "What would you like to eat this morning, milady? Cook will prepare whatever you like."

"Has everyone else eaten?" Esme asked.

"His Lordship is an early riser, and so, apparently, are his grandparents. They all broke their fast hours ago."

"Where is Lord Alston now?" Esme asked, feeling stupid for not knowing where her husband had gotten off to.

"At work in the study. Your breakfast, milady—what shall I tell cook?"

"I usually just have tea and toasted bread, but this morning I'd like eggs and ham if it's not too much trouble."

"No trouble at all. I'll tell cook and send your tea in with Grimes."

"Would you inform His Lordship that I'd like a word with him?" Esme asked.

"Right away, milady."

Grayson left. Dante entered the dining room a few minutes later. "Grayson said you wished to speak with me."

"Will you join me? I don't like to eat alone."

Dante pulled out a chair across from her. "I already ate, but I'll have coffee."

Grimes appeared with a carafe each of coffee and tea. He poured according to their wishes and left.

"Is there something important you wished to discuss?" Dante asked.

Why is he acting so cold? Esme wondered. "I wanted to know your plans for the day."

Dante's dark brows snapped together. "Is there a reason for this line of questioning?"

What was wrong with him? Had he forgotten our closeness last night? "If you're in danger, I want to know where you're going."

Dante sent her an oddly tender look. "I can take care of myself, Esme."

Esme glared her disapproval. "Does that mean you're not going to let me help you?"

"Help me do what?"

"Protect yourself."

Dante had the audacity to laugh. Esme fumed. His arrogance was exceeded only by his stubbornness.

"Except for calling on Mr. Bartholomew, I have no plans for today. I'd like to spend time with my grandparents while they're here."

Esme's breakfast arrived. She waited until Grimes left, then said, "I thought they were staying with us indefinitely."

"That's what I'd like, but they are nomads, unaccustomed to mansions and servants to wait upon them. They might decide to leave at any time."

Esme dug into her eggs and ham. The food tasted especially good this morning.

"You must be hungry," Dante observed.

"Famished. I scarcely tasted our wedding feast."

"I noticed." His dark eyes glinted mischievously. "You didn't get much sleep last night, either."

Esme's cheeks burned. "Whose fault was that?"

"I didn't hear you complain."

"No, Dante, I didn't complain. My wedding night was everything I hoped it would be."

Her serious reply seemed to surprise Dante. Visibly flustered, he changed the subject. "Is there anything in particular you'd like to do today? Newlyweds are expected to be seen out and about. I thought a drive through the park would be nice; the weather is especially fine for a late autumn day."

"I would like that," Esme replied. "What about your grandparents?"

"I asked, but they declined. If you've finished eating, they are waiting to welcome you to the family. Mrs. Clarke, the housekeeper, will show you around later."

Esme rose. "I'm eager to see your grandparents and acquaint myself with your home. It's far grander than I imagined."

Dante escorted her to the back parlor. Carlotta sat mending while Sandor peered restlessly out the window at the garden. They both smiled at Esme.

"I'll leave you alone to get reacquainted," Dante said, leaving her at the door. "I'll be in the study with my secretary if you need me."

Sandor reached Esme first and gave her a quick hug. "Welcome to the family, milady. We are pleased with our grandson's choice of wife."

"Thank you," Esme said, touched by Sandor's warmth.

Carlotta joined them and grasped Esme's hands. "Sandor speaks the truth, milady. We couldn't be happier. We've waited a long time for Dante to find love."

"Oh, but . . ." What could Esme say? That Dante held no tender feelings for her? That the Alston title and wealth meant more to him than she did? That she loved while Dante didn't?

"Come sit down," Carlotta said, leading Esme to a chair close to where she had been sitting. "There is something you wish to tell us, is there not?"

How did Carlotta know? Esme hesitated. Did she dare unburden her heart to Dante's grandmother?

"Do not be shy, milady. When I look into your eyes, I see love for my grandson."

Esme squirmed in her chair. Was Carlotta clairvoyant? "Please call me Esme. We are family."

Carlotta nodded. "Very well, Esme. You may say anything you wish to us."

"I don't know if I dare. My maid has been my only confidant since my mother died. But there is something I want you to know. It's important that you believe I had nothing to do with the attempt on Dante's life."

"We know that," Sandor interjected. "But our grandson is a stubborn man. He never came to grips with the fact that he had been abandoned by his noble parent. Though we provided all the love he needed, he still felt his life was missing something."

"Dante has always been comfortable in his own skin," Carlotta added, "but beneath that skin beats a wounded heart."

"My prejudices against gypsies didn't help," Esme admitted. "But I no longer feel that way and regret that I ever did. I love Dante. Making him believe I care isn't going to be easy. He thinks I planned his death with Lord Lonsdale."

"Did you?" Sandor asked.

"No! I met with Calvin in the woods the day Dante was shot but it wasn't to plan his death. I wanted to tell Calvin that I planned to marry Dante. I didn't want to leave Dante, but Calvin forced me. I didn't even know Dante had been shot until he returned to London."

Carlotta stared deep into Esme's eyes. Esme couldn't look away, couldn't even blink. With one piercing look, it seemed as if Carlotta had reached down inside Esme to her soul. Did she find it lacking?

"I believe you," Carlotta said.

Esme nearly collapsed with relief. "What can I do to convince Dante?"

"You will find a way. Nothing I can say will convince him. That must come from you." She held out her hand. "May I read your palm?"

Without hesitation, Esme placed her hand in Carlotta's. Carlotta turned her palm up and stared intently. "You and my grandson will live a long and happy life," she said in a singsong voice, "but first you must resolve a dangerous situation. I see children . . . more than one."

Dangerous was the word that jumped out at Esme. "Tell me about the danger."

Carlotta's brow furrowed in concentration. "That part is not clear to me."

"You said we would live a long and happy life."

"And so you shall . . . if you and Dante survive this roadblock to happiness."

"Does Dante know he's in danger?"

Carlotta nodded sagely. "He knows, but he brushes it aside."

"Make him believe it," Esme urged. "Make him promise to be careful."

Dante chose that moment to reappear. "Who needs to be careful?"

"You. I told your wife that you need to be cautious in your dealings."

Esme gave Carlotta a grateful smile.

Dante glanced from Esme to Carlotta, and then to Sandor, who nodded without comment. "I can take care of myself. Please don't worry. I stopped by to tell you I'm going out for a while."

"Where are you going?"

The concern in Esme's voice touched Dante. "Mr. Bartholomew has some papers for me to sign, and I want to pick up the financial statements he has prepared for me. I thought I'd drop by his office and take care of it this morning. I'll be back in plenty of time for our outing in the park."

"Perhaps I should come with you."

Frustrated, Dante shoved his hands through his hair. "Esme, marriage doesn't mean we should be connected at the hip. Haven't you got something to do this morning? Calls to make, that sort of thing? I thought you wanted a tour of the house."

"What if someone makes another attempt on your life?"

Dante stared at her. "Are you trying to tell me something? Has Lonsdale planned another surprise for me?"

"How could I possibly know what Calvin is planning?"

"I don't have time for this," Dante said. "I'll see you later."

"He's angry," Esme said after Dante left. "How can I protect him if he won't let me?"

"You'll find a way," Carlotta said with a certainty that Esme wished she felt.

Dante found his horse waiting at the front entrance. He mounted, took the reins from the stable lad and cantered down the street. He smiled at Esme's offer to accompany him, chuckling all the way to the solicitor's office. He had married a tigress.

When Dante had encountered her in the breakfast room, he wanted to scoop her into his arms and carry her back to bed. What was wrong with him? He couldn't stop thinking about her. His mind refused to function on any other level. He could picture Esme naked, Esme beneath him, on top of him, his cock inside her.

He could almost feel her mouth on him, his mouth on her, in her, her taste on his lips. He shifted in the saddle; his trousers suddenly felt too tight. His loins ached. He couldn't wait to bed Esme again. It was going to be a struggle to contain his lust until bedtime. Esme already had more power over him than he had intended to give her, more than she deserved. If he could trust Esme, he would be free to love her with his whole heart. But would that day ever come?

Dante finished his business with Bartholomew quickly and decided to stop in at White's. He spotted Viscount Lonsdale and headed in another direction. Lonsdale caught up with him, forcing Dante to acknowledge him. "I understand congratulations are in order," Lonsdale said. "I read the announcement in the *Times* yesterday. I'm surprised to see you out and about already. Apparently, marriage doesn't agree with you."

"Be careful, Lonsdale, you go too far," Dante bit out in a voice that should have warned the viscount.

"Everyone knows why you wed Esme."

"Lady Alston to you."

Disregarding the harshness of Dante's voice, Lonsdale forged ahead. "You were forced to wed *Lady Alston* in order to keep my uncle's title and fortune. I'm actually glad you took her off my hands. Whores are cheap and readily available."

The muscles in Dante's jaw tautened and his dark eyes narrowed as waves of rage seethed through him. "No one insults my wife and gets away with it."

Dante was unaware that a crowd had gathered around them until he heard someone whisper, "A duel!"

Dante had no intention of challenging Lonsdale. His education hadn't included fencing lessons. He was well acquainted with firearms but didn't want to kill Lonsdale. Not until the viscount confessed to his myriad crimes. Instead of issuing a challenge, which the avid onlookers expected, Dante clenched his fist, drew back his arm and felled Lonsdale with an uppercut to the chin.

"The man's an animal," one fellow said, not without admiration.

"Uncivilized," another proclaimed.

"Simply not the way to handle these things," a third man sniffed.

Unfazed by the remarks, Dante faced the crowd and calmly asked, "Has anyone seen Lord Brookworth?"

"Here I am," Brookworth said, pushing his way through the crowd. "Very nicely done; couldn't have managed it better myself. This calls for a drink. Will you join me?"

The crowd parted as Dante and Brookworth headed toward a secluded corner where two chairs awaited them.

"Lonsdale had no business goading you," Brookworth said. "I suspect he wanted you to challenge him. I hear he's an exceptional swordsman, and equally skilled with a pistol."

"Dueling is illegal. Besides, I have no intention of giving Lonsdale a chance to kill me. I'll meet him on equal terms, but not on the dueling field."

"Within the hour this incident will become fodder for the gossip mill. I wouldn't be surprised if your popularity increases after today."

Dante gaped at Brookworth; then his lips curved into a smile. "I can just hear it now. 'The gypsy is an animal. He laid Lonsdale low with one blow. He's too uncivilized to duel like a gentleman.'"

Brookworth nodded. "All that and more. I wouldn't be surprised if invitations to the most fashionable events begin pouring in. All of the *ton* will want to see the man who duels with fists instead of sword or pistol. I daresay the women will swoon over you."

"I'm sure Esme will *love* that."

"So tell me, what happened while you were away from London? We had little opportunity for a private chat at your wedding. Where did you go?"

"Chasing after Esme. Don't ask; it's a long story. There is one thing that might interest you. I was shot while visiting my grandparents at their encampment near Heath. I remained with them until I healed enough to return to London."

"What? Who did it?"

"I don't know, but I suspect Lonsdale. He was known to be in the vicinity at the time."

Brookworth's gaze slid over Dante. "You look healthy enough now."

"Aye, thanks to Grandmother's healing skills. Have you learned anything helpful about Lonsdale in my absence?"

"One piece of information I uncovered might interest you. I followed Lonsdale down to the docks one day. He met with a couple of unsavory-looking characters. I didn't want to be seen, so I didn't hear what they said."

"What business could Lonsdale have with waterfront riffraff?" Dante wondered. "Thank you; that information could prove useful." He rose. "If you'll excuse me, I promised my bride I'd take her riding in the park."

"I'll keep my eye on Lonsdale, and so will Carstairs," Brookworth promised. "Fear not—we'll get to the bottom of these attempts on your life."

Dante was given a wide berth as he strode out the door. He knew what the *ton* was thinking and didn't care. No man, whatever his rank or popularity, was going to insult his wife and get away with it.

Dante arrived home in plenty of time to change clothes for his outing in the park. He was quite looking forward to letting society know that Lonsdale's slurs against Esme had little effect on him. Esme was his wife now, and under his protection. He had fulfilled the terms of his grandfather's will, and nothing could change that.

Esme entered their chamber shortly after Dante; she held several envelopes in her hand.

"What have you there?" Dante asked.

"Invitations," Esme said, waving the envelopes in front of him. "They just arrived. It appears we are suddenly all the rage. I never expected this."

Dante slipped his arms into the coat Simpson held for him. Brookworth had been right. Everyone wanted a look at the "uncivilized gypsy" who had attacked Viscount Lonsdale. "Do you wish to attend any of them?"

"I think we should make an appearance at most of them. It's expected of us."

"Very well. I'll leave that up to you since I know little about these things. Are you ready for our outing?"

"Oh, yes. I love the park. I dressed for a carriage ride; that's what you intended, isn't it?"

"Yes. But if you prefer something more strenuous, we can ride our horses along Rotten Row tomorrow morning, weather permitting."

"I love to ride. Uncle Daniel sent my mare over with a groom this morning."

"Where are my grandparents?" Dante asked.

"They went to the mews to check on their wagon. I don't think they like living in a house, and yours is so grand. Your grandfather certainly did live well."

"Yes, didn't he," Dante said dryly. "I talked to Bartholomew this morning about doing something worthwhile with my money. He didn't seem too pleased, but it's my money to do with as I wish. I'm still mulling over options."

Esme looked stunned and pleased at the same time. "No one can claim you're not a generous man, Dante. What charities do you have in mind?"

"Let's discuss this later. Weather this time of year is unpredictable, and I want to take advantage of what little sunshine is left before clouds move in." He offered his arm. "Shall we go?"

A well-sprung curricle and a matched pair of bays were standing at the curb, another of the former Lord Alston's luxuries. Dante handed Esme up, then climbed onto the driver's bench and released the brake. It was a fine autumn day with a hint of winter in the air. Most of London society must have had the same idea, for the walkways and roads were crowded with strollers, carriages and riders. As soon as Dante was recognized, people turned to stare and point.

"Whatever is the matter?" Esme asked. "Why are people staring at us?"

"Perhaps it's because of the altercation I had at White's this morning."

Esme gaped at him. "What kind of altercation?"

"It need not concern you."

"It most certainly does concern me," Esme huffed. "I'm your wife, or have you forgotten?"

Dante's smile could easily be taken for a leer. "How could I have forgotten after our wedding night? I can hardly wait for a repeat performance. No one can say we're not compatible in that area."

"Don't change the subject. I want to know what happened at White's."

Just then a young dandy rode up beside them, forcing Dante to slow down. "We haven't met yet, my lord. I'm Lord Hurlton. Your expertise at fisticuffs was most impressive, my lord. Perhaps you'd care to join my friends and me one day at Gentleman Jim's establishment. We could use a few pointers."

"I rarely engage in fisticuffs, Lord Hurlton," Dante said. "This morning was an exception."

Dante flicked the reins against the horses' rumps and they stepped out smartly, leaving Lord Hurlton behind.

"What did you do?" Esme asked. "You may as well tell me, since everyone seems to know but me."

"I took exception to something Lonsdale said today at White's."

"You struck him?"

Amusement colored his words. "I didn't have my knife handy."

"How many people saw you hit him?"

"I didn't count."

Esme groaned. Obviously, Dante wasn't aware of the seriousness of his offense. How could society approve of him if he went around hitting people?

"What did Calvin say to anger you?"

"You don't need to know."

Esme flushed. It was obvious that Calvin had insulted her, forcing Dante to defend her honor. She needed to speak with Calvin before any more damage was done.

When the wind shifted around to the north, people

began scurrying for their homes. Dante turned the carriage around and joined the exodus from the park.

Lord Parkton was waiting for them. Grayson had put him in the study and provided him with refreshments. Esme reached the study first, with Dante close on her heels.

Esme kissed her uncle's cheek. "What brings you here, Uncle?"

"I heard some disturbing news today," Parkton said, looking directly at Dante.

"If you're referring to that unfortunate altercation at White's, I already know about it," Esme said. "Calvin goaded Dante, my husband had no choice."

"I worry about you, Esme. Lonsdale is spreading some nasty gossip. I thought it would die down after you wed Alston, but apparently it hasn't."

"I'll take care of Lonsdale, Lord Parkton," Dante said.

Parkton stared at him. "I like you, Alston, I really do, but you handled things badly today. Most men would have issued a challenge. Resorting to fisticuffs is unseemly."

"I didn't want to kill Lonsdale. Not until I have what I need from him."

"He might challenge you after you attacked him today."

Dante laughed. "He's too much of a coward."

"I'm worried about Esme. I don't want her caught in the middle of your vendetta."

"Perhaps I should have a talk with Calvin," Esme suggested.

Both men spoke at the same time. "No!"

"There is nothing you could say to him that either Alston or I can't," Parkton said.

Esme glanced at Dante. He glared a warning at her. His message was clear. He didn't want her anywhere near Calvin, because he still didn't trust her.

Parkton went on his way. Then Dante left to find his grandparents. Esme found herself at loose ends. She sat down to think. She didn't care what Dante said, or how much he disapproved, she needed to speak to Calvin. Not one to put off till tomorrow what she could do today, Esme left the study and hurried to her room to retrieve her reticule and cloak.

She left the house through the kitchen door while cook had her back turned. She knew where Calvin lived and hailed a passing hackney. During the short drive to Calvin's townhouse, a plan began to form in her head. She needed to learn the truth about the elder Lord Alston's death before another death occurred . . . a death that would destroy her.

The hackney rolled to a stop. Esme alighted and paid the driver. Marshaling her courage, she marched up the stairs and rapped on the door. The dour butler who opened it looked down his haughty nose at her.

"Is Lord Lonsdale at home?" Esme asked.

"He's not receiving."

"Would you please inform him that Lady Alston is here? I'm sure he'll see me."

"He's not to be disturbed for any reason, milady. Perhaps you can leave a card and come back another day."

"I'm sure he'll see me if you'd just tell him I'm here," Esme insisted, her voice rising in anger.

"What in blazes is all the ruckus about?"

Esme turned at the sound of Calvin's voice. He stood at the top of the stairs, a scowl darkening his face. He started down the steps, but faltered when he recognized Esme.

"Is that you, Esme?"

"I know you weren't expecting me, Calvin, but this will only take a few minutes of your time."

Lonsdale continued down. "You may go, Bumble."

Bumble sniffed and shuffled off.

Lonsdale sent her a knowing smirk. "I knew you'd turn to me for help. Come into the study and tell me what happened. We won't be disturbed there."

Praying she was doing the right thing, Esme followed Calvin into the study.

Chapter Eighteen

Lonsdale seated Esme on a worn leather sofa and sat down beside her. "Tell me what brings you here," he asked.

Esme saw the dark bruise marring his chin and quickly looked away. "I'm sorry about what happened at White's today, but you shouldn't have taunted Dante."

"He told you?"

"Of course he did. Dante might not have acted like a gentleman, but neither did you. Whatever possessed you to spread gossip about me? I don't know what you said, but it must have been despicable for Dante to react as he did."

"Not as despicable as a gypsy bastard assuming control of one of the oldest and most respected titles in the kingdom. It's inconceivable and totally wrong. The title should have been mine."

"How badly did you want it, Calvin? Enough to kill for it?"

"What in blazes are you talking about?"

"More than one attempt has been made on Dante's life since he came into the title. You're the only one who would benefit from his death. Were you behind those attempts? Did you shoot Dante that day you met me in the woods near the gypsy encampment?"

Calvin shot out of his chair. "Good God! Do you really believe me capable of murder?"

"Dante does, and I'm beginning to think he's right. You have everything to gain from his death and nothing to lose."

Calvin began to pace. "I admit I was angry and still am, but murder?" He swung around to confront Esme. "I can't believe you just accused me of a heinous crime."

"If not you, then who?"

"I have no idea. Apparently, the gypsy has enemies."

Esme searched his face. "Are you one of them? Why did you goad Dante at White's? Why are you spreading malicious gossip about me?"

"Why does any man lash out at people who hurt him? Being disinherited nearly destroyed me. My pride suffered, and I wanted to strike back. I was using you to hurt Alston, but I realize now that it hurt you too. I apologize."

"Apologizing will do little to mitigate Dante's suspicions. He believes you murdered his grandfather."

Calvin's face drained of all color. "Murder! That . . . that's preposterous! His death was a suicide. I was only trying to make trouble for the gypsy when I accused him of murdering Uncle Alston. I never once thought his death was anything but suicide."

"Apparently, Dante has reason to believe otherwise. He's determined to prove you guilty of the crime."

Calvin sat down . . . hard, his fear palpable. "You've got to help me, Esme. I didn't kill anyone, nor did I try to harm your husband. I did attempt to stop you from marrying the gypsy, and I did force you to leave the gypsy encampment, and I might have told you some lies about Alston, but that's all I did. You have to believe me."

The wild look, the fear Esme saw in Calvin's eyes convinced her of his innocence. Though Calvin might be guilty of many things, murder wasn't one of them. "I may regret it, but I do believe you. But it's Dante you have to convince, not me."

"Will you help me? Will you defend me to Alston? If you don't, I fear your husband will kill me."

Esme shook her head. "Dante won't kill you, but if he finds evidence against you, he'll turn you over to the law."

Calvin lowered his head to his hands, his voice filled with despair. "I'm in enough trouble as it is. I'm deep in dun territory and hounded by creditors and unscrupulous moneylenders who didn't seek payment until now because they believed I was in line to inherit Uncle Alston's wealth. But now that I've been disinherited, I'm being pursued. If I don't pay soon, I'm going to end up dead or in debtors' prison."

"Do you swear you didn't murder your uncle or try to kill Dante?"

Calvin lifted his head. His eyes were desperate, pleading. "I swear on the graves of my parents. I'll find the family Bible and swear on that if you'd like."

Esme considered him for a long time, recognizing his desperation, his near panic. She had never thought Calvin capable of murder, and after hearing him out, she knew she had been right. But convincing Dante wasn't going to be easy. One of the problems was the lack of suspects once Calvin was eliminated. No one else would gain from Dante's death.

Esme rose to leave. "I'll do what I can, but I'm not a miracle worker, and believe me, it's going to take a miracle to find another suspect. Meanwhile, don't do anything further to anger Dante."

Calvin walked her to the door. "Thank you, Esme. I would have made you a good husband, whether you believe it or not. Today at White's I was hurt and angry and reacted in an ungentlemanly way. I hope you will forgive me."

"Let's not talk of forgiveness, Calvin. It's too soon for that. As for Dante, I can't promise he'll listen to me, or even take his investigation in another direction once I voice my opinion that you're innocent."

Esme left Lonsdale's townhouse deep in thought. During the hackney ride home, she pondered everything Calvin had told her. Was believing in his innocence a mistake she'd live to regret?

Dante had been beside himself with worry when he couldn't locate Esme. None of the servants had seen her leave the house, which added to his concern. Where could she have gone? Why hadn't she told him she was going out? Did Esme's leaving have anything to do with Lonsdale?

He sincerely hoped not.

When Esme hadn't returned after an hour, Dante sent footmen out looking for her. He imagined all kinds of terrifying scenarios. If something had happened to her, heads would roll. Dante was preparing to join the search when he heard the front door open and close, and then the murmur of voices. He opened the study door and nearly collapsed with relief when he saw Esme handing her cloak and reticule to Grayson.

Relief was soon replaced by anger, and then by rage. How dare she frighten him like that? Didn't she know the streets of London were dangerous? She hadn't even taken her maid with her. Dante stood in the doorway, fists clenched, waiting for Esme to join him.

"Grayson said you wanted to see me," she said.

"Come in," Dante ordered.

Esme walked past him into the study, faltering beneath the weight of his disapproval. The door closed behind her. She sent him a tentative smile. "You look angry."

In a voice scarcely above a whisper, he said, "Anger doesn't begin to describe what I feel. Whatever possessed you to sneak off without telling anyone where you were going? Didn't you think I'd worry about you?"

"I wasn't in any danger."

"We won't know that until you tell me where you went."

Esme hesitated, her smile wobbling, then disappearing altogether when Dante's expression remained implacable.

"Please don't be angry."

Dante remained resolute. Though he didn't want to intimidate Esme, she had to know that he had enemies who might use her to get to him. "I want an explanation and I want it now."

Esme lowered herself into a chair and gazed up at him. She appeared wary but not frightened of him, though he thought she should be.

"Sit down, Dante. I don't like you towering over

me. What I'm going to tell you isn't what you want to hear, but you need to hear it nonetheless."

Dante sank into a chair, not in the least mollified. "Very well, you may begin."

"I want you to hear me through before you say anything."

"Bloody hell, Esme! Just tell me and get it over with."

"I went to Calvin's townhouse."

Dante lurched from his chair. "You did what?"

"Please, Dante, sit down and listen. You can voice your disapproval later."

Dante counted to ten. When that didn't ease his temper, he loosed a string of curses.

"Do you want to hear this or don't you?"

"Of course I do. I can't wait to hear why you felt compelled to visit Lonsdale without my knowledge."

"I wanted to find out if he was guilty of murder."

"You wanted . . . Damnation! Did you expect him to confess to you? Never mind, continue. I'm anxious to know what he had to say."

"He didn't murder your grandfather, Dante, nor did he try to kill you. I'm convinced of it."

Dante threw up his hands. "How gullible can you be? Let me get this straight. You went to Lonsdale and asked him flat out if he was guilty of murder."

Esme nodded.

"He denied it, and you believed him," Dante stated.

She nodded again.

"I never thought you were a fool, Esme, but what you did was foolish as well as dangerous. You didn't expect Lonsdale to confess to murder, did you? No man in his right mind would. *I* wouldn't."

"You didn't see him, Dante. He was truly shocked when I told him you suspected him of making attempts on your life. He's in deep trouble; merchants and moneylenders are hounding him, and he has accumulated gambling debts he can't pay."

"All the more reason he needs the Alston fortune. You don't want to believe Lonsdale capable of murder because you harbor tender feelings for him."

"That's not true!"

Dante began to pace. "You deliberately disobeyed me. I forbade you to see or speak to Lonsdale, and you agreed."

Esme's trembling chin angled upward. "I may be your wife, but you don't own me. I wanted to help you. I wanted to know if you should forget Calvin and look elsewhere for your grandfather's killer."

His words issued forth on a low growl. "Do you honestly believe Lonsdale is innocent?"

"I do. If his reaction was an act, he's the best actor I've ever seen."

"Forgive me for not agreeing with you. Lonsdale has a great deal to gain from my death. He killed Grandfather Alston because he thought he would inherit and desperately needed the money. When he learned Grandfather had changed his will in my favor, he came after me."

Esme shook her head. "You're wrong. I'd stake my life on it."

Dante searched her face, then issued a challenge. "Would you stake our marriage on his innocence?"

Esme regarded him gravely. Dante could almost see her mind working. He prayed she'd give the right answer, but knew she was naive enough to actually believe in Lonsdale's innocence.

305

After a long, tense pause, Esme said, "Yes, I would stake our marriage as well as my life on Calvin's innocence. Why can't you see that I'm trying to protect you? If all your attention is focused on the wrong person, the real killer is free to strike until he succeeds."

"That's enough, Esme! Do you think I'm stupid? No one—do you hear me?—no one stands to gain anything from my death but Lonsdale. I'm sorry you hold our marriage in such low regard."

He turned away from her. "You may go. Now that I know you're safe, I need to get back to these financial statements Bartholomew sent me. I can make no sense out of them, and neither can Luther."

Hands on hips, Esme pinned him with a pugnacious glare. "Why won't you believe me?"

He stared at her, the stark planes of his face hard as granite. "How do I know you didn't discuss my demise with Lonsdale? How can I believe anything you say?"

Esme's breath caught on a sob. "Dear God, you hate me."

Dante's expression softened. "I don't hate you. I want to trust you, I really do, but you're making it difficult."

"That's because you married me for the wrong reasons."

Damn her! Didn't she know he wanted her? His soul wanted her. His heart wanted her. His only issue with her was trust.

"I'm sorry, Dante, for both of us."

She turned and walked away.

"Esme."

She didn't stop. He reached her in three long strides, spun her around. He hadn't known what he intended until he touched her. One simple touch and the magic returned. The magic that was Esme.

He dragged her against him, stared into the deep purple of her eyes and then crushed her mouth with his. The kiss overwhelmed him with feelings, feelings that he tried to ignore, *had* to ignore. But still the kiss went on. She parted her lips, moaned; he thrust his tongue inside, tasting her, perhaps for the last time.

Something inside him shifted; he refused to heed the sensation, aware that it could lead to terrible consequences. Trust had to be earned, and thus far Esme hadn't earned his. He started to ease away from the kiss before he was driven to the point of no return. Esme's lips followed him. He shook free of her and thrust her away.

"That's just a sample of what you'll be missing, what your lies have cost us."

"I didn't know there was an us. You've made it abundantly clear that you don't trust me, couldn't love me, and that you married me to keep your title and wealth. Doubt me all you want, Dante; it won't stop me from trying to save your life."

Her head held high, Esme stormed off. Dante returned to his desk, too distraught to focus on business matters. All he could do was stare into space, wondering if he had been wrong to dismiss Esme's doubts about Lonsdale's guilt.

Carlotta and Sandor found him in a strange mood when they encountered him in his study later.

"What happened?' Carlotta asked. "The whole household heard you and Esme arguing. What did you do to her?"

"What makes you think I did anything? Why don't

you ask Esme what *she* did? The woman is incorrigible. She tried to convince me of Lonsdale's innocence. She put our marriage at risk because of it."

Carlotta shook a finger at Dante. "If there is trouble between you and Esme, you must heal it."

"It may be too late, Grandmother. We're at a stalemate. If she apologizes after I prove Lonsdale's guilt, we can move forward. But it won't be easy. Esme lost my regard when she contacted Lonsdale against my wishes."

"Perhaps she had good reasons," Sandor suggested.

Dante didn't want to discuss his wife with his grandparents. "Don't push, Grandfather. I'll handle Esme as I see fit."

Carlotta grabbed Sandor's sleeve. "Dante needs to be alone right now."

"I'll see you at dinner tonight," he said, already regretting his abruptness.

Dante returned his attention to the financial reports Bartholomew had prepared for him. Though he was pretty good with numbers, these didn't make sense. The financial health of his vast estate needed more than mere scrutiny, and he intended to take all the time necessary to figure things out.

Dante emerged from his study in time to dress for dinner. Apparently, Esme had already dressed, for he found himself alone in their chamber with Simpson. Before he went down to dinner, he gave his valet explicit orders concerning his new sleeping arrangements.

Esme and his grandparents were waiting for him in the parlor. Dinner was announced almost immediately, and they all filed into the dining room. Dinner was an awkward affair. At first Carlotta tried to keep the conversation going, but she soon gave up. Immediately following dinner, Dante excused himself, stating that he had made plans for the evening, plans that didn't include Esme.

"What about the Porterhouse ball tonight?" Esme asked. "I already accepted."

"You may go if you wish," Dante said coolly. "The carriage will be at your disposal."

"You want me to go alone?"

Though his manner was polite, his eyes seethed with banked fury. "If it pleases you; I have no intention of attending." Then he delivered the killing blow. "Perhaps you'll find Lonsdale there."

Esme felt as if her world was spinning out of control. She wanted to lash out at Dante, but refused to involve Carlotta and Sandor in their problems. The old couple thought the world of their grandson, and she didn't want to make him look bad in their eyes.

Esme pushed her chair back. "Please excuse me. I'm exhausted and shall seek my bed."

Carlotta and Sandor exchanged worried glances but said nothing.

The moment Esme entered the bedchamber, she realized something was wrong. She soon saw what it was. All of Dante's clothing and personal things had been removed. Esme sank into a chair and let the terrible consequences of her visit to Calvin sink in. Apparently, Dante wanted her out of his life and out of his bedroom, the only place where they had been compatible.

Jane bustled into the chamber. "Simpson said His Lordship has moved out of your bedchamber. What did you do this time?"

Esme bristled. "What makes you think it's my fault?"

"I know you so well, milady. You disappeared for a time today and didn't ask me to accompany you. You had to be up to no good."

"Honestly, Jane, you sound just like Dante. All I wanted to do was help him. I had a long talk with Calvin; he convinced me he didn't kill Lord Alston, and that he wasn't responsible for the attempts on Dante's life."

"You believed him?"

"You should have seen him, Jane. He was shocked when I told him that Dante suspected him of murder."

"I suppose you expressed your opinion to His Lordship."

"I did. We exchanged harsh words. I told him I'd stake our marriage on Calvin's innocence."

Jane clucked her disapproval. "Look what *that* got you. A cold bed."

Esme heaved a wistful sigh. "I wonder where Dante went tonight."

Jane turned Esme around so she could unbutton her dress. " 'Tis best you don't think about it."

Dante found Brookworth at Brooks's, but Carstairs was attending the Porterhouse ball with his fiancée.

"I thought you were supposed to attend the ball with your bride," Brookworth drawled.

"There was a change of plans." Brookworth opened his mouth to speak, but Dante forestalled him. "Don't ask," Dante warned. "I'm here to have a good time."

Brookworth shook his head. "Trouble in paradise already? How droll. Ah, well, what say we join a friendly game? If I remember correctly, you consistently won my money at university."

"You had so much of it," Dante replied.

They found two empty seats at a table and joined in a game of whist. Dante's luck held, and he won several hundred pounds; Brookworth lost and suggested another sport.

"Lady Harrison is having a private party tonight at her townhouse. I was lucky enough to snag an invitation. I'm sure she won't mind if I bring you along."

Dante hesitated. He was well aware of the kind of parties Margaret held. They always ended in orgies. He had attended a time or two during his carefree days as a gypsy lover in search of bored women who would welcome him into their beds. He had never been one to pass up an opportunity.

Until now.

"I don't think . . ." His words ground to a halt. He didn't owe Esme his loyalty after her betrayal. "Sounds like a good idea," Dante amended.

Brookworth bent Dante an odd look. "Are you sure?"

"Very sure."

The party was in full swing when Brookworth and Dante entered the front parlor, where an assortment of people had gathered. Dante recognized some of the women and a few of the men. Lady Harrison greeted them effusively.

"Welcome, my lords. How thoughtful of Lord Brookworth to bring you to our little gathering, Alston. There's a buffet set up in the dining room, and cards in the card room for those who prefer gambling to . . . er . . . more pleasurable sport."

Her glittering gaze settled on Dante. "I'm gratified to know that marriage hasn't changed you." She wound her arm through his. "Come along, Alston. I'm sure Brookworth can find his own entertainment."

An uncomfortable feeling began in the pit of Dante's stomach as Margaret led him toward the staircase. "What do you have in mind, milady?"

"Since you're here, I presume your new wife is unwilling to accommodate you in bed tonight. I consider it my duty to take up the slack."

Dante's steps dragged as he followed Margaret up the stairs to her bedroom. This really wasn't something he wanted to do. He remembered telling Esme he would never stray, that he would always remain faithful to their marriage vows, but that had been before she went to Lonsdale's townhouse unattended. How did he know what she and Lonsdale did while alone? Probably the same thing he was going to do with Margaret.

Margaret stood on tiptoes and looped her arms around Dante's neck, drawing his head down so she could reach his mouth. The moment her lips touched his, Dante knew he had made a terrible mistake. Unlike Esme, Margaret had done this with countless men, while Esme belonged only to him. At heart he knew that no one else had touched her.

Margaret's lips were warm and inviting. She opened her mouth to him, and when he refused the invitation, she prodded his lips open with her tongue and thrust it deep into his mouth. Her taste was foreign; he didn't like it. Even her scent repelled him. It was heavy, cloying. Her body was too fleshy, her makeup too thick.

She wasn't Esme.

Placing his hands on Margaret's shoulders, Dante set her away from him. "This isn't going to happen, milady."

Margaret sent him a look that would have pounded a lesser man to his knees. "What kind of man are you?" she challenged. "We've done this before, if you recall."

"I'm married now."

"Since when has that mattered to men like you?"

"Men like me," Dante repeated, hating the sound of it. "I am not the carefree gypsy you once knew. I have responsibilities now."

"So do most of the men here tonight," Margaret huffed.

"I'm sorry. Tell Brookworth I'll catch up with him another time." He headed toward the door.

"Coward," Margaret spat.

Dante stopped, swiveled around, pierced Margaret with a quelling look. "Good night, milady."

Dante opened the door and stepped into the hall. Margaret's insult followed in his wake. "Bastard."

Esme couldn't sleep. She missed having Dante beside her. After only one day of marriage, her world had fallen apart. All she'd wanted to do was protect Dante. She'd thought that once he learned Calvin wasn't the murderer he would look for another suspect. Because Dante refused to listen to her, the real killer was free to strike again.

The mantel clock struck midnight. Shortly thereafter, she heard Dante's footsteps in the hallway. She held her breath when he paused outside her door.

Her breath left her in a whoosh of disappointment when he continued on. She had wanted him to stop, to open the door, to come to her bed and make love to her. He didn't. What if he never made love to her again?

Esme was too overwhelmed by remorse to sleep. Not because she thought she'd done wrong, but because Dante refused to listen to logic and had accused her of betraying him. Whom had he been with tonight? Was it a woman? Had they laughed together at Esme's inability to hold her husband's interest after a single day of marriage?

Esme's morbid thoughts skidded to a halt when she heard her bedroom door open and the click of the latch falling in place as it closed. The patter of footsteps approached the bed. She recognized Dante's scent, a scent she would never forget. The candle on the nightstand flared. Esme eased up against the headboard.

Dante loomed over her, his face set, his eyes dark as sin. "You're my wife," he said.

"I'm surprised you remember."

He sat down on the edge of the bed. "Oh, I remember, damn you."

Esme peered at him. "Are you foxed?"

Dante held up his right hand. "Sober as a judge."

An overpowering whiff of flowery perfume drifted to her from his disheveled clothing. His cravat was askew, his jacket hung open, and his shirttails were out of his trousers. Esme's temper flared. "You've been with a woman. You reek of her perfume."

One dark brow shot upward. "How astute of you to notice."

"If you woke me up to gloat, you needn't bother. I expected no less from you. Go away and let me sleep."

"You're my wife," he repeated.

"I think we've already covered that subject."

Esme was puzzled. What did Dante want from her?

"I want to make love to you."

That *did* surprise Esme. "How many women does it take to satisfy you?"

"I made a promise to you when we wed. I haven't broken that promise."

His statement stunned Esme. "Are you saying you didn't have a woman tonight?"

"I never lie. I had an offer but turned it down."

"Her scent is all over you."

"I walked away."

"Why?"

He looked away. "I'm not certain. It's difficult to explain."

"Perhaps you care for me," Esme dared.

"Perhaps, even though it's difficult to admit it right now. You went to Lonsdale against my wishes, and wagered our marriage on a false assumption. What if he'd tried to harm you?"

"He didn't. And I wagered our marriage on something I believe to be true."

He shook his head. "I thought . . . I hoped . . ."

"What did you hope?" She held her breath, praying for the words she wanted to hear.

His fists clenched, his jaw firmed. "I don't know. You've bewitched me—there's no other explanation. You're the only woman I want in my bed."

He reached for her and pulled her into his arms. Esme wrinkled her nose and pushed him away. "I don't want to make love to a man who reeks of another woman's scent."

"Dammit, Esme, I told you the truth. Why are you being so difficult?"

"*You're* being difficult. Do you believe me about Calvin? Will you consider other suspects in your investigation of your grandfather's murder?" She glared at him. "I'm not the one who moved out of our room."

"I was angry and acted hastily. Though I don't believe you, or trust you when it comes to Lonsdale, I'm not willing to give up the only area of our marriage where we are compatible."

Esme's heart withered and died. She had hoped for more. "I'm sorry, Dante, that's not enough. If you wanted a reconciliation, you should have come to me without the scent of another woman on you."

"I didn't . . ." Dante began. But the protest died in his throat when he realized Esme was right. No matter that he hadn't bedded Margaret—the intention had been there, and her scent was on him to prove it.

Chapter Nineteen

Dante stormed out of Esme's bedchamber in a huff. Being rebuffed by one's own wife was a humiliating experience. Damn Margaret for smelling like a cheap whore. He didn't blame Esme for turning him away, but still it hurt. Since it was too late to order a bath, he made use of the pitcher of warm water and towels Simpson had left for him. Then he donned a robe and sat in a chair, staring at the dying embers in the fireplace while he pondered everything Esme had told him.

Kernels of doubt began to form. Had he been wrong about Lonsdale? But if the viscount were not the culprit, then who could it be, and why? No answers were forthcoming.

The thoughts whirling in his head were giving Dante a headache. He rose and began to pace. It didn't help. The room where Esme slept beckoned him. Without conscious decision, he left his chamber and stealthily entered Esme's. He approached the bed. She was sleeping. The sputtering candle provided sufficient light for Dante to study the sweet outline of her face. She looked as innocent as a child, too innocent for him to believe that she had conspired with Lonsdale.

Surrendering to the clamoring need to hold her, he slipped out of his robe and climbed into bed naked beside her. His arms went around her. She murmured something unintelligible and snuggled against him. Thrilled to have Esme where she belonged, he closed his eyes and drifted off to sleep.

Esme awoke to daylight, too warm and comfortable to open her eyes and start her day. She stretched her legs, gasping in surprise when she realized she wasn't alone. Her eyes flew open. Dante's arms surrounded her, his hard body provided heat at her back.

"Dante!"

"Right here, love. You're awake—good. I've been waiting for you to awaken."

He felt her stiffen in his arms. "Why?"

"I've done a lot of thinking since you turned me away last night."

She shifted in his arms, her violet eyes apprehensive. "Did you come to a decision?"

"I did. I don't like sleeping alone."

Was it disappointment he saw in her expressive eyes?

"What else?"

"Despite everything I've said to the contrary, I want to trust you."

"I've never lied to you."

"I decided to take your advice and look elsewhere for Grandfather's killer. If you're willing to risk our marriage on Lonsdale's innocence, perhaps I should listen to you. You've known him longer than I have."

Esme rose up on her elbow, her face suffused with happiness. "You don't know how long I've prayed for your trust. I've never done anything to harm you and never will. I . . ." her voice faltered. "I love you, Dante. Even though you don't love me, I will never stop loving you."

"Little fool," Dante murmured. "I loved you long before I knew your name. I've loved you through all your insults and condescending remarks about my gypsy blood. Nothing you've done has changed my feelings. But trusting you is more difficult than loving you."

"What made you decide to trust me?"

"I realized that if our marriage is ever going to have a chance, I have to give you my trust as well as my love. After our argument I was hurt, and I wanted to hurt you too. The only reason I went out last night was to prove I didn't need you in my life."

"Did you prove it?"

"No. I knew my love was genuine when Lady Harriston failed to coax me into her bed. After I returned home and you rebuffed me, I did some serious thinking. I asked myself if I could love a woman I didn't trust. I thought long and hard about it and realized that love and trust go hand-in-hand. To have one you must have the other."

A sob caught in Esme's throat. "You don't know how long I've waited to hear you say those words. I realize I've said things to hurt you, and I deeply regret them. What matters now is that we love and trust each other. We can work together to solve the mystery of your grandfather's murder before another attempt is made on your life."

Dante had spent hours trying to figure out who besides Lonsdale would profit from his death, but he had drawn a blank. Though he had told Esme he thought Lonsdale might be innocent, and that he would broaden his search, he didn't expect to turn up any new suspects.

"Nothing is going to happen to me, my love."

He cleared his mind of everything but Esme—the weight of her body in his arms, her warm feminine flesh melding with his, her sweetly curved mouth that begged for his kisses. Esme must have read his mind, for she clasped his head in both hands and brought his mouth to hers. Dante needed no further encouragement. He had waited forever for the unconditional love Esme offered. To have her willing and eager in his arms was a blessing he most definitely didn't deserve after his misspent youth. He accepted the gift of her love gratefully.

He kissed her sweet lips, kindling a flame he knew would never be extinguished. Lightning leaped between them, surging through them, violent in its intensity. His mouth ravaged hers, insatiable, demanding more. Need took over, need so great it threatened to consume him.

Dante threw off the covers, his mouth leaving hers long enough to remove her nightgown and toss it away. Then he flipped her over on her stomach. Esme moaned beneath him as his mouth began a leisurely journey down her writhing body. He stopped briefly to worship the twin mounds of her buttocks with his lips, and then kissed his way down each leg, pausing to nuzzle the backs of her knees.

He grasped her hips, raised her up on her knees, spread her thighs apart and moved between them. Leaning over her, he licked a path down her spine, gathered her breasts in his hands and gently squeezed her nipples.

His hands left her breasts, caressing her raised bottom, running his fingers along the exposed cleft of her sex. His cock reacted violently to the scent of aroused female. All the blood seemed to have left his brain and settled in his rampant erection. If he were a selfish man, he would thrust inside her and drive himself to completion, but his pleasure came from giving Esme pleasure. Dragging in a steadying breath, he managed to maintain a modicum of control.

A shiver of anticipation slid down Esme's spine when she felt Dante's fingers open her, probe her and then plunge inside the scented entrance to her body. She wanted to scream, to beg him to enter her, while at the same time she wanted to savor what he was doing to her with his fingers. When he found the swollen nubbin beneath the fold of flesh that shielded it, she did scream. He stroked her until she hovered on the brink of a cataclysmic explosion, and then he withdrew his fingers.

"Dante!" She uttered his name on a fractured cry.

"I'm here, my love."

He nudged her entrance with his cock, then thrust inside, moving in and out, driving himself to the hilt, then withdrawing and thrusting again, deeper and harder each time.

"Come with me, love, you're nearly there," Dante urged.

He leaned over her, sliding his hands around to her breasts, molding them with his palms, plucking her nipples with his thumb and forefinger. The pleasure was so intense, Esme raced toward climax with unstoppable speed. She felt him thrust and then hold still, buried deep, so deep inside her, sweeping her with him into a whirlpool of raw passion, battering them with a force that fused their souls. She heard Dante whisper her name, soft and reverent, and felt his engorged sex pump mindlessly inside her. Then she was there, joining him in ecstasy.

She cried out, molding her bottom against his loins as he pumped his joy and love inside her. Her knees collapsed beneath her and Dante followed her down. Boneless, she relaxed beneath him, savoring the sheer weight of him on top of her, the heat of their joining still pulsing through her veins, the glory of him raging through her body.

Dante lifted himself away and flopped down beside her. She flipped over on her back, breathing deeply, listening to the ragged cadence of Dante's heart.

He turned on his side and grinned at her. "Did I die and go to heaven?"

"Dante, don't even joke about dying," Esme chided. Then she smiled. "That *was* quite wonderful, wasn't it? If you'd like to stay in bed the rest of the day, I'm sure we can recapture the magic."

"Magic—what an appropriate description of what we just shared," Dante agreed. "I've always known we belonged together, but convincing you presented more of a problem than I had anticipated." He sighed. "However much I'd like to oblige, I fear I must tend to a tedious matter in my study. Neither my secretary nor I can make sense of those financial reports Bartholomew sent over. Shall we exercise our horses in the park later?"

"I'd love that!" Esme said enthusiastically.

He kissed her hard, then climbed out of bed. "I'll ask Simpson to move my things back in our chamber. Why don't you ring for Jane and order a bath for yourself while I take mine?"

Esme watched Dante retrieve his robe and pull it on, admiring the sculpted breadth of his chest, the hard lines of his buttocks and muscled legs. His manhood, even at rest, was impressive. Her gaze turned to the dark planes and bold features that made his face unique. She gazed at his swarthy complexion, the tousled blue/black hair that curled naturally over his forehead and eyes as deep and dark as sin, and smiled.

Dante paused at the door and glanced back at her. "I hope that smile means I make you happy."

"Extremely happy," Esme purred, "in more ways than one."

With Esme's words echoing in his head, Dante returned to the spare bedroom and rang for Simpson. An hour later, bathed and dressed, he joined Esme for breakfast.

"Where are my grandparents?" Dante asked Grayson as he poured his coffee.

"They wanted to explore London before they returned to their people," Grayson explained.

"Oh, no—I should have gone with them," Esme cried. "They shouldn't be wandering the streets of London alone."

"They aren't alone, milady," Grayson informed them. "I sent them in the carriage with John Coachman and Grimes. Grimes is a big, strapping man and knows London well. He won't let any harm come to them."

"Thank you, Grayson," Dante said. "I don't know what I would do without you. Grandfather Alston was lucky to have you."

A shadow passed over Grayson's eyes. "I was lucky to have been employed by your grandfather," he replied. "Lord Alston was a good man, he died before his time. We both know he'd done things in his life he shouldn't have, but in the end he made everything right."

Dante mulled Grayson's words over in his head as he ate. Most of his life he'd hated the noble parent and grandparent who had abandoned him. Whether or not Dante deserved the marquisate was moot; his grandfather had trusted him to keep the estate solvent for future generations, and that was precisely what Dante intended to do. He glanced at Esme. Their son would inherit—a son Esme might even now be carrying.

"You're staring at me. Is something wrong?" Esme asked.

Dante forced a smile. "Can't I look at my beautiful wife?"

"That's not what your expression is telling me. You're thinking about your grandfather's killer."

"Can you blame me?"

"No, but I can't help worrying about you."

Dante rose and kissed the top of her head. "Think pleasant thoughts. I'll be in the study if you need me. I may have to call on Bartholomew soon so he can explain the numbers in the reports he prepared for me."

Dante pored over quarterly reports and financial statements, unable to make head or tail of the numbers. He didn't consider himself dense; he had excelled in mathematics at university, but these numbers didn't add up, and he didn't like what he was thinking. Something strange was going on. He was ready to give up when Lord Brookworth was announced.

Dante welcomed the interruption and asked Grayson to show him into the study.

"What happened to you last night?" Brookworth asked after he was seated comfortably with a snifter of brandy in his hand. "Margaret said you'd left rather abruptly. The last I saw of you, she was dragging you up to her bedroom. Did you have an attack of conscience or something?"

"You could say that," Dante replied. "I don't know what I ever saw in Margaret. I met her at a fair some years back. That a noblewoman should find a gypsy attractive was a heady experience for me, so I accepted her invitation to visit her bed. I soon learned she wasn't the only bored noblewoman eager for a gypsy lover."

"I heard tales about the randy gypsy lover as far north as York. You certainly got around."

Dante shrugged. "Gypsies travel. But I'm married now to a woman I . . ." He sent Brookworth a sheepish look. "I love my wife."

Brookworth nearly dropped his drink. "When did this come about? I assumed yours was a marriage of convenience."

"I fell in love the first time I met Esme. It was at the Bedford Fair. I didn't even know her name. I kissed her. It's a long story, one I won't bore you with. But now women like Margaret no longer interest me. I went with you last night because I was angry, but I couldn't go through with what I intended."

"Are you still angry?"

Dante grinned. "No, but I won't bore you with those details either. Suffice it to say, Esme and I are in complete harmony. I'm glad you're here. I wanted to talk to you about Lonsdale. Esme believes he's innocent. She made several good points in his favor, but I'm still not entirely convinced. All the same, I promised her I'd look elsewhere for the killer."

Brookworth gulped down his brandy and set the glass down. "Look where? Who else stood to benefit from your grandfather's death?"

"What do you know about Bartholomew?"

"The solicitor? Not much. He's been your grandfather's solicitor and financial adviser for years. I've never heard anything derogatory about him. I've seen him in gambling halls, but that's all I can say about him. Whatever else he is, he's discreet in his dealings. Why do you ask? Do you suspect him of trickery?"

"No, not really. He's a respected solicitor. I'm sure he can explain the discrepancies in the financial reports he sent me." He took his pocket watch from his vest and checked the time. "It's almost noon. I promised Esme I'd join her for lunch. We're going riding in the park this afternoon."

Brookworth stood. "If you don't mind, I'll continue investigating Lonsdale. He's still our prime suspect."

After Brookworth left, Dante penned a note to Bartholomew and sent it off with Grimes. Then he joined Esme and his grandparents in the dining room for lunch. For some reason, Carlotta seemed distracted and fidgety.

"Is something wrong, Grandmother?" Dante asked. "You look troubled. Didn't your outing go well?"

"I've seen all of London I care to see," Carlotta

replied. "I prefer the smell of grass and trees, and food cooking over an open fire. But that's not what is bothering me."

"You're worried about Dante, aren't you?" Esme asked. "Do you know something we do not?"

"It's not something I know, it's what I feel, what my senses tell me. Do not go out today, Dante."

Dante smiled at Carlotta. "Don't fret over me, Grandmother."

"Perhaps we shouldn't go riding this afternoon," Esme suggested.

"Nonsense," Dante replied. "What could happen to me in the park? I'm not going to alter my life to accommodate someone who might or might not be stalking me."

"Your grandmother is a wise woman, Dante," Sandor cautioned. "You should listen to her."

"I should take my wife riding," Dante insisted. "To please you, I shall carry a pistol and be very cautious."

Esme started to protest. "Dante, maybe—"

"No, love, we're going riding and that's final." He rose. "I'll meet you in the foyer in one hour."

"Dante has ever been a stubborn man," Carlotta said after Dante left.

"Can you tell me anything specific?" Esme asked.

Carlotta sighed. "No, 'tis just a feeling I have. The miasma swirling around Dante has become blacker and denser; I fear that an eruption of those dark forces is imminent."

"What can I do?"

"This is something Dante has to do on his own." She smiled into Esme's eyes. "I sense a new understanding between you and Dante. You both radiate happiness."

"We *are* happy," Esme agreed. "We settled our differences this morning. Dante loves me and I love him. There's nothing stopping us from living a long and happy life except . . ." Her next words burst forth on a sob. "I don't know what I'd do without him."

"Are you sure you want to do this?" Esme asked Dante before they left the house for their ride.

"Positive. I'm not going to hide, love. I want to lure the killer into the open."

"You have protection?"

He patted his pocket. "I have a pistol in my pocket and a knife in my boot. And just to be on the safe side, since you'll be with me, I've asked Grimes and Jordan to follow us. They're the brawniest of our footmen. Are you ready?"

Their mounts were waiting in the gravel driveway. Esme patted her mare's nose before mounting with Dante's help. Dante swung his leg over his own horse, and then they were off. Esme looked back as they trotted down the street and saw two footmen riding a short distance behind them.

The day was cool, damp and dreary, but that didn't stop Esme's enthusiasm for the outing. It felt wonderful to be riding again. She hadn't ridden her mare since leaving the country. Neither she nor anyone in their party noticed the man trailing behind Grimes and Jordan at a discreet distance.

They entered the park and cantered along Rotten Row. The traffic was light today, due to the weather, Esme supposed, but she felt freer than she had in a long time. A fine mist bedewed her face, invigorating her and making her feel a bit reckless.

"I'll race you to the trees," she challenged.

"We should stay together," Dante said, but it was too late. Esme had already given her mare her head. Muttering a curse, Dante galloped after her. Despite his apprehension, Dante had to admire Esme's seat. She rode as if she were born to the saddle. She rode like a gypsy. That was the best compliment he could pay her.

Dante had almost caught up with her when a movement in the shrubbery to his left caught his attention. He pulled Condor up short. The horse reared, and when he settled, Dante guided him into the shrubbery. He heard a pop, recognized it for what it was and ducked low over Condor's neck. The bullet whizzed over his head. Dante rode as far as he could go into a bramble patch without injuring his horse and then dismounted, continuing his chase on foot. He caught a glimpse of a man crashing through bushes and shrubs but soon lost sight of him.

"Milord, are you all right?"

"I'm fine, Grimes. Stay where you are. I'll be right out."

Esme had already joined the anxious footmen when Dante led Candor back onto the path.

"What happened?" Esme demanded. "Are you hurt? I heard a gunshot." She wrung her hands. "I knew we should have listened to Carlotta and stayed home today."

"I'm perfectly fine," Dante assured her. "The bullet missed. I tried to catch the culprit, but he slipped through the thicket. He may still be in the park, but I wouldn't recognize him if I saw him."

Esme shivered. "Let's go home."

Dante agreed, and they left the park. Esme was shaking so badly when they arrived home that Dante had to steady her after she slid from the saddle. With his arms around her waist, he guided her up the stairs and into the house.

"Can I be of assistance, milord?" Grayson asked, hovering over them.

"No, thank you, Grayson. Lady Esme isn't feeling well."

"Someone shot at Dante," Esme blurted out. "I knew we shouldn't have gone out."

"As you can see, Grayson, we are both unharmed. Will you order the carriage brought around? I'm going out again as soon as I get my wife settled."

Esme clutched his lapels, nearly frantic with fear. "No! Don't go."

Dante scooped her into his arms and carried her up the stairs. "You'll feel better after a nap. You didn't get much sleep last night."

She gave him a wobbly smile. "Neither did you."

Dante opened their chamber door and carried her inside. He seated her on the edge of the bed. "I'll help you out of your clothes." He removed her cloak and reached for the top button of her gown.

She caught his hands. "Jane can help me. Tell me where you're going."

His hands dropped to his sides. "I have an appointment with Bartholomew. I shouldn't be long." He kissed her hard. "Meanwhile, try to get some rest."

Jane bustled into the room and skidded to a halt. "Oh, forgive me—I thought milady was alone."

"She is; I was just leaving. I ordered her to rest; see that she does."

"What was that all about?" Jane asked once Dante was gone.

"There was another attempt on Dante's life today.

Grimes and Jordan were with us in the park, but that didn't deter the killer. He is becoming bolder and bolder."

Jane's hand flew to her throat. "Grimes was with you? Is he all right?"

"Why, Jane—is there something you'd like to tell me about you and Grimes?"

Jane giggled. The sound surprised Esme, for Jane never giggled. "We're friends."

"Just friends?"

"We have an understanding. It happened so fast, I'm still reeling. He wants me to meet his family. His sister lives nearby in the country. He's a widower; his sister takes cares of his two children. I hope you're not angry. I know I'm past marrying age, but Grimes and I, we're of an age and both of us free."

"I approve, Jane. You deserve to be happy."

Jane heaved a relieved sigh. "I knew you'd approve, but I'm not sure about His Lordship."

"Leave His Lordship to me. I'm sure he'll be as happy for you and Grimes as I am. Just don't rush into anything."

"I won't, but you're a fine one to talk, miss. Now, shall I help you undress?"

"I'm not going to bed, Jane. I'm going to follow Dante."

Jane shook her head. "What kind of mischief are you up to?"

"It's not mischief, Jane. I'm worried about Dante. Do you know where I can find a pistol? I'm sure Dante took his with him."

Jane's eyes widened. "That sounds like mischief to me."

"Please, Jane—I need your help."

Before Jane could answer, Carlotta rapped on the door, then burst inside. Sandor followed on her heels. Both looked upset.

"Forgive me," Carlotta said, "but I'm looking for Dante."

"He's gone out," Esme replied, beginning to experience real fear. "Why? Is he in danger?"

"He's faced danger since the day he became marquis, but this is different. This time he's walking straight into the jaws of death."

Esme's hand flew to her throat. "I know where he's gone! Don't worry, Carlotta—I'll find him." She turned to her maid. "Jane, that pistol I asked for—I'll need it immediately."

"I'll try, milady, but I don't think any of the servants own firearms."

Grayson appeared in the open door. "Milady, Viscount Lonsdale is here. When I told him His Lordship wasn't at home, he requested an audience with you. He said it was urgent."

Carlotta swayed, her gaze focused inward. "You must see him, Esme."

Carlotta's word was good enough for Esme. Calvin wouldn't have come here unless something dire had happened. "Tell Lord Lonsdale I will be down directly and show him into the study."

"Shall I come with you?" Carlotta asked.

"No, I'll see him alone. He might be reluctant to speak freely before strangers. I'll let you know what he has to say the moment he leaves."

Calvin was pacing restlessly when Esme arrived in the study. He glanced up, came to a halt before her and took both her hands in his. Esme pulled her hands free.

"What's this about, Calvin? Why did you want to see Dante? You know how he feels about you."

His words came out in a rush. "Where is Alston? It's important that I speak with him."

"He had an appointment with his solicitor."

Calvin cursed, then grasped Esme's hand and pulled her out the door. "We need to leave immediately."

Esme resisted. "Calvin, stop! Where are we going? Tell me what this is about."

"It's about saving your husband's life and clearing my name. Are you coming or not?"

Esme didn't hesitate. She had looked into his eyes, seen his sincerity and decided to trust him. "I'll fetch my cloak and find a weapon. You can explain everything to me on the way to wherever we're going."

"I have a weapon, and I asked the footman to fetch your cloak. There's no time to lose." As if on cue, Grimes appeared with her cloak.

"This had better not be another of your tricks, Calvin."

"Believe me, Esme, I'm being completely honest. If you love your husband, and I believe you do, you'll come with me."

That decided it for Esme. She snatched her cloak from a startled Grimes and followed Calvin out the door.

Chapter Twenty

Dante arrived at the solicitor's office in a troubled mood. For Bartholomew's sake, Dante hoped the man had answers to his questions. Talbot, Bartholomew's assistant, greeted him with a sly smile that immediately aroused Dante's suspicions. He couldn't imagine why Bartholomew had hired a man of questionable character, for Talbot had never struck him as honest.

"Mr. Bartholomew is expecting me," Dante said. "I sent a note around earlier."

"Indeed, my lord. Mr. Bartholomew said to show you into his office the moment you arrived." He opened the door to the inner office and ushered Dante inside. But instead of leaving, he shut the door and leaned against it. Bartholomew invited Dante to sit down.

A shiver of apprehension slid down Dante's spine as he lowered himself into a chair across the desk from Bartholomew. Dante had learned long ago to trust his instincts, and right now they were screaming danger. He opened his coat to allow better access to his pistol.

"What I have to say is private, Bartholomew," Dante said. "Dismiss your assistant."

"Talbot is privy to all my business dealings," Bartholomew replied. "You can talk freely in front of him. Now, how may I help you?"

"My secretary and I have carefully scrutinized the financial reports you sent over and cannot account for discrepancies we found in the documents. I'm hoping you can provide answers."

"Perhaps your education isn't advanced enough to understand the reports," Bartholomew suggested. "Don't bother your head about them. I took good care of your grandfather's affairs and intend to do the same for you."

Dante felt his temper rising. "Grandfather Alston provided me with a fine education, and well you know it. I was particularly adept at mathematics. Granted, my secretary isn't a mathematician, but he has a fine head for figures. All I require is your explanation as to where the missing funds have been invested. I'm sure it's simply a case of documents gone astray."

Bartholomew cleared his throat. "Yes, of course, that's precisely what happened."

"I'll have the missing documents now, if you please," Dante said. "I don't like leaving loose ends."

"Well . . . er . . . it might take a few days."

Dante's gut told him that Bartholomew was lying. Had he told Grandfather Alston the same lies? Things began adding up, things that put Bartholomew in a bad light.

"Exactly what are you up to, Bartholomew? I thought

I could trust you. I know Grandfather did, unless . . ." His words fell off, his unspoken insinuation hanging in the air like autumn smoke.

"I'm not accustomed to having my integrity impugned, Alston."

"I want a full accounting of the Alston portfolio. If my suppositions are wrong, I will, of course, apologize."

"Well, well, what do you know?" Bartholomew said nastily. "It looks like the gypsy is smarter than we thought, Talbot."

When Dante reached for his pistol, it was already too late. Talbot had moved silently behind him; he felt the cold steel of a gun barrel pressed against the back of his head.

"Remove your pistol and set it on the desk," Bartholomew said. "I know you are carrying one."

"So your assistant is in this with you," Dante said as he carefully placed his weapon on the desk. Bartholomew took it and shut it in the bottom drawer of his desk.

"Of course he is. Do you think I could have pulled this off alone?"

A red haze floated before Dante's eyes. "You killed my grandfather." His softly spoken words held a wealth of seething hatred.

Bartholomew shrugged. "I had to."

"Why?"

"He discovered the discrepancies. I thought I had them well hidden, but Alston finally caught on. He was going to expose me. I couldn't let that happen. I killed him and made his death look like a suicide."

"You made a mistake," Dante said. "Grandfather was left-handed. You placed the pistol in his right hand. I knew it was murder from the beginning, but I never suspected you. All this time I thought Lonsdale was the guilty party."

Bartholomew sneered. "Lonsdale. Ha! I had a good laugh over that. My mistake was due to haste. I knew Alston was left-handed."

"Did you think me too stupid to notice the discrepancies?"

"Not after I met you. Once I saw that you intended to keep the marquisate, I realized you had to die. You were too clever not to see through our machinations."

"Had Lonsdale inherited, you still wouldn't have been in the clear," Dante reminded him.

"Lonsdale is a dunce. He never would have looked closely into the estate's finances. As long as he had money to gamble and pay his debts, he would have been content. I wanted to find Alston's new will the night he died and exchange it for the old one, but Alston said he'd given it to you. I had no choice but to kill Alston and try to convince you I was your best friend. It almost worked."

"Almost isn't good enough, Bartholomew. What do you intend to do now that I'm on to you?"

Until now Talbot had remained silent. "Let me kill him. When his body is found floating in the Thames, no one will suspect us of doing him in."

"Go ahead and shoot," Dante taunted. "A gunshot will bring everyone within hearing distance to your office. Maybe even the Watch."

"He's right, Talbot. We can't kill him here."

"What have you done with all the money?" Dante asked, trying to buy time. He needed to maneuver around so he could reach the knife in his boot without being shot in the head for his efforts.

"Talbot and I live very well, better than we could on

our meager earnings. I have a wife and keep a mistress; you can imagine how draining that is on one's funds. Then there are the gambling debts. There is always a need for money."

"Grandfather paid you a substantial retainer, and so do I."

Bartholomew dismissed Dante's words with a wave of his hand. "Is one ever paid enough?" He tapped his chin. "You have to die. Any other option is out of the question."

Dante decided he wasn't going to become fish food as long as he had breath left in his lungs. Talbot didn't dare fire his pistol in such close quarters, and that gave Dante a slight advantage.

He inched his hand down his leg toward his boot while keeping his focus on Bartholomew. Once he had his knife in hand, he intended to swing around and plunge it into Talbot's heart. Then he would take care of Bartholomew. But he wouldn't kill the solicitor. He'd let the law take care of the weasel.

Unfortunately, Talbot was watching Dante closely. Dante had the knife in his hand when Talbot brought the butt of his pistol down on Dante's head. Dante felt pain explode in his head, and then everything went black as he pitched sideways onto the floor.

"Why did you do that?" Bartholomew demanded. "I wasn't ready to end the conversation. Is he dead?"

Talbot knelt beside Dante's prone form and pried the knife from his hand. "This is why," he said, tossing the knife on the desk. "Never trust a gypsy." He checked Dante's pulse. "He's not dead. I didn't bash him hard enough to kill him."

"What are we going to do with him?"

"Bind and gag him and hide him for a few hours.

When it gets dark, we'll carry the body to your carriage, take him to the docks and dump him in the river."

Bartholomew nodded, liking the idea. "There's rope in the storeroom." He chuckled. "Alston won't be going anywhere until we're ready to dispose of him."

"After his body is found, Lonsdale will inherit and we're home free," Talbot crowed.

Bartholomew bent down and grasped Dante's feet. "Take his shoulders; we'll drag him into the storeroom."

"Do you think anyone will come looking for him?" Talbot asked as he hefted Dante's shoulders.

"We'll say we haven't seen him," Bartholomew replied. "He never arrived. After we finish here, I want you to take his horse to the livery down the street. We can get rid of it later. No one will suspect us of wrongdoing. I'm a respected businessman, after all."

Esme found Calvin's story hard to believe. It didn't seem possible that Mr. Bartholomew was the villain Calvin had described.

"Are you sure, Calvin? Very sure?" Esme asked, not for the first time.

"I know what I heard, Esme," Calvin insisted. "I went to Bartholomew's office to inquire if I could get an advance on my inheritance to stave off some creditors. His assistant wasn't in the front office, but I noticed that the door to the inner office was ajar. I intended to knock to announce my presence, when I heard Bartholomew and his assistant talking."

"You didn't mistake what they said, did you?"

"No indeed. They were talking about getting rid of your husband because they feared he was on to them. They said that Alston had sent word that he was coming to question them about discrepancies in the estate's financial reports."

"You don't think Bartholomew would harm Dante in a public office, do you?"

"I don't know, Esme. I hoped to warn Alston of Bartholomew's duplicity before he left home."

"Dante must have suspected something. He and his secretary were holed up in his study for days. I didn't know what was going on." She glanced out the carriage window. "Are we there yet?"

"Bartholomew's office is just around the corner."

"What are we going to say if Dante isn't there?"

"I don't know. We'll think of something."

Lonsdale stopped the carriage in front of Bartholomew's fashionable office building.

"I don't see Dante's horse, and I know he didn't take the carriage," Esme said.

"Stay here while I go inside," Lonsdale instructed. "Bartholomew won't suspect anything if I pay him a visit; I've been hounding him ever since Uncle Alston's will was read. I can take a look around inside and let you know if Alston is there. It wouldn't look right if we showed up together."

Although Esme didn't like it, Calvin's logic made sense. If she arrived with Calvin, Bartholomew might become suspicious. "Very well, I'll wait outside. If you don't return in a reasonable time, I'm coming in."

Lonsdale entered the building where Bartholomew kept his office. No one was in the outer reception area when he entered. As he approached the inner office door and reached for the knob, the door swung open. Talbot stood in the opening, as surprised to see Lonsdale as Lonsdale was to see him.

Bartholomew exchanged a wary look with Talbot.

"My lord, what are you doing here?" Bartholomew asked.

Lonsdale made a visual inspection of the room and saw nothing to indicate that Alston had been there. "I've come to inquire if you'd considered my request concerning my uncle's will."

"Unfortunately, the will is ironclad. Your uncle was a thorough man, and he didn't want you to have access to money in advance. He said he feared you'd squander it.

"I've done all I can within the law. However," he confided, lowering his voice, "I doubt the gypsy will hold the title for long. I understand attempts have been made on his life. Should the next attempt succeed, the marquisate is yours."

Pretending eagerness, Lonsdale said, "Even though it isn't right to wish for a man's death, I hope you're right. But what if Lady Alston is increasing? Wouldn't the child, if it's a son, inherit?"

"That's possible but highly unlikely. They've only been married a few days. Even if Lady Alston is increasing, life is so fragile." He shrugged. "One never knows."

"Of course, as you say, one never knows. Unfortunately, I fear Alston is too canny to fall victim to an assassin."

Lonsdale knew something was amiss when Talbot and Bartholomew exchanged glances that could only be described as gloating.

"No man is indestructible," Bartholomew observed dryly. "Go home, my lord, and await further developments. Good things come to those who wait. Who knows, perhaps Alston's delectable wife will be yours when all is said and done. That's what you wanted, isn't it? The title *and* the woman."

"Indeed," Lonsdale said. "That's all I've ever wanted."

Lonsdale's departure was delayed when he heard a loud thump.

"What was that?" he asked.

Bartholomew put on an innocent face. "What? I didn't hear anything."

Another thump, this one so loud no one could deny its existence. "There!" Lonsdale said. "Didn't you hear it? It's coming from behind that door."

"Rats in the storeroom," Talbot said. "The building is infested. We spoke to the landlord about them and he promised to do something."

Lonsdale decided to accept the explanation rather than cause a ruckus that might result in his death as well as Alston's. The best way to help Alston was to fetch the Watch.

Lonsdale shrugged. "Nasty creatures, rats. Good day, gentlemen, and thank you for your time."

The door opened. "Oh, I didn't know you had a client," Esme said, stepping into the room. "No one was in the outer office."

Lonsdale stifled a groan. Why couldn't she have waited another few minutes?

"Lady Alston," Bartholomew greeted her smoothly. "What an unexpected pleasure. What can I do for you?"

"I'm looking for my husband. He said he had an appointment with you."

Bartholomew shifted his gaze to Lonsdale. "You know Lord Lonsdale, of course."

"We are acquainted," Esme said coolly.

"He was just leaving," Bartholomew said. "Talbot, show His Lordship out. And then fetch my carriage. It's nearly closing time."

Talbot nodded his understanding. "This way, Lord Lonsdale," he said, ushering him out the door.

Esme could tell that Calvin didn't want to leave, but there was no reason for him to delay without raising suspicion. When the door closed behind Calvin, Esme returned her attention to the solicitor.

"Was my husband here, Mr. Bartholomew? It's important that I locate him. An emergency has occurred at the house; he's needed right away."

"Why didn't you send a servant, my lady?" Bartholomew asked smoothly.

"They are occupied with the emergency," Esme explained.

"Lord Alston failed to arrive at the appointed time," Bartholomew informed her.

"He's not here?" Esme asked with wide-eyed innocence. "How odd. He said he was coming straight to your office."

"Perhaps he changed his mind, my lady."

Esme pretended confusion. "Perhaps, but—"

Thump.

"What was that?"

Bartholomew cursed beneath his breath. "Rats in the storeroom."

Thump.

Esme had never heard rats make that kind of noise. There was only one explanation for the sound.

Without a thought for her own safety, she raced to the storeroom and flung the door open. The small room was dark, but once her eyes adjusted to the lack of light, she saw Dante. He was lying on the floor, trussed up like a Christmas goose, a gag tied over his mouth. Spinning on her heel, she glared at Bartholomew.

"What is the meaning of this? Release my husband at once."

"Nosy bitch," Bartholomew cursed. "What in the devil am I going to do with you?"

As he started toward her, Esme bent and removed the gag from Dante's mouth. "Are you hurt?"

"Dammit, Esme, what are you doing here?"

"I'll explain later, after Mr. Bartholomew unties you."

"You're delusional, my lady, if you think either of you will leave here alive," Bartholomew spat.

"Exactly how do you intend to get rid of us?" Dante challenged. "My hearing is excellent. I heard you speaking to Lord Lonsdale. He saw my wife here. He'll suspect murder if we both disappear."

Bartholomew sneered. "I can handle Lonsdale. He wants the Alston wealth. He'll keep quiet as long as he benefits from your deaths. You will quietly disappear, both of you. In a few days your bodies will be discovered floating in the Thames. Lacking suspects, your deaths will remain an unsolved mystery."

"That's not a smart move, Bartholomew," Dante argued. "Lonsdale is my heir. He will become the prime suspect."

Bartholomew tapped his chin. "That could work to our benefit. I'll drain the Alston estate dry while Lonsdale awaits trial and testify that the estate had been going bankrupt for a long time. That's it!" he crowed, pleased with his shrewd thinking. "A bankrupt estate would explain your grandfather's suicide, too. I win no matter what happens to Lonsdale.

"Now, my lady, I'm going to silence you until such a time as Talbot and I can get rid of you and your dear husband."

"My pistol is in Bartholomew's bottom desk drawer," Dante whispered so only Esme could hear.

Esme knew it was all over for them unless she could reach the pistol. But the way things looked now, it would snow in hell before that happened. Bartholomew was advancing toward her, his menacing snarl spelling her and Dante's doom.

Determination stiffened her spine. If she intended to act, she had to do it now. Lowering her head, she charged at Bartholomew like an enraged bull and butted him in the stomach. He staggered backward, the breath whooshing out of him.

As Esme rushed past him, he snagged her skirt and dragged her back. Raising his arm, he backhanded her. Esme went flying. The last thing she heard was Dante's enraged roar. Then darkness closed around her.

"I hope you rot in hell!" Dante raged. "You're going to pay for striking my wife. Untie me."

"Untie you? So you can kill me? I think not, gypsy."

The door opened and Talbot slipped inside. He took one look at Esme lying limp on the floor and asked, "What happened?"

"I had to silence her. She got to the storeroom before I could stop her. She knows everything."

"Is she dead?"

"I don't think so, but she's out for a while."

"This changes everything," Talbot said. "We can't wait; we have to kill them now. I'll strangle the gypsy with rope first and then his wife."

Esme didn't move, didn't bat an eyelash. She had lost consciousness for only a moment and had been fully alert when Talbot had entered the room and begun talking about killing her and Dante.

She saw Talbot bend over Dante with the rope, but apparently Dante wasn't prepared to die yet. Drawing back his bound ankles, he kicked Talbot in the stomach.

Bartholomew rushed to pin down Dante. During the ensuing ruckus, Esme crawled to the desk. She removed the pistol, opened the bottom drawer and used the desk to lever herself to her feet. There was a moment of dizziness and then it was gone, replaced by grim determination.

Esme peered into the storeroom, rage fueling her when she saw that Talbot had placed a rope around Dante's neck. Though Dante struggled, he could do nothing to save himself. Bound tightly, he was no match for his captors. Esme cocked the pistol and advanced toward the storeroom.

"Stop or I'll shoot!"

All three men looked up at her, two of them stunned to see her, the other smiling despite the rope tightening about his neck.

"You heard me. Drop the rope and move away from my husband. This pistol holds two bullets, and I assure you I can shoot with remarkable accuracy."

Neither Talbot nor Bartholomew moved. Esme could tell by the looks on their faces that they didn't believe her. She didn't blame them. She had never fired a pistol in her life, but she wouldn't hesitate to do so now. One glance at Dante's purple face reinforced her rage; she had to bluff her way through this or lose the man she loved.

Aiming the pistol with both hands, she walked into the storeroom. Summoning her courage, she approached Bartholomew, who was holding Dante down while Talbot held the rope around his neck. Trying to keep her hands from shaking, she pressed the pistol against Bartholomew's head.

"Tell your partner to release the rope and step away from Dante. I can't miss at this range."

"Dammit," Talbot cursed. "Do something, Bartholomew. She's just a woman."

"A woman with a gun," Bartholomew gulped. "If you don't do as she says, she'll kill me."

"I should let you die," Talbot growled.

"I wouldn't advise it," Esme warned. "I don't think you could reach me before I fired the second round. Remove the rope from Dante's neck or Bartholomew dies."

"Do it!" the solicitor rasped.

Talbot dropped the rope. Esme was pleased to note that the purple was slowly leaving Dante's face. Her problem now was finding a way to release Dante while holding the two villains at bay. She didn't want to kill anyone if she didn't have to.

Bartholomew must have sensed her indecision. "You won't shoot me; you're not capable of murder."

"Try me and find out," Esme bluffed. "Both of you step to the back of the storeroom." They hesitated a moment, then obeyed. "Dante, can you move?"

"Just barely," Dante rasped.

"Can you scoot out the door? I don't dare lower the pistol to help you."

Using his heels and bottom to propel himself, Dante scooted the short distance to the door. Once he cleared the threshold, Esme slowly began to retreat.

"We can't let her get away with this," Talbot hissed. "Rush her—she won't shoot. If they get away, it's all over for us."

"Shoot, Esme," Dante cried. "You have to shoot."

Talbot lunged at Esme. Her hand began to shake, but Dante's words gave her courage. Closing her eyes, she fired the pistol at Talbot. When she opened her eyes, Talbot lay at her feet, writhing and cursing violently. Esme fled out the door, slamming it behind her.

"There's a bolt on the door, shove it in place," Dante rasped. Though her hand was shaking, Esme shoved the bolt home, then collapsed against the door.

"You were magnificent," Dante praised. "My knife is on the desk; use it to cut me free."

Esme found the knife and quickly sliced through the ropes. Dante stretched his arms and legs to work out the kinks and then rose to his feet. Seconds later, Esme was in his arms.

"Little fool," he said. "I didn't think you knew how to fire a pistol."

"I . . . I don't," Esme stammered. "I had to bluff in order to save us."

"By the way, that pistol holds only one bullet."

Esme's knees began wobbling like jelly. Dante's arms tightened around her.

"What made you come here?" Dante asked.

"Calvin told me you were in danger. He had visited Bartholomew earlier in the day and overheard him and Talbot planning your murder. He came to the house to warn you, but you had already left."

"Lonsdale? That's hard to credit."

"Believe it. He made me wait outside while he took a look around Bartholomew's office. He was gone so long, I became anxious and decided to follow. You know the rest. I expect Calvin to return with the Watch soon."

"I was nearly wild with fear when I heard you in Bartholomew's office. Though I don't condone your reckless behavior, it was the bravest thing I've ever seen a woman do. Bloody hell, you don't even know how to shoot straight, or how many bullets my pistol holds. I'm surprised you had enough sense to cock the hammer. Is it any wonder I love you? No other woman would risk her life for me."

Esme gave him a misty smile. "I couldn't let you die. I love you too much. Will you be my gypsy lover forever, Dante?"

He lowered his head and kissed her, offering his love, his body and his soul, all in the space of one heady kiss. If he had lost Esme, he wouldn't have been able to go on. She was his soul mate. He owed her his life. If their children inherited their mother's courage, he would ask for nothing more.

Dante ended the kiss when the door burst open, admitting Lonsdale and several members of the Watch.

"What happened?" Lonsdale asked. "I got here as soon as I could. Where are Bartholomew and his assistant?"

"Locked in the storeroom. There's a wounded man in there," Dante told the Watch. "Both men are guilty of attempted murder and embezzling. Take them to jail; I'll come around tomorrow to press formal charges."

A Watchman unbolted the door and ordered the two men out. Bartholomew shuffled out, a defeated man, but Talbot had to be carried, cursing and struggling all the way. His wound didn't appear life-threatening. They would both live to face the hangman.

After the two men were taken away, Dante turned his regard on Lonsdale. "I owe you an apology, Lonsdale. I didn't suspect Bartholomew until today. He made a serious mistake in believing I was too stupid to examine the financial health of the estate or question his honesty."

"Enough said, Alston," Lonsdale replied. "I account myself partly responsible for your problems. Though I didn't try to kill you, I did attempt to steal your intended bride." He held out his hand to Dante. "I hope we can put all this behind us. We are related, after all."

Dante stared at Lonsdale's outstretched hand for a long, tense moment before grasping it with his own. "I don't know if we can ever be the best of friends, but I'll never forget that you came to my aid when I needed it. Although," he added sternly, "you never should have brought Esme here. You should have summoned the Watch immediately."

"I couldn't agree more," Lonsdale replied. "That's exactly what I intended to do after I heard the thumping coming from the storeroom. But Esme became impatient and arrived unexpectedly. I left immediately to summon the Watch. I had a pistol on me, but feared Esme would be hurt in the fray if I used it."

He looked at Esme, still held tightly in Dante's

arms. "Are you all right, Lady Esme? I hurried as fast as I could."

Dante turned her face so Lonsdale could see the bruise. "Bartholomew struck her. He intended to kill us both and make you the new marquis. He planned to continue siphoning money from the estate after you inherited. He didn't think you'd question his dealings as long as you had enough blunt to pay your gambling debts and live in style."

Lonsdale paled. "Good God! What a dunce I've been. Did Bartholomew kill Uncle Alston?"

"He did."

"Why?"

"Grandfather suspected Bartholomew was embezzling from the estate. Bartholomew killed him before he could act on his suspicions. After he killed Grandfather, he intended to replace the will in Grandfather's possession with an older will that named you his heir. His scheme failed. Grandfather had given his copy of the will to me for safekeeping. That's how little he trusted Bartholomew."

"It's difficult to believe Bartholomew would stoop to murder," Lonsdale said.

"He was desperate. He knew Grandfather was on to him and he was facing years in prison—or worse, the hangman. It's over now." He smiled at Esme. "I'm taking my wife home."

"I think Calvin should be rewarded," Esme suggested.

"I don't know why; he's caused us a lot of trouble."

"He saved your life."

"I don't deserve anything," Lonsdale protested. "I only did what needed to be done."

"If we are going to cry peace, Lonsdale, I'm willing to do what I can for you. Gather your vowels and bring them by the house tomorrow. I'll see that they're paid. But this is the last time. Mend your ways or end up in debtors' prison, it's your choice. Now move aside. It's time I took my wife home."

"I'll drop you off in my carriage," Lonsdale said, holding the door open for them.

Scooping Esme into his arms, Dante carried her away from the scene of their narrow escape from death.

Epilogue

"I'm going to miss your grandparents," Esme said wistfully. "I wish they would stay longer."

Dante and Esme had just retired to their bedchamber after a rather subdued dinner in which Carlotta and Sandor revealed their plans to return to their people.

"They're not comfortable living in a grand house like this," Dante said. "They're happiest in their wagon, roaming the countryside with their own kind. We'll see them in the summer when we return to Bedford Park. They promised to camp in our meadow the entire summer. I don't intend for us to live permanently in London, we will only return to Town for the opening of Parliament, if that's agreeable with you."

"I like London no more than you do, but I agree that you should take your seat in Parliament. Your Grandfather Alston would want that."

"Turn around so I can unfasten your dress. Or would you rather I called Jane?"

Esme gave him a seductive smile. "I'd rather you did it."

"Minx." Dante grinned. "I know what you're about. You want to torture me."

She reached up and pulled his head down to hers. Dante obliged her with a searing kiss that told Esme exactly how this night would end. He would get no argument from her. The gypsy lover was all hers now; no other woman would ever experience the magic of his passion.

The kiss went on and on. When Dante drew away, they were both breathing heavily, both aroused. Their clothes suffered in their haste to have each other naked. Then they fell onto the bed, limbs tangled, Dante's lips finding hers, kissing her with the same exquisite skill she'd come to expect from him.

"What would milady like tonight?" Dante whispered against her lips.

"You," Esme sighed, "inside me."

Dante chuckled, a wicked sound that sent liquid fire though her veins. Just the tone of his voice aroused her.

"I can be much more inventive than that. Should I start by kissing your breasts and sucking your nipples? You always enjoy that."

Esme stretched out her arms. "Have your way with me, gypsy."

"As you wish, milady."

Dante nuzzled her breasts and teased her nipples with the rough pad of his tongue. Esme bit back a moan, arching up into his caress. Each time Dante made love to her, he drove her to new heights. When she breathed her last, she wanted it to be in Dante's arms.

Emotion flared in Dante's eyes as he slid down her body, caressing her sensitive skin with his tongue and mouth. Lifting his head, he whispered, "I love you, Esme, so much that I ache with it. Open your legs so I can feast on you."

He drank deeply from her fountain of honey, until he heard her sob, felt the shudders wracking her. Shaking with urgency, he eased up her body, mounted her and thrust his hard, virile length into her throbbing heat, shuddering at the pure glory of it. He whispered her name, his voice husky as he worshipped her with his body, driving inside her deeper, harder, faster. Desire and love flowed in a rush from his body into hers. He felt the walls of her sex contract, heard her cry out, and knew they had found paradise together.

Sweet contentment filled him as he sought the strength to lift his weight from her. Rolling onto his side, he cuddled Esme to him and pulled the covers over them.

"Dante? Are you asleep?"

"No. I'm counting my blessings. After all this time I still can't believe you love me."

"Believe it," Esme said, resting her head on his shoulder. "You're the only man I'll ever love, the only man I want." Her fingers strayed to his chest, toying with the soft dark hair growing there. "We've never talked about children."

A tense silence ensued. "I wasn't sure you wanted children with me."

"Why ever not?"

"I thought that was obvious. I'm a gypsy."

"You've never done anything to prevent me from conceiving."

"I thought I'd let nature take its course and pray that you'd love the children I gave you."

Esme's hand stilled. "You *do* want children, don't you?"

His gaze locked with hers, held. "I'd love children as long as you're their mother."

Esme released the breath she had been holding. "I'm glad, because I'm carrying your child."

Dante went still—very, very still. "You're having my child?"

"Didn't I just say so?"

She feathered her mouth across his. "Our babe will have both my blood and yours in his veins. We'll teach him to be proud of his gypsy heritage."

"He? How can you be sure?"

"I confided in Carlotta earlier today. She predicted a son for us; first a boy and then a daughter."

Dante grinned. "I wouldn't mind if we had a daughter who looked like you first. I just want our child to be healthy."

"I love you so much, Dante.

I want everyone to be as happy as I am. Even Calvin seems to have reformed. He's found himself an heiress, and their engagement will be announced soon."

"Forget them, Esme. We're in love, we're in bed, and the night is still young. Shall I love you again?"

Her eyes sparkled mischievously. "I'd like that. Show me again how the notorious gypsy lover delights his mistresses."

"I have but one mistress, milady, the woman in my arms," Dante murmured as he swept her beneath him.

Author's Note

Gypsy Lover evolved from a visit to Eastern Europe. While traveling in Hungary and Bulgaria, I came across countless gypsy wagons parked along the road-side in empty fields. Curious about the people, I stopped one day to observe. An old gypsy woman beckoned to me. Though we couldn't speak each other's language, we managed to communicate. When she offered to show me around, I accepted.

The camp, consisting of twelve wagons, was populated by men, women, children and dogs. All seemed happy despite the primitive living conditions and lack of proper sanitation. Before I left, I pressed some money in her hands and thanked her.

When I returned home, the gypsy caravan continued to intrigue me, and I began writing *Gypsy Lover*. I hope you enjoyed it.

I love hearing from readers. For a newsletter and bookmark, please send your request to me at P.O. Box 3471, Holiday, FL 34690. A long self-addressed stamped envelope is appreciated. Visit my Website at www.conniemason.com and e-mail me at conmason @aol.com.

The Pirate Prince
CONNIE MASON

She is a jewel among women, brighter than the moon and stars. Her lips are lush and pink, made for kissing . . . and more erotic purposes. She's a pirate's prize, yet he cannot so much as touch her.

Destined for the harem of a Turkish potentate, Willow wonders whether she should rejoice or despair when her ship is beset by a sinfully handsome pirate. She is a helpless pawn in a power play between two brothers. She certainly had no intention of becoming the sex slave of a sultan; and no matter how much he tempts her, she will teach her captor a thing or two before she gives her heart to . . . *The Pirate Prince*.

CONNIE MASON
The Last Rogue

All London is stunned by Lucas, Viscount Westmore's vow to give up the fair sex and exile himself to St. Ives. The infamous rake is known for his love of luxury and his way with the ladies, just as the rugged Cornish coast is known for its savagery, its fearsome gales and its smugglers.

But Luc is determined to turn away from the seduction of white thighs and perfumed flesh that had once ended in tragedy. He never guessed the stormy nights of Cornwall would bring unlooked-for danger, the thrill of the chase, and a long-legged beauty who tempts him like no other. As illicit cargo changes hands, as her flashing green eyes challenge his very masculinity, he longs for nothing so much as to lose himself in . . . *Bliss*.
